A MOTIF OF SEASONS

OTHER BOOKS IN THE HERZBERG TRILOGY

The Music Book

A young English woman, on the run from her father, and a retired Prussian military officer sent to England by King Frederick the Great are plunged into the London demi-monde and a pursuit across Europe in search of fulfilment. The young woman's music book bears witness to what unfolds.

Fortune's Sonata

English by birth, Prussian by marriage, rebellious by nature, the beautiful Arabella von Deppe steers her family through turbulent historical times in this thrilling story of love and loss, betrayal and revenge, ambition and beliefs, friendship and fate. With music as her inspiration and a murderer as her friend, she proves a worthy adversary of Fortune as she weathers winds beyond her control.

A Motif of Seasons

EDWARD GLOVER

THE OAK HOUSE

Published by The Oak House
High Street, Thornham, Norfolk PE36 6LY

Copyright © 2016 Edward Glover

Cover images:
Tegeler See by Margarette von Zavadsky, reproduced by permission of
Edward and Audrey Glover
Detail from Antonio Vivaldi's *Violin Concerto No. 4 in F Minor – Winter –*
from *The Four Seasons*
Over the Top by Paul Nash © IWM (Art.IWM ART 1656)

ISBN: 978-0-9929551-2-0

Dedicated to the memory of

Private Charles Alfred Lawrence

23702
The Norfolk Regiment
Killed on the 15th of September 1916
Remembered at the Thiepval Memorial
to the Missing of the Somme

CONTENTS

Genuine victories, the sole conquests yielding no remorse, are those gained over ignorance.
Napoleon Bonaparte 1769–1821

There is all the difference in the world between good-natured, good-humoured effort to keep well with your neighbours and that spirit of haughty and sullen isolation which has been dignified by the name of "non-intervention". We are part of the community of Europe, and we must do our duty as such.
Lord Salisbury 1830–1903

Love and desire are the spirit's wings to great deeds.
Johann Wolfgang von Goethe 1749–1832

Man's mind is so formed that it is far more susceptible to falsehood than truth.
Erasmus 1466–1536

FOREWORD

The Herzberg trilogy is a tale of two families – the Whitfields in England and the von Deppes in Prussia – linked by the unexpected marriage, in 1766, of the young, headstrong and beautiful Arabella Whitfield, an accomplished musician and singer, to the older, retired Prussian military officer Count Carl Manfred von Deppe.

The Music Book, the first novel in the trilogy, tells of the dark and turbulent circumstances leading to this union, forged out of a mutual search for personal redemption. The second, *Fortune's Sonata*, relates what happens to the Count and Countess after 1766, against the backdrop of the later years of Frederick the Great, the French Revolution and the Napoleonic Wars. The Countess, who outlives her husband, becomes famous for the chamber orchestra she creates and her friendships with successive Prussian kings, Catherine the Great of Russia, Mozart and Beethoven; far less well known is that she is protected from her frequent enemies by a brutish royal spymaster and arch manipulator. Her most treasured possession is a music book given to her by Frederick the Great on her marriage. *Fortune's Sonata* ends with Napoleon's defeat in 1815 and the Countess's death a year later.

In the following years, the von Deppes – now one of the most prominent and respected families in a post-war Prussia of renewed strength and rising European ambition – flourish on the imposing estate of Herzberg, renowned for its orchestra and cultural heritage. Leading members of the family occupy influential positions at court and in government. In England, George Whitfield, the head of the Whitfield family – from which the Countess remained estranged throughout her life in Prussia – owns a large and prosperous Norfolk estate, Meltwater Hall, but has important connections to London's social and political life. By the 1840s his wealth has further increased, exemplified by his expansion and embellishment of Meltwater and the acquisition of further expensive property in London. Bequeathed these assets, his son, Robert Emerson Whitfield – an ambitious man with valued political and financial contacts in the capital – seeks to enhance his influence and reputation. He finds at Meltwater an earlier, long-forgotten music book, which had once belonged to Arabella, his father's half-sister, before her marriage, and, as part of his wider self-aggrandising plan, travels to Berlin in the autumn of 1853 to retrace her journey from London to Prussia eighty-eight years before.

A Motif of Seasons resumes the story of the two families, still overshadowed by past estrangement, following Robert Whitfield's return from Berlin. The tale reaches its First World War climax on the 1st of July 1916, the first day of the Battle of the Somme, when the British army suffered over 57,000 casualties, of whom more than 19,000 were killed – the single biggest loss of life on a single day in the army's history. By the end of the battle five months later, more than 900,000 British and Empire troops had perished. The epic scale of this remorseless battle and the earlier bloody confrontations across the trenches of France and Flanders exacted a dreadful toll on families across Britain, sparing no one, regardless of class. The opposing German army, along with its allies, suffered equally, with communities in the imperial Reich paying a heavy price in death, hardship and despair. The Whitfield and von Deppe families were no exceptions, inexorably swept along by this tide of sorrow and loss, like corks bobbing on spate-swollen water.

* * * * *

Vivaldi reflected the cycle of seasons in his four much-loved violin concerti. Taking him as my cue, I have divided the period of this third book (1853–1918) into four parts, in keeping with the four seasons of the year – Victorian seasonal snapshots you might say.

As for the "motif" in the title, it is said by some musicologists that there is a single recurring theme in Beethoven's *Fifth Symphony*: the repetition throughout of the opening bars of the first movement, which in their opinion represent Fate knocking on the door. The motif in my book is not only a reference to the recurring seasons of a year, reflected in the varying fortunes of the two families, but also a reminder of the enduring legacy of the lifelong bitter feud between Arabella von Deppe and her father, still dividing the actions and opinions of both families long after her death.

This story with its twists and turns is one of hope, music, love and optimism as portrayed in the promise of spring and the warmth of summer, but it is equally one of mistrust, arrogance, deception and betrayal, as represented by the mists and uncertainties of autumn and the unforgiving bleakness of winter. It reveals – in both families – weaknesses, fears and foibles, and of course the damage that personal secrets can sometimes inflict, all of which contribute to the darker side of human behaviour and to the fragility of relationships in crisis. But my story is also one of how the human spirit can prevail.

All the dates in the book, used to mark the passage of time, are drawn from the actual calendars for the year in question. While some of the characters in the book were real, the words I have attributed to them are from my pen and therefore entirely invented.

As in my two previous books I have once again created several fictional women as central characters. First, I enjoy writing about women, their interaction both with other women and with the opposite sex and the delightful complication they add to life through their presence, manifest in their gestures, their voices, their expressions, their tastes and opinions. Second, in history there have been many examples of women who have played an important and sometimes courageous part in a particular course of events, or who have contributed to the arts and sciences. With limited notable exceptions their deeds have often gone unsung. *A Motif of Seasons* is my small personal tribute to the role that many real-life women, often unsung, have played in the shaping of the human dimension.

Edward Glover
North Norfolk
26 May 2016

DRAMATIS PERSONAE PRIMAE

Germany
Count Joseph Wilhelm von Deppe, elder son of the late Count Carl Nicolas von Deppe
Beatrice, his wife
Count Frederick Paul von Deppe, younger son of the late Count
Anne, his French-born wife
Countess Anne-Sophie, daughter of the late Count
Countess Elisabeth Mariette von Böhm, cousin of the late Count
Victoria Elise, her daughter
Count Daniel Frederick, elder son of Joseph
Nicolas Carl, younger son of Joseph
Arabella von Eisenwald, his granddaughter
Ernst Kiefer, investigator
Rebecca Bartlett, governess
Alice, her daughter

England
Robert Emerson Whitfield, only son of the late George Whitfield
Emily, his wife
Charles Whitfield, elder son of Robert Emerson Whitfield
Arthur Whitfield, younger son of Robert Emerson Whitfield
Florian Whitfield, his son
Charles Hardinge, barrister
Herbert Pettigrew, private investigator and former policeman
William Folliot, Foreign Office official
Aurelia, his wife

PROLOGUE

As his coach turned into Downing Street, Robert Whitfield looked at his pocket watch. It was shortly before one o'clock on the afternoon of Tuesday the 20th of December 1853. Though he had returned from Berlin at the end of the previous week, he had delayed calling upon the Secretary of State in order to settle some investment matters requiring his urgent attention. Having done what was necessary and with his wife, Emily, and their son, Charles, already at Meltwater awaiting his arrival for Christmas and the New Year, he wished without further delay to tell the Minister of the outcome of his journey to Prussia and to seek endorsement of his decision to pursue reconciliation with the von Deppe family. The previous evening he had received word that the Foreign Secretary would see him this afternoon.

The coach drew to a halt. The street bustled. Amidst carriage wheels and horses' hooves hawkers plied their wares, alongside pretty dressmakers, street singers, prostitutes and those already inebriated from early drinking at the nearby Cat and Bagpipes and the Rose and Crown. As he stepped down he caught sight to his right of two frock-coated men emerging from the Prime Minister's residence deep in conversation, whispering lest they be overheard, though how that could possibly happen in such noise defeated him. To his left stood three black mud-spattered carriages; perhaps they had brought the latest despatches from Her Majesty's ambassadors in Paris, Vienna, St Petersburg or even Constantinople. Behind the conveyances was a shabby terrace of dilapidated two-storey houses, some shored up by wooden posts to stop them sinking further into land made boggy by an underground stream. He noticed that since his last visit to the street one post had finally succumbed to the weight of its load, allowing the structure to collapse. It was hard to imagine that this rickety line of failing houses comprised the premises of the Foreign Office.

Beyond the terrace and adjacent Fludyer Street lay the rest of Westminster, with its accretion of parliamentary power, its deepening crust of gilded splendour reflecting increasing brash imperial swagger. Beyond Westminster to the east and north was a larger uncouth, dangerous and volatile London with its thievery, murder and filth, its opium dens and human misery – all so different from the smaller, industrious city he had recently seen, full of purpose, good order and strong commitment to the promotion of Prussia. Though he had only stayed a few days, he had nonetheless gained the impression of a self-confident Berlin, the hub of a new European power in the making. On the long journey home he had pondered how in the future it might view England. Would it be as a respectful friend and ally or as a competitor? There were historical similarities between the two nations that would suggest the continuation of natural friendship and a mutual alliance of opinions; Prussia had proved in the end a valiant opponent of Napoleon Bonaparte. But some forty years on, would it continue to see its place in Europe as a secondary power or might it seek a more selfish and prestigious role?

He had speculated upon what might best be done to ensure continued harmony between the two but had decided not to share his thoughts with Lord Clarendon – at least not now. His present purpose was to thank him for the passport he had kindly provided and to tell him of his contacts in Berlin, which he intended to cultivate for personal reasons and, if they flourished, for possible wider national benefit at a later stage. He also wished to demonstrate again his knowledge of European affairs, to show that he was more than just a wealthy landowner and successful investor, that he was a man of political skill with a contribution to make beyond England's shores if he were given the opportunity. Tall, somewhat foppish, sometimes pompous like his father and with an extensive circle of friends and acquaintances, he longed to secure a baronetcy such as his grandfather had enjoyed. It would bring that extra measure of respect that money and land could not provide, and such an honour would greatly please his wife, Emily, who would see the title "Lady" as a just reward for her own social efforts. Perhaps a continuing and useful association with George Villiers, the 4th Earl of Clarendon, might advance the prospects of such recognition, particularly if he could demonstrate that he might be of service in foreign affairs.

Whitfield entered one of the unprepossessing houses and climbed the staircase, decorated with unseemly cracks in the wall, to the Private Secretary's office on the first floor. The din within the building was almost as loud as the noise outside in the street and he caught a faint whiff of a noxious odour from a broken sewer. He could even feel the vibration from a churning printing press somewhere in the attic. Surely his country's Foreign Ministry deserved better, more impressive premises than these, premises that should display the true power and splendour of England? There had long been talk of a new building but so far words had not materialised into any firm plan.

"Robert, it is indeed good to see you back. Welcome home! How did you fare? And how is Monsieur le Baron, our esteemed Minister Plenipotentiary to His Majesty the King of Prussia?" Wreathed in cigar smoke, Her Majesty's Secretary of State for Foreign Affairs beckoned him to take a seat at a large polished table beneath a portrait of the Queen.

"His Excellency greatly flourishes, Secretary of State," replied Whitfield. "We had a long talk shortly after my arrival in Berlin, and he arranged for me to meet Count von Deppe. He asked me to pass on his best wishes and to convey some despatches to you, which I have left with your Private Secretary."

"Bloomfield is a good man," replied Clarendon. "He did well in St Petersburg as our envoy, so he seemed a sound diplomatist to send to Berlin. The Prussians are habitually suspicious of the Russians and the Russians of them. His experience of both sides enables him to understand and interpret their respective motivations. The Prussians are an ambitious lot, always have been. Frederick the Great began it all – a brilliant opportunist at pinching other people's territory, helped by an outstanding army. I am sure there will be a unified Germany one day if they have anything to do with it – with Prussia as top dog. Bloomfield says there are already some strong voices for it, despite the King's earlier decision to decline the monarchy of all Germany. But enough of my thoughts. Tell me all. Did you find out about your intriguing ancestor – your father's half-sister, I think you said? About her life in Prussia, and who her descendants might be? I always like to get a flavour of what lies behind the scenes of some of our friends and foes, and to hear some gossip, which Lady Clarendon devours with avidity."

The handsome, refined and engaging Clarendon sat back in his large high-backed chair, taking another deep puff on his cigar.

"My expedition, if I may call it that, went well, sir, very well. It is my opinion that Count Joseph von Deppe, a senior man at the parliament in Berlin, and his family – including his brother, who is a courtier at the royal palace – may not be averse to the prospect of restoring friendship with mine. If that were to prove possible it might bring other rewards and new connections. Of course, it may take time to heal the wounds of the deep rancour between the late Countess Arabella von Deppe and her father – my grandfather – and to remedy the subsequent bad feeling it caused between the two families throughout the remainder of her life and beyond. But nothing is impossible."

"Fascinating," replied the Foreign Secretary. "Tell me more about the Countess."

Robert Whitfield recounted what he had learnt about the Countess Arabella's life in Prussia following her marriage, about her musical achievements and her friendship with the late Prussian King and his wife, Queen Luise, and explained how he intended to begin his efforts towards reconciliation.

As he listened, Lord Clarendon was at first inclined to think this matter would most likely prove inconsequential, just another family quarrel and attempted repair with no direct relevance to any affairs of state. Yet the more Whitfield went on the more he was struck by the unusual emotional link between two influential, well-heeled families in two strategically significant countries, which might perhaps, in due course, if there were reconciliation, be exploited to English advantage. He knew from his own time as Her Majesty's representative in Spain of the damage that unchecked family passions could cause. He had seen that all too clearly in the troubles of the Spanish royal family. Whitfield, while not always likeable, was still a man whose judgement he had come to trust. For that reason, though the attempt at family reconciliation might come to nothing, he should perhaps encourage him to make it after all, not least on account of two members of the von Deppe family apparently holding influential positions in the Prussian hierarchy. If Whitfield did achieve success in creating some strong personal family ties in Berlin, that could well provide in due course a potentially revealing insight into Prussia's aims, which might in turn prove useful in building a closer friendship with the Hohenzollerns once England's likely war with Russia had ended. In any peace conference London would need all the allies it could muster to reach a satisfactory treaty. To improve the cards in his hand it would be desirable to have Prussia on his side at the conference table. Why not begin the pursuit of that option now – but in the hands of an external self-appointed agent?

Whitfield finished.

"Let me be frank with you, Robert, and by the way what I will say now you must not disclose to others."

"You have my word, sir. You can trust my discretion," replied Whitfield, relishing the prospect of being given confidential information.

"Good," responded Clarendon. "I confess that when you asked me for your passport I had never heard of the English-born Countess Arabella von Deppe, which was remiss of me. From what you have just told me she achieved much during her many years in Prussia, not least in music, and by all accounts remains a revered figure. However, despite my interest, this is not a matter of state – at least not for now – and therefore, while you are right to seek a rapprochement between your family and the von Deppes, you should do so alone, without my public encouragement. Our government is heavily preoccupied with the prospect of war against Russia. The Czar thinks the Ottomans are getting steadily weaker and is therefore eyeing some of their territory, which we cannot allow him to acquire. Finding a peaceful solution that satisfies everyone takes up all my time daily. I fear, however, my efforts may fail and therefore we have to contemplate a military campaign. If there is war, it is paramount that I do whatever is necessary to ensure that we and the French stick together against the Czar, regardless of any views the Prince Consort down the road may have on the matter. At the same time we must be vigilant for other protagonists who may choose to take advantage of our preoccupations for their own ends – either now or after the outbreak of war."

"And Prussia?" interrupted Whitfield.

"Though I am optimistic they will not cross us if we go to war, our vigilance must indeed extend to them," replied Clarendon. "Berlin is neutral now but the question arises, for how long? If they were to abandon their neutrality, would they join us? I hope they would, but we cannot be sure. For the present we should do what we can – discreetly – to be on good terms with them, and to ensure as far as possible that whatever interests they have do not conflict with ours, that we tread the same road in harmony, though not forgetting the French do not like the Prussians. So, Robert, you have done well in your fortuitous personal quest. I repeat that you should proceed with your plan, because any success may just, at some later point, be in our diplomatic interest. But there can be no personal fanfare from me or reference to our discussion. I know I can rely on your discretion. Please do let me know privately if the situation develops favourably. And of course you have my agreement to entrust to Bloomfield the conveyance of your correspondence with the von Deppe family. Now, let us turn to some other matters on which I would welcome your view."

After leaving Downing Street, Robert Whitfield returned to his house in the shadow of Westminster Abbey to write immediately to Count Joseph von Deppe. Though the broad-fronted residence was large and imposing for a man of his wealth, and little changed from his grandfather's time, he still considered it his family's London pied-à-terre rather than a grand property. Meltwater Hall, the family country seat, remained his real home. His wife preferred it, too, though more in the summer than in the dismal, chilling months of winter. After a late light lunch he retired to his study and before the afternoon had ended his letter to Joseph von Deppe was with Lord Clarendon's Private Secretary for onward transmission to Baron Bloomfield. That evening, sitting alone by the fire in his library, he recorded in his diary what he had done. The die had been cast. Early the next day, the 21st of December, he left for Meltwater to join his family and friends for Christmas.

PART ONE: ALLEGRO AND LARGO
THE PROMISE OF TRUST 1853–1858

CHAPTER 1

The Invitation

It was a bitter winter. Lake Wannsee had been frozen for more than a month. The snow along the shore remained as deep as ever. Each new day opened with the same cloudless crystal sky. The comfort of the villa kept at bay the numbing cold wind that blew incessantly from the east. It was hard to remember a winter as glacial as this.

Count Joseph, a tall, thin, good-looking man who moved with grace and ease, turned from the library window and reread the letter he had received the day before through Baron Bloomfield's special messenger.

"Joseph, you look so preoccupied. You have read that letter I do not know how many times. Does it contain bad news?" asked Beatrice, his wife, in a soft voice.

He looked up.

"No, my dearest, it is not bad news. It is a letter from Mr Robert Whitfield who, as you will recall, came to Berlin last November. It contains an unexpected and surprising proposal."

He handed her the letter.

Dear Count von Deppe,
Following my return to London, I wish to thank you and Countess Beatrice for so kindly receiving me, my wife, Emily,

1

and my son, Charles, in Berlin last November. It was a great honour to meet you and to learn more about the remarkable life of the Countess Arabella von Deppe, your great-grandmother and my father's half-sister. She was clearly a woman of great distinction, courage and accomplishment and has brought lasting lustre to your family and the kingdom of Prussia.

As I journeyed home to London I reflected on how it is never easy, in matters of the most sensitive human emotions, to put right grievous wrongs of the past, to drain the well of bitterness. This is never more so than in the case of the Countess, who was poorly treated by her father. It was evident to me from our conversations that the family name Whitfield, which she bore at her birth and which she was relieved to cast aside on her joyful marriage to Count Carl Manfred von Deppe, continues to this day to convey for your family an unhappy and unwelcome association.

As she was so sorely tested while bearing the Whitfield name, I wish to do what I can to make amends for past injustice and callousness. While I regret deeply this did not happen in her lifetime, please allow me to do what is necessary now, even though you may consider my gesture belated and that by itself it will not remove the stain of prior misdeeds. However, what I propose may help to lighten the stain and so lead eventually to its erasure.

Towards this desirable end, it is with great pleasure that I wish to invite you, the Countess Beatrice and other members of your family who may feel similarly so disposed, to come to England at a mutually convenient time as our guests, in order to enjoy our hospitality in London and at our estate in Norfolk and to acknowledge and celebrate the life of your great-grandmother. Nothing would give my wife and me greater joy than to welcome you in this way. Your presence in England would enable us to become better acquainted and so begin what I earnestly desire – the reconciliation of our two families to our mutual satisfaction and advantage, and even, perhaps, to the eventual mutual benefit of our two countries. If you choose to accept this invitation, as I earnestly hope you will, I leave the timing of your visit in your hands, though if it were possible an arrival in late spring or mid-summer would allow you to see

2

England at its best.

I say again how conscious I am of the pain the name Whitfield continues to cause you and your family, but I beg that you give this heartfelt invitation the most serious consideration.
With my best wishes,
Robert Whitfield
Westminster
Tuesday the 20th of December, 1853

"How do you intend to reply?" asked Beatrice.

"I cannot answer his letter until I have consulted those in the family who will be inclined to listen, including Cousin Elisabeth Mariette. Her mother, Elise Catherine, was by all accounts closest to Arabella, as her only daughter. Elisabeth's opinion we must consider carefully."

Beatrice looked at her husband.

"I can imagine what her opinion will be," she replied. "She has been so vehement in her criticism of the Whitfields. She will say that Frederick Daniel, your grandfather, Arabella's son, would turn in his grave if he knew there was a prospect of renewed contact with them. Do not forget, Joseph, that Sir Robert Whitfield drove his daughter from the family home through his intransigence over whom she should marry, and her brother, it is said, tried to abduct her, even kill her. According to Elisabeth Mariette, for those reasons, your grandfather and his sister, Elise Catherine, both so protective of their mother, considered the link with the Whitfields to be dead, not to be resurrected. You have told me many times that your great-grandmother died a Prussian, honoured by the late King. Surely it would be an insult to her memory to go to England and dine at the Whitfield table?"

"Beatrice, I always welcome your opinions but in this instance the decision does not lie with me alone. I say again: I cannot answer Mr Whitfield without consulting everyone, since the invitation extends not just to you and me but to other members of the family. Tiresome though this business may be – raking up old memories – it is still necessary that I hear everyone's view, and to do that we must meet at Herzberg as soon as the weather eases. After all, it was there that this story began, long ago. I will write to everyone tomorrow."

* * * * *

Two weeks later, on Friday the 10th of February 1854, the von Deppe family gathered for the weekend.

Schloss Herzberg had originally been a classic rectangular construction but during the latter part of the eighteenth century it had expanded, notably to accommodate the beautifully decorated and furnished *Spiegelsaal* that Arabella had designed for the performance of her beloved music. Now with two wings, whose walls were covered by climbing roses that almost encompassed the upper windows, the soft and mellow red brick house was even more imposing, its enlarged front door further highlighted by a more substantial pediment bearing the von Deppe crest. Beyond the surrounding patio and well-kept lawn lay open farmland. Yet despite its substantial architectural additions Schloss Herzberg still conveyed a simplicity and warmth that impressed and embraced all those who entered its commanding hall. Everyone who visited it regarded Herzberg as a lovable house of calm and understated balance, a skilful combination of Prussian substance interwoven with discreet traces of French and English style, as one might expect of a woman of French and English origin.

Though the winter remained as deep as ever, the family were delighted to be together again after months of separation, their last reunion having taken place in the previous autumn, to mark the eighty-seventh anniversary of the foundation by Arabella of the Schloss Herzberger Camerata in 1766, at the command of Frederick the Great. Fires had been lit in every room, the house was illuminated by a multitude of candles, laughter could be heard everywhere and the house staff hurried hither and thither. After supper, in the *Spiegelsaal*, the Camerata's chamber orchestra, still nationally acclaimed, played some of the family's favourite pieces from Haydn and Beethoven, including the latter's *Septet in E Flat Major*, together with pieces by newer composers. The Countess Elisabeth Mariette von Böhm, now in her sixtieth year but still as graceful, flirtatious and magnetic as her late mother, Elise Catherine, presided over proceedings with barely concealed pride and joy. She and her philandering husband, Philip Otto, spent more time than others at Herzberg, though Elisabeth was more often there alone, provoking gossip of her own affairs within its walls, despite her insistence that she was only there to ensure the house was cherished and retained its reputation as a place of taste and outstanding music. Joseph von Deppe, his younger brother, Frederick Paul, and Anne-Sophie, their sister, were content to indulge the strong-willed Elisabeth, as was her daughter, Victoria. There were few in the family who would gainsay this formidable woman.

The next day some went riding; a few of the men went shooting, while others declined to face the cold and chose to relax in the library. Joseph went for a walk around the garden trying to spot early signs of spring. He saw some snowdrops and promising buds on the trees but spring seemed to him a distant prospect still. His brother, Frederick Paul, though young for his age, was a respected official at the court of King Frederick William IV; he was already proving a sure-footed survivor in the machinations that had continued since the upheaval in Prussia in 1848, when revolution had swept through Europe. His companion at court was the older, somewhat stiffer Heinrich Stefan von Rostow, their sister's husband. The two brothers wandered for almost an hour, discussing Prussia's prospects, the strength of the conservative faction – of which von Rostow was part – in parliament and among those closely around the King, the war between Russia and Britain, in alliance with the French, and its implications for their homeland. As they turned back towards the house, their sister, Anne-Sophie, joined them.

"You two look so serious – and so cold. Both of you, come inside and join the rest of us. There is much wonderful gossip to be heard. It is truly good to be together again."

Neither brother could long resist her urging.

"Let's have a race to the house," said Frederick Paul.

"You two can, but I cannot run in my long skirt. What I can do, though, is throw snowballs."

"How far can you throw?" said Joseph.

"Let me see," she replied.

She made two snowballs and walked towards the house, her brothers following behind. She suddenly turned and threw a ball at each, her good aim catching them unawares. Then hitching her skirt above her knees to reveal long slender legs she ran as fast as she could, chased by her brothers, doing their best to match her accuracy with the snowballs.

"I won the race," she shrieked, laughing, from the patio.

"You always do outsmart us, Anne-Sophie. You are a tribute to your father – or perhaps more to your grandmother Jacqueline. Few could ever get the better of her," said Joseph.

Dinner that evening was a grand affair. While fresh snow fell outside, the family – the great, the good and the younger generation – gathered in splendour in the dining room. As the elder son of his late father, Joseph sat at one end of the large square early-eighteenth-century dining table, his wife, Beatrice, at the other. On his immediate right, in place of honour, sat Elisabeth Mariette, while her husband, Philip Otto, took a similar position on Beatrice's right. The remaining family – Elisabeth's daughter, Victoria, now separated in marriage from her husband, Herr von Eisenach; Fredrick Paul and his elegant wife, Anne, the only daughter of the Comte and Comtesse de Morville, a family that had managed to survive the ravages of the French Revolution; Anne-Sophie and her husband, Heinrich Stefan; the Countess Anna Maria von Deppe, the mother of Joseph, Fredrick Paul and Anne-Sophie, who had never recovered from the premature death of her husband, Carl Nicolas; Ernst Walter Henning, widower of Alexandra Véronique Lorraine, Carl Nicolas's sister, who had died young of typhoid; and Elisabeth Mariette's brother, Johann Matthias, and his wife, Margarethe – were interspersed with Ernst Walter's son, Wilhelm Louis, and his wife, Julia Victoria, and his daughter, Antoinette Jacqueline, and her husband, Christian Ludwig Clemens. Conversation around the table was lively and amusing, as might be expected in any contented family, though everyone knew that Joseph would soon seek their views on the letter he had recently received from Robert Whitfield.

After they had finished dessert, Joseph asked the staff attending them to leave until summoned. Then he addressed his family.

"As you are aware, I have received a letter from Mr Robert Whitfield, who came to Berlin late last year to learn more about his father's half-sister and our ancestor, the Countess Arabella. An obviously wealthy man, with connections to the British Foreign Office, he came to see me twice at the parliament building, on the second occasion with his wife, Emily, and his young son, Charles. He brought with him the music book that Arabella's mother, Lady Thérèse Whitfield, who was French, had given her on her seventeenth birthday and which, as Elisabeth will confirm, Arabella brought with her all the way to Prussia in 1766. I did not know that on her marriage to Carl Manfred, Arabella had returned this music book – which I observed contained several precious items of music and some personal writings – to her mother as a keepsake, since Frederick the Great had given her a new music book as a wedding present. Elisabeth Mariette keeps the second book securely in this house. In answer to his questions I told Mr Whitfield what I knew of Arabella's life at Herzberg and the unique contribution she made to Prussia. He was deeply impressed. It is best that I read you his letter and then I would like your opinions as to what my reply should be."

There was silence after he had finished reading, eventually broken by the Countess Anna Maria.

"My late husband, Carl Nicolas, told me how his father, Frederick Daniel, had often spoken harshly of the way his mother had been poorly treated by her father. He insisted this behaviour had been unforgivable and whilst she had devoted her life to the von Deppe family and had brought great happiness, acclaim and respect to this estate, the pain of what her father had done to her – and indeed what her brother had tried to do – overshadowed the rest of her life, though she rarely said so. I am sure that if Carl Nicolas were here this evening he would favour a reply that politely but firmly rebuffed Mr Whitfield's invitation."

The Countess Margarethe spoke next.

"As many of you know, I can be blunt at times. I will be so on this occasion. Although I know less than some around this table about what happened in the past, I see little merit in a positive answer and therefore join Anna Maria in advising you, Joseph, not to accept. While money is not everything, in this instance it is my opinion that the Whitfield family are parvenus who wish to do nothing more than wheedle their way into our affections in order to bask in the good name and reputation of this family. Why should we grant them that, when they sought to destroy a beautiful and talented young woman who, through willpower and great devotion, rescued this family from near extinction and brought it much national praise and musical glory? I am sorry to be so dismissive but that is my opinion, for what it may be worth."

Johann Matthias too saw no merit in a positive reply. He had an open mind on most matters but on this one he could see no alternative. The two families should continue to go their separate ways.

Antoinette Jacqueline intervened. "I take an opposing position. If this letter represents contrition on the part of a new generation of the Whitfield family, then surely it is right to recognise it as such and to respond accordingly. We should avoid taking a sanctimonious and high moral view. None of us is unblemished. Did not the Countess Arabella keep the company of a dreadful man called Drescher, to whom there is even a memorial stone in the garden, and did not her husband have a hand in the fate of her brother?"

"Antoinette Jacqueline, enough of that," retorted Anna Maria. "We seek to be honourable. Do not confuse that with being sanctimonious."

"Oh Aunt Anna, don't be so stuffy! Do not hide inconvenient facts."

"I agree," said Anne-Sophie. "We must be open-minded on this matter, not keep old grudges alive."

"Anna Maria and I are certainly not keeping old grudges alive," Margarethe replied. "We draw on our experience of human nature to express our opinion of what is best in this instance. We should not let the Whitfields damage this family again. See what is happening already – discord among us."

"Ladies, please, please," interrupted Joseph. "Frederick Paul, what do you think?"

"The final decision on what to say in reply rests with you, since the letter was addressed to you. Previous feuds apart, I have my doubts about the wisdom of a positive reply, not least because we have no idea where Mr Whitfield's proposal may lead. Besides, with so much happening in government and at court I am not sure that it is practical to undertake a journey to England at this time, particularly with war between Britain and Russia. I would advise that it is best to send Mr Whitfield a suitable reply thanking him for his invitation but saying that because of other circumstances we are not in a position to make a decision at this time. Leave matters there."

"Frederick, you would make an excellent diplomatist, if you were not at court," replied Joseph drily.

Heinrich Stefan agreed with Frederick. This was not the time to consider such a visit. Moreover, raking over the coals of a past family dispute would be unhelpful.

"Cousin Elisabeth, you have been silent so far. What is your advice?" Joseph asked.

"My mother often told me that my grandmother's hatred of her father had been visceral," began Elisabeth Mariette. "Though a strong Catholic, she could never bring herself to forgive him, particularly in the absence of any remorse for his actions. As Arabella's granddaughter I can well understand her refusal to forgive and I am sorely tempted to add my voice to those advising you to decline the invitation. However, few of you will know that in 1786, in response to a letter from her brother, Arabella replied that, although she would never see her childhood home or England again, she hoped that one day in the future the descendants of the two families would meet and by so doing lay a foundation for true and lasting friendship. Though I must confess it pains me to say this, I believe we should fulfil her wish in this regard. I therefore recommend, Joseph, that you reply affirmatively. Moreover, you should know that I am prepared to accompany you to London."

Everyone was surprised by her unexpected opinion. Her daughter, Victoria, who had said little during the evening, agreed for once with her mother's sentiments.

For a minute or so, no one spoke.

"How do you know Arabella replied in such terms to her brother?" asked Anne-Sophie.

"Because," said Elisabeth, "that is what my mother told me shortly before her death and there is a scrap of paper in my grandmother's music book on which she recorded what she had done. My mother said that, although it had been distressing for her to write in such terms, Arabella believed it was nonetheless right to do so."

"Joseph," said Julia Victoria, "I am a newcomer to this family and am sincerely touched by the warmth with which I have been welcomed since my marriage to Wilhelm. I do not wish to cause offence on a matter regarding which I may yet still be considered an outsider who should remain silent. Nonetheless I will speak. It is tempting for us – in this beautiful house, in this gilded existence – to seek to wrap ourselves in a rich cloak of purity and refinement to the exclusion of all other things. But surely to do so would be to condemn ourselves to self-imposed loneliness in a world that is changing dramatically? Moreover, to take such a step would surely contradict what I believe the Countess Arabella sought to do with great courage – to reach out to those she met, whoever they happened to be, whether it was through music or granting free tenure to those families who for generations had worked the Herzberg land for this family's benefit. I have seen Caspar David Friedrich's painting *Wanderer above the Sea of Fog*, painted two years after Arabella's death. I urge this family not to become like that faceless figure, surveying the distant horizon but unable to see the valley below because of the fog that obscures it. For me this family of which I am honoured to be part must avoid the risk of preoccupied mastery over an idyllic landscape of music, culture and social refinement. Instead we should surely strike out in new and more practical directions. We have to sail oceans, not lakes. The letter should be considered a challenge. If Mr Whitfield wishes to hold out his hand in friendship we should take it, put his sincerity to the test and show him and others the courage of our convictions, our willingness to tackle the unfathomable. That is what the Countess Arabella did. I have learnt much about her from Elisabeth Mariette. She bravely left Paris for the east as a young woman – on her own – all those years ago because that is what she believed she had to do in search of fulfilment and redemption. That same restless, courageous impulse later drove her, in 1792, to go back to Paris to rescue the Comtesse de Vervins from the Revolution. I urge you all not to turn the wrong way. Let us follow her example."

"I agree," whispered Anne-Sophie. So did Antoinette Jacqueline.

The room once again fell silent.

"I conclude," said Joseph, "in the light of what Elisabeth has revealed and Julia Victoria's eloquent opinion that I should send Mr Whitfield a favourable reply. I might add that, even without Elisabeth's disclosure of the letter, I had intended to say that it was my and Beatrice's opinion that we should accept the invitation. Whatever we may think about past events we must acknowledge that some English blood flows in our veins, just as French blood does, though in greater measure. This family has benefited from such blending. Nor should we forget that there has long been friendship and at times alliance between Prussia and England. It would be churlish of us not to weigh such facts in the balance, even if in the scale of things some may regard them as inappropriate of consideration. Unless anyone strongly disagrees, I will write accordingly."

With that they left the dining room for the *Spiegelsaal* to listen to Mozart's *Clarinet Quintet in A Major* and then Michele Stratico's *Violin Concerto in G Minor*, a favourite of Elisabeth's because of its instrumental virtuosity. As they did so, Joseph pondered not only the decision they had reached but some of the opinions that had been expressed. He feared that some fractures in the family had been exposed.

The next morning he replied to Robert Whitfield.

> *Dear Mr Whitfield,*
>
> *Thank you for your letter of Tuesday the 20th of December 1853, which reached me in the middle of last month by kind courtesy of His Excellency Baron Bloomfield. The delay in its delivery was on account of the cruel winter that has held us tightly for many weeks, though I am pleased today to see in the garden the first signs of its loosening grip.*
>
> *I am sure you will appreciate that, as the contents of your letter were unexpected and of concern not just to me and the Countess Beatrice, it was desirable to withhold a rapid response so that I could seek the opinions of others in our wider family. I have now done so.*
>
> *It will not surprise you that our discussion was thoughtful. As you wrote in your letter, the late Countess Arabella von Deppe was sorely tested and poorly treated by the family of her birth. This cast a long shadow over her remaining life and has troubled her descendants ever since. It was therefore tempting to leave the ashes of past events undisturbed in the hope that the winds of time would blow them away and the previous connection between our two families be consigned to forgotten history. However, we concluded that, difficult though it may be, it was indeed time to try to address the past in a more positive*

spirit as you have proposed. I therefore write to inform you that we wish to accept your kind and generous invitation to come to England in order to join with you in marking the Countess's life in an appropriate manner. Only time will tell what may ensue thereafter.

I am not yet in a position to say precisely when the Countess Beatrice, our two children and I may come to England but we intend it should be this year, possibly in early July when the parliament goes into recess. Nor am I yet able to say who else may accompany us, though I am pleased that it is likely the Countess Arabella's granddaughter, the Countess Elisabeth Mariette von Böhm, will do so, together with her husband, Herr Philip Otto von Böhm, and their daughter, Victoria. I will write to you again before long about this.

I wish to thank you for your kind gesture of reconciliation. Despite the pain of past years, you may be assured that we at Herzberg will do all that we can to ensure our visit is a success. I will now pass this letter to His Excellency Baron Bloomfield for his kind assistance in ensuring you receive it.
Joseph von Deppe
Herzberg
Sunday the 12th of February, 1854

Four weeks later Robert Whitfield received a message from Lord Clarendon's Private Secretary advising that a letter from Berlin awaited his collection. That afternoon he sat in his study in Westminster and read the Count's reply. He sat back satisfied. The next day he wrote to inform Lord Clarendon of the news he had received, after which he wrote a cheque for the purchase of Number 35 Chesterfield Street in Mayfair, which he intended should accommodate the von Deppe family on their arrival in London.

CHAPTER 2

Rite of Passage

Early on Thursday the 6th of July 1854, the steamer slipped its moorings and slowly edged from the harbour. England lay just twenty-eight miles across the Channel, placid in the morning sun. Joseph, his wife, Beatrice, and their children, Daniel Frederick and Nicolas Carl, together with Joseph's sister, Anne-Sophie, and her daughter, Victoria, were on the top deck with Elisabeth Mariette's husband, watching ships coming and going. Frederick Paul had been obliged to withdraw at the last moment on account of pressing business at court.

Elisabeth sat apart, her mind still troubled so many days after leaving Berlin. Was this journey a betrayal of her grandmother's steadfast commitment to Prussia to the exclusion of everything to do with England – a commitment Elisabeth's mother had herself honoured and which she had urged her own daughter to follow – or was the inherited commitment an unnecessary isolation that had to stop without further ado? Had Joseph been right to end this taboo after she had disclosed what Arabella had written in her music book, thus breaking her vow that she would never reveal its secrets and indiscretions? If only she had said nothing, had held firm to the belief that what she was told as a child had a worthy, lifelong purpose, and had therefore insisted on refusing the invitation – despite Joseph's reference to the connection of blood –

it was likely they would not be on board and she would not be vexed in this way. But the sudden irresistible impulse to reveal the content of the scrap of paper perhaps reflected her inescapable belief that the older she became the more she was obliged to confront the accumulating absurdities of life, the stupidity of obstacles constructed long ago, the misplaced fears of things that existed only in the mind. She had come to realise – late – that life was not always what it seemed to be. Beneath its surface lay darker, unknown depths. The older she became the more these depths should be plumbed in order that truth could be established and myth banished. The seagulls shrieked above as though mocking her troubled thoughts. Whatever the answer, it was too late to turn back. With the decision made at Herzberg they had passed the proverbial fork in the road. Whatever discomfort might lie ahead it was time to face the past, to see whether those fears that had long preoccupied her were real or just a figment of her imagination.

As the harbour of Boulogne receded into the distance, Elisabeth recalled her happy childhood at Herzberg, surrounded by the very certainties of life she now questioned. Her mother, Elise, had been a remarkable woman – beautiful, graceful and feminine and much admired as an accomplished musician and singer, the instigator of even greater fame for the Camerata Herzberger. She was, some had said, a force of nature, almost a goddess stepped down from Mount Olympus. Her husband adored her, gave her everything for the pleasure of her smile, and regarded their daughter as her mirror image, worthy of equal adoration. But Elisabeth's mother had a secret, a dark secret that she had hidden from everyone until her daughter uncovered it by accident at Herzberg.

One afternoon when her father was away she went to her mother's bedroom, that famed bedroom once belonging to the Countess Arabella, with its imposing tapestries. The door was ajar. She heard whispering. Gently pushing the door open, she saw her mother, unclothed, in the arms of another woman. Elisabeth stood frozen to the spot. Realising she was there but showing neither embarrassment nor shame, her mother smiled at her, beckoning her to the bedside.

"Elisabeth, this is Lisl, my friend and companion. Lisl, this is my beautiful daughter, Elisabeth Mariette."

Lisl touched her face. She was young and tender like her mother.

"Elisabeth, you are indeed beautiful. Perhaps one day you will be even more beautiful than your mother, and pursued by Eros."

"One day she will be," replied Elise. "Now, my little one, go down and wait for us in the garden."

She and Lisl kissed her.

Elisabeth left. For a moment she listened behind the closed door. There was no sound. Shortly afterwards, her mother and Lisl joined her on the patio. The three talked and laughed about many different things. Elisabeth observed that occasionally her mother's and Lisl's hands touched.

That evening, after supper and Lisl's departure, Elise turned to her.

"What you saw this afternoon in my bedroom is our very own secret. It is a most special secret, a secret only you may know. Not even Papa must know."

"Mama, why do you wish to be with another woman? Why do you not love Papa?"

"I do love Papa, deeply, but in another way. Sometimes he cannot give me what I seek."

"And what is that?"

"It is hard to explain, my child. Lisl has a softness that touches my inner being. Once upon a time your grandmother, Arabella, had a secret like mine – in Russia. To be with Lisl enables me to break free, as Arabella did – to be expressive, uninhibited, to have freedom of choice."

"I do not know what you mean."

"As a child it is right for you to learn the accepted way to do things – such as good manners at table and how to behave in the presence of others, to respect one another. But when you too become a woman, and that will be soon, I have little doubt you will understand what I mean. Yes, when we are grown-up we remain good-mannered and respectful but we explore new ways to live our lives in search of personal happiness. I cherish your father's love for me but I also seek the companionship that sometimes only we of our own sex can give to one another. Sadly, the search for this special friendship has to remain a secret as it is likely others would disapprove and try to end it. So for these reasons, some of which you may not yet understand, you must solemnly swear to me that you will never disclose to anyone what you saw today. Because if you do the goblins may come and devour us both."

"I promise, Mama. I promise upon my heart. But please love Papa."

"I will, Elisabeth. I promise you I will continue to love him as much as he loves me. And if you keep your promise to me, as I am sure you will, one day I will let you see grandmother's music book, in which there are many secrets. And one day when I am old I will give you her book to hold and keep. From then on it will be yours to guard. No one else must know of its contents."

"Yes, Mama, I understand."

Thereafter, Lisl often came to Herzberg, for tea or musical soirées, and when she did so she always asked to see Elisabeth and to read some stories to her in the library. Only once did Elisabeth again witness any physical contact between them, when she saw them sitting together in the garden – two beautiful women bathed in sunlight. As she approached she saw Lisl tenderly kiss her mother's hand before relinquishing it. The secret she had sworn to keep bore heavily upon her during her remaining childhood, even more so in her adolescence, when she saw her father embrace her mother on his return to Herzberg after long absences. Often she could barely conceal the truth. Yet each time, at the last moment, she pulled back from uttering the fateful words.

Later she came to understand what her mother had meant. Though marriage to Philip Otto von Böhm was fulfilling, she needed more than he could offer beneath his stiff Prussian exterior. Like her mother she felt sometimes she would suffocate from the stifling accumulation of morality in which she was encased. So she came to enjoy the charged frisson of flirtatious dalliances with other men, though they were never, despite what she knew others alleged, affairs such as her husband enjoyed. But she too had a secret. She had once allowed herself to be kissed by a woman. Though the kiss reminded her of what she had once seen in her mother's bedroom, and of the guilt she had endured from withholding a secret from her beloved father, the instant thrill of another woman's lips on hers ignited a passionate sensuality she had never experienced before. But nothing came of the fleeting kiss. The woman who might have become more than a friend died

16

soon after of consumption.

Shortly before her death six years before, her mother, as she had promised long ago, handed her the key with which she opened the secret hiding place. Together they leafed through the handsomely bound music book, presented to Arabella by Frederick the Great, looking at the letters and writings within, at the miniature of the young Thérèse de Miron with the still unsolved mystery of the letters *FB* in the lace around her décolletage, and at the bold words of a young woman on a sheet of faded paper: *I will do what people want but only as I want it to be.* They unwrapped the painting of the Russian Empress Catherine the Great and Arabella in their unbuttoned military uniforms, talking intimately, hand in hand.

"Elisabeth, all this, this treasury of secrets, I bequeath to you. It is for you to guard and one day share with your daughter, Victoria, if that is what you decide. But for others it must remain closed, inaccessible. That is what I promised my mother, just as my mother promised her's. I ask you to promise me that you will never divulge its content to anyone else."

"I promise, Mama, just as I did as a child about Lisl. I will keep its secrets. I promise."

Yet she had broken her oath; the dam of silence holding back past secrets had cracked. There was now a risk that it could burst altogether, exposing a torrent of deception, absurdities and curiosities. Withholding the music book from family scrutiny would now become that much harder. So long as she lived she would do her best to deter requests to see the book. But to whom should she eventually entrust it? To her daughter, as her mother had done? Victoria had inherited the beauty, magnetism and feminine allure for which the von Deppe women had always been famous. Also like the female line before her, she had an impressive musical talent and a strong intellect that often caused her to be unpredictable in her opinions, frequently controversial and sometimes outrageously outspoken. Could she trust her daughter to be the guardian of a trove of family secrets? If it were not to be Victoria, who else? Surely it could not be Joseph or his brother? Men were not keepers of women's secrets. Or perhaps it should be Anne-Sophie? Or perhaps she should destroy the book – its contents forever out of reach? It was a decision she would take after her return to Berlin.

"Cousin Elisabeth, come quickly," said the children, breaking her thoughts. "Come quickly, we are almost there – the cliffs of England. You must come."

* * * * *

"Welcome to England, honoured guests," said a young man in a smart crimson livery. "My name is Joiner. My companion, Fletcher, and I work for Mr Whitfield. He has instructed us to assist you on your journey to London, where he and Mrs Whitfield eagerly await your arrival. He has arranged for you to stay nearby tonight at a fine guest house. This will give you time to rest after what I am sure has been a long and arduous journey. Tomorrow morning I will escort you on the train to Reigate, where you will change onto another train to London. Any luggage you do not require tonight Fletcher will take ahead by special carriage, to await your arrival in London. I too will lodge at the guest house, in case I can be of any assistance during your brief stay."

"Thank you, Mr Joiner, and you too, Mr Fletcher," said Joseph. "We will take an early stroll followed by supper and then retire for the night. What time should we be ready to leave tomorrow morning?"

"At eight thirty a.m., sir, if that is convenient to you and your party."

"I am sure it is," Joseph replied.

Early in the afternoon of the next day, Friday the 7th of July, the von Deppe family arrived at London Bridge station, where they were warmly greeted by Robert Whitfield, accompanied by his wife, Emily, and their son, Charles.

"Count and Countess von Deppe, distinguished guests, children, we are delighted to welcome you to London. To have you with us is a great pleasure, privilege and honour. Your advance baggage has already been safely conveyed to 35 Chesterfield Street, where it awaits your arrival. I have carriages ready to take you there. Joiner and Fletcher will escort you. My staff at the house will make you comfortable. I am sure you will find everything you may need. If it is convenient to you, Mrs Whitfield and I would like to call upon you early this evening, to confirm that everything is indeed in order and to ensure that my proposed arrangements for this weekend in London and next week at Meltwater, our country estate, meet with your satisfaction."

"Mr Whitfield," said Count Joseph von Deppe, "on behalf of my family and Herr and Countess von Böhm, I wish to thank you for your hospitality and most excellent arrangements. You have already been an extremely kind host. I am sure everything will be in order. We look forward to your visit this evening."

Formality was the watchword when the two families, from different backgrounds and different countries, sat together in the library at Chesterfield Street. Politeness and civility were matched by circumspection and vigilance. Behind the bland words of conversation there was unspoken calculation of one another. There was residual suspicion on the part of Elisabeth and her husband as to the real reason for the intended rapprochement. Joseph von Deppe, used to the rough and tumble of Prussia's parliamentary debates on the case for German unification, had an open mind, his wife less so, though as might be expected she deferred to her husband's judgement. Anne-Sophie was undecided, her attention already diverted by the frenzy of London's streets, giving her no time to consider what might lie behind the Whitfield solicitation. Victoria von Deppe continued to say little other than utter polite pleasantries.

On his return to Westminster, Robert Whitfield was pleased with the way he had broken the social ice and how the von Deppe family had responded. He had managed to bring a family of considerable distinction and apparent influence all the way from Prussia, overcoming their obvious reservations about his motive in doing so. He thought there was a didactic touch about the soft-spoken Count Joseph, though still flexibility of mind. Philip Otto von Böhm was stiff and formal, almost at times a cartoon representation of a Prussian landowner, though with a perpetual twinkle in his eye. His wife was more of a conundrum: refined, self-confident and striking in look and appearance but defensive in the face of his charm. Her daughter, Victoria, was attractive, delicately feminine in posture and manners, and inquisitive, but so far had said little, though he had noticed few details escaped her observant eye. Her thin lips perhaps indicated the potential for acerbic comment. In contrast her cousin, Anne-Sophie, was pretty, light-hearted and amusing, a good foil for her more serious brother. Whitfield hoped that by the time they reached Meltwater the proverbial ice would have thawed sufficiently for them to enjoy what he had planned.

On the evening of Monday the 10th of July, after a weekend of riding, walks in the parks and visits to the capital's landmarks, the von Deppes were guests of the Whitfields, with some of their friends, at the Royal Italian Opera House in Covent Garden. With the composer still as popular as ever in London and lionised in Paris, Whitfield thought a performance of Rossini's *The Barber of Seville* would be an excellent example of the lighter side of London's operatic life. For Elisabeth Mariette, Victoria and Anne-Sophie, it was an evening of delightful musical frippery, in sharp contrast to the entrenched and more heroic German opera of von Weber, whose opera *Der Freischütz* had opened a Romantic path for other composers to follow. One such composer was Felix Mendelssohn, with whose family Elise von Deppe had become close friends, the friendship opening up a new repertoire for the Camerata. But for Elisabeth, Anne-Sophie and Victoria the sheer musical froth of *opera buffa*, the heady bustle of London's traffic late into the night and its avant-garde dress fashions were pure indulgence. To them, for a while, Herzberg seemed a world away. As for Joseph von Deppe and Philip von Böhm, an evening out in London, followed by after-theatre supper, was a reminder, if one were needed, that although Berlin was an expanding city, still opening its arms to immigrants, it was not yet a sophisticated metropolis to match the heart of the growing British Empire. To Böhm in particular it was a plain statement of the pressing need for Prussia to pursue more vigorously the unification of the German states, thus creating a powerful, greater Germany which, with Berlin as its capital, could begin to match the industrial strength and military might of England. Prussia deserved to be at the top table in Europe.

The next day the von Deppes readied for their departure for the Whitfield country estate. Their stay in London had been well arranged and enjoyable, yet, while they would not for one moment deny it had been comfortable, they would not shed a tear at leaving

Chesterfield Street. Number 35 was a handsome, well-appointed house in Mayfair, double-fronted, with a fine entrance, spacious rooms on all three floors, a good library and, for the ladies, an excellent, well-tuned piano. The furnishings represented a different style from the more classical and lighter ones at Herzberg; they were heavier but still of rich quality. The acquisition of such a property, with its wide, imposing staircase, indicated a family of significant wealth, a fact that was equally evident from the striking Whitfield house in Westminster, where they had taken tea. Elisabeth speculated privately on the matter of the family's income. Where did the money for such acquisitions come from? Another reason for their relief at leaving Chesterfield Street was to be rid of Fletcher and Joiner. Their constant presence and involvement in the daily arrangements had begun to grate, particularly on Anne-Sophie and Victoria, in contrast to the men, who took it in their stride. As for Elisabeth, she felt some unease while in the house. Though the windows were large, letting in an abundance of light, some of the rooms had darker recesses where it did not penetrate, particularly the bedroom she used on the second floor, overlooking the street. These shadowy spaces made her feel uncomfortable at times, notably at night when she extinguished her bedside candle. Victoria and Anne-Sophie admitted to similar feelings about their rooms too. Their collective judgement, which they did not share with the men as it would have been dismissed as nonsense, was that the house lacked warmth, it failed to embrace, and that embedded in its fabric was a touch of seediness. Victoria wondered what secrets it retained in its walls. Several times she passed a landing bookcase behind which, unknown to her, was a tightly folded scrap of yellowed paper with almost illegible writing, wedged at the foot of its interior panelling. Had it been read it would have unlocked the past.

The journey to Meltwater took two days. First, the two families travelled from Bishopsgate station in London to Ely, where they disembarked to visit the cathedral, and then on to Norwich, where they stayed overnight. Whitfield had planned the stop in order for them to attend a concert in the Assembly Rooms, of which the highlight for Victoria was John Field's *Piano Concerto No. 5 in C Major*, and to do some sightseeing the next morning, particularly the city's own cathedral; Anne-Sophie was relieved not to be asked which of the two she preferred. After a light lunch they travelled by coach to Meltwater. For Robert Whitfield this would be an opportunity to seek to put the von Deppes at even greater ease. Dismounting from their coaches, that late afternoon of the 13th of July 1854, Elisabeth, Anne-Sophie and Joseph stood and gazed in silence for a moment at the large, broad-fronted brick-and-flint house before them – the house from which, eighty-nine years before, Arabella Whitfield had fled in great distress, to begin a journey that had eventually taken her to Herzberg, to marriage and the foundation of a new generation of the von Deppe family.

The house, much altered since that year, was now grand in its architectural scope; yet another manifestation of the expenditure of significant amounts of money. The Tapestry Hall, now the main entrance to the house, was a nineteenth-century addition, as its style revealed. On the upper-staircase wall hung a large and striking seventeenth-century Brussels tapestry of Zeus in his chariot amidst the clouds. On the lower landing was a smaller tapestry of Judas pointing at Christ in the Garden of Gethsemane. In the wing to the right was the so-called New Gallery, carpeted in rich red, with an array of pictures, some indifferent in style and quality. Above the gallery were guest bedrooms. To the left of the Tapestry Hall was the older part of the house with its impressive Long Gallery, featuring some fine portraits and landscapes, where once the young Arabella had danced. Adjacent were the living room (or parlour as it had once been known), the large dining room, the Oak Room, and the library. It was in this room that the von Deppe family saw the stern, uncompromising portrait of Sir Robert Whitfield, Arabella's father, who had caused her so much unhappiness. The small chapel, in which she and her Catholic mother, Lady Thérèse Whitfield, had received communion, had now become a billiard room. The furnishings throughout were impressive, a mixture of seventeenth, eighteenth and nineteenth century. Elisabeth, Victoria and Anne-Sophie tried to guess which items might have been in place when Arabella lived in the house.

After their arrival the von Deppes walked in the garden, went by carriage on a tour of the mainly arable estate, and saw some of the villages with their small flint-and-brick cottages. Labourers toiled in the fields preparing for the harvest. Robert Whitfield was treated with respect wherever they went. The next day, the 14th, there was a picnic on the hills above the estate looking out towards the sea beyond. In the evening they enjoyed music in the Long Gallery played by a string orchestra from Norwich. The following day Robert and Emily Whitfield went with their guests to Meltwater church to unveil a simple plaque alongside other stone memorials to local worthies. It read:

In honour of
Arabella, Countess von Deppe, once of Meltwater and the Whitfield family
1743–1816
Proud of England, her country of birth
A patriot of Prussia

It was a poignant moment for Joseph and his family. Elisabeth did not enjoy the simple ceremony as she considered it an unnecessary and painful reminder of what had driven her grandmother to leave England, events she had tried so hard to expunge. Nor did Elisabeth approve of the reference to Arabella's Prussian patriotism. That was inappropriate. Arabella's patriotism had been for Herzberg and her family. The guilt about the journey to England that had often troubled Elisabeth since departing Berlin resurfaced. Standing in the small medieval church, watching Robert Whitfield and the parish priest unveil the plaque, she felt sure her mother, Elise, would not have approved but it was too late.

It had been many years since the social elite of the surrounding countryside – some forty or so of the great and the good, the wealthy and the aspiring – had received such an impressive invitation as that to dinner and dancing at Meltwater on Saturday the 15th of July; it was a week after news had reached England of a Russian defeat in the Crimean War, and some four months after England and France had declared war on Russia, and the subsequent declaration of Prussian and Austrian neutrality. The house throbbed with bonhomie, social élan, wealth and of course novelty – it had been several decades since foreigners had come to Meltwater. Before and during dinner the von Deppes were asked many questions about Herzberg, their views on the war, about the Prussian kingdom and its European aspirations, and naturally their perception of the prospect of an alliance with England against Russia. The von Deppes responded with care, skilfully deflecting

23

questions about an alliance and the origin of the connection between the two families. They in turn asked about the interests and activities of their dining companions and about life in rural England in the face of the country's rapid industrial expansion, though Philip von Böhm sought views on England's imperial interests.

Robert Whitfield ended the dinner with a toast to his guests.

"Distinguished guests, ladies and gentlemen, it has been a profound pleasure for Mrs Whitfield and I to welcome you all to Meltwater Hall. It has been a particular honour and privilege to have with us this evening from Prussia the Count and Countess von Deppe and other members of this distinguished family. Their presence at Meltwater is to recognise the late Countess Arabella von Deppe, who one hundred and eleven years ago was born in this house. A gifted musician and singer, she left here as a thoughtful and spirited young woman. Later in life, following her marriage to the late Count Carl Manfred von Deppe, she contributed significantly to the future of Prussia and its place in Europe. It is indeed an honour to have her memory represented tonight by her family.

"Sadly, our country is at war in the Crimea in defence of what we believe is right. I hope, as I am sure you all do, that the conflict will soon end. But, until it does, I hope that we in this country and that of our esteemed visitors will remain steadfast in our commitment to the right outcome, whether as protagonists or neutrals.

"I now ask you to stand and toast His Majesty Frederick William IV King of Prussia."

Joseph von Deppe rose to his feet.

"Mr and Mrs Whitfield, distinguished guests, ladies and gentlemen, it is not easy for me to respond to a toast on behalf of His Majesty, my King, in English. Please forgive any mistake I may make.

"Mr and Mrs Whitfield, the von Deppe family wish to thank you warmly for your most generous hospitality in London and here at Meltwater. We are honoured to have been your guests. It was a hard journey for us to make. It is too easy to leave unattended attitudes shaped by the past, to leave previous outcomes as they are and not, instead, concentrate on what lies ahead. Mr and Mrs

Whitfield, I welcomed your visit to Berlin last year and the opportunity it presented to inform you about a remarkable woman born in this house. On this visit we have remembered her, which is as it should be.

"Early next week we will return to Prussia, to our concerns about the future, just as you and others in this room will do here in England. My family hope that from this beginning we can remain in touch with yours. How that may help remains to be seen in this difficult world. It is up to all of us to do what we can to find a sweet wind to carry forth our endeavours and to hope that our two countries, with their different interests, may benefit from good relations in the years ahead.

"I now ask you to stand and toast Her Majesty Queen Victoria."

After dinner, there was dancing. With the waltz more than ever established in England as the dance of choice, it was of course the favourite that evening and, naturally, as it had begun in Vienna in the eighteenth century and then later taken hold in Berlin, the von Deppe families were already adept at the steps required, making them much in demand as dance partners. The handsome – and unattached – Mr Charles Hardinge, a well-to-do lawyer, formerly with chambers in Norwich, now in London, waltzed four times with Victoria, each time pressing her ever closer to his breast.

"Mr Hardinge, I am delighted you are such an accomplished dancer of the waltz but if you do not let me rest from your arms I am sure I will be suffocated!"

"Countess Victoria, I apologise if I have been too energetic. It is a rare pleasure to have such a beautiful and exquisite partner. I will of course let you rest – though, if I may be so bold, on condition I may have the last dance with you."

"Perhaps, Mr Hardinge, perhaps I will permit it. Let us see how the rest of the evening transpires."

However much she tried to elude him Victoria was obliged to allow him her last dance. Again he held her tightly to him. This time she did not resist.

The following day, once those dinner guests who had stayed overnight had breakfasted and departed, was quiet. In the early afternoon, while Victoria accepted an unexpected invitation to walk with Mr Hardinge, Beatrice, Elisabeth and Anne-Sophie sat in the library – avoiding any glance at Sir Robert Whitfield's portrait over the mantelpiece – to leaf through the battered brown music book that had once belonged to Arabella. They saw her musical exercises, some transcriptions, her thumbnail sketch of Herzberg and the minute drawing of her and Carl Manfred sitting beneath a tall tree in the garden; they played some of the compositions it contained on the piano in the Oak Room. It was with great reluctance that they returned the book to Mrs Whitfield.

Later that afternoon Joseph von Deppe and Robert Whitfield walked together close to the sea shore. Beneath the veneer of smiling bonhomie and politeness, they circled each other with venomous suspicion, their metaphorical swords tip to tip ready to draw the first blood.

"Count von Deppe, I wish to thank you again for coming to England with your family. It was evident to me, as I have previously written to you, that what happened in the past had left a deep wound. I was much surprised by what I learnt from you in Berlin about the Countess Arabella. It made me even more determined to take steps to try to heal the wound. It was brave and honourable of you and your family to come. I hope, as I said last night, that much will come of it."

"Mr Whitfield, I thank you for your great generosity over these last few days. It is true, as I admitted yesterday at dinner, that the decision to come was not easy, but I believe it was the right one. What will happen now is difficult to say. There will be much for my family to reflect on as we travel home."

"Count von Deppe, I earnestly hope that we will not let matters rest after this visit. There is much that can be done to mend further the damage of the past. You and I should do what we can to see that our reconciliation strengthens, for the sake of our two families and indeed for our respective countries."

"'Should do', Mr Whitfield, 'should do'? What is it that you really want? You have lavished so much on us. Is it your way of seeking atonement merely? If that is so, atonement depends surely not on the expenditure of money but on simple statements, sincere gestures and quiet deeds. I can see that you are an ambitious man, Mr Whitfield. There is nothing wrong with that. Each to his own. But if you have another motive in this matter I wish to know what it is, because if it is a step towards political ambition, such as your grandfather appeared to have, then we do not wish to be part of it.

All we seek is to regard this visit as a kind personal gesture on your part. I am sorry if my bluntness offends you. But then we Prussians can be blunt. We do not have the extensive vocabulary to be found in the English language with which to express our thoughts and emotions in nuanced meaning or allusion."

Whitfield paused and then, picking his words carefully, replied. "Count von Deppe, I assure you I am not offended. I agree that it is right we should be frank with one another, be pragmatic. My motive in inviting you and your family to England was solely honourable. I am glad that as a consequence of your visit our families have joined in taking the first steps to assuage the anguish of the past for which my forebears must carry responsibility. Let us leave it at that for the present, though I truly hope that in the future we may be bolder in recognising ways to deepen our friendship."

"I accept your assurance, Mr Whitfield, and note your hope for the future. But for the present let us leave our sentiments where they are. As I think you say in English, one swallow does not make a summer."

"That is the case, Count, that is indeed the case. Yet I would say that even one swallow heralds the promise of spring and greater warmth."

"That may be so, Mr Whitfield, but as our great poet Goethe once wrote, 'Precaution is better than cure.' We must exercise precaution as we put our words to the test. Now I wish to suggest that, as the sun is setting, we end this verbal fencing, pocket our pledges of friendship and see what happens."

"Of course, Count, let us do that."

They returned to Meltwater, saying little to one another. Everything had already been said.

That evening, after an early supper, the families adjourned to the Oak Room.

"Mr Whitfield," said Joseph, "the Countess Elisabeth and her daughter, Victoria, would like to play to you as a small farewell gift of thanks for your kindness over these past days."

"We would be honoured," said Robert Whitfield.

Victoria opened her music book.

"I wish to play Johann Nepomuk Hummel's *Piano Sonata No. 2 in E Flat Major.* My mother took me to meet him shortly before his death in 1837. I think too few people recognise his contribution, not least his advocacy of music copyright."

As she played, Whitfield glanced at Joseph von Deppe. He was a fine, elegant man, with understated self-assurance. But over the past days the graceful manners and ease of confidence that came from the Count's privileged birth had come to irritate him. Moreover, his remarks during their walk had tested his temper. How dare the man question his motives? As he listened to the gifted young woman at the keyboard, he realised he was guilty of the sin of unadulterated envy. Yes, he had wealth, an impressive family seat, properties in London, a son and heir and, most important of all, a pretty wife who had told him in London she was going to have another child and whose family had contributed substantially to the Whitfield wealth. But he lacked that polish, that peace of mind the Count portrayed. His envy was the greater because it was his father's half-sister, Arabella, who had given to the von Deppes what he believed he lacked. Why had her qualities not graced his father? Perhaps he should not have gone to Berlin. Perhaps he should not have written the letter he had. If he had not, he would not be troubled by envy now. There was nothing to be done now, however. He had to master his emotions, whatever they might be, for the greater purpose decreed by his questionable scruples.

He was woken from his thoughts by the Countess Elisabeth.

"As a final piece I would like to play Johann Sebastian Bach's *Prelude and Fugue No. 1 in C Major.* It was a favourite of the Countess and she wrote that she played it often to the Empress Catherine of Russia when they were alone."

As she played, the flames of the candles on the piano shivered for a moment. When she finished no one spoke until the echo of the last chord had long since vanished. The visit had ended on a poignant note.

The following morning the two families said goodbye, warmly pledging to correspond in order to promote their reconciliation as circumstances permitted. Yet the art of letter-writing had already been exercised even before they got into their carriages, with Victoria's receipt of a letter from Mr Hardinge, delivered before breakfast. With a slight blush she declined to disclose its content to her inquisitive mother.

Weary but satisfied, and in the company of Joiner and Fletcher, the von Deppes returned to London and after one more night at Chesterfield Street and another at Folkestone they left England on Thursday the 20th of July. On their long journey back to Prussia there was much for them upon which to reflect. As for Robert Whitfield, he shortly wrote to Lord Clarendon.

CHAPTER 3

Redeeming Pledges

In early September 1854 Robert Whitfield received a letter from Count Joseph.

Dear Mr Whitfield,

I take this opportunity upon my return to Berlin to write on behalf of my family to thank you and Mrs Whitfield most warmly for your gracious hospitality during our visit to your country. Your attention to our comfort and pleasure knew no bounds. We hope that you are safe from the outbreak of cholera in London.

We have returned to Prussia with a clear impression of England and the important and desirable contribution it seeks to make – in keeping with its political and economic interests – to the pursuit of peace in Europe. I have little doubt, from opinions I hear expressed by those around me, that my own country's assurances remain equally strong in that regard, if, of course, no impediment is placed in the way of either Prussia's wish to play such a role or its defence of the interests that enable it to do so. I am of the opinion that our two governments, in their wisdom and mutual interest, will do all that is necessary to encourage this process. Peace in Europe has no opponent in Prussia.

In contrast, the establishment of good friendship between our two families may take longer. Though we are joined by blood, we have since 1766 followed different paths — like two trees of the same species whose growth, set apart by great distance, history and natural conditions, has varied. It is accordingly my opinion that our mutual friendship can only flourish if there is a common commitment, the existence of favourable circumstances and an abundance of patience. Moreover, whatever we may do must accord with my family's warm memory of the late Countess Arabella and the high esteem in which she continues to be held not only by us but by the kingdom to which she devoted so much of her life. I assure you we will do all that is desirable in this matter, but you will understand, I am sure, that it should be at a pace and with steps of our choosing. Only that way will we overcome the past and build a more enduring reconciliation.

As a first step along this road, the Countess Beatrice and I intend to seek before too long an English governess to come to live at Herzberg in order to teach our children the English language and other skills and delights of England. We consider that to be an appropriate first consideration, the fruit of which may permit our children to come to England more frequently to continue the association of our two families. We also hope that your son may soon visit Herzberg for some months to learn more of us and Prussia.

With my compliments and renewed assurances of our highest consideration,

Count Joseph von Deppe
Villa Wannsee
Friday the 11th of August, 1854

Unaware of the care the Count had taken in the composition of his letter, which had been preceded by intense family debate, and not allowing for the fact that the Count was writing in a foreign language, Whitfield considered the letter pompous, lacking in warmth and disappointing. He had held out his hand in friendship. In return the Count sought to place in his own hands control over the pace of the reconciliation he sought. But on rereading the letter he considered there were perhaps two positive aspects. The remarks about the pursuit of peace in Europe and the defence of their respective interests being to the mutual advantage of both countries would surely please Lord Clarendon, anxious to keep Prussia neutral in the present conflict with Russia. Furthermore, the Count's announcement that he and his wife intended to appoint an English governess for their children not only signalled an inclination to follow a prevailing Victorian social fashion; it also might provide an opportunity for him to suggest a suitable woman of modest dress, good deportment and impeccable reputation, should such a person come to his or his wife's attention. If so, that in turn might provide him with an expedient means to observe the von Deppe family at closer quarters.

He quickly replied.

> *Dear Count von Deppe,*
>
> *My wife and I wish to acknowledge receipt of your kind letter of the 11th of August. She and I were reassured to hear that you and your family had returned safely to Prussia. We continue to have warm memories of your visit. We have been untouched by the cholera epidemic in London, which I am pleased to report is now abating.*
>
> *I share your sentiments about our two countries at this difficult time of conflict in Europe and our respective interests in the pursuit of lasting peace. It is my wish, which I hope you will share, that we continue to correspond from time to time about such matters as our personal contribution to increasing friendship between our two families, however long that may take.*
>
> *Mrs Whitfield and I note your intention to appoint in due course an English governess for your children. The engagement of such women with impeccable reputations is increasingly widespread in England and, I gather, becoming more frequent abroad. Should Mrs Whitfield or I come to hear of any suitable candidates contemplating such a position in Germany, I will write to you accordingly, in case you pursue the matter further.*
> *Yours most sincerely,*
> *Robert Whitfield*
> *Meltwater*
> *Wednesday the 6th of September, 1854*

* * * * *

While Whitfield sought a meeting with Lord Clarendon, there was a more private exchange of correspondence between the Countess Elisabeth's daughter, Victoria, and Mr Charles Hardinge, with whom she had danced several times at Meltwater. Just before she had left Meltwater to return to Prussia, he had written to her; before her departure from London she had replied. Reading her letter, Hardinge was encouraged to respond.

It was in late August that Victoria received his response. She sat alone in the garden at Herzberg as she read it.

Dear Countess,

I wish to thank you for your kind reply to the letter I sent to you on your departure from Meltwater. I much appreciated its sentiments. I have often thought of our acquaintance since then.

You said in your letter that you frequently travel on behalf of your mother, the Countess Elisabeth, on account of the affairs of the Herzberger Camerata. I have ascertained that the orchestra is playing in Vienna for two evenings in the week beginning the 27th of November. It so happens that I will be in Venice shortly before then, to pursue some legal matters on behalf of a client.

With apologies for my unprecedented boldness, I write to seek your permission to join you in Vienna at a performance of the much-famed Camerata and, if you would similarly permit, to ask you to accompany me to the opera later in the week before I return to London. We might even find an opportunity to dance together. I would quite understand if you thought such a plan inappropriate. However, I live in hope that I might receive a positive reply.

Yours most sincerely,
Charles Hardinge
Gray's Inn, London
Monday the 7th of August, 1854

Victoria pondered the letter. She was aged thirty-four, trapped in a marriage to a man who had deceived her and from whom she was now separated on account of his mistress, Carolina de Vos. From the early months of their marriage she realised she had chosen poorly. She had no children. Much to her mother's chagrin, she had removed her wedding ring. Though she enjoyed wealth, the pleasure of Herzberg, the excitement of the Camerata, with which she often played, and a wide circle of intellectually stimulating friends, her bed was cold. Now in her hands was a letter from an unattached, handsome, somewhat rakish English lawyer who had caused her to tremble fleetingly as he held her close while dancing. It had reminded her of what she missed. On her return to Berlin the stiffness of Prussian society, the moralising attitudes of the circle in which she moved and her lack of personal freedom to do what she wished were suffocating, just like the uncompromising corset into which her maid laced her tightly each morning. She longed to escape, to be different, to throw caution to the wind. Was this the moment to do so? If her husband had a mistress, why should she not have a lover, a lover who was not German? She went to bed resolved that if she was of the same opinion in the morning she would reply to Mr Hardinge granting his request to join her in Vienna, regardless of the possible consequences. She slept fitfully that night. Rising before dawn with her mind made up she wrote to Charles Hardinge, sending her letter on its way after breakfast without further hesitation. As the messenger sped down the long driveway to catch the post to Berlin, she recalled the words she had carefully written:

Most Personal
Dear Mr Hardinge,

I thank you for your letter, which arrived yesterday. Its receipt gave me great pleasure.

How well informed you are! The Camerata will indeed play in Vienna in November — on the evenings of the 28th and 29th, to be precise. On the latter evening I intend to perform Mr Haydn's Keyboard Concerto in D Major, *a favourite of mine, which is always enjoyed in Vienna, and then perhaps another, the* D Minor, *by one of the Bach sons, Carl Philipp Emanuel. Though he was overshadowed by his father, I particularly like the lyrical second movement.*

If you enjoy music it would please me greatly to know you

were present for the performance that evening.

I intend to stay at the König von Ungarn, in whose building Mr Mozart composed The Marriage of Figaro, *remaining there until Saturday the 2nd of December. I hope that you may be able to remain in Vienna until then, so perhaps permitting us opportunities to go to the opera, to sup together afterwards, to dance a Strauss waltz at Dommayer's and, if time permits, even to enjoy tea and some Viennese Sachertorte.*

Yours most sincerely,

Victoria von Eisenach

Herzberg

Monday the 28th of August, 1854

Her mother enquired later in the day who had written to her.

"Mr Hardinge, Mama," she replied.

"What news did he bring of the Whitfields?"

"No news, Mama. He asked if his information was correct, that the Camerata would be performing in Vienna in November. If so it was his intention to travel from Venice to be there. I said his information was correct and, moreover, that I would be there too and pleased to see him."

"Hmm," replied Elisabeth.

"Mama, I know what is in your mind. But if he proffers friendship – his letter indicates that he does – then I intend to accept, not least because during the brief time I was with him at Meltwater I enjoyed his company. Besides, he is a good dancer and I would like to put his skill to the test in the Viennese waltz."

"Victoria, I urge you to be careful. You have a reputation to protect."

"Mama, you are so stuffy. My husband has deserted my bed for another woman's. I wish to be free like him, to be friends with whomever I wish. Just like you and the rest of our family I will do nothing to tarnish the good name of Herzberg, but I have no intention of sacrificing my right to freedom or my personal happiness. You have done the same, your mother did so, and before her the virtuous Arabella, from whose tiresome shadow we never seem to escape. If the three of you were free spirits, so must I be. That's an end to it."

*

A month later, Victoria received another letter from Charles Hardinge, who, much to her relief, had not been dismayed by her forwardness.

> *Dear Countess von Eisenach,*
> *I was delighted to receive your letter of the 28th of August. I will call on you at the König von Ungarn, where I too will stay, on the morning of the 29th of November, to renew our acquaintance before attending the Camerata's performance later that day. Thereafter I will ensure that I am at your disposal for the remainder of the week, to enjoy whatever pleasures may delight you in Vienna.*
> *Yours most sincerely in friendship,*
> *Charles Hardinge*
> *Gray's Inn, London*
> *Thursday the 21st of September, 1854*

Victoria told her maid the following morning to pull her corset even more tightly, to ensure her figure was well practised to fit into the flattering tight-fitting dresses she intended to order for Vienna.

* * * * *

Frederick Paul contacted his brother, Joseph, in some urgency to draw his attention to *The Times* of London newspaper, copies of which were often received at court, for Tuesday the 14th of November. In addition to a war despatch from William Howard Russell on the front at Sebastopol, recounting the valiant charge of the British Light Brigade against Russian guns on the 25th of October, it also contained the following advertisement:

> *A gentlewoman aged 26 years, of spotless reputation, accustomed to tuition, recently returned from Paris after a residence of three years, wishes to meet with an ENGAGEMENT as DAILY GOVERNESS in Europe. She instructs in English and French in all their branches, Italian, drawing and music. Satisfactory references can be offered. Address to RB, Post Office, High Wycombe.*

"Victoria," said Joseph, "your mother tells me that you are leaving tomorrow for Vienna, and that while there you are likely to meet Mr Charles Hardinge."

Victoria prepared herself for a reprimand for arranging to meet a young Englishman unescorted in frivolous Vienna. She thought of an acerbic response.

"If that is so," Joseph continued, "I should be most grateful if you would ask Mr Hardinge if he would be kind enough on his return to England to arrange to convey this letter from Beatrice to the stated address as quickly as possible."

"Now that is mysterious!" said Victoria, smiling. "May I have some hint of its content?"

"It is a response to an advertisement from a young woman seeking a post as governess. Beatrice wishes Daniel, Nicolas and boisterous Catherine to be well schooled in appropriate manners and conduct, and to have the benefit of a good teacher of English. This is all the more necessary with the imminent birth of another child. If Mr Hardinge is unable to oblige I will have to find other means to respond."

"Cousin, if I may say so you are being rather pompous. Why should you wish to employ an English governess?"

"I am sorry if you have gained that impression but the English do this kind of thing rather well. I do not like all that they do, but in this instance Beatrice and I see no difficulty in following in their footsteps. Besides, Victoria, if you choose to be in Vienna with an English acquaintance then we can choose an English governess."

"Touché. I am sure Mr Hardinge will oblige. That is the least he can do," replied Victoria in a soothing manner.

* * * * *

Victoria arrived in Vienna. She had been there many times before in the company of the Herzberger Camerata, whose fame had breached the city's musical walls during her mother's lifetime. An accomplished pianist, as her mother, grandmother and great-grandmother had been, Victoria – and indeed the Camerata – relished performing to audiences drawn from throughout the Austro-Hungarian Empire. To play compositions by Haydn, Mozart – with whom the renowned Arabella had once played at Herzberg –

and Beethoven, who had once flirted with her grandmother, and those of Schubert and Mendelssohn, easily conveyed any unhappiness and frustration to the realm of welcome amnesia. In truth, she found the city's lively spirit, its fashions, its waltzes and the public acclamation for superlative musical performances intoxicating. While a miniature portrait of her husband would, on her mother's insistence, hang about her neck as a testament of love, the many friends she would encounter in the city would know it was a meaningless gesture in a loveless marriage. On this occasion her excitement was almost childlike in her anticipation of being in the company of the handsome Charles Hardinge. Tongues would wag, as inevitably happened in a city that thrived on gossip and hypocrisy, but for Victoria this was of no consequence.

For Charles Hardinge this was his first visit to Vienna. The city amazed him: music everywhere, a plethora of spoken languages – German, French, Italian, Hungarian, Bohemian, Polish, Flemish, Turkish, Slavic and Romanian – and so many beautiful and finely dressed women. And to top it all he was to meet a married woman from a gilded world with whom he had briefly danced and with whom he had shared a short but enticing correspondence. Though a confident lawyer who had flirted with many women, he was apprehensive at what lay ahead, not least daunted by the prospect of being in the company of such a skilled musician. A letter of welcome from the Countess awaited his delayed arrival at the König von Ungarn, together with a ticket to the concert that evening at the *Musikverein*.

He sat in evening dress in the third row. There at the keyboard was the Countess Victoria von Eisenach, dressed in a close-fitting gown of blue taffeta shot with salmon pink, softly bathed in the surrounding candlelight. As she sat on a gold upholstered stool, her sculptured face – framed by loosely pinned-back, rich-dark waved hair – and her straight-backed posture displayed a combination of imperious self-confidence and beguiling femininity. He watched her intensely as she played the poco andante movement of the Bach concerto, her fingers barely touching the keys, her gaze fixed in the distance. He had never heard music played so sublimely. He could not believe that this was the woman he had pressed close to him at Meltwater. He was transfixed. It was thus with understandable diffidence that he accepted her invitation to join her, her friends and members of the orchestra afterwards. Though he and she laughed and joked together as they mingled, there was little opportunity to talk alone. They agreed that they would meet the following morning so she could accompany him on a tour of the city and, did he but know it, fulfil her stratagem to be alone with him.

The next day was crisp beneath a cloudless rich-blue sky. Despite the cold, they hired a barouche for their tour of Vienna. Sitting side by side, facing the driver's solid back and partially hidden by the half-hood, they spoke with ease, their conversation interspersed with occasional bursts of laughter, particularly when Victoria, wearing a long black mink coat with matching hat and muff, made her companion repeat German phrases in the Viennese accent. She longed to touch his hand but dare not, unsure of what his reaction might be and fearful in case friends in a passing carriage might observe. After two hours they stopped at a coffee house for tea and Sachertorte. Before resuming their journey back to the hotel she asked him to accompany her that night to the imperial residence for a ball to mark the imminence of Advent. Though pleading that he was unsuited for such an aristocratic event, he accepted her invitation, albeit with some trepidation.

They entered the vast *Redoutensaal*, its walls covered in rich tapestries and illuminated by glittering chandeliers, Victoria's arm on his. She wore a powder-blue satin dress, severely nipped at the waist, with its hem and off-the-shoulder neckline edged in white fur; behind, at her waist, was a large darker-blue bow with long trailing ends. Her hair was pinned up into a chignon by a diamond clasp, and around her neck was a diamond necklace she told him had once belonged to her grandmother. He wore elegant evening dress. For a few minutes they circulated amongst the guests, many congratulating her on her fine musical performance the previous evening. She introduced the somewhat shy Charles Hardinge as a family friend. Then the music began.

"Well, Mr Hardinge, shall we dance?"

"Of course, Countess. I have not come all this way not to renew our acquaintance on the dance floor."

"That is excellent, Mr Hardinge. But please remember that the waltz in Vienna is twice as fast than is the case elsewhere."

"So I have read, Countess!"

They began to dance – facing each other, his right arm and hand behind her back, clasping her close to him, her left arm and hand on his right shoulder, drawing him tightly to her, while her right hand was locked in the fingers of his left. With each dance, interspersed with sips of champagne, they drew ever more tightly to one another. The chemistry intensified. At midnight they danced for the last time. As the music stopped she pressed him close to her as though to whisper to him. Instead she brushed her lips against his cheek and squeezed his hand.

They rode back to the hotel in silence, her hand just touching his.

"Goodnight, Countess. I thank you for the great honour and privilege of dancing with you. This evening has been unforgettable. I hope that tomorrow we may have lunch together before you depart for Berlin."

"Of course, Mr Hardinge. I would not let you leave without saying goodbye."

He escorted her to the door of her room. As he was about to turn away, she took his hands in hers.

"Mr Hardinge, I wish you to seduce me."

Hardinge was momentarily lost for words. She drew him close to her and kissed him. Holding his hand, she unlocked the door and they entered the room together.

"Countess, you are a married woman. I would not wish to harm you or your reputation in any way."

"It was Abelard who once said, 'Through doubting, we are led to enquire, and by enquiry we perceive the truth.' The truth of this matter, Mr Hardinge, is that you have turned my world on its head. I do not know how it has happened but the fact remains: I believe I have fallen in love with you. That may shock you because, yes, I am a married woman – married to a man who has deserted me for another. I assure you my feelings towards you are not an attempt to match his deeds but to seek out a little of the happiness that has so far eluded me. My boldness may have greatly offended you. I earnestly hope it has not. I wish you to make love to me now, in the privacy of my room. It will be our secret." She kissed him again.

"Countess, I am indeed lost for words – not because I am scandalised by your request but because you and I come from different worlds. Yours is far removed from mine – a world of fine music, gifted speech and wealth. Mine is the more prosaic one of law and the milieu in which I mix in London is a vast distance from what I have experienced here in Vienna. What can I offer you that you do not already have at your fingertips?"

"Do you not see, Mr Hardinge? That is precisely the point. While you may think I lead a frivolous life of enjoyment, I do not have the happiness or ease of mind you do. I wish to share your happiness, if only for this moment."

"Countess, I am not dismayed by what you have said. To the contrary, I am deeply honoured and flattered that you should reveal your feelings. It would be dishonest of me not to admit that since my arrival in Vienna I have admired you even more – the deftness of your fingers on the keyboard, your lightness of conversation and your beauty and elegance. I will confess that I have said to myself more than once that if you were not married I would fall at your feet."

"Thank you for your honesty, Mr Hardinge."

They embraced.

"Please undress me, Mr Hardinge."

Taken aback by her directness, he undid her dress and removed her corset.

Unclothed in front of the fire, her hair released from its chignon, she undid his shirt. They drew the curtains around the bed and made love. Coming quickly, she had secured the release she had long been denied.

Instead of leaving Vienna the next day they stayed together for another two – arm in arm by day and entwined in her bed by night. Arriving in the city as acquaintances they left Vienna on Monday the 4th of December as lovers, pledging to correspond and to meet in Paris as soon as possible in the new year. For Victoria there was now another urgent task – to seek the annulment in Rome of her barely consummated marriage. She would not be thwarted. Charles Hardinge had already agreed to provide the legal arguments she would have to deploy. Both were resolved that until she had prevailed in this matter their love for one another had to remain secret.

* * * * *

On Wednesday the 13th of December 1854, a messenger went to High Wycombe post office to collect mail for Miss Rebecca Bartlett. The next afternoon, in a pleasant-looking house in Paddington, she opened the Countess von Deppe's response to her advertisement, the latest addition to those already in her possession. She read it carefully.

"Miss Bartlett, the letter in your hand is the one to which I should like you to reply in the affirmative without delay. It will be a most fitting appointment for a young woman of your talents and demeanour. I have it on good authority that the von Deppe household is of considerable importance. You would be highly suited to the tasks they would have you do."

The slim, pretty, fine-featured woman nodded.

"I will write immediately as you direct. Should I hand my reply to you to be posted?"

"You should, Miss Bartlett," he replied softly. "I await its completion. But in your reply, which I shall read, there must be no mention of the matter that binds us together, neither must there be if the Countess von Deppe appoints you. Do you understand?"

"I understand, sir."

"Good. Now write your reply as I have recommended. If you secure the position, you will be contacted in Berlin in due course by someone else, who will from time to time ask you some questions about the family you serve as governess. Nothing difficult, I emphasise. Let's say it's keeping in touch. Of course, any answers you provide will be strictly confidential. By the way, should you disclose what you have been asked to do, I fear there may be unpleasant consequences."

She nodded. Even now she would not be free of this loathsome man who had blighted her life.

An hour later, Miss Bartlett left to return to High Wycombe. Any feelings she once had for Mr James Lambert had been extinguished long ago. His brusque manner and evident impatience as she wrote the letter underlined her fatal mistake in having allowed him to seduce her with false protestations of love. What he had made her do subsequently had caused her grievous distress. She had hoped that her response to the advertisement would release her from him, but now that appeared unlikely. Before nightfall her reply was on its way to Prussia, while Mr Lambert had returned to Westminster. Shed of his pseudonym Robert Whitfield left London early the next morning for Meltwater.

That evening, riding alone in his carriage from Norwich railway station to his estate, this determined, devious and ambitious man concluded it had been a good year for his prospects.

His income had further increased as a consequence of further shrewd investments, many of which were known only to him. His wife, Emily, had given birth in April to his second son, Arthur, a sickly child but whose health doctors had assured him would improve. The von Deppe family had accepted his invitation to come to England, where they had joined him in unveiling a memorial to his father's half-sister and pledged, despite some evident misgivings, to collaborate in building a new albeit lukewarm friendship. At their most recent meeting, Lord Clarendon had congratulated him on this achievement, reiterating that until the war with Russia was over Prussia had to be kept neutral at all costs, to avoid antagonising France, London's partner in war. The continuation of private correspondence with the Count might help in that regard. Once the present conflict had ceased, however, it would, Clarendon had repeated, be necessary to have Prussia at the conference table as an ally, though keeping their expectations in step with British interests would not be easy. Clarendon had emphasised again how, fragile though it may still be, the Whitfield connection to the von Deppe family might help there too by providing a valuable private channel – not dependent on the intervention of Queen Victoria or her husband – to King Frederick William's court in Berlin, together with another channel to Prussia's parliament. He had encouraged him to persevere with the rapprochement of the two families, however slow its nurturing might be, and to report to him personally any helpful snippets of meaningful information.

This last remark had immediately prompted him, following receipt of Count Joseph's letter of the 11th of August, to attempt to manipulate – without their knowledge – the family's search for a young woman to fill the post of governess. If his current manoeuvring bore fruit, he was confident that Rebecca Bartlett, with discreet assistance from those acting on his behalf, would prove an excellent observer and reporter of the family's activities and well-being. As her social salvation and reputation depended upon him, she would have little choice but to comply with his instructions. There were of course risks in taking this step but he was used to such stratagems, just as his father had been. If his plan worked, he could much improve the quality of information he might offer to the Foreign Secretary, which might prove of use in the discharge of government policy towards Prussia. Success in that quarter might earn him the corona of recognition he sought more than anything else – the restoration of the Whitfield baronetcy.

However, more important still than that, Rebecca Bartlett might provide him with an even greater opportunity – not simply to receive reports about the family but to seek to manipulate the intentions of the von Deppe family to his personal satisfaction, perhaps even to engineer their possible misfortune, so helping to slake his unquenchable thirst for revenge, fuelled by an irresistible jealousy of their status and continuing success. For too long the Whitfield family's fortunes had been outshone by the Countess Arabella and the legacy of fame she had bequeathed to the von Deppes. Moreover, might it be possible to prove an assertion his grandfather had once uttered in rage, that Arabella had behaved so abominably she could not possibly be his daughter? If that were true, whose daughter was she? Even if what he planned could not undermine the von Deppes' prominence and influence, at least he would have a unique insight, the source of which he intended never to disclose, into their secrets. He would be a voyeur. To be so would be a dangerous game, but as an accomplished card player he was ready to test his hand.

* * * * *

Rebecca Bartlett arrived in Paris on Wednesday the 14th of March 1855 in the company of Mr Charles Hardinge, who happened to have legal business to attend to in the city. There she met the Countess Victoria von Eisenach, with whom she would travel to Berlin to meet her prospective new employers. A few days later the two women arrived at Wannsee.

The previous week the Countess Beatrice had given birth to Elisabeth, her fourth child, and it was with some relief that she greeted the new governess. Slim, petite, but pale and unsmiling,

Miss Bartlett immediately settled into the rhythms and routines of the von Deppe household. Initially stiff with the older children – Daniel, Nicolas and Catherine – she soon began to thaw. The more relaxed she became the more her educational skills became apparent. By the summer she had learnt to speak good German, though as instructed the principal lingua franca was English for the children, followed by French. By the end of 1855, Rebecca had developed such a warm rapport with Daniel, Nicolas and Catherine that the Count and Countess asked her to stay for the foreseeable future. She had become an essential part of the household and they were particularly touched by her manner towards the months-old Elisabeth; in her care of the young child she displayed an ease and familiarity unusual for a single woman. Beatrice put it down to her previous experience in Paris.

In November Beatrice and Joseph left Berlin for several days to attend some important events in Munich. Returning to Wannsee in the early evening ahead of her husband, Beatrice found Rebecca tenderly cradling a sleeping Elisabeth. The two women sat together in front of the nursery fire, talking about the year past and the one to come. As the Countess rose to say goodnight, she noticed that Rebecca, still cradling the sleeping child, turned her face away.

"I do believe you have been crying. What is the matter? You must tell me. Have my children offended you? If so I will reprimand them in the morning."

"No, they have been well behaved, as they always are."

"Then please tell me, Rebecca, what is it?"

"It is nothing, Countess, nothing."

"Rebecca, Herzberg may have its secrets and absurdities but there are none in this house. We are impressed by your work. If my husband and I have made you unhappy you must tell me so that we can put matters right."

"You and the Count have been most kind and generous. It is nothing, just a silly mood."

Beatrice looked intensely at the young woman and at the tender way she held the child in her arms.

"Have you a child of your own?"

Rebecca's eyes welled. She nodded in the affirmative, handing Elisabeth to Beatrice.

"I will leave your employ immediately."

"Rebecca, please sit down and tell me your story."

Rebecca found herself unable to withstand the Countess's solicitous concern.

"Some four years ago, before I went to Paris, I met a gentleman. We walked together. He flattered me, bought me expensive clothes. Later we lay together. Shortly afterwards I realised I was carrying his child. He immediately gave me an advertisement for a Madame Costello, who helped women wishing to be treated for the obstruction of their monthly menstruation. I insisted I would not do that. He ordered that I should. Again I refused. As I could not wholly resist his cruel blandishments, he arranged instead for me to have the child where no one would recognise me or enquire into my circumstances. I gave birth to a daughter. She was beautiful. I called her Alice, but I knew I would have to give her up, as he had insisted, and to travel abroad to avoid any scandal. He did all that was necessary. That, ma'am, is my story. I have tried so hard to forget Alice, but every now and then your beautiful daughter reminds me of her."

"Who was this man who behaved so unconscionably?"

"I cannot say, ma'am, though I am convinced that the name I know him by is not his true one. This matter is now in the past. I will not pursue it. I was obliged to promise him I would never disclose his identity – whether it be true of false – because he said that if I did so he would ruin the reputation I was trying so hard to restore. But it is not my reputation I care for, though it wounds me to say that. It is the safety of my daughter. He knows where she is. I do not."

Rebecca could not hold back her tears.

"What a cruel, heartless man. How could he do such a thing?"

The young governess buried her face in her hands, gently sobbing.

"You say you do not know where Alice might be now?"

"I believe she may be with a family in Whitechapel, in the east of London. He talked once of a poor family he knew there. When the time came for me to part with Alice, he assured me the family he had chosen would take good care of her." Recovering her composure, she thanked Beatrice for listening to her sad tale. "I think it is best if I leave in the morning. I described myself in my

47

advertisement as a woman of spotless reputation. I am not and therefore I must go."

"Rebecca, I cannot make you stay but I urge and wish you to remain. Your bond with my children is strong and I do not want it broken. So tomorrow morning, please give me your answer. If you wish to leave, our hearts will be heavy but we will let you go. If you decide to stay, as I hope you will, then we will be greatly pleased. And perhaps one day we may be able to help you find Alice."

Later that evening Beatrice told her husband.

"If Miss Bartlett stays, we should help her to find her daughter," she concluded.

"How can we possibly do that? And even if we located her, it would be impossible to overturn a legal adoption in another country. Let her go, Beatrice. Do not bear her cross. We have our own affairs to attend to."

"Joseph, don't be so selfish. There are hundreds of abandoned women in Berlin and beyond, victims of men having their way and then moving on to the next warm bed with no thought for those they have cast aside. And in the backstreets there are daily disposals of unwanted children because of reneged promises. None has a legal basis. The Countess Arabella benefited from the services of a man called Drescher who, though unpleasant, was by all accounts intensely loyal. He kept her safe. Her high opinion of him is evident in the memorial she placed at Herzberg. I urge you to find someone like him to make enquiries in London about the man who has ruined the life of the woman caring for our children. Have a heart, Joseph."

He was momentarily overwhelmed by the vehemence with which his wife had spoken. But he was unable to oblige her.

"That will not be possible, Beatrice. Those days are gone."

"Are they, Joseph? Are they really gone? I doubt it. What about Mr Charles Hardinge, Victoria's friend? Perhaps he could make enquiries in London on our behalf."

"Beatrice, I cannot forbid you from discussing this matter with Victoria. But if you do so please be careful. I am not sure how far she can be trusted."

"I will be careful. But I am not going to leave matters as they are. Miss Bartlett's situation has struck my conscience and to ease it I must do something."

*

In February the following year, 1856, at Victoria's request, Charles Hardinge appointed a private detective to begin the search for Alice Bartlett.

* * * * *

A month later, in Berlin, a thin mean-looking middle-aged man in a shabby coat approached Rebecca Bartlett on the Unter den Linden, where she had been shopping for a new dress with the income she had carefully saved. Doffing his hat and speaking in heavily accented English, he enquired if she were Frau Bartlett.

Startled, she replied she was.

"Frau Bartlett, I do not wish to stop you from your business in this town but my client has asked me to ascertain your whereabouts and, if I found you, to enquire after your well-being. I will be pleased to tell him that I have indeed found you and that you appear in good health. I will also report to him that, as he requested, I reminded you of your obligation to him to impart, from time to time, such information as you might consider of use to him. He said you would know what I mean."

Rebecca gave a stumbling reply.

"Sir, I do not. I know neither who you are nor what you mean."

"Come, come, Frau Bartlett, I believe you do."

He pressed into her hand a business card on which was written a name and address:

Herr Franz Toller
18 Holzmarktstrasse
Berlin

"Please get in touch with me at this address when you have your first information ready. It is near the Schlesischer Bahnhof, close by the Spree River. I look forward to hearing from you, as indeed does my client."

He doffed his hat and walked away. Rebecca stood ashen-faced and shaking. What was she to do now? Comply with odious blackmail for the sake of Alice's safety – wherever she might be?

Or refuse, inform her employers about her blackmailer and possibly lose her job? She walked for a minute or two, trying to collect her thoughts before rejoining the Countess Beatrice. But she could not decide what to do. Oblivious to her surroundings she bumped into a young, neatly dressed man.

"Are you all right?" he asked. "You look unwell. Can I be of assistance?"

Tearful, Rebecca shook her head.

"Are you English?" he asked.

She nodded.

"Come with me, Fräulein," he said in good English. "You look as though you might faint. You need a strong coffee. By the way, my name is Ernst Kiefer, at your service."

Taking her arm he led her to a nearby coffee house.

They sat together, Rebecca barely speaking, hardly sipping her coffee.

"I wish he were dead," she whispered.

"Who is he?" Kiefer asked, scarcely able to hear her words.

"I cannot say," she replied.

As she reached for her handkerchief the crumpled business card fell from her grip.

He picked it up.

"Does this man have anything to do with it?" said Kiefer, reading the name.

"Yes," replied Rebecca.

"Tell me what's troubling you, Frau Bartlett."

"How do you know my name, Herr Kiefer?"

"Now it is I who cannot tell you. But what I can say is that I may be able to help you as a friend. You can trust me, even though we have never met before."

Rebecca looked at him. He was good-looking, with dark, wavy hair and a sun-touched complexion; well-educated, judging by his demeanour and the way he spoke.

"Please, Frau Bartlett, tell me what you wish to disclose before it is too late. I represent people here who wish you well, not harm."

"Herr Kiefer, I have been let down before by those who pledged loyalty. How can I trust you? I do not know you. I could not bear to be betrayed again."

"I will not betray you or what you tell me. I will protect you."

Rebecca, her face taut, looked at him. To him, she was a woman in great distress.

"Frau Bartlett, you have my word. It is as strong as the word that was once given to the Countess Arabella von Deppe, of whom I am sure you have heard. Now please tell me."

She hesitated, still looking at him intently, her face white with fear.

He placed his hand on hers. Looking into her desperate face he said, "You must believe me. I will prove a steadfast friend. You can be assured."

She turned her eyes to the crumpled card, recalling Herr Toller's chilling smile.

"I hope I can trust you. If you betray me, I will no longer wish to be of this world."

Tearfully, she then told him her story, much as she had explained it to the Countess Beatrice.

"Thank you, Frau Bartlett. What you have told me coincides with information I have from another reliable source. There is nothing further to be done for the present. Go home and be about your business. Your safety is in my hands and is assured. But please say nothing to anyone about our conversation."

"Thank you, Herr Kiefer, for listening. I have told you my story. What is yours? Are we to meet again? How will I find you?"

"Frau Bartlett, my story is an old and long one and not for telling today. We may meet again or we may not. If you are in need of my assistance, leave a note with the proprietor of this café. He will know where to reach me quickly. If I have information I need to share with you, I will send a message to where you live. Yes, I know where that is. Rest assured all will be well."

With that they parted. Rebecca hurried along the street for her rendezvous with the Countess and their return to Wannsee. Her mind was in turmoil. What had she done? To reveal her misfortune to a complete stranger had been foolishly ill-judged. That night, after she had put the children to bed, she sat by the fire in her room. She felt as though her life hung by a thread. Who might tug or cut that thread – Herr Toller, Herr Kiefer or Mr James Lambert? Surely it would not be him? What had he to gain by her removal or death? He wanted her to remain with the von Deppes because, for motives unknown to her, he wished her to spy on the family. Surely he would not wish to unmask her for not providing personal information about her employers? If he did so he could not be sure she would not reveal what he had asked her to do. Perhaps her position was not as precarious as she had thought earlier in the day. But then there was Herr Kiefer. Why had he suddenly emerged? And who was his reliable source?

CHAPTER 4

Affairs of State

The signing of the Treaty of Paris on the 30th of March 1856, bringing the Crimean War to an end, was greeted with relief in London. The war had been deeply unpopular ever since the Light Brigade's defeat at the Battle of Balaclava in October 1854 and had even brought down the government. After the Treaty, Robert Whitfield heard frequent talk of the resumption of the business of statecraft in the manner practised since Napoleon's defeat in 1815. But the financially sharp-eyed, the informed and the wise in his circle of friends sensed, as he did, that this was wishful thinking. New rules by new players, including Prussia, at the international card table were inevitable in the pursuit of national interest and geographical influence. Nothing could be taken for granted any longer. Just as in the pursuit of financial affairs and personal ambition, to both of which Whitfield attached the utmost importance, it was necessary to be constantly adaptable.

He decided it was time to engender fresh momentum in his infrequent correspondence with the von Deppe family. His particular preference would be for the exchange of letters to result in an invitation to him and his family to visit Berlin. But much as he would like this he knew it would be unwise, since he should avoid any step that might link him to his agent in Berlin, Herr Toller, chosen by Joiner and Fletcher, his two trusted personal confidants, to do his business in Prussia. That particular channel had so far revealed little other than occasional worthless social snippets, without mention of the von Deppe family, so adding nothing to the information being conveyed through British diplomatic channels. According to Herr Toller he was doing his best, though to Whitfield his best was not up to the standard of famed Prussian thoroughness. Nor, if he went to Berlin, would he wish to encounter Rebecca Bartlett. He knew he could display indifference to her presence but he could not be sure she would show indifference to him. Besides, an encounter would reveal to her his true identity. He was aware of reports at his club that Charles Hardinge was sometimes in the company of the Countess Victoria von Eisenach in Paris and Vienna. Whether their association constituted an affair, as some had speculated, or was merely for the exchange of legal advice concerning the rumoured annulment of her marriage, was unclear. He had once approached Hardinge at his club but the latter had said little. Indeed, he had found their meeting somewhat frosty. But then Hardinge often displayed a curt manner.

On the other hand, Whitfield had heard persistent rumours that the friendship between Queen Victoria's eldest daughter, the fifteen-year-old "Vicky", and Prince Frederick William of Prussia was blossoming and that marriage might be imminent. If that were the case, and the wedding were to take place in London, it would surely provide the opportunity to invite the von Deppe family to stay once again at Meltwater, particularly if Count Frederick Paul were to accompany Prince Frederick William. He decided, therefore, to write to Count Joseph in a spirit of friendship.

> *Dear Count Joseph,*
>
> *As considerable time has elapsed since we last corresponded, I thought you may wish to know of the widespread satisfaction in England at the end of the wretched war in the Crimea. Though the cost in casualties has been high, I and my fellow countrymen are pleased that the Czar did not achieve his unacceptable ambitions. We thank Prussia for its support and understanding in this affair.*
>
> *I join others in expressing the hope that, following the peace treaty in Paris, matters will return to normal as best they can, particularly in regard to the free intercourse of trade and the*

opportunity for greater contact between our two countries, in whatever form that may take.

In that connection I wish to say that if the occasion arises for you and your family – or indeed other members of your wider family – to travel again to England, I would be delighted to act as your host as I did before, both in London and on my estate. It would be a great pleasure to have you with us and to continue the personal rapprochement we began on your last visit. In cordial friendship and with my warmest best wishes,
Robert Whitfield
Westminster
St George's Day, Wednesday the 23rd of April, 1856

The reply he received was polite but inconclusive, other than the hint in the last paragraph of possible nuptials:

Dear Mr Whitfield,

I wish to thank you for your letter just received, the content of which I have conveyed to my family. They have asked me to reciprocate your best wishes.

Prussia too is pleased that the conflict between Russia and its opponents, France and England, is over. The loss of life and the hardship on both sides are deeply regrettable. It is indeed right that peace should now prevail in Europe. Prussia will lend its weight to achieve this and hopes that our respective efforts will be recognised in the pursuit of new objectives.

Our family have no plans to travel beyond Berlin at this time and certainly not as far as London. But if Cupid were to persuade the spirit of winter to warm us then nothing might be excluded.
Yours cordially,
Joseph von Deppe
Wannsee
Thursday the 29th of May, 1856

He showed the reply to Lord Clarendon's Private Secretary, who considered it a likely hint from a separate reliable source that a marriage between the Princess Royal and the Prussian royal family might indeed perhaps happen soon.

* * * * *

Since their stay in Vienna in the late autumn of 1854 the friendship between Victoria von Eisenach and Charles Hardinge had not languished. Indeed it had deepened. As she could not risk compromising her pursuit of an annulment by careless liaisons that might be observed by those possibly acting on her husband's behalf, their correspondence was secret, each letter written in a code only they knew and delivered by the most discreet of go-betweens. Their occasional encounters not in the presence of others were furtive. With rare exception, desire was limited to a brush of hands, the touch of a fingertip or a hurried kiss, or to a passionate embrace hidden in the billowing steam of a locomotive. When they were together in the company of others Victoria gained pleasure in crossing her legs beneath her slim-fitting dress because she knew that it excited him and it thrilled her to know that it did.

In their correspondence and in their encounters Victoria slowly and methodically built the case for the annulment of her marriage. She knew she had a huge obstacle of prejudice to overcome and that her husband would not easily stand aside on account of both his pride and the financial advantage of being part of the von Deppe family. She had decided not to seek a judgement on the grounds that the ordination of the Lutheran priest who had married them had been invalid, or that the Catholic priest who had been present at the ceremony to bless them had been equally invalid. For her it was necessary to prove that her husband had been committed in mind and body to another woman at the time of their marriage and that this fact, supported by her possession of an indiscreet letter she had found amongst her husband's personal possessions, overrode the consummation of the marriage. Though the odds of success were against her, she was determined to succeed in securing a judgement in Rome on this basis. By the middle of 1856 she was ready to disclose her secret.

"Mama, I intend to seek in Rome an annulment of my marriage. What I value above all in life is loyalty. My husband has been the purveyor to me of manifest disloyalty. He may feature large in the social life of Berlin but he has failed to match my exacting standards. Annulment, if I succeed in securing it, may exact a cost to my reputation. But I care not. I wish to be rid of him and be rid of him I will."

"My dear child," replied Elisabeth Mariette, "the world is everywhere corrupted by disloyalty and men figure prominently in its extent. His dalliance with Carolina de Vos, which no doubt lies at the heart of your disaffection, may be upsetting. Mozart's opera *Così fan tutte* maintains that women are all the same – faithless. But Mozart was wrong. It is the men who are faithless. It was ever so and ever it shall be. Be patient and forgiving, and in the meantime satisfy your needs with an affair of your own. That may hasten Hermann Klaus back to your bed."

"Mama, I am not your child, nor will I be patient and forgiving. My husband has committed treachery and for that I will never forgive him. Nor will I remain any longer in a marriage of pretence, turning a blind eye. Those days are past. The English Duchess of Devonshire may have tolerated a *ménage à trois*, but not this countess."

"Victoria, has Mr Hardinge turned your head?"

"I love him. I declared myself to him before any such declaration crossed his lips. I wish to marry him and I will seek his hand. I know he will behave honourably until I am free."

"You intend to propose to him? My God, child, what can you be thinking of! You are already married."

"I repeat, Mama, I am not your child. I am a woman with desires and appetites that need to be satisfied by a man I love and respect, a man who truly loves me. I wish to end my present marriage as soon as possible and I am resolved so to do."

"There will be gossip. We will be engulfed in scandal."

"If that happens, then let it be so," Victoria retorted. "It is time for a fresh wind to blow through this stuffy family."

The conversation paused, both women momentarily exhausted by their verbal sparring. In the silence Elisabeth von Böhm recalled the indiscretion of her mother – her liaison with another woman. She had been forgiving of her mother. She should not oppose her own daughter but support her.

"How will you achieve the annulment you seek?" she asked Victoria.

"On the grounds of invalid consummation," Victoria replied.

"And what does that mean?" her mother asked.

"It means that he was already committed to another in mind

and body on our wedding day."

"What you seek to prove will be fraught with difficulty and your husband will oppose you."

"I recognise I must climb a mountain of opposition," said Victoria, "but I will succeed. Besides, the payment of a handsome sum to one of those greasy cardinals in the Curia will pave the way. I have already found someone to put a finger on the greasiest."

"Victoria, I have long considered you unreliable and your actions often incomprehensible, testing my patience to the limit, but now you have lost all common sense. When will you begin this outrageous scheme?"

"I have already started. My application has already been lodged in Rome. I have arranged to take the Camerata to play some sweet music to His Holiness and when I perform at the keyboard I will dazzle him with a décolleté dress."

"You are truly scandalous, Victoria."

"Perhaps I am," her daughter replied. "But let it happen. As I say, our boring Herzberg façade needs to be shaken by a strong March gale."

"What am I to tell your father? Are you going to tell Cousin Joseph? And ought you to inform Cousin Frederick in case this news reaches the palace?"

"I will write to them all on the eve of my departure, as I will write to my so-called husband. By the time they have absorbed the shock I will be on my way."

"And what of Mr Hardinge, may I ask?"

"He will be far away in England, about his business. When I have my annulment, he and I hope to declare our love for one another publicly shortly therefter."

"I still cannot understand why you wish to do this in such a hurry."

"I wish to be rid of Hermann Klaus von Eisenach and unlink his name from mine. I wish to bear the name Hardinge as well as his child."

"Victoria, are you already carrying his child?"

"Yes, Mama, I am. It is my intention that it will be born in Vienna."

Her mother appeared as though she might faint.

"I know this will cause scandal. It will be the talk of Berlin. But this is how it must be. My summer of happiness is coming. Nothing will stop it." She embraced her mother. "Nothing will stop me, Mama," she repeated.

"My darling Victoria, you have always been a free spirit, like your ancestor, Arabella. Let God be with you. Go with my blessing and send me regular news from Rome. I want to know when I have my first grandchild."

"I will, Mama, I will."

Within a week, on Tuesday the 8th of July, Victoria von Eisenach left for Rome. Two weeks later, wearing a beguiling off-the-shoulder tight black dress, her hair pinned into a chignon and a Herzberg diamond necklace around her neck, sparkling in the candlelight, she performed Beethoven's *Piano Concerto No. 3 in C Minor* before a large audience, in the front row of which were several cardinals, dazzled by her beauty and brilliance. There was not a cough, not a movement as, spellbound, they watched her soft white fingers delicately play the second movement, and her virtuosity and flourish in the final rondo-allegro. This was the remarkable woman who had made clear in her earlier audience with His Holiness what she required and the price she was willing to pay to secure his signature. Watching from the gallery was Charles Hardinge, mesmerised by this impeccably dressed woman, poised and self-confident – indeed so well dressed was she that in his opinion she was close to being unclothed.

* * * * *

Since his first encounter with Victoria von Eisenach, Hardinge's legal career had made good progress in the Fortescue chambers in Gray's Inn. His forensic skill in cross-examination had won him praise and increased Fortescue's income. Few knew about his liaison with the German countess but he had been observed, when not in court, studying Catholic canon law – made and enforced by the Church to ensure obedience and common practice but also to order the personal activities of all Catholics. Those who saw him thus engaged assumed he was possibly considering changing from the Anglican faith to Catholic. Those who asked got no answer. He had also sought with alacrity the task of travelling frequently to Paris and to Vienna in respect of commercial litigation by

Fortescue clients. While some considered commercial cases rather boring, Charles Hardinge thought the opposite.

The unusual request from Victoria, to find someone to search for a five-year-old child on behalf of her cousin's wife, Beatrice, had taken him by surprise. He asked her some questions in an attempt to shed light on the background to the request but had received little elucidation. His curiosity tempted him to persist, but as it was evident from her tight-lipped replies that, despite his professional skills, further information was unlikely, he decided he would oblige however scant the details.

Late on the afternoon of Friday the 22nd of February 1856, when few lawyers were in chambers, Hardinge received a message that his visitor had arrived.

"You sent word that you wished to see me, Mr Hardinge."

Herbert Pettigrew was a tall though stooping man. His creased sallow face was thin with sunken cheeks and dark eyes. His hair was black, possibly dyed. A former sergeant in London's police force, he had proved an excellent and trustworthy informer and observer, and had located with considerable ease a number of missing people.

"Take a seat, Pettigrew."

They sat before the fire, each with a whisky.

"I have a task for you, which may take time and therefore require patience. It will be akin to finding the proverbial needle in a haystack. But a man of your experience, diligence and discretion will surely find it. I will pay you well for your efforts."

"I am always pleased to help. You, sir, have been particularly good to me, seen me right. So what is the task?"

"The task, Pettigrew, is to find a child, a girl aged about five or six, born to a young woman called Rebecca Bartlett, living at the time in Clapham. She was obliged by a man whose name I do not have – the father, we believe – to give the child away to a family in Whitechapel. I do not have the name or address of the family either. They may still be there or they may have moved. But in all probability they will not have done so – as you well know, Whitechapel is a good place to hide. What I can tell you is that the child was given the name Alice at birth. When she was removed from Miss Bartlett, Alice had around her neck a locket as a keepsake. Sealed inside were a strand of the mother's hair and a minute piece of folded paper on which were written the words: 'Please forgive me, Alice. I will never forget you. With love, RB.'

"The only other fact in this slender tale is that the intermediary who arranged the removal was a wealthy man, possibly the owner of several properties in London, one of which was in Paddington. If he is the natural father, as we believe, it is conceivable that he may continue to keep an eye on the child's well-being and indeed may possibly make payments to the family to ensure they stay silent. That is all the detail I can offer you. You will of course be well paid for your trouble in this matter, which must be pursued discreetly. If the father is indeed still observing the child, he must not be aware of your enquiries. As I said, Pettigrew, we offer you a difficult case. But if anyone can find the child it is you."

"Thank you, Mr Hardinge, for your faith in me. If I were to establish the whereabouts of the child, what am I to do?"

"You should report to me at once – only to me, do you understand?"

"And what happens thereafter?"

"I will consult my client. In all likelihood, she will wish to be reunited with the child."

"And where might that reunion take place?"

"Not in this country, Pettigrew."

"Am I to understand that, if I find the child, I am to abduct her from the family with whom she is living? That would be illegal, Mr Hardinge."

"It would indeed be unlawful, Pettigrew, and I have no wish, as a lawyer, to break the law. I have to earn a living as a respectable man. No, we would seek to persuade the family to relinquish the child into someone else's temporary care, if they are so willing."

"How would that be?"

"I would offer the family a handsome reward for giving up the child, whom they had no legal right to accept in the first place as the arrangement was against the mother's wishes."

"Mr Hardinge, forgive me, but women have no rights, including with respect to the care of children."

"That is sadly so, Pettigrew. Nonetheless, such a statement may frighten the family into being cooperative."

Pettigrew looked dubious.

"What we will do," Hardinge explained, "is to appeal to the

good nature of the family and offer a substantial payment as opposed to a day in court being cross-examined as to how they acquired the child. In such circumstances common sense ought to prevail. After all, everyone has a price. Is that not true, Pettigrew?"

"Yes, sir," he replied.

"So, Pettigrew, do you wish to take the case?"

"I do, sir, gladly."

"Good, I am pleased. Here is thirty pounds to set you on your search for the needle. But be vigilant. The natural father of the child, whoever he may be, must never know of this venture, at least not until it is completed and the child out of the country."

"Have no fear, Mr Hardinge. I will find her."

Pettigrew stepped out into the night of a bustling Gray's Inn Road. In Whitechapel, where he had once served before his dismissal from the police force, all human life moved amid a miasma of misery – overcrowding, insanitary conditions, workhouses, opium dens, crime and poverty. The divide between those who flourished in this squalor and those who buckled beneath its weight was money – often the profit from theft and human addiction. Trace the money to its source and more often than not the arch villain was uncovered. If he found the girl, the family that had taken her might well be tempted by the prospect of more money to spend, whether on liquor, illegal activities or on more comfortable lodgings. It was rare for someone living in Whitechapel to sit on money. Even if the family were initially uncooperative, he was sure, like Hardinge, that a big enough sum would eventually persuade them to change their mind, particularly if they thought there was a real prospect of prosecution for illegally concealing a child from its natural mother, from whom it had been unlawfully removed. It would be a case of taking the money and getting out of Whitechapel as quickly as possible, before their neighbours knew.

He would start with shop owners and stallholders, since there were always some amongst them ready to trade information for money – snippets of gossip that might shed light on the identity of the family that had given the girl a home. Nor would he overlook old friends in the force. Despite these possible sources, he knew his task would require patience, as Hardinge had forewarned. And he would have to watch his back, since friendship counted for little in the streets of Whitechapel. Moreover, there were those in the criminal fraternity keen to settle some old scores with him. It would help if the girl's first name – Alice – had stayed the same. From his experience, while a surname was usually changed in cases like this, a child's first name often was not, not after a certain age anyway, since that was the one to which it had previously answered. But if the name had been changed it would make it even more difficult to trace the girl. Still, he would rise to the challenge and, if he succeeded, Mr Hardinge might give him a handsome bonus. That would greatly please Mrs Pettigrew.

* * * * *

Kiefer knocked on the door of 18 Holzmarktstrasse.

"Herr Toller?" he asked.

"Yes. Who are you?"

"My name does not matter. May I come in?"

"No," replied Toller, becoming agitated.

"I think I must," said Kiefer, pushing past him.

"Hey, what do you think you're doing?"

"I'm coming in to talk to you about your client in England. We don't want any nosy neighbours to hear us, do we?"

Kiefer entered a small living room, furnished sparely in a nondescript fashion.

"Let's sit down, shall we?"

Toller looked nervous.

"You gave your card to a young woman a day or two ago on the Unter den Linden, did you not? She was English, I believe. You implied that she would be in trouble if she did not do what you said."

"What I may or may not have said to her is no business of yours. This conversation has gone far enough. Please leave."

"But Herr Toller, what you said, your threatening tone towards her, is indeed my business."

"And why is that?"

"You left this innocent woman distressed in a public place. I comforted her. She showed me your card. That is why I am here."

"Listen, whoever you are. My client in London has given me instructions and I am obliged to discharge them in return for the money he has paid me. Now, get out."

"Ah, Herr Toller, now we know your client lives in London. Do you know his name?"

"I don't," replied Toller. "I correspond with an intermediary called George Smith."

"George Smith?" Kiefer interrupted. "How common a name can you get! That's not his real name. It's an obvious alias."

"Look," said Toller, beginning to sweat, "I have entered into an agreement which I must discharge. If I don't, I will have to repay the money I was given and I no longer have it."

"Herr Toller," said Kiefer, leaning towards his interlocutor in a menacing manner, "I will honour the agreement with your client in your name. I will take it upon myself to speak to the girl, encourage her to be my friend. I am sure I can persuade her to loosen her tongue, to spill whatever beans there are to spill. And if more money is forthcoming for information I supply in your name – which I assume you telegraph to Mr Smith – then, who knows, I may share a sum here or there with you. All you have to do, Toller, is to get out of the way. I hope I am clear?"

Toller looked at the unknown man staring at him – suave, well-educated, neatly dressed, young but with the iron of age in his ice-cold merciless eyes. He had dealt with this sort in the past, using his tricks of the trade, but there was something deeply chilling and cunning about this one.

"If I don't do what you ask?"

"It is simple, my friend. I will kill you – not now, but when you're least expecting it. You will be constantly looking over your shoulder but even then you won't see me coming. That's my style. Unexpected."

Toller turned ashen.

"I agree to your terms."

"Good, Herr Toller, a man to do business with."

Sweating profusely, Toller gave the telegraph details for Mr Smith – no address, only a poste restante. So far he had only sent temporising replies because it had been difficult to intercept the girl, a governess for a wealthy family in Wannsee called von Deppe. Mr Smith had recently shown signs of impatience with his responses and warned that there needed to be better information if there were to be more payments.

"Thank you, Herr Toller, for your cooperation. Oh, I nearly forgot. Not a word to anyone about our transaction. Do you understand?"

Toller nodded.

"If you do, you will regret it. Good day, Herr Toller."

An hour later Toller walked down the street. He listened carefully for footsteps behind him and frequently turned to see if he were being followed. There was no sign of the man with the unforgettable eyes. He entered the telegraph office and began to write a message at the desk.

"Herr Toller, we meet again and so soon."

Toller froze as the man took the form from his hand and read it.

"So, an advance warning to Mr Smith, I see. How predictable you are. Come with me."

They left the telegraph office.

"Let's go for a walk."

The following morning some boatmen fished a body from the River Spree. There was no sign of violence, only some stones in the coat pockets.

A week later Kiefer walked with Rebecca Bartlett as she pushed the pram along the shore of Lake Wannsee.

"How pleasant to see you again, Frau Bartlett. I thought you might be here walking with your charge. It's such an agreeable spot."

"It is indeed, Herr ..."

"Herr Kiefer, Ernst Kiefer, at your service."

"Of course, Herr Kiefer, it was silly of me to forget."

"Do you walk here often?"

"Yes," replied Rebecca. "I come to forget the past."

"Has that man, Herr Toller I think his name was, troubled you again?"

"No, not since he accosted me on the Unter den Linden," she said with a sweet smile of relief.

"Good, I don't think he will."

"How can you be so sure?"

"Just an instinct, Frau Bartlett, just an instinct," he replied. "I hope that eases your concern about things."

"Indeed it does a little. Thank you. But there will always be sadness in my heart. It will never go. I lost something and I will never get it back."

"Frau Bartlett, you should never say never, that's my motto."

They walked on.

* * * * *

Two days after his call at the Fortescue chambers, Herbert Pettigrew began his search. He looked older than his age of forty-five. Long years on the east London beat and eventual misfortune had taken their toll. He had been dismissed from the force for allegedly taking a bribe – a sum of £15, which he had agreed to keep safe for an old informant serving two years' hard labour. Another officer, long jealous of Pettigrew and anxious to fill the post of station sergeant, had reported him. Though sorry to see him leave, the deputy commissioner said he had no choice but to dismiss him. As a gesture of support he had passed Pettigrew's name, with his personal commendation, to Fortescue's clerk of chambers, who was always seeking to add to his list of investigators to pursue cases of marital infidelity and other misdemeanours.

The east end of London teemed with children, some feral and homeless, recruited in early childhood as pickpockets and thieves, easily disposable if the execution of a crime went awry; others in school, if they could get a place. It was in the schools that Pettigrew began his search. It helped that he knew some of the teachers from his previous patch, but none was able to help. Although some had pupils with the name Alice, none, nor their families, fitted the vague description the lawyer had given him. He turned to the harder task of walking the streets, frequenting the pubs, knocking on brothel doors and calling at workhouses. There were several promising leads but each had a dead end. He reported his lack of progress to Hardinge. If he were to continue he would need more money. Hardinge did not contest his request and gave him fresh moral encouragement as well as financial.

"Pettigrew, the deputy commissioner told me you were one of his best – dogged. Please don't give up. If anyone can find this girl, it is you."

"I hope you're right, sir."

After Pettigrew left, Hardinge contemplated the possibility that before too long he might have to write that the girl could not be found.

A week later, as he was coming to the end of another day of fruitless searching, listening to stallholders' cries and the shouts of barrow boys, Pettigrew stopped near an alleyway to buy a hot toddy to revive his low spirits and aching feet.

"Sissy, come here, girl. Stop running ahead, walk beside me."

Pettigrew looked up. Along the alleyway he saw the back of a stooped woman, two small children tugging at her skirt, another, older child running ahead of her.

"Sissy, come back. I will tell Mr Fitch about you. Do not run off. I need to keep my eyes on you. I can't if you run ahead."

Suddenly, a thought crossed Pettigrew's mind. Alice, sis, Sissy as a nickname, Mr Fitch – could this be it? The girl and the family for whom he had been searching all these weeks? He followed the woman down the alley, across a dismal street, down another alley and then into a passage behind a rank of tenement buildings. A short distance down the passageway the woman opened a door and disappeared. Still following them, he heard her voice yelling at the children to get inside quickly. He peered through a crack in the passageway door. The woman was gathering sheets from the washing line – not patched, grey-looking sheets but fresh-seeming white ones. He returned to the front of the tenement building and stood outside Number 7, which, he calculated, was the one he had seen from the back. Unlike the rest of the tenement the window beside the front door and on the floor above had proper curtains, apparently of the same design. This suggested single occupancy.

"Who lives in Number 7?" he asked a woman selling half-used candle ends.

"If I told you, what's it worth?"

He held up a bright shilling. The woman tried to grab it.

"Oh no, tell me first."

"It's a family called Fitch. He used to be a clerk in a tailor's shop the other side of the river but sometime ago the tailor closed and rumour has it he lost his job. They used to have their noses in the air but not any longer. Three children but word is that one of them – she calls her Sissy – is not hers. Hey, what I've told you is worth more than a shilling. I want more, Mr Nosy Parker."

Pettigrew tossed a sixpence at her.

"You mean bastard!" she called after him.

Pettigrew went at once to Gray's Inn. If he were right, if there had been serendipity, the time had come to approach the family.

"Good man, Pettigrew. Good work," said Hardinge. "I authorise you to visit them, to see if they do indeed have Alice and, if so, whether they would respond to an approach from me."

Later that evening Pettigrew went back to Number 7, taking a street boy with him to wait outside and keep lookout.

He knocked on the door. He heard the running of feet on floorboards and muffled cries.

"Who's there?"

"Mr Pettigrew at your service," he replied.

"We don't want any hawkers here, especially not this time of day."

"I am not a hawker. I would like to talk about Alice."

Suddenly the door was flung open and a hand grabbed at his coat lapel, pulling him in. The door slammed behind him.

"What about Alice?" said a tall broad-shouldered man. His crumpled clothes had once upon a time been fine but were now past their prime. "Has she got into trouble again? That girl never does what Mrs F tells her. I thump her every now and then but it seems to make no difference. Anyway, who are you?"

"My name is Pettigrew," he offered again. "I am conducting enquiries on behalf of a client. No, I am not a policeman. I was once but not now. My client is anxious to trace the whereabouts of a young girl called Alice who may have been brought to Whitechapel some five years ago for adoption as an unwanted child. Does your Alice fit that description, Mr Fitch?"

"Sit down, Mr Pettigrew. I will fetch my wife. She should be here."

A few minutes later Mr and Mrs Fitch confessed they had been approached by someone – no name – acting on behalf of a wealthy gentleman who wished to help a friend place an unwanted little girl. They were not sure why they had been approached. Perhaps because at the time he was working in a tailor's shop in Mayfair, and once, he remembered, in answer to a client's question, he had said that so far he and his wife had been unable to have children. The "someone" had said he might be able to help. Some weeks later this same person had offered them Alice, the sum of £20 to buy her some clothes, and the promise of a similar allowance annually. No such payments had been received for the past two years and now he had lost his position. He did odd jobs around Whitechapel and his wife took in washing but times were hard, life no longer promising as it had used to be.

"Did the child come with the name Alice?" asked Pettigrew.

"Yes, but without a surname. We asked at the time but it was unknown because she was an orphan, that's all we were told. So it was suggested we give her our surname."

"Why is she called Sissy?"

"Because we told our firstborn, Meg, that Alice was her sister. Meg started to say Sissy and the name stuck."

"Did any documentation come with Alice?"

"There was none," answered Fitch. "We were told not to report we had her. If we did so, we would not receive any money and we would get into trouble. As she was a pretty little girl and we were so pleased to have her, we complied. You are the first we have told our story to."

"When Alice came to this house, did she bring a locket with her?" Pettigrew asked.

"Yes," replied Mrs Fitch. "I pawned it last week for two guineas."

"Where was that?"

"At Steiner's in Southwark," she replied. "He said it was solid silver but the miserable devil would only offer me the price I told you."

"Mrs Fitch, would you come with me to Steiner's – now? We need to find the locket as it is the key to your possible salvation and Alice's too."

"But we have no money to buy it back."

"I do," Pettigrew answered quickly.

Within two hours they were back at Number 7, the locket in Pettigrew's pocket. They sat down. Carefully, he prised the locket open with his pocket knife. Inside were the strand of hair and the tightly folded piece of paper as Charles Hardinge had described. He unfolded the piece of paper; it bore the words the lawyer had told him.

"Mr and Mrs Fitch, the hair you see and the wording you read on this scrap of paper belong to Alice's true mother. Now in better circumstances, she wishes to reclaim her daughter. I must ask you if you would let Alice go, for a handsome but confidential settlement in return. It would be necessary for a proper agreement to be drawn up. If you were to consent, we would have to move quickly."

Silence fell on the room. Then, "Yes," they replied together.

"But what about the other gentleman?" asked Mrs Fitch.

"Since he has not shown up for the past two years to honour his word, we must consider him no longer part of the matter."

"Who will prepare this agreement you spoke of?"

"Lawyers in Gray's Inn will act in this regard. Do not fear. There will be no retribution for the past, only a happy ending for you both as well as for Alice," Pettigrew assured them.

On Tuesday the 20th of May 1856 Mr and Mrs Fitch signed a confidential agreement surrendering their responsibility for Alice. In a private room they said goodbye to the girl for whom they had cared since her arrival in Whitechapel some six years before (the exact date remained a matter of conjecture, as did her age, since her birth had never been registered). She said little as farewells were exchanged. Mrs Fitch shed a tear or two but the news that a bank account had been opened for them containing the sum of £500 meant that they could face a fresh future beyond Whitechapel. If the "gentleman" who had delivered the child to them ever knocked on the door again they would be long gone to an undisclosed address.

Alice spent the next three weeks with Charles Hardinge's mother and father in Norwich, where she received fresh clothes, had her hair cut and was taught improved table manners. On Monday the 16th of June she left England in Hardinge's charge, the resealed and freshly polished silver locket around her neck and in Hardinge's attaché case a passport in the name of Alice Bartlett, signed by the Foreign Secretary; it had been lying on Lord Clarendon's desk for signature when Robert Whitfield made one of his periodic calls on him. Three days later, in Paris, Hardinge conveyed the child into the safe hands of the Countess Beatrice von Deppe before travelling on without delay to Rome.

The following week, the Countess and Alice arrived in Berlin.

"Alice, later today we will arrive at my house by a lake. It is to be your new home."

"Are you my new mother?" the girl asked, bewildered.

"No, my child, I am not your new mother. But at my house you will meet your true mother. Her name is Rebecca. She lives there with me, my husband and my four children. Now that you and she will be together again, you will live there too."

"Will the house be big enough for us all?"

"Yes, Alice, it will, as you shall see."

That afternoon, they arrived at Wannsee. They sat in the music room awaiting Rebecca's return from her daily walk along the lake shore. Beatrice stepped out to greet her on the steps of the villa.

"Countess, I am so pleased to see you back. The children have done well at their lessons."

"Rebecca, there is someone waiting to see you."

The governess's face drained.

"Who is it, Countess? Have I done anything wrong?"

"No, Rebecca, nothing is wrong. We have found Alice. She is in the music room. I hope you and she will remember this as one of the happiest days of your lives. There is nothing more we need of you today. Get to know your child. She badly needs your love."

Rebecca did not move, struck dumb. Tears welled in her eyes.

"Hurry, woman, go to the music room – now."

* * * * *

Victoria played twice more with the Camerata in Rome before the orchestra's departure for Vienna and Berlin. At last she and Hardinge were alone, sitting hand in hand on the terrace of their villa in the sweet warm air of a Roman evening.

"I know you must leave soon for London, but you may be pleased to know that earlier today I received a message from the cardinal, advising that His Holiness has approved my annulment. It will be in my hands tomorrow. It took much effort to secure – a décolleté dress or two and a large sum of money. But the deed is done. Upon its receipt by my lawyers in Berlin and its public notification I will at last be a free woman." She kissed him, a long tender kiss. "Now I must find someone to marry me. I do not wish to remain alone. I want to be truly loved." She kissed him again.

"Countess, you are a remarkable woman – beautiful, tempestuous, mercurial, a purveyor of the finest music, seductive and a sensuous dancer."

"Is that all you have to say, Mr Hardinge?"

"No, it is not."

They stood up. He placed his arms around her waist; she cupped his face in her slender fingers.

"So, Mr Hardinge, what else have you to say?"

"Countess, will you honour me by becoming my wife? I have not the wealth or the –"

She put her finger to his lips.

"Charles, please, enough of that. There is one matter you should know, however, because I must be honest with you."

"And what is this matter?"

"I am bearing your child. This fact may cause you to withdraw your proposal of marriage. If you choose to do so, I will understand and will think no less of you. But in those painful circumstances we must part, as I would not wish you to be tainted by my shame. Yet I will be honest. And though it will break my heart to see you go, I will be brave. You will have left me with memories of profound happiness."

His arms tightened around her waist and pulled her closer to him.

"My darling sweetest Victoria, my most highly favoured lady, I am honoured to be the father of our child. My proposal remains for you to accept, if that be your wish."

She kissed him, long and gently.

"Charles Hardinge, I accept your proposal without hesitation because I love and respect you deeply. I have done so ever since we danced at Meltwater. Together, you and I and our child will be – wherever we choose to live – a force of nature, blowing a wind of change through my family."

They kissed again, another slow lingering kiss.

"Shall we have supper and a good wine to celebrate?" he asked.

"That can wait, Mr Hardinge. I want you in my bed without further delay."

And so it was they went to her bed to make erotic love in a Roman villa worthy of Lucrezia Borgia.

Later that year Hardinge returned to Rome and escorted his fiancée to Vienna. There, following news of the legal confirmation in Berlin of her marriage annulment and after the dust of anger, surprise, gossip and innuendo had settled, they married before the high altar in the Jesuit church, beneath the picture of the Assumption of the Virgin Mary. She signed the register as the Countess Victoria Elise Hardinge von Böhm.

* * * * *

The year 1857 passed quickly. On Wednesday the 11th of March, Victoria gave birth to a daughter, Aurelia, in Vienna, baptised in St Katherine's Chapel in the Stephansdom, Vienna's ancient cathedral. After a short stay at Herzberg, Charles Hardinge accompanied his wife and daughter to London. There he resumed his place in chambers at Gray's Inn as a much sought-after lawyer, while Victoria entered the Royal Academy of Music to teach and continued her musical performances – at the Royal Opera House in Covent Garden when it opened the following year and with the Royal Liverpool Philharmonic Society. She also arranged for the Camerata to perform in London. When not performing and teaching she was a figure of considerable acclaim in London's upper social circles.

Rebecca Bartlett became a greatly admired governess to the von Deppe children in Wannsee. Her daughter, Alice, was quickly fluent in German and soon fully part of the Wannsee household. Ernst Kiefer became a frequent walking companion to Rebecca but their friendship elicited little display of passion on her part.

Robert Whitfield received periodic telegrams reporting snippets of pointless social gossip in which the von Deppe family were occasionally mentioned. Telegrams sent to Herr Toller via Fletcher or Joiner simply elicited the response that such information was all he could obtain from his informant and that to press for more might compromise their employer's identity. Ernst Kiefer intended to maintain the correspondence in the hope that one day he might unmask the identity of the man who had caused his companion

Rebecca so much unhappiness. Though this telegraphic exchange offered little of substance, Whitfield was a master at overlaying it with skilful touches of fiction to enhance its apparent significance in his occasional meetings in the Foreign Office. Later in 1857, his investment success, his favourable loans to those in high places and the inevitable word in the right ears resulted in the restitution of the baronetcy his grandfather had once had. Though his jealousy of the von Deppe family remained as fierce as ever – stoked by the arrival on the London social scene of the glamorous Countess Victoria – he and Lady Whitfield were guests at the wedding of the Princess Royal to Prince Frederick William of Prussia at the Chapel Royal, St James's Palace, on the 25th of January 1858; the assembled congregation heard Richard Wagner's *Bridal Chorus* from his opera *Lohengrin*, by request of the bride.

Two days before the wedding, Count Frederick Paul von Deppe, courtier to the Prussian King, and his French wife, Anne, accepted an invitation to dine at 35 Chesterfield Street. It was a dazzling evening with an illustrious array of guests, including Victoria and her husband. The conversation was light-hearted and, by and large, amusing, except for a somewhat abrasive brief exchange between Sir Robert and the Count on the matter of the prospects for German unification. After supper Victoria played Beethoven's *Piano Sonata No. 25 in G Major*. The applause for her talent irritated her host. However hard he tried to escape, and despite his subterfuges, he still remained trapped in the von Deppe shadow. Yet that might still change. He took comfort from his observation that in spring, in his garden at Meltwater, there were sometimes unexpected gusts and eddies of chilling wind in dark corners that the sun was not yet high enough to reach, and also occasional frosts setting back the flowers' blooms. But when the sun rose higher in the sky, warmer days at last arrived and all was well in the garden. So it would be with his schemes.

PART TWO: ADAGIO AND PRESTO
A LIFE OF PLEASURES 1869–1873

CHAPTER 5

A Summer at Herzberg

It was a warm, hazy, languid August afternoon at Herzberg. Thirteen years had passed since the marriage of Victoria and Charles; twelve since the birth of their daughter, Aurelia; and eleven since the wedding of Princess Victoria to her beloved Prince, now, since 1861, the Crown Prince of Prussia. The laughter from the game of croquet, the afternoon tea with cream and gossip that followed, and the accompanying elegance of tight-waisted dresses and broad-brimmed hats distracted from the changes beyond the lawns and leafy groves of the estate.

An opponent of liberal easy-going tendencies, Otto von Bismarck, the King's chief minister since 1861, had become, in effect, the ruler of the land. Though deferential to His Majesty in public he manipulated the monarch at will, using royal decrees to outwit elected officials. Those who chose not to succumb to this master of high-handed strategy and intrigue soon became dispensable. His machinations had even caused ratchets of strain within the von Deppe family. Frederick Paul sympathised with the continuing efforts of the Crown Prince and Princess to educate their son Wilhelm in the more laissez-faire British approach to government, even though the determined young man repeatedly rebuffed their efforts, favouring instead his tutor's predilection for autocratic rule. In contrast, Joseph von Deppe was inclined towards the chief minister's policy, directed towards the enhancement of Prussian power and influence in Europe, so visibly displayed in 1866 in the annexations of Holstein and Hanover and the defeat of Austria. As a servant of parliament he had little alternative. Accordingly, the two brothers rarely discussed matters of government, such was the increasing frequency of their differences of opinion. In all other respects family harmony prevailed, as was evident that afternoon as the ladies sipped their tea à la mode English and the men slapped their thighs in bonhomie. The world seemed good.

To one side of the elegant ladies sat an attractive, slim young woman, almost out of a painting, dressed in a white high-collared, high-waisted dress with long puffed sleeves and lace cuffs. Her small almond-shaped face with large blue eyes was framed by tresses of long dark-brown hair that reached almost down to her slender waist. Beneath a white parasol, she appeared at ease, smiling as she talked in fluent German. It was Alice, now aged eighteen. Her mother, Rebecca, gazed at her through the library window. Alice turned and they waved gently to one another.

Rebecca too had changed. Though she still possessed the title of governess, the von Deppe boys and their sister Catherine Elise had long left her charge. Only the youngest child, Elisabeth Beatrice, remained. Aged fourteen, even she was on the brink of leaving the nursery classroom. Several times Rebecca had suggested to the Countess Beatrice that she should leave the household as her work was done. The Countess prevailed upon her to stay, since in her opinion she had become an integral part of the Herzberg ménage; her view was echoed by all four children, primarily because Rebecca had become their trusted confidante. What they could not tell their parents, they could divulge to her. Nor did Ernst Kiefer wish her to leave the von Deppe household, since he was still occasionally inspiring her to write further worthless messages to the mysterious Mr Smith in London. Rebecca often found his reasons for asking her to do this unconvincing but he flattered her and, to be truthful, she enjoyed the young man's company on walks along the shore of Lake Wannsee and occasionally along the Unter den Linden when they took coffee together.

Yet though still most welcome at Wannsee and living in

considerable comfort, Rebecca was lonely. Aged forty-one, she realised that her chances of marriage had evaporated. She lived in limbo, not eating with the servants and without a place at the von Deppe dining table. Occasionally, when everyone else was away, she and the Countess would eat together, talking easily but never quite equally. When there were Camerata performances she was always given a privileged seat but separate from the family and their friends. With Alice now an inseparable part of the von Deppe family, a good pianist and a close companion of the beguiling Catherine Elise on journeys to Berlin, Rebecca was all too aware she had lost her daughter to adulthood and the comfort of privilege. At night when she undressed and unpinned her tightly twisted chignon she sometimes stood unclothed before the mirror to view her figure and to cup her breasts to check their firmness. She longed for a man to take her, to give her that intense pleasure she had briefly enjoyed with Alice's father long ago. In her empty bed she often lay awake envious of her daughter's latest fancies and fripperies or listening to Alice and Catherine laughing in the bedroom they shared along the nursery corridor. The time was not far away when Alice's future would require a decision, not least whom she might marry. And where was her life to be, in Prussia or in England, returning to a country she did not know, to become a governess like her mother? Whatever might happen to Alice, Rebecca was resolved she herself would have to go her own way. She had no wish to become an aged dependant of the von Deppe family, however hard they might press her to stay.

* * * * *

If Rebecca was frequently preoccupied with her future, the young Ernst Kiefer was equally so with his. In 1851 he had travelled from Spain where his grandfather, the handsome Anton, had spent the rest of his life since journeying to Andalusia as the companion of the Countess Arabella in the closing years of her life. Though he had preferred the company of men, with whom he felt most physically at ease, Anton had also slept with the occasional woman who was anxious to enjoy the pleasure of his body. The most notable of these had been the beautiful young widow Doña Elena Marquez of Seville, an acquaintance of Don Alfonso Ordóñez, the

Countess Arabella's lover. Their brief affair in 1817 had resulted in the birth of a girl who, as a result of her mother's marriage to Anton Kiefer, albeit a marriage in name only, soon became the heiress to her mother's estate, bearing the name Maria Carmen Kiefer Marquez. At the age of sixteen she had married an Andalusian, Don Enrique García, becoming known at her specific wish as Doña Maria Carmen García Kiefer. They had two boys, the younger of whom was Esteban Jesús.

Born in 1836, he was restless like a gypsy and hearing from his mother about the life of Anton Kiefer he decided, at the age of eighteen, in the chaos of Spain, to leave home to go to Prussia to trace his grandfather's footsteps. Adopting the name Ernst, he had gone to Herzberg asking to view the memorial stone to Waldemar Drescher and Robert Trudaine. There he had met the Countess Elisabeth Mariette who had told him – indiscreetly – all she knew about Anton and his association with Drescher, drawing on notes and anecdotes in the Countess Arabella's music book. It was she who had told him about the sad story of the newly appointed English governess and who, when he had offered to be useful to the family in return for some financial assistance, had encouraged him to speak to Miss Bartlett, to delve deeper into her background. Agreeing to do so, it had been fate that on the day he had followed her to Berlin to make her acquaintance he had encountered the mysterious Herr Toller.

Since that encounter, Kiefer had found his métier: as a so-called private detective acting on behalf of discreet clients, "tying up loose ends", as he chose to put it. Though he enjoyed Rebecca's occasional company and from time to time had tea with the Countess Elisabeth Mariette, he was desirous of more lucrative business. The sporadic messages to Mr Smith in London earned him a little loose cash but he wanted more. Some years later the Countess suggested that in due course he might wish to go to London, to carry messages to her daughter. That, she said, with a twinkle in her eye, would be the opportunity to see Mr Smith at close quarters. She would be intrigued by his report. He had confided this proposal to Rebecca but she pleaded with him not to go, wishing to avoid any risk to her daughter's future. He had acceded to her entreaties, though he remained determined to go to London at some point. Staying in Berlin had of course the silver lining that he would be able to observe Alice at regular intervals, since the Countess Elisabeth had requested that he make sure "the girl" did not lead her cousin Catherine Elise astray. Kiefer did not disclose that it was the reverse. Be that as it might, to observe Alice would be a pleasure. She dazzled him and he sometimes imagined what it would be like to kiss her. But he knew their lips would never touch. She had become socially superior to him.

* * * * *

Meanwhile, in London, Victoria greatly enjoyed her musical and social life. Though still an acclaimed teacher at the Royal Academy of Music and an occasional performer at public concerts, where she was particularly respected as an accomplished interpreter of Beethoven, it was her salon for which she was most lionised. Artists, musicians, writers and politicians sought invitations to her dinner parties in the house she and her husband had bought in Carlton House Terrace. To everyone she was the gregarious Victoria, thriving amid the creative throng that constantly surrounded her. They relished the way she presided over these often noisy gatherings, cajoling her social protégés to do whatever crossed her mind for roles she wished them to play or schemes to pursue. The loss of her second child a few weeks after birth and another two years later had caused her lasting inner sadness but outwardly her vivaciousness went undiminished. Her daughter, Aurelia, now twelve, showed every sign of repeating her mother's beauty and outspokenness. Many echoed Elisabeth Mariette's opinion that the goddess Fortuna continued to favour with grace and striking looks the female descendants of the now almost fabled Arabella. For his part, the quietly spoken Charles Hardinge, greying but still handsome, and deeply in love with his wife, flourished in his legal practice, becoming a notable Queen's Counsel in the higher courts. Clients queued for his services.

Sir Robert and Lady Emily Whitfield spent most of each week in London. Their elder son, Charles, a quiet boy now aged twenty-five, remained in Norfolk. A lawyer at his father's request and about to marry Miss Sarah Thornberry – naturally from a wealthy Norfolk family, as his father insisted – he divided his time between Charles Hardinge's old chambers in Norwich and the Meltwater estate, where his father's land investments required frequent careful attention. The marriage of the young couple in Norwich cathedral, early in the spring of 1869, was an impressive countywide social event. Charles's fifteen-year-old brother, Arthur, was best man. The Hardinges were invited and accepted, but declined a celebratory soirée at Meltwater at Victoria's insistence. Robert Whitfield and his veneer of money were not to their taste. For her he was a parvenu, an opinion her husband was somewhat inclined to share.

On account of his substantial wealth, his investment acumen and his political connections, which he kept in good repair whatever party might have a parliamentary majority, Whitfield had established a strong reputation as a man who could get things done, who had a sound financial touch. He had decided long ago that he had no wish to stand for parliament as his grandfather had wanted so much to do. A baronet, he would have preferred to join the Foreign Office to become an ambassador, but the several hints he had dropped with Lord Clarendon had not delivered the opening he sought. Besides, entry to the diplomatic service was no longer entirely dependent on who you knew. Unknown to him, it had been noted more than once in private Foreign Office diaries that, though talented, persuasive and equipped with sufficient money to fund an embassy's social diary, he was "not at heart one of us". Had more been known of his more private dealings that conclusion might have been more widely shared.

The owner of a growing number of properties in London, which formed part of his ever larger investment portfolio, Whitfield depended on his two trusty assistants, Fletcher and Joiner, operating from an inconspicuous office in Clerkenwell, to manage this important business and to attend to other sensitive and private matters, including receipt of the erratic snippets of information from Berlin. Whitfield paid them well. Fletcher, who was largely responsible for the irregular payment by telegraph of small sums of money to several informants, had various aliases for such tasks. In the case of Berlin it was Mr George Smith. From time to time he suggested that he might go there to meet Sir Robert's so-called local agent, Herr Toller, to see if there were ways to improve the quality of the reports. His employer repeatedly dismissed such suggestions. What he was engaged in was shady business and he could not risk putting his reputation at risk, not least with the Hardinges.

Though London's social circles overlapped, it was not often that the Whitfield and Hardinge paths crossed. The Whitfields were not musically inclined, though they professed they were. Their frequent excuse for declining concert invitations was the pressure of other social commitments. Occasionally Lady Whitfield would accept invitations to ladies-only events at Carlton House Terrace but she often felt overawed by her fellow guests, among whom intellectual discussion was often the flavour. Sometimes the Whitfields invited Victoria and Charles Hardinge to dinner parties in their Westminster home and out of good manners and curiosity the latter generally accepted, but they often proved tedious affairs. There followed reciprocal invitations to Carlton House Terrace and again out of respect the Whitfields would attend. On such occasions, if ever the activities of the von Deppe family in Prussia arose, Robert Whitfield deftly turned the subject in case he let slip information he had received privately from Berlin. He often said to himself that he should cease the arrangement with Herr Toller. Yet though the reports he received were almost useless, he could not bring himself to instruct Fletcher to send the necessary instruction. Whitfield's obsession with the von Deppe family had steadily eaten into his soul.

* * * * *

The family gathering at Herzberg on Saturday the 28th of August 1869, before everyone went their separate ways, was a grand affair. While Elisabeth Mariette still mourned her husband, Philip Otto, who had died in 1863, and greatly missed her brother, Johann Matthias, whose death had followed two years later, and had been saddened most recently by the demise of her cousin, Ernst Walter Henning, she took heart from the presence of the younger generations of the von Deppe family and, of course, of that of her daughter, Victoria, and her granddaughter, Aurelia. Mingling with the family were close friends from government and the court.

The evening began with the Camerata's performance in the *Spiegelsaal* of Haydn's *Symphony No. 101 in D Major*, long a family favourite. Everyone swayed to the beat of the ticking clock in the second movement. Elisabeth Beatrice stood and waved her arms in similar motion, periodically overcome with fits of giggles. Afterwards, Frederick Paul's son, Paul Wilhelm, played Haydn's *G Major Violin Concerto*, much to the pride of his mother, Anne. Few had heard him play with such skill. Victoria played Brahms' *Sonata in F Minor*, which Clara Schumann had first performed in public in 1854, and then Beethoven's *Für Elise*, the score of which her grandmother had received in a letter from the composer. The Camerata's final item was the intermezzo from Puccini's opera *Suor Angelica*.

Victoria addressed the audience.

"Before I ask the Camerata to finish with a rousing piece to mark summer's end, I have a surprise for you. Alice, please come to the piano."

Alice took her seat. The *Spiegelsaal* fell silent as she began to play Chopin's *Berceuse in D Flat Major*. Everyone was entranced by the lightness and fluidity of her keyboard skill. Rebecca fought hard to hold back her emotion. Nicolas Carl gazed at Alice in amazement. A once somewhat awkward young girl had emerged from her chrysalis as a beautiful butterfly. The *Spiegelsaal* rang with hurrahs as Victoria hugged her pupil.

"Now, everyone, please stand, sing and clap in time as the orchestra plays Rameau's *Les Sauvages*, introduced to the von Deppe musical repertoire long ago by the Countess Arabella."

Anne-Sophie became mistress of the beat. No sooner had the music ended than the orchestra burst into an encore, with Frederick Paul's daughters, Jeanne Françoise and Jacqueline Anne, singing the French lyrics and Catherine Elise, her sister, Elisabeth, and Alice doing courtly steps to cries of "Bravo!"

Everyone adjourned to the candlelit gallery where, beneath the von Deppe portraits, family and friends mingled in groups as the Camerata quietly played some inevitable Bach and Mozart. While the men in evening dress were the epitome of Prussian self-assurance, they were outmatched by the ladies, displaying stylish ornamentation, sublime beauty and skilful manipulation as they gossiped about friends, acquaintances and the latest taste in fashion.

"Mama," said Victoria, looking up at the portrait of Arabella painted in Spain, "I hope she would be pleased with what we have made of her legacy."

"I am sure she would," Elisabeth Mariette replied, "though in her days it was still fashionable to reveal one's breasts to a greater extent than is the case today. I no longer have anything to show but judging by their profile I am sure Anne's girls and Joseph's have much they could flaunt."

"Mama, you shock me."

"Victoria, no one could shock you – the woman who set her cap at an Englishman, had him in her bed and more, I might say, while still in possession of a husband. How are things with Charles?"

"He flourishes in his law practice, he remains good in bed and he allows me great licence to do what I wish. What more could a woman want? But like me he worries about the state of affairs in Prussia, the signs of silly competition with England. The vaunting ambition of His Excellency the Minister President never ceases. Where will it end?"

"I do not know," replied her mother, shrugging her shoulders. "And please do not raise the matter with Joseph and Frederick. They take opposing views of Herr Bismarck. In these times one has to be careful what one says and to whom. For me politics is a distasteful business, and always has been. Our legacy is music and we must protect it, see that it continues to flourish. If we do not, no one else will. I am getting old and frail and I fret over who will carry the Herzberg musical responsibility after I have gone. I had hoped it would be you, but as your home is in England that would appear not to be possible."

"I might be able to persuade Charles to let me return to Berlin for several months each year. But surely the Camerata can largely pursue its own interests. If you mean fresh musical talent, you have heard much tonight – Anne-Sophie, Anne's daughters, Catherine Elise, Elisabeth, and there is Paul Wilhelm too. And don't forget Alice. She has been an excellent pupil."

"How could such a girl help to bear the von Deppe legacy? Alice is not one of us," her mother replied frostily.

"Mama, don't be so snobbish. She may be the daughter of the governess but she has acquired the social manners and musical ability of the best of us. Her future will soon require a decision because before too long she will be eyed by many young men. Indeed I noticed that Nicolas kept glancing at her surreptitiously. I hope her future will be here."

"We will see," murmured Elisabeth Mariette, looking at Alice from the corner of her eye. "There is another matter, Victoria. In my room upstairs, under lock and key, is the Countess Arabella's music book, which Frederick the Great gave to her. Its musical contents are priceless and it is full of secrets and indiscretions. She entrusted it to my mother's safe keeping and then it was passed to me. Upon my death, I wish you to have it, to keep it safe and to ensure that its contents are not shared within the family. We have a name and a reputation to preserve. Her private life must not, even after all this time, become common currency, the subject of Berlin gossip. I have thought hard about asking you to do this. Though you have always been outspoken and often urged the family to bend in the wind of change, I still believe you are the best person, the person I can trust. Before you leave for England I wish you to sit with me so you can have a glimpse at what the book contains."

"Mama, I will do as you ask, even though you have not been entirely honest. If you were sworn to secrecy by your mother, as you say, then you must confess that you have broken that oath more than once by revealing occasional selected snippets of its contents to suit your promotion of an argument. I am sure you would consider that to be the privilege of the archive keeper but I consider such a tactic shameless. But then you have always been selective with the truth. That is what makes you so deliciously outrageous — the family dragon when it suits you, a truth you cannot possibly deny, Mama."

Her mother smiled. "It is a delicious privilege of old age, Victoria, as you will one day find."

Victoria laughed. "I will see the book for myself and decide whether I wish to accept the responsibility you seek to place on my shoulders. If I do, I will exercise it as I think best. But rest assured, Mama, while this family often drives me to great distraction with its impression of living in the past, of pretending to be some imperial dynasty in a gilded palace instead of opening its windows to changing times, I would never undermine it. Its reputation of probity is too precious for me to do that. Besides, Charles would not let me do it."

Her mother nodded, somewhat reassured by her daughter's words.

"Victoria, the book must remain at Herzberg. It cannot go to England."

"We will see, Mama. Trust me to do what is best. Now, let us circulate and look less like conspirators."

The evening continued as it had started, with the Camerata's well-practised *Tafelmusik* of the past, to which few listened, the admiration of gowns, idle gossip and uninformed speculation about what the autumn might hold. The young giggled and whispered their indiscretions, while the older generation reflected on times past and how manners had changed. In the background, though few wished to acknowledge its existence, was the lurking shadow of war and, increasingly evident to some, Bismarck's moves towards a greater Prussia as part of a unified Germany, for which there appeared to be an ever greater public clamour. Whether such a clamour was a fiction created by the Minister President or a reality, it was hard to say. If people had an opinion that evening some tended to keep it to themselves.

"Joseph, what new war does Herr Bismarck have planned?" the French-born Countess Anne asked her brother-in-law. "It cannot be Austria. Is it my country next? I ask Frederick almost every day but he says he cannot tell me. Either he does not know, which is unlikely, or he does know but, like so many husbands, chooses to believe his wife is too frivolous to hear his opinion."

"My dearest Anne, how beautiful you look this evening. You, Anne-Sophie and Beatrice outshine the candles around us. And what talented children you have."

"Joseph, don't patronise me."

"That is the last thing I would do," he replied, smiling.

Anne poked him in the ribs.

"I know you too well. You flatter to deflect me from the truth. I ask you again: is another war imminent?"

He smiled.

"I flatter you because I enjoy flattering beautiful women. It gives me great pleasure to do so. The Countess Arabella has left an indelible legacy to Herzberg – a succession of beautiful women, of whom you are one."

"Joseph, I pocket your compliment. A woman always responds well to flattery. But now you are beginning to irritate me. As one of the most informed men in this room, answer me, I demand you. If my husband won't, I expect you to do so."

"Anne, I cannot say. I am only an official in the parliament. I do not sit in the Minister President's office. There are others in this room who may know the answer you seek."

"Joseph, you are so slippery."

"Perhaps that is the reason I have survived so long."

They laughed. Beatrice and Frederick Paul joined them.

"What do you intend to do about Alice and indeed about her mother?" asked Anne.

"That is a good question," said Beatrice. "I did not realise that during Alice's short time at Herzberg Victoria has turned a shy young girl into a blossoming, self-assured pianist. Her mother has said several times that she and her daughter should leave, though where they would go is unclear. So the answer to your question is that Alice's future has not been discussed. I know Catherine Elise would be devastated if she were to leave Wannsee."

"I think," interjected Anne, "that Victoria would be keen to see Alice stay in Berlin and become an adornment to the Camerata."

"I do not see how that might happen," replied Beatrice. "A plain and timid young girl from a tarnished London background has turned into a beauty who turns the heads of young men, including, I observe, my son. How she would manage the highs and lows of love I do not know. What is certain is that her growing capriciousness, learnt from my daughter, may break more than one young man's heart."

"There may be a solution for her mother," said Frederick Paul.

"And what might that be?" asked Beatrice.

"I hear that the Crown Princess seeks an English companion in her household. Perhaps your governess would be suitable? I can make further enquiries if you so wish."

"I should be grateful if you would."

"And if she were to become part of the royal household, what would happen to Alice?" asked Joseph.

"My dear husband will, I am sure, understand that is a matter for us ladies to contemplate – but not this evening."

Victoria, her husband and Anne-Sophie joined them.

"Anne-Sophie and I have decided we've had enough of this Bach and Beethoven," said Victoria. "I have asked them to play some waltzes. We have to dance – all of us. And Charles agrees, don't you Charles?"

"My darling Victoria, how could I not do so."

With that the Camerata began to play Johann Strauss's *Tales from the Vienna Woods*, composed the year before. The Hardinges took to the dance floor with alacrity, while Nicolas suddenly appeared and without waiting for her answer swept the shy and unsuspecting Alice onto the floor in their wake.

And so that summer of 1869 at Herzberg ended in a whirling flourish of colour and chemistry. The music drifted onto the patio where Rebecca and Ernst Kiefer sat in the warm summer-night air. He took her hand and they began to dance in the gentle breeze. As the music rose and fell, he drew her closer to him and kissed her, but she restrained any inclination to express her inward emotions to him.

CHAPTER 6

A Matter of the Heart

In the following weeks and months the shoreline of von Deppe family life changed little – at least perceptibly. The daily tides of routine ebbed and flowed in shafts of sunlight but all the while the horizon darkened further, heralding an approaching ferocious storm of the like one sees from time to time during blissful summertime.

The storm broke on the 16th of July 1870 when the French parliament voted to declare war on the kingdom of Prussia, a declaration that, in the opinion of many, Bismarck had skilfully engineered in pursuit of his policy to achieve German unification. Following sweeping Prussian military victories in France, culminating in the Battle of Sedan in September, the Second French Empire fell and a government of national defence declared the Second Republic. The war between the two belligerents, coupled with internal insurrection in Paris, rumbled on until peace was secured in May the following year. Meanwhile January had seen the proclamation at Versailles of King Wilhelm as German Emperor, and Bismarck's appointment as Imperial Chancellor followed in early 1871. With these events the old 1815 balance of power had been swept away. Overnight, a united Germany had become the main power in continental Europe, possessing the most professional and, by all accounts, most ruthless army.

The Countess Anne, of the well-known de Morville family in Lorraine, was deeply depressed by news of the French defeat and the ensuing months of insurrection in Paris. Though loyal to her husband and the country to which she was now committed, she found the jingoism in Berlin distasteful. She told Elisabeth Mariette privately that she feared no good would come of unification, only to receive the unsympathetic reply that the French had merely tasted what Prussia had suffered under Napoleon, including the attempted rape by French soldiers of her late uncle's wife, Jacqueline d'Anville, in her Herzberg bedroom. Anne received greater understanding from her children and Anne-Sophie, her sister-in-law. Her husband, Frederick Paul, remained silent on the matter, as did his brother, Joseph. Further sympathy came in a private letter from Victoria Elise in London, telling of disquiet amongst some of her friends about the apparent new, more assertive and competitive tone in messages from Berlin, a view she had heard Sir Robert Whitfield express at a dinner party. She believed his words carried some weight as he was known to have close friends high in the Foreign Office. Victoria added the comforting words that, though the von Deppe family might appear by their silence to be loyal to the new Empire, she was sure there was within the family's bosom a significant measure of unspoken alarm about what had happened, including the tasteless proclamation of the Empire at the Sun King's Palace, on account of the extent to which French blood ran in their veins – from Jacqueline d'Anville, from Anne herself and, of course, from the Countess Arabella, who had been half French. This mingling of French and German blood, she wrote, had helped to give the von Deppe family its unique blend of humanity and cultural and musical curiosity. It would be a tragedy if this were lost in subservience to a new regime. Accordingly, she urged Anne to continue to speak for France in her quiet persuasive way.

* * * * *

Another more sensitive matter closer to home intervened to divert family attention.

Upon Alice's nineteenth birthday, and then again on Elisabeth Beatrice's fifteenth – marking her final departure from the nursery corridor – Rebecca had once more spoken to the Countess Beatrice about her own future, to no avail. She raised the subject again on the occasion of Catherine Elise's engagement to the handsome Major Otto Wilhelm Thurnhoffer, attached to the Prussian General Staff.

"I believe it is time I should take my leave of you. You and the Count have been gracious employers but now that all of your children have left my care I no longer have a role to play worthy of the remuneration you give me. It would be wrong for me to become infirm and an unnecessary burden on the household. I have saved some money, so I should be able to care for myself while I find fresh employment as a governess or as a companion."

"Rebecca, it would be a sad moment for us if you were to leave. You have been a faithful governess to our children. You have taught them well and I know they have valued your discretion when they have told you matters they preferred not to share with me. What is more, you gave them wise advice, similar to that which I might have given them myself, but which they would not have welcomed from their mother. Have you another prospect in mind?"

"Not at present, ma'am, but I am sure I will find something. I have a friend who would be ready to offer me temporary accommodation in Berlin while I decide whether to stay in Germany, which I would like to do, or to return to England."

"Rebecca, you said you might consider a post as companion. My brother-in-law says he is aware of a position that might appeal to you."

"What might that be, ma'am, if I may ask?"

"The Crown Princess is, he understands, seeking an English companion to join her household – not as a lady-in-waiting but as a discreet friend with whom she can discuss certain matters in private. I can think of no one better to fill such a role."

Rebecca was taken aback.

"I am hardly the person, given my background, to serve a princess."

"Rebecca, you should not be self-deprecating. If you can flourish in this family, I have no doubt you would serve the Crown Princess Victoria well. If the post is offered to you, I would urge you to accept."

Rebecca remained doubtful.

"Thank you, ma'am. I am most grateful."

"Good. I will speak to my brother-in-law accordingly."

"Ma'am, there is another matter."

"And what is that?"

"It is my daughter, Alice. If I am to leave Wannsee, whether to stay in Berlin or to return to England, she must leave you too. It would not be right for her to stay, dependent upon your generosity. She is now grown-up and must make her own way in the world."

"Rebecca, do not worry in this way. We adore Alice, we admire her and Catherine Elise has already asked her to be a bridesmaid at her wedding to Major Thurnhoffer. We wish her to stay. So let the future on that score rest as it is. What is most desirable now is for you to be settled in a way that will make you most happy."

* * * * *

On the morning of Saturday the 15th of April 1871 Catherine Elise von Deppe, an Easter bride, married the newly promoted Lieutenant Colonel Otto Wilhelm Thurnhoffer at the Garrison Church in Potsdam. It was a grand affair, followed later by an elegant soirée at Herzberg attended by the great, the good and the powerful, including Field Marshal Helmuth von Moltke, Chief of the General Staff. It had been a long time since such a lavish event had taken place at Herzberg – an early manifestation of the new Empire. Though some members of the von Deppe family felt a certain hidden discomfort at the extensive array of military uniforms in the Schloss, nothing was said or done to cast any shadow over the nuptials of the handsome couple. Later that evening, as the guests left, the Countess Beatrice passed a personal letter to Rebecca, asking her to attend the Crown Princess Victoria the following week.

The interview with the Crown Princess was far from the intimidating affair Rebecca had expected. The two walked in the palace garden – with the Princess, remarkably well informed about Rebecca, asking many questions, from education to household economy. Their walk lasted almost an hour. When the Princess signalled it was time for her visitor to leave, Rebecca curtsied deeply. As she rose, the Princess asked if she would care to join her household as a companion. There would be no title but the creation of a bond of trust, which she hoped would grow in strength as they became better acquainted. Rebecca could barely utter the words of acceptance, so tested was her composure. Once she had done so, the Princess smiled and turned away. The following week Rebecca received a letter by hand of Count Frederick Paul requesting her to arrive with her belongings at the Crown Prince's palace on Monday the 22nd of May.

Before her final departure from Wannsee on the preceding Friday Rebecca summoned Alice to her room. Mother and daughter held each other tightly.

"Mama," said Alice, "I am delighted you have been asked to be a private companion to Her Royal Highness. No one could be a better friend to her than you. You have been a remarkable and loving mother in the absence of a father I have never known. You have taught me so much, not least the importance of humility, and striven so hard to ensure the shelter, privilege and comfort of this family. Your wisdom and experience will be of great use in your new role."

"You make me feel so old when you talk of wisdom."

Alice laughed. "Please let me know when I may call upon you from time to time."

"Alice, of course I will. I am not to be a lady-in-waiting, only a private companion to Queen Victoria's daughter, a priceless honour to me. I hope to see you often, if, of course, you have the time to see your mother amid your busy life in Wannsee, Herzberg and Berlin. You are a beautiful young woman, an excellent pianist and full of self-assurance. I know the family will take good care of you. Many young men in the city will seek your hand. You must choose wisely, unlike me. But remember, Alice, you cannot remain part of this family for ever. In due course you too must leave to seek your future in different circles. That is all I ask."

"I understand, Mama. I truly understand. And I hope Herr Kiefer will continue to keep a watchful eye over you."

"He is only a friend, Alice, only a friend."

And so it was that Rebecca Bartlett left Wannsee and, after a weekend in the company of Herr Kiefer, who seemed extraordinarily knowledgeable in his advice about those who would cross her path at the palace and who might be friend or foe, she arrived at her new employment. She and Kiefer agreed they would meet occasionally to exchange pleasantries and share gossip. He assured her that his correspondence with Mr Smith would end, but in truth that was not to be the case. He believed as strongly as ever that an important person stood behind Mr Smith and he was determined to be the unmasker. But so long as the Countess Elisabeth Mariette lived he could not move. He did not wish to besmirch his own grandfather's reputation, which the old lady held in high esteem.

* * * * *

As the dust of the declaration of empire settled and daily life in the new Germany resumed, so the social life of the von Deppe family become more calm – just as the final movement of Beethoven's *Sixth Symphony* has its cheerful and soothing rural allegretto following the passage of the storm in the fourth movement. Everybody went about their business. Alice continued to spend time with Catherine Elise when her new husband was preoccupied with General Staff affairs, and sometimes with Catherine's younger sister, the precocious Elisabeth Beatrice. In between these pleasures she went to concerts, performed several times at the Camerata's invitation, answered occasional letters from Victoria in London, asking about her progress on the keyboard, and sometimes called on her mother at the palace. Moreover, as Herr Kiefer diligently reported to Rebecca, she was often in the company of Nicolas Carl, the Countess Beatrice's younger son, now aged twenty-four and a lawyer. Again, Rebecca warned Alice on one of her visits of the risk such a friendship might carry. She must not let the lure of the von Deppe name turn her head. Her daughter assured her that she was well aware of the social boundary she could not cross, and that she knew she would have to leave Wannsee in due course.

Some weeks later Alice attended a concert by the Camerata at the Hofoper in the Unter den Linden, sitting with members of the von Deppe family in the royal box, arranged by Frederick Paul. It was an elegant evening, with the ladies in their finest clothes. At first Alice had steadfastly declined the invitation she had received. But Beatrice issued a stern ultimatum: Alice must accompany them. She had come to regard Alice as her "extra" daughter and therefore wished her to be seen more often with the family in public, even though the Countess Elisabeth Mariette opposed such a step. Her husband's support was lukewarm but, since he was preoccupied with the Imperial Chancellor's machinations and therefore had no wish to pick a fight with his wife, he left such a domestic matter to her. Spurred on by a letter from Victoria, urging her to ignore family snobbery and embrace Alice, Beatrice ensured that the young woman that evening was eye-catching in a pink off-the-shoulder full-skirted evening dress overlaid with layers of tulle. Her hair was gathered into a plait decorated with minute flowers and around her neck she wore a diamond necklace belonging to the Countess. As the tall, shy young woman moved to take her seat many in the stalls below looked at her through their opera glasses, struck by her beauty and poise, asking one another who she might be. Expecting to sit in the second row of the box, she was instead bidden by Nicolas Carl to sit beside him in the front. The concert began.

Following Haydn's *Trumpet Concerto* the concert's principal item in the first half was Beethoven's *Seventh Symphony*. After the interval, during which Alice was the object of even closer scrutiny, the family resumed their seats for a selection of baroque arias. The second one was *Fra quest'ombre* by Johann Adolf Hasse from his opera *Solimano*. As the soprano sang the words:

> *If among these shadows you spy*
> *A wandering shade in search of rest,*
> *'Tis that of your faithful husband,*
> *Come to beg you for mercy.*
> *Sweet will my final breath be*
> *If, after my death, you live on for me.*

Nicolas placed his hand gently on Alice's, whispering in her ear, "If I were your husband, those would be the very words I would sing to you." For a moment his hand lingered on hers before slowly withdrawing. Alice did not move, did not look towards him. She could not believe what she had just heard. She felt herself blush, terrified that the Countess may have observed what her son had done.

That night Alice lay in bed unable to sleep, recalling the aria over and over again. What had Nicolas meant? She enjoyed his friendship, his kindness and his apparent affection for her, which she had always assumed was of the sort a brother might show a beloved sister. She had sometimes flirted with him. Catherine Elise had taught her how certain coquettish female gestures could easily manipulate a man's attention towards a young woman, tricks Catherine had confessed she had used to bewitch her future husband. Though she might employ some of these tricks herself, Alice was always mindful of her promise to her mother that she would resist any temptation to seek to cross the social boundary between her ordinary English background and that of the von Deppe aristocracy. She decided in the depth of the night that she would say nothing – pretend what Nicolas had said and done had never happened – but also resolved that the time had surely come to take her leave of the family, heartbreaking though that might be.

Two weeks later, on the 26th of July, after declining two invitations to join Nicolas in Berlin, Alice asked to see the Countess.

"I have decided I should leave you to return to England, the country of my birth, to begin a new life there. It has been a hard decision but I believe it is the right one. I wish to thank you and the Count for your gentleness and generosity towards me since my arrival in your family as a young child. But I cannot stay."

Alice found it difficult to speak these words. She ached inside and at any moment would burst into tears.

"Alice, I do not believe you are being honest with me or yourself. Honesty is amongst the greatest of virtues, to be nurtured and practised every day. Dishonesty is a sin of commission. Please tell me the truth. Why do you suddenly wish to leave?"

Alice summoned up her remaining courage.

"I come from a poor simple background in London. I have been brought up by a deeply caring and loving mother but without a father. What I lacked in childhood, you, the Count, your children have provided in boundless quantity and generosity. I must now build on that legacy in my own way in England, not in Germany."

"Alice, I do not understand what you are trying to say."

"Countess, I have to leave because I cannot continue to live a life to which I was not born. To do so would be a lie."

She had uttered the words she had dreaded. What more could she say? She wanted to flee the room and to sob in the privacy of her bedroom. She did not think she could bear the Countess's concerned persistence any longer.

"Alice, listen to me. I still believe you are deceiving me and more importantly yourself. You are not speaking the truth. I believe I understand the reason why you wish to leave, but I am not sure you do."

Then she heard the words she had least expected – the cruellest of words.

"Are you in love with my son?"

Alice's face reflected her inner anguish. What was she to reply? Be honest, the Countess had said.

"I don't know. I really do not know," she said as her tears welled. "And even if I was, he and I could never be married for the reason I have given. We come from different worlds."

"Let me help you, Alice, towards the truth. My son has told me that he has fallen in love with you. Like many Prussian men, he does not wear his emotions easily on his sleeve. He is young and still has much to learn of life, and there will be some in the von Deppe family, not least the Countess Elisabeth Mariette, who will stand on their pride and seek to oppose his wish to have you as his wife. But he will have no opposition from me or his father. Instead, he will have our support. And the Countess Victoria is a robust ally. Alice, let me come to the heart of the matter. Your background is beside the point. My son says he loves you and I believe he does. It is for you to decide whether you wish to receive his proposal. These are uncertain times. There are many in this land who are puffed up but, as it is often said, pride comes before a fall. When a fall might come to this nation no one knows. In the meantime, all of us, including you, should grasp and pursue happiness as best we can."

"Countess, do you not see that I am of low birth? My humble circumstances do not fit with this august family whose famed portraits line the gallery at Herzberg. I could never give what they have given. I do not wish to stay and become in due course an object of pity, to be discarded when people are tired of me."

"Alice, please stop. I have been silent for too long. I agree with the Countess Victoria that this family must stop living on past glory and upholding stuffy traditions, that we must display our emotions more often, that we must be more honest with ourselves. The circumstances of your birth are of no consequence. What matters is what you have become – a self-assured and striking young woman with great musical talent. You have much to give, but you must allow others to give to you. My son loves you and because of that wishes to seek your hand in marriage so he can share his life with you. If you choose to accept his proposal – and that must be your decision and no one else's – I have no doubt that you can give Nicolas much happiness in return. Now, if I have convinced you of the real truth, which I believe you have been avoiding, do you still wish to leave us?"

Alice looked up, her eyes full of tears. The room was spinning. She was in such turmoil. The Countess took her hands in hers. Alice tried to summon the courage to speak.

"Alice, be brave. Speak the truth that is in your heart."

The room fell silent.

Alice let slip the burden.

"Countess, yes I do love Nicolas. I love him because he fills me with joy whenever we are together. You have helped me to understand that is so." She paused. Should she utter now the fateful words and so go against all that she had promised her mother? "I would be deeply honoured to receive your son's proposal. But what should I tell my mother?"

"Your mother is already informed and has no objection. Please, Alice, put my son out of his misery as soon as you can so he can revert to his legal career."

They laughed.

A week later a notice appeared in the Berlin press announcing the engagement of Fräulein Alice Bartlett to Count Nicolas Carl von Deppe. The marriage took place in the small chapel at Herzberg on Saturday the 9th of September 1871, followed by a musical soirée at Herzberg, where they were to lodge temporarily under the watchful eye of the family matriarch, the Countess Elisabeth Mariette. Much to Rebecca's pride that day, her daughter had become Alice von Deppe and a Countess by marriage.

* * * * *

A few days later Ernst Kiefer sent another of his messages to Mr Smith in London. In its contents about this and that, he reported that fresh English blood had entered the veins of the von Deppe family. On its receipt, Robert Whitfield raged. His plan to rid himself of an unwanted mother and daughter had resulted in Whitfield blood once again mingling with that of a German family who continued to haunt the fortunes of his own. To add to his injury, the woman he had abandoned had become the companion of the Crown Princess Victoria. When would this insanity stop?

He sent immediate instructions to Fletcher to summon Herr Toller to London, not only to pay him off but, if necessary, dispose of him. Whitfield realised that the risk of the exposure of his devilment had now become too great for this correspondence to continue a moment longer.

CHAPTER 7

A Promise of Enduring Friendships

It is a feature of late summer that, while daylight warmth may linger into evening time, twilight inexorably advances its territory almost by stealth. With the encroaching eventide comes the prospect of longer nights and darker horizons. It is a time of year when summer's memories are cherished and promises of enduring friendship through autumn and winter pledged.

In July 1872, Victoria and her daughter, Aurelia, returned to Herzberg for two months, ostensibly for the purpose of seeking to persuade Paul Wilhelm and Alice to perform in London. She knew this would be hard to achieve but was nonetheless determined to try. Another and more pressing reason for her return was her mother's frailer health and the decision, which still had to be taken, about the fate of Arabella von Deppe's music book. The uncertainty, Victoria knew, was beginning to distress her mother, the sole surviving member of the family who had known and adored the famous Countess.

Her mother resting beside her, Victoria sat in the library one afternoon to discharge her promise to consider whether she should become the keeper of this secret book – a decision she had long fought hard to avoid. She undid the frayed gold ribbon, allowing the contents of faded documents, slips of paper and musical transcriptions and compositions to spill onto her lap. For the next two hours she sat transfixed by all that she read. Too often she had hastily dismissed Arabella as a relic of a bygone age. Now she judged her in a new light – a woman who had created an orchestra, who had abhorred convention; a woman who had taken profound risks during the French Revolution; who had frequented the company of risqué men, such as Waldemar Drescher; and who had enjoyed friendship with *Der Alte Fritz*, Catherine the Great and Mozart; and a woman who had, it appeared, been sexually free. Reading them for the first time, she was struck by the written words: *I will do what people want but only as I want it to be.* They summarised pithily Victoria's own approach to life. They would now become her clarion call and she would encourage Aurelia, Alice and the other younger members of the von Deppe family to echo them too. On the death of her mother, a new and younger generation of the family would step forward, ready to take Herzberg and its legacy in a new direction. It would be thrilling to ride the tide of history following the example of an inspiring woman. Yes. She would become guardian of the book.

As she replaced the contents inside the leather binding Victoria noticed a small object wrapped in paper. She slowly undid it to discover the beautiful miniature of Arabella's mother, Thérèse de Miron. On the reverse of the paper wrapping was a note in the handwriting of Arabella's daughter, Elise, explaining how she had learnt the likely identity of the painter but so far had been unable to discover the meaning of the letters *FB*, skilfully disguised in the sitter's décolletage. That secret remained to be unravelled. Victoria turned the miniature in her fingers to read the inscription on the back. This was a mystery she decided she would resolve.

The Countess Elisabeth stirred.

"Well, are you going to become its guardian?"

"Yes, Mama, I will."

"Good, but how are you going to care for it if you are in London? The book with its secrets cannot leave Herzberg and it must not be left in the keeping of the other side of the family. They are all so untrustworthy."

"You cannot say that."

"Can't I? But I do. I am not sure, for that matter, why I trust you, but as you are my only child I have little choice. Since you married Mr Hardinge –"

"*Sir*, Mama," interrupted Victoria. "He is now *Sir* Charles Hardinge, QC."

"Since you married Sir Charles Hardinge, you appear to have become more sensible."

Victoria smiled. Her mother was right in her judgement.

"So, Lady Hardinge, what is the answer? Where will you keep the book?"

"I will find a suitable hiding place here at Herzberg and come every year to ensure that it has not been disturbed. But I would like to take the miniature to London."

"That is out of the question. It belongs to the music book and must remain with it."

Elisabeth Mariette became agitated.

"Mama, if that is your wish it will remain here. But I am resolved to discover the bearer of the letters *FB*."

"Victoria, please leave matters alone. I did. It is old history."

"Mama, why should I leave matters alone? Is it because you fear the discovery may cast doubt on the identity of Arabella's father?"

"We would not be here," the elderly Countess replied sharply, "if it were not for Arabella's pursuit of Carl Manfred von Deppe. They fell in love and together they renewed the family. What may have happened before that should remain closed. It was none of our business then and that is equally the case now. So please do not pursue matters."

Victoria paused before replying.

"One person who intrigues me from what I have read is Anton Kiefer. I wonder whatever happened to him."

"There you go again, that irritating curiosity of yours. He is but a footnote in the music book. Do not pursue it, please!"

"Why not?" retorted Victoria.

"Because I ask you not to do so," replied Elisabeth Mariette brusquely.

"I sense, Mama, you know more about Herr Kiefer than you are telling me. If you wish me to be the keeper of this book of secrets and to defend Herzberg's reputation, you must confide in me what else you may know. If challenged later, how can I ask if you are dead?"

Elisabeth Mariette scowled.

"I have met Kiefer's grandson – some years ago. He is of

Spanish blood."

"How did you meet him?"

"He came to Herzberg shortly after arriving from Spain to view the memorial stones. He asked me what I knew about his grandfather's association with that awful man Drescher. I revealed – selectively – what I knew. He offered to be of assistance to the family. I told him about poor Miss Bartlett. He said he would speak to her discreetly about her circumstances to see if he could help. I gave him some money. He later told me that they had met, that the matter was in hand, but he did not divulge their conversation and I did not enquire as I had no wish to know."

"Has he asked for more money?" demanded Victoria.

"No, he has not. But he has written from time to time, renewing his offer of assistance."

"Assistance with what, may I ask?"

"He has long wanted to go to England to find out more about Alice's father. He has also arranged the occasional despatch of some urgent private letters from me to you in London."

"I suppose you did that so he had a pretext to pursue Alice's father?"

"Yes," Elisabeth Mariette replied simply.

Victoria was aghast at this revelation.

"Have you kept his letters?"

"No. I burned them."

"What you have done is unforgivable. You must have no more correspondence with him. Do you understand? If it ever became public knowledge that you, the great defender of the von Deppe name, had instructed and paid for such a man – with an uncertain background – to investigate Miss Bartlett, governess to Joseph and Beatrice's children and now companion to the Crown Princess, and, moreover, to seek to trace the father of her daughter, now married to Joseph's son, there would be a public scandal."

"Victoria, you are vexing me. I did it because I thought it was for the best. That's an end to it."

"Mama, I am not sure that you have told me the full truth. But let me be clear. If he contacts you again, you must tell me. Neither Miss Bartlett nor Alice must know about this – ever. Do you understand?"

Elisabeth Mariette did not respond.

*

At the beginning of September, 1872, Victoria and her daughter returned to London. Two days later, Elisabeth Mariette and Ernst Kiefer met for coffee in Berlin. Mindful of her daughter's pledge to guard the music book, which she had no wish to jeopardise, she made Kiefer promise that under no circumstances would he ever travel to London to unlock the identity of Alice's natural father. Alice had now married into the family and there was no longer any point in pursuing her background. Any skeletons surrounding her birth were, she insisted, better left undisturbed, since their exhumation would only fuel gossip at best, cause scandal and lasting damage at worst, and therefore cast an unwanted shadow just as everyone was adjusting to the pecking order of the new German Empire. Kiefer attempted to refute her view, maintaining that it would be better to find out now and be prepared in case of unfavourable disclosures later. The Countess insisted robustly that such a step was not in the family's interests. Any unwanted disclosure, she emphasised, could have serious consequences for Herzberg's reputation, that of Alice's mother and possibly even him, the source of the harmful information. Was that a threat, he wondered? Bringing the conversation to a close, she paid him a handsome sum of money. In return, Kiefer pledged to remain silent, to do nothing. But after they had said farewell, his curiosity about Mr Smith and the reason for the sudden instruction to provide no further reports remained unabated. The Countess would not live for ever. Once she was dead he would surely be relieved of any obligation.

A short while later Kiefer met Rebecca Bartlett at the palace, where from time to time they took tea together. He had remained fond of her, regarding the Crown Princess's companion as a wise and trusted friend in whom he could confide. He told her of his conversation with the Countess. Rebecca was relieved to hear of his promise not to pursue the matter of her daughter's father. She had become the Crown Princess's respected confidante and, though she sometimes found the stifling pomp and rigour of the imperial family hard to bear, she was proud of what she had achieved since her arrival in Germany. She still longed to find lasting love and happiness in the arms of a man but it could not be

Kiefer. As he had pledged to take no further action and she believed him, Rebecca decided that it was time to bring their friendship to an end. So when they said goodbye that afternoon she declined his suggestion to agree a date on which he might call again, choosing instead to be vague. As Kiefer walked away from the palace he knew they would not meet again.

* * * * *

At the beginning of February 1873, in London, Victoria received an urgent message that her mother's health was failing fast and that it would be desirable for her to return to Herzberg as soon as possible. Within a few days of her daughter's arrival, the Countess Elisabeth Mariette von Böhm died in the grand bedroom where her grandmother, the Countess Arabella, had done so fifty-seven years before. A week later, on Friday the 21st of February, her funeral took place in the Garrison Church at Potsdam, after which she was laid to rest in the grounds of Herzberg alongside her husband, Philip Otto, and close to her mother and brother. The Camerata gave a memorial concert in her honour, attended by many notables and friends of the family. A number of those present sensed that the family now faced a new future in the hands of a younger generation.

Despite Victoria's insistence that Herzberg belonged to the family, not to her, it remained the family's unanimous wish that use of Herzberg should rest nominally with Victoria and, moreover, that it should remain the official home of the Camerata. It was also agreed that Nicolas Carl and Alice, and any children they might have, should continue to live at the Schloss, thus caring for the estate during Victoria's absences in London. Before leaving Herzberg, with the first signs of spring becoming manifest in the garden, Victoria placed the music book in a new safe, hidden behind a panel in her late mother's bedroom, but not before a photograph had been taken of the miniature for her to take back to London.

* * * * *

Ernst Kiefer read of the Countess's death and had been a bystander as the funeral cortège passed on its way from the

Garrison Church to Herzberg. Deciding that her death had released him from his promise not to go to London, he had accordingly telegraphed Mr Smith to say that he would arrive there before too long as they had some unfinished business to settle. Receipt of yet another tiresome message from the persistent Herr Toller, who had, it appeared, become an exponent of blackmail, resulted in instructions from Fletcher's paymaster to deal in whatever way necessary with the unwanted visitor should he indeed step foot in London.

* * * * *

At the beginning of 1873 Robert Whitfield decided it was time to begin to put his affairs in order.

Troubled frequently by the aches and pains of old age, he drew up a fresh will. Aside from providing generously for his wife, Emily, should she outlive him, he decided that the Meltwater estate should pass to his elder son, Charles, who enjoyed the financial benefit of the estate, supplementing his legal income. Moreover, Charles's wife, Sarah, was a good chatelaine and had given birth there to her son, Sebastian, and most recently her daughter, Priscilla Emily. To ensure the regularity and health of the estate's income, particularly as the Meltwater staff increased in number, Sir Robert had appointed an astute land agent, William Bickers. He had proved an adroit protector and promoter of the estate, ensuring always the best price for the product of the land.

Sir Robert's younger son, Arthur, once a sickly child, had grown into a mature young man, more earnest than his elder brother but with great independence of mind. Sir Robert had hoped that he would assume responsibility for Whitfield affairs in London. However, though Arthur dutifully paid attention to them, under his father's close scrutiny, it was apparent that his real interests lay elsewhere, not least in portrait painting for some of his young friends.

* * * * *

In June Alice received a letter from Victoria in London.

Dearest Alice,

I have now received the warmest reports of the acclaim that greets you whenever you perform with the Camerata. I heard in particular that recently you were given a standing ovation for your interpretation of Mozart's Piano Concerto No. 18. *Bravissima!*

It is now time for you to come to London. The Camerata has been invited to perform at the Royal Albert Hall. I have promised to play some Beethoven. I think you should play too — some Mozart or Haydn. I know you will have serious reservations about coming to England but please consider it — please, Alice, please. It would be so exciting to have you with us — London's social life is so intoxicating with music, dancing, fashion and gossip — and such a relief for you from stuffy Berlin. It is good for us Prussians to be exposed to London's splendour.

So, Alice, you must come. Besides, Charles has arranged for Nicolas to spend some time at his chambers. You simply cannot stay behind at Herzberg. I command you to come. So there, you have to. And I have told Paul Wilhelm to come too, with his wife, Wilhelmina. What a noise we will all make.

Yours adoringly,
Victoria
Carlton House Terrace, London
Thursday the 5th of June, 1873

Alice pondered Victoria's letter. Her husband was full of excitement at the prospect of up to three months at one of the best-known chambers in London and gaining access to some of the best legal contacts. If Prussia were to be great, it had to be on a par with London in so many ways. But Victoria was right: she had distinct misgivings about returning to England. Her life was in Prussia; she knew little of the country of her birth, and besides, to go would remind her of her childhood there as a waif. It took considerable persuasion on Nicolas's part to secure Alice's agreement and he only succeeded after her mother had given her own somewhat tentative blessing. Accordingly, it was fixed that they would arrive in London on Monday the 21st of July, after a short stay in Paris with Nicolas's cousins Jeanne Françoise,

Jacqueline Anne and Paul and their families. Moreover, said her husband, Alice would be able to see – and buy – some of the latest fashions.

* * * * *

Like Paul Wilhelm and Wilhelmina, Nicolas and Alice were immediately overwhelmed by London's hustle and bustle – the never-ceasing roar, its cafés and theatres, and the unending multitude of people. Victoria and Charles welcomed them with great excitement to their now larger home in Carlton House Terrace, an indication of Charles's increasing legal income, augmented by his wife's inheritance from her late mother. During her first month in London, Alice prepared with Victoria and Paul Wilhelm for the Camerata's three concerts at the Royal Albert Hall. On the first night, Victoria played Beethoven's *Piano Concerto No. 5* to rousing applause. On the second night, Paul Wilhelm performed Brahms' *Violin Concerto in D Major*. On the last night, Alice, almost overwhelmed with nerves, played Haydn's *Keyboard Concerto in F Major*, to an enthusiastic ovation lasting several minutes. *The Times* of London gave a pleasing review of all three concerts and of the remarkable talent of three musicians from the same German family. Robert Whitfield ignored it. Music had never been a source of enjoyment for him, and in this instance his correspondence with the von Deppes had petered out long ago. He and his wife confined themselves to occasional social encounters with the Hardinges. The less he had to do with the von Deppes the better, not least on account of Herr Toller.

After a restful late summer, spent partly in Cambridge and Cornwall, Nicolas and Alice rejoined the Hardinges in Carlton House Terrace. One evening shortly after their return, Victoria announced that they had all been invited to a soirée at Buckingham Palace as guests of the Prince and Princess of Wales.

"Alice, this is such an honour. Everyone will be so jealous of us in Berlin. The Kaiser is one thing but the Prince of Wales is another! We must go and buy suitable dresses – and close-fitting too. You have such a slim figure even without your corset."

Alice could not speak. For her, a poor-born English girl, to go to Buckingham Palace was unthinkable. What was happening to her was surely a dream from which she would one day wake as Cinderella had woken the morning after the ball. Victoria cradled Alice's hands in hers.

"Alice, this is not a dream."

Sir Robert and Lady Whitfield also received an invitation to attend the soirée, as a private gesture, he surmised, for quietly settling the small matter of a debt the Prince of Wales had incurred at a game of baccarat. Though Whitfield had come to dislike the swirl of such occasions, his wife persuaded him that it would be discourteous to decline the invitation.

* * * * *

There was one task Alice wished to fulfil before her departure from London. Without telling her husband or Victoria, she had asked Charles Hardinge to arrange for her to go to Whitechapel, where her mother had told her she had been found. He organised for Herbert Pettigrew to accompany her.

They went by carriage. The cobbled streets of the east end of the city seethed with people, horses and handcarts, hawkers, thieves, drunks, prostitutes and the destitute. The poverty and filth were palpable. Under Pettigrew's guidance the small carriage eventually arrived at a side street. Dressed in a long grey coat and wearing a broad-brimmed black hat with a veil, Alice walked down a passageway, Pettigrew at her side. They passed half a dozen children playing hopscotch, their clothes dirty and patched. They came to an alleyway.

"That's where I first glimpsed you, along there. Where I first heard you being called and realised I might finally have found you. Then the yard and the house offered more evidence."

"I would like to see them, Mr Pettigrew."

"Of course, ma'am, but we must be quick before we attract too much attention. This is not a place to linger."

She followed him down a series of dingy narrow alleys until he stopped to point silently at a door. She gazed through the crack in the panelling into the yard. An elderly, hunched woman in ragged clothes was collecting patched shirts from a washing line. Pettigrew took Alice's arm and led her to the front of the tenement block.

"Which was my house?" she asked.

"That one," replied Pettigrew, nodding towards it.

The building was shabby, with broken guttering. Alice stood for a moment in silence.

"If I may say so, ma'am, you were lucky. Many unwanted children disappear in these parts to become beggars or prostitutes or to die of the pox or some other epidemic. Their lifespan is short."

He thought he observed a tear behind her veil.

"Do the people who cared for me still live there?" she asked.

"No, ma'am, they do not. Mr Hardinge, as he then was, arranged for them to be compensated for their care of you. Though they had children of their own, they looked after you. They did their best."

"Were they sad when I left?"

"Perhaps for a moment they were. But you were a commodity, after all. They had been paid some money to take you and had been promised more. It never came. With the sum from Mr Hardinge they quickly left to live in a more genteel place, where I believe they have flourished. Now we must go, ma'am. We are attracting attention."

They turned to head back to the carriage.

"Who do you think you are, some la-di-da lady, come to gawp, to enjoy the misfortune of others?" cried a toothless grey-haired woman.

"I once lived here," replied Alice.

"Then you were lucky that some fancy man paid enough for your services. All the more reason not to return and gloat," said the old woman. "Be off with you! If not, there are some who will relieve you of that coat of yours."

Before Alice could reply Pettigrew hurried her back to the carriage.

"Thank you, Mr Pettigrew. I will never forget what I have seen today. I am so lucky you found me."

"It is Sir Charles you must thank. I would add that the man who placed you in Whitechapel was a scoundrel with no scruples."

Alice did not reply. They sat in silence until the journey ended.

Later that evening, Alice spoke to Charles Hardinge.

"I wish to thank you for arranging for Mr Pettigrew to take me to Whitechapel. He was kind and most protective. He reminded me of how much I owe you. Without you I would not be here."

She kissed his cheek.

"And without Victoria, neither of us would be here."

"Indeed," replied Alice. "I owe so much to her too – from teaching me music to understanding love and its enemy, cruelty. To see those children in rags this afternoon was horribly distressing."

"Alice, when I see them in court for crimes and misdemeanours, or view their bodies in the morgue, it greatly distresses me too. The world in which we live is patently unjust, grinding poverty and its counterpoint, opulence. I suggest you do four things on your return to Berlin. First, you must become an even more accomplished pianist and let as many people as possible hear you play. Second, there are, I am sure, suffering and abandoned children in Berlin. See what you can do to help them. But above all, Alice, do not dwell on your past and so risk creating an obsession that destroys the love you and Nicolas have for one another. One day he will be a great lawyer and you a renowned musician. That must be your legacy."

"And the fourth thing I should do?" she asked.

He paused.

"Be careful who you trust. Be constantly vigilant for the betrayer, keep your family close and any secrets you may have even closer."

"Thank you, Sir Charles. I will do my utmost to follow your advice."

* * * * *

Thursday the 2nd of October 1873 was indeed a grand affair at Buckingham Palace – dinner followed by dancing, with over two hundred guests in attendance. Sir Robert and Lady Whitfield sat at a table adjacent to the royal high table. The evening, beginning with cocktails, followed the normal ritual of such an occasion – a combination of small talk, pleasant wine and large portions of food. Lady Derbyshire, sitting on Whitfield's left, having exhausted conversation with her neighbour, suddenly whispered in his ear.

"Sir Charles and Lady Hardinge are here tonight. When we adjourn to the ballroom, I should like you to introduce me as I have never had the pleasure of meeting her. I am not on her salon list. Besides, I am curious to meet her cousin, Alice, who is also here tonight."

Whitfield froze.

"Sir Robert, you look pale. Are you not feeling well?"

He forced himself to reply.

"Lady Derbyshire, have no fears on my account. This room is too hot for my liking after the draughts of Norfolk but I will survive."

After interminable chatter and inevitable speeches, dinner ended and guests were shepherded to the ballroom. Whitfield longed to escape to the safety of his home but knew it would not be possible to do so until the royal couple had withdrawn. At least he had managed to separate himself from Lady Derbyshire, by ensuring that he and his wife went to the opposite end of the dance floor. Surrounded by friends he thought there they would be safe. But it was not to be.

"Sir Robert and Lady Whitfield, what a pleasure it is to renew acquaintance after such a long time. Charles spotted you from a distance."

He spun round.

"Lady Hardinge, indeed it is a pleasure to meet you again after so long. And Charles, it is good to see you too. I hear business is flourishing in your chambers."

"Please, gentlemen, no legal conversation tonight," interrupted Victoria. "It is my honour to introduce His Excellency Georg Herbert zu Münster, the new German ambassador to the Court of St James, and my cousin, Count Nicolas, and his wife, the Countess Alice, born in England but, like the Countess Arabella von Deppe, married to Prussia. There, I have done it."

Charles Hardinge patted his wife's shoulder in appreciation.

As he turned to look at the young woman Whitfield felt faint, the blood draining from his face.

"Why, Sir Robert, are you not well?" enquired Victoria – the second time the question had been asked of him that evening. "You look as though you have seen a ghost. I know we have not seen one another for some months but I assure you there are none here, only the living."

Everyone laughed. They were mocking him, he thought. Pull

yourself together, man.

"Alice, Sir Robert is one of the wealthiest men in London – a finger in every financial pie. And his grandfather was father to Arabella –"

"Victoria, enough please," interposed Charles Hardinge. "Alice does not want a family history."

As Lady Derbyshire joined them, Alice stepped forward and curtsied to Whitfield and his bemused wife. He was barely conscious of his actions as he bowed and kissed her hand.

Struggling to regain his composure, he saw before him a tall, dark-haired young woman of slender build with exquisite lips. Her obviously long hair had been bound into a bun in keeping with the prevailing fashion. She had a gentle smile and deep-blue eyes. Was this his daughter? He could not resist the burning question, odd though it might be to others.

"It is an honour to meet you, Countess." The words stumbled from his lips. "Lady Whitfield and I welcome you to London. Have any of your family accompanied you to this great city?"

"No," replied Alice, "my mother has remained in Berlin, where she is a companion to the Crown Princess." She spoke softly, with a slight German accent.

Once more, Whitfield struggled to keep his composure. His faintness returned.

Her answer confirmed what he knew to be the truth. This elegant young girl whose hand he had kissed was his daughter. The girl whose mother he had abandoned; the girl who, when she was a child, he had placed with a family in Whitechapel, leaving her there without promised financial support, hoping never to see her or her mother again. This girl with his blood in her veins was now part of the family he had come to loathe. He found it hard to contain his conflicting emotions of rage and despair. For the rest of the evening social pleasantries came from his lips though he was barely aware of what he was saying.

An hour later he and Lady Whitfield returned to their home in Westminster, but not before he heard that his wife had accepted the German ambassador's invitation to dine at his residence the following week with the von Deppes. Despite her husband's protestations and foul mood, Lady Whitfield insisted that they would have to attend, reminding him of his pledge long ago to mend fences between the two families. After retiring to his bedroom, Whitfield looked into the mirror. A frightening image confronted him: a face of rage, lips wet with venom, eyes moist with contempt. Was this tortured face a consequence of being outwitted yet again by a family he had come to hate just as much as his father and grandfather had done? Or did it reflect his depraved betrayal of a defenceless woman, who had loved him, and of his daughter – all because of his hubris, his love of money and above all his Faustian pact to achieve the means to destroy everything associated with that accursed woman, Arabella Whitfield? He sank back in the chair, overwhelmed by the opposing forces of resentment and remorse. He felt drained; spiritually decayed; bereft; grief-stricken. Supping with the Devil, he had destroyed others and himself in the pursuit of his own vanity. He began to taste the bitter remorse that must have afflicted Judas after his betrayal of Christ. Unlike Judas he did not have the courage to end his life. A coward, he would have to live with the shame of what he had done – shame he could not assuage since he could never avow the girl as his daughter. Such an avowal would lead to his public disgrace. He had thus condemned himself to private damnation made worse by the necessity to continue to take whatever steps were required to ensure she never found out that his blood ran in her veins.

Across St James's Park, Charles Hardinge sipped a whisky, perusing the closing arguments in favour of the defendant that he was to present in the morning. His beloved Victoria lay asleep, her sheets of music fallen from the bed and scattered on the floor. He gathered them up, stroked her still-auburn hair, loosely tied back with dark-blue ribbon. He softly kissed her cheek. She smiled at his touch.

Along the corridor Alice looked into the mirror as she watched her hair, released from its pins, cascade in gentle waves onto her delicate shoulders. She saw Nicolas observing her from the bed in expectation. Her life as a small child in Whitechapel had hung by a thread. Now she was woven through divine fate into a rich family tapestry in a world of legendary rivalries amongst the acclaimed of the social, political and musical spheres, where the struggle for fame and prestige was passionate. Her visit to the east end of London two days before had been an unforgettable reminder that she should constantly strive to retain her husband's love and loyalty, never to take them for granted; and also a reminder that a close companion in her life would forever be the fear of her existence once again hanging by a single strand. She had resolved as they returned from the palace hand in hand that from now on she would play the part of Scheherazade, with her husband as the king, to be sure he never relinquished her.

She stood to face him, letting slip the crimson shawl she held against her breasts and revealing her slender alabaster body just as a butterfly silently sheds its silken chrysalis to reveal the beauty of its unfolding wings. With a bewitching smile Nicolas had not seen before she beckoned him. Entwined in each other's arms, they stood pressed together, skin against skin, barely breathing. Then they lay together, warmed and illuminated by the flickering fire. He slipped easily into her, her arms pulling him in ever deeper. Alice had become the magical princess enticing her king with the promise of more. Their love, she vowed, would be enduring.

* * * * *

A week later, on Wednesday the 8th of October, the von Deppes and the Whitfields joined other German and British guests for dinner at the residence of His Excellency the German Imperial Ambassador in honour of the departing Herzberg family. Elegant ladies, some in full skirts and some in the new silhouette fashion, mingled with sleekly spruced men in their finest evening dress. Laughter and the latest gossip amongst the ladies and talk of foreign affairs amongst the men dominated the conversation before and at dinner, though it must be said that Sir Robert Whitfield looked ill at ease, saying little, which did not go unnoticed by some of the guests used to his frequently offered financial opinions. He simply replied that he felt somewhat fatigued from recent undisclosed activities and on this occasion preferred to listen to the observations of others. Before the ladies rose to powder their noses so the men could pass around the port, the ambassador rose to speak.

"Excellencies, ladies and gentlemen, I welcome you all to my dinner table. Your presence this evening gives me much pleasure, as I know it does to His Majesty the Kaiser and His Excellency the Imperial Chancellor. They attach the highest importance to the strong relationship between Great Britain and the German Empire. Ever since Waterloo, and indeed before that, we have had shared interests on the continent of Europe. Now, following the unification of the German states into the new Empire, we are even more ready to be a strong ally of Great Britain, with mutual respect on both sides. Moreover, what glories you have we too should be allowed to have. If that approach leads us to friendly competition, that will only be for the better, because it will help both countries, as equals, to play an eager and important part in the pursuit of peace.

"Before I propose a toast to Her Majesty Queen Victoria, I wish to acknowledge our special guests Lady Hardinge, a lady of impeccable Prussian background, Count Paul Wilhelm von Deppe and his cousin the young Countess Alice von Deppe – English by birth, I believe – and to thank them for their exquisite German contribution to the musical life of London during their stay in this country. Their performances and those of the Camerata Herzberg are a prime example of what Germany has to offer. These three artistes are a remarkable demonstration of the strength and quality of the enduring mutual alliance between London and Berlin, where the alliance continues to flourish under the Kaiser's leadership. I wish also to acknowledge the contribution of Sir Robert Whitfield, whose family is linked by marriage to our special guests and who, during his close contacts with successive Foreign Secretaries, has done much to inform them of events in Berlin.

"Excellencies, ladies and gentlemen, I propose a toast to Her Majesty the Queen and Empress."

Everyone rose and clinked glasses.

You blathering fool, why don't you shut up, thought Whitfield. No one was meant to know of his contacts with the Foreign Office. What would the von Deppes and Hardinge be thinking? On the point of sitting down, he was nudged by his wife, who whispered, "Robert, stay on your feet and respond to the ambassador. Remember the ambassador's words: we are linked to the von Deppes by marriage."

"Don't I know it," he whispered back, before pulling back his shoulders and raising his voice to address the room.

"Excellency, on behalf of your guests I thank you most warmly for your generosity this evening and for your kind words. It is a pleasure for us to sit at your table.

"I too wish to convey sincere thanks to Lady Hardinge, Count Paul and the charming young Countess Alice, whom I recently met for the first time at Buckingham Palace, for their exquisite music. Lady Whitfield and I were regrettably unable to attend their concerts in London but I have read of the acclaim they received. It is richly deserved. Perhaps we may hear them play before we leave."

He paused for the flutter of encouragement and anticipation that greeted this suggestion to die down, then resumed:

"Excellency, I am not an exponent of the art of diplomacy as you are. I can only speak of the facts as I see them. I agree that my country and your Empire have much in common and we should build on that – each in our different ways. But as we do, we should ensure that friendly competition, as you call it, does not become the sole arbiter of our relationship. There is surely much more to it than that. The von Deppe family, with their skills, prestige and well-deserved acclaim, are a fine example of how an enduring friendship can be consolidated without dependence solely on the acquisition of military or industrial might. Rest assured, Excellency, from what little I know my government regards yours as a worthy ally in the pursuit of peace. I am convinced that with an approach such as that to which I believe you were alluding we can indeed build a strong alliance of mutual interest.

"Excellencies, ladies and gentlemen, I propose a toast to His Majesty the Kaiser and to enduring friendship."

As they sat down amidst murmurs of approval, Victoria rose to speak.

"I know it is frowned upon for women to dare to give after-dinner speeches. I do not wish to challenge the convention. I only wish to thank you, Excellency, and you, Sir Robert, for your kind words about my cousins and me. We deeply appreciate it. We too would echo your and Sir Robert's words about the pursuit of peace between Germany and Great Britain, with music as a significant strand in whatever pattern is woven to achieve it. Thank you."

After dinner, Paul von Deppe played Beethoven's *Violin Sonata*

No. 5 in F Major and Victoria Robert Schumann's *Kinderszenen*, while Alice finished with Chopin's *Waltz in E Flat*. With that the guests disappeared into the London night, Sir Robert still unable to look Alice in the eye as he said goodbye. His failure to do so did not escape Victoria's attention. She found it puzzling.

Before their final departure, scheduled for Tuesday the 14th of October, the von Deppes, accompanied by Victoria, journeyed north to Liverpool to attend a concert given on the 11th by the Royal Liverpool Philharmonic Society. The programme was German in content. The first item was Johannes Brahms' *Violin Concerto in D Major*, followed by Beethoven's *Fifth Symphony in C Minor* with its mighty, stirring final movement. As the last note echoed Nicolas leapt to his feet with cries of "Bravo." More enthusiasm was to come. After the interval the orchestra performed Felix Mendelssohn's inspiring *Symphony No. 2*, the *Lobesgang*. The final words sung by the chorus moved Victoria:

> *Let all give thanks to the Lord.*
> *Give thanks to the Lord and sing his name aloud.*
> *Let everything that has breath praise the Lord.*

Those words convinced her that her determination to persuade Alice to come to London had been vindicated. Since her arrival, Alice had changed from a shy, deferential young girl into a poised, self-confident and highly striking young woman, who had revealed in public a remarkable musical ability. Regardless of who might have been her father and the sadness of her early childhood, both of which had troubled her, she had become a well-respected member of a famous family. With further encouragement and tranquillity she would surely enrich the von Deppe reputation and heritage.

In Nicolas Victoria had noticed something new – the early signs of a more strident advocacy of Prussian patriotism. He had said after the Beethoven symphony that its climax had kindled his willingness to serve his country in whatever way might be necessary to advance its cause. Victoria was no advocate of German patriotism. Its growing shrillness, the emphasis on competition, which the German ambassador had accentuated, was beginning to worry her as it did Nicolas's mother, Beatrice. In contrast, Nicolas's brother, Daniel, had so far displayed little such tendency. Herzberg, for all those who had grown up and lived within its walls, had always been a place where change but not war had been advocated. She resolved to speak privately to Nicolas and to remind him, if it proved necessary in their conversation, that his paramount responsibility was to meet not the wishes of the Kaiser but those of his wife, who would surely have a child before long. Victoria's observation was shared by Alice. She had already decided on her method of dissuasion: as Scheherazade she would entice her husband to stay close in never-ending expectation of more to come.

* * * * *

Robert Whitfield noticed a short report in the London *Times* recording the von Deppe family's departure for Germany. Though he was relieved, his tribulations were far from over.

The troublesome Herr Toller, who had been in London for some days, had met Fletcher – under his alias Mr Smith – in a Wapping warehouse on the evening of the Liverpool concert. Despite the offer of a substantial payment Toller had insisted on meeting Smith's paymaster, about whom he claimed he had important and damaging information worth significantly more money. He was determined to be paid. A struggle ensued, during which he had fatally knifed Fletcher. The more brutal Joiner, now Whitfield's sole assistant and master fixer, caught Toller as he fled. Under duress he revealed he was Ernst Kiefer and admitted having killed Toller in Berlin some years before. He insisted that he had incontrovertible evidence establishing the true identity of Alice von Deppe's father and that this evidence, which he had placed in a safe box in Vienna, would be damaging to the reputation of Joiner's employer, if it were ever published. Under further pressure from Joiner, Kiefer agreed to hand over his proof in Vienna for one last large payment.

After being kept under lock and key in a damp Wapping cellar for a day, Kiefer received Joiner's reply. His employer had agreed to meet him in person in Vienna on Tuesday the 28th of October at a place he, Joiner, would arrange. There, Kiefer's evidence would be scrutinised. If it was worthy, he would be paid. If not, he would suffer a penalty. Kiefer nodded his compliance but, before he was allowed to leave, was obliged to sign a confession that he had killed, in a premeditated act, an innocent man called Fletcher as well as Toller. Joiner threatened Kiefer that if he did not keep to the bargain they had struck, his confession would be made public and he would become a hunted man carrying a large enough price on his head to guarantee he would be pursued until found. To make sure he kept the rendezvous in Vienna, Joiner had arranged for a hireling named Spicer to accompany him. Kiefer completed and signed the confession under the watchful eye of Spicer, a large, thuggish individual who spoke little. Joiner pocketed the confession. The next day, the 14th of October, the blackmailer and his escort boarded the train for Dover and the onward journey to Vienna.

Joiner briefed Robert Whitfield. Accompanied by his fixer, Whitfield left London for the same destination six days later, ostensibly to discuss an investment with an Austro-Hungarian client. Telling neither family nor friends of his intention to go to Vienna, he knew he was taking a significant risk in this venture, but this running sore – of his own making – had to be treated once and for all and, moreover, he had to ensure that it was done. Under no circumstances could he allow his identity as Alice von Deppe's father, or the circumstances of his betrayal of her and her mother, to be revealed. Ageing and unwell, he found his rage at his self-inflicted injury swelled. He was sliding further into a dark and damnable abyss. If Kiefer had to be silenced, so Joiner too. That final act would leave blood on his hands. What a price the Devil was driving for his silence.

As the train steamed out of Victoria Station the last rays of the summer sun were eclipsed by the early clouds of autumn.

CHAPTER 8

The Viennese Affair

It had proved a largely congenial journey across Europe, full of pleasant distractions. As each day began, Robert Whitfield remained convinced that, if he was to retrieve the information Kiefer claimed to possess, it was right to confront him. Despite the risks involved, it was a necessary price to pay to protect a secret of great personal and financial import. Revelation of paternity would inevitably lead to the ridicule, shame and ruin of the family name and, even more painfully, to the scorn of the von Deppe family. His exacting investment in secrecy had therefore to be preserved at all costs and, with the careful preparations already made, together with Joiner's skill, it would be. However, once the train crossed the Austro-Hungarian border, on the 26th of October, Whitfield suddenly began to lose his nerve, doubting the wisdom of their intentions. As the train drew into Vienna's Staatsbahnhof the following day, Joiner, in a repeated effort to allay Whitfield's anxiety, sought to convince him all would be well – that the city's hubbub would provide the desirable degree of diversion so they could do what had to be done. No one in London knew they had come this far and in the backstreets of Vienna they would surely be out of sight and mind.

In accordance with their plan Whitfield went immediately by carriage to the Hotel Imperial, where a comfortable room awaited him. The city was full of people since it was now only a short while before the World Exhibition on the Prater would close its doors. He had read about it months before in *The Times* of London – a valiant effort on the part of the Austro-Hungarians to match the previous exhibitions in London and Paris by mustering beneath one roof all of the best that the city and the Empire had to offer. Not long after the exposition had opened the Vienna stock exchange had crashed – too many shares for too many unsound enterprises – and there had been a cholera epidemic. This had sparked *Schadenfreude* in London, still proud of its own 1851 international exhibition. Yet the Vienna exposition had survived, despite the mounting debts he and his financial friends had forecast. He would be intrigued to visit it if his own personal business was satisfactorily and expeditiously settled. That would depend on Joiner and his accomplice, Spicer.

Fatigued and having barely brushed the dust from his clothes, Whitfield was resting in his room in the early evening when he received a telegram. The contents shook him.

> *Lady D informs me you are in Vienna. I have arranged dinner invitation for you. Details will follow.*
> *Victoria H*

Whitfield cursed. How had that damn woman, Lady Derbyshire, found out that he was in Vienna? What mistake had he made? He could only imagine that Thomas Cook, who had provided him with the coupon for his hotel, had sent – against his instructions – a receipt for his payment to his house in Westminster and that upon reading it his wife had told some of her friends. The messenger boy asked if there were a reply. Tempted to say something offensive, he instead wrote on the telegram form:

> *Thank you. Attendance dependent on prior conclusion of other business.*
> *RW*

Some two hours later there was another knock at the door. A man in imperial uniform delivered a large crested envelope. Whitfield opened it to find an invitation to a soirée at the Hofburg Palace on

Tuesday the 28th of October, given by Prince Leopold of Bavaria and his wife, the Princess Imperial Gisela of Hungary, in honour of the Crown Prince Frederick Wilhelm and his wife, the Crown Princess Victoria.

"What answer should I convey, Sir Robert?" the messenger asked.

Whitfield realised he had little choice. The Crown Prince and Princess were often in London, not just to attend royal events but to escape the rigour of the German imperial court. On account of the fact his name was known to them, and because of his own private association with the Prince of Wales, he could not decline, though on this occasion he keenly wished it were otherwise.

"I accept the invitation with great pleasure."

"A carriage will collect you at seven o'clock. Formal attire is required."

Whitfield sent for some light refreshments and wine. His plans for a discreet presence in Vienna had disintegrated.

Later that evening he received a further message. A man, who declined to give his name, had asked to see him. Should he be sent up or did he wish to see his visitor downstairs? Whitfield knew it was Joiner. He sent word that he would be down shortly. Some twenty minutes later Whitfield and Joiner left the hotel to walk a short distance to a nearby café, unaware they were being followed.

"Has Kiefer appeared?" asked Whitfield.

"Yes," Joiner replied. "We are to meet at this address." He passed a piece of paper across the table. "It's in a small cobblestoned alleyway behind Ballgasse in the city's first district. Kiefer preferred it to one I had found through a contact. He is ready to provide his evidence to you personally – but only to you. When are you coming, so we can get this business over with? Tomorrow evening will be best, since Spicer and I can then dispose of him, once he has given you his so-called evidence, under cover of darkness. There is a graveyard nearby. Afterwards, Spicer can be paid and leave. The sooner we are on our way the better too."

Whitfield explained he could not arrive at Ballgasse until after midnight. Joiner and Spicer would have to prevail on their own until then. Joiner was unhappy at this news as Kiefer was becoming increasingly restless. Whitfield returned to the Hotel Imperial, unease mounting, not least because the place for the meeting had been Kiefer's choice, not Joiner's. It broke the military rule that a battle was best fought on the ground of your choosing, not the enemy's. But it was too late to change.

* * * * *

As Whitfield went to sleep, Frederick Paul and his wife, Anne, who had accompanied the Crown Prince and Princess, retired to their rooms in the Hofburg. Along the corridor was Rebecca Bartlett, the Crown Princess's companion. Known to the Crown Princess as Miss Becks, she had recently received the honorary title of baroness in recognition of her loyalty and discretion, not least over witnessing some of the tempestuous scenes between the Crown Princess and her son Wilhelm, concerning his behaviour towards his parents. At the Grand Hotel on the Ringstrasse, her daughter, Alice, was alone in her room, writing to her husband.

> *My dearest Nicolas,*
>
> *If only you were here with me.*
>
> *We all arrived safely from Prague yesterday. Our brief visit there was a great success and I greatly enjoyed a performance of* Così fan tutte. *I travelled with Mama in her carriage. We gossiped so much. She, a baroness, and I, a countess – in charge of the royal baggage; how amusing is that!*
>
> *I have never seen such a grand city as Vienna – so much hustle and bustle and so many people rushing hither and thither. Viennese ladies are most splendid and fashionable and the men exceedingly handsome, particularly the officers in their uniforms. Everywhere there is music, especially the sound of the waltz, and the cakes are irresistible. I have had two already today. If I have any more I shall burst my corset. Men are so lucky that they do not have to wear such a dreadful garment. What we women do to ourselves to attract men!*
>
> *For most of today I have been practising for tomorrow night's soirée – a concert, dancing and promenading. It will be impressive, and my first opportunity to see the Empress Sisi if she is there. I have seen a painting of her in the hotel. She is exquisitely beautiful. And the famous Russian ballerina,*

Natalya Plisetskaya, is likely to be there as well. The Empress is said to admire her greatly. There will be so much talking and laughing at the soirée that I am sure no one will hear me. But Uncle Frederick says that is no excuse. I must be perfect. So tomorrow morning I will practise again and again. I have chosen one of Mozart's piano concertos – No. 23, the one you like me to play often – instead of Herr Haydn.

The bed in my room is a beautiful four-poster with red-velvet drapes. If only you were here with me, dearest Nicolas – to kiss me, to undo me, to sweep me into bed and to make passionate love to me. As I play the second movement tomorrow night I will imagine my fingers on the keyboard are your fingers caressing my breasts. I cannot wait for you to do so when I return to Berlin.

And yes, in my excitement I nearly forgot that Aunt Anne has told me Sir Robert Whitfield has suddenly and mysteriously arrived in Vienna. Cousin Victoria has, it seems, arranged through her connections for him to attend tomorrow's soirée. I do not think that Uncle Frederick is too pleased but then who can ever say no to venerable V.

Lastly, my dearest prince, thank you for allowing Martha to come with me to Vienna. She is such a sweet and helpful girl. I know it is a luxury to travel with a maid but to be without her on this occasion would be hard as there is so much to do. And it means I am not dependent on those fierce maids who care for the Crown Princess.

I hope that you will get this letter soon.
With my deepest love,
Alice, your Scheherazade
The Grand Hotel,
Vienna
Monday the 27th of October, 1873

* * * * *

The new day brought increased activity. Frederick Paul was finalising the arrangements for the visit of the Crown Prince and Princess to the exhibition, ensuring that the right people would be available to answer the inevitable penetrating questions about the many exhibits and ensuring that the German presentation was perfect. Rebecca had risen early to prepare the gown and accessories the Princess would wear later in the day to the imperial soirée. Martha had similarly prepared her mistress's own gown, which the Countess would soon have to put on before her departure for the Hofburg Palace for her final practice. At the Hotel Imperial Robert Whitfield stirred. This would be a day of devilish contrasts – a royal soirée and a bleak encounter with Kiefer at midnight. To be sure of finding the meeting place late at night, Whitfield took a tour of the city in a hansom cab during the day, asking the driver to make a detour in the vicinity of Ballgasse. Neither driver nor passenger was aware another cab followed.

* * * * *

At four o'clock in the afternoon Alice, in a beautiful powder-blue off-the-shoulder gown, her shoulders protected by a dark-blue velvet cloak, left the Grand Hotel for the imperial palace in a carriage. She was accompanied by Lieutenant Albrecht von Dassanowsky, her escort for the evening, and Martha, who two hours before had laced her mistress into her corset more tightly than ever, following the insistent instruction that her waist should be truly slim to catch the Empress's eye. Later, after her final practice, as Martha refreshed her coiffure, Alice watched from a window as the guests for the soirée began to arrive by carriage. Her mother, in a brief respite from her royal duties, joined her for a short while. Together they stood holding hands, gazing down at the scene of elegance and privilege below, at the women in their finest clothes, portrayals of dignity and doubt-free self-worth. Neither spoke, each alone with their thoughts. Though they were part of this opulent world, both privately considered themselves mere observers rather than participants.

For Robert Whitfield attendance was tiresome. Beneath his evening dress his heart beat quickly. Joiner had sent a message that Kiefer was becoming increasingly impatient. He would wait only a few hours more.

As the guests mingled in the splendid *Redoutensaal*, Whitfield sought the company of a banking acquaintance he had met in London some years ago. They had barely begun to discuss the prevailing financial situation in Europe when he heard a voice behind him. It was Alice's.

"Sir Robert Whitfield, welcome to Vienna. I am honoured that you should have come so far to hear me play," she said with a gentle laugh.

She was even more fetching than the last time he had seen her in London. Her hair was down but pinned back in a loose pony, intertwined with tiny pink roses. Her slim waist accentuated her pleasing bust. She proffered her hand. He brushed it with his lips. He had kissed his daughter once again.

"Sir Robert," Alice continued, her composure unnerving him, "I wish to introduce Count Frederick Paul von Deppe – you met his brother in London some years ago, I believe – and his wife, the Countess Anne. They accompanied Crown Prince Frederick Wilhelm and Crown Princess Victoria to Prague and now here to Vienna to see the exposition before it closes."

The two men shook hands.

"I am delighted to meet you, Sir Robert, as is my wife. My cousin Victoria has told me much about you. What brings you at short notice to Vienna?"

"I had to deal with a business matter that could not wait. I hoped to combine its resolution with a visit to the exposition."

"Have you been yet?" enquired Frederick Paul.

"Not yet," said Whitfield.

The two men continued to exchange pleasantries.

"Alice, what are you going to play tonight?" asked the Countess Anne.

The two men turned towards Alice.

"Forgive me, I should have asked you," said Frederick. "It was most rude of me not to do so," he added.

Alice turned her eyes down in a coquettish manner Anne had not observed before. She had clearly blossomed since marriage, which for a woman was as it should be.

"It was difficult to choose without my mentor Victoria's advice," replied Alice. "I had thought of a Haydn keyboard concerto. Then I considered a concerto by Daniel Steibelt but, as he is supposed to have lost to Beethoven in an improvisation contest in Vienna in 1800, I decided discretion was the better part of valour. So I have chosen a Mozart concerto. Better safe than sorry, as Mother sometimes says."

"We wish you well, Alice," said Frederick.

"As do I," interjected Whitfield.

"I compliment you on your attire," said Anne. "It is a pity that Nicolas is not here to see for himself. But you have a handsome soldier to escort you. Lieutenant, take good care of her."

"I most certainly will," he replied.

Alice once again turned her head in the same flirtatious way Anne had noticed before, only this time she blushed as the handsome lieutenant offered his arm to escort her to the platform. Anne made one other observation. Alice's eyes and her smile seemed for a fleeting moment to mirror Sir Robert's own features. Dismissing what she had seen as a trick of light, she thought no more of it.

The evening, bathed in candlelight, amply fulfilled the expectations of those present. Following the short concert, with an accomplished performance by Alice, guests circulated, dallied and danced, by popular demand, to the waltz. Lieutenant von Dassanowsky pressed Alice to partner him several times.

"Countess, I could dance with you all evening."

"Lieutenant, I enjoy dancing with you but before long I must dance with Count Frederick and perhaps even Sir Robert Whitfield, who looks somewhat uncomfortable."

"Countess, I beg – just one more waltz please. I fear that once I let you ago you will disappear just like Cinderella."

"One more dance it will be. Then I must join the others and rest assured, Lieutenant, I will not disappear at the stroke of midnight. My stroke of fortune came long ago."

He was tempted to ask the meaning of her Delphic remark but decided that even if he did he would not secure an answer from a woman flirting with him as he was with her.

It was shortly before midnight that carriages started to be announced. Slowly the guests began to file out of the *Redoutensaal*, taking their leave of their hosts, Prince Leopold of Bavaria and his wife, the Princess Imperial Gisela of Hungary, as they did so. As she joined Frederick Paul and Anne in the farewell line, Alice thought she caught a glimpse of the Empress Sisi.

"Is that the Empress?" she whispered to Lieutenant von Dassanowsky.

"Yes, it is," he replied.

"Please take me closer," Alice requested.

They moved as close as they dared. Alice gazed at the Empress. She was truly beautiful. Recognising Alice from her performance, the Empress smiled and beckoned her.

"You played beautifully. If only I could do the same."

With those words she turned away.

Alice and the lieutenant joined the von Deppe family in the ante-room as guests waited for the announcement of their carriages.

"Dearest Alice, you were magnificent. I was so proud of you."

"Thank you, Mama. Lieutenant, I would like to introduce my mother, the Baroness Bartlett."

"I am honoured to make your acquaintance, Baroness. Your daughter is not only an accomplished pianist, she is also an exquisite dancer. You have taught her well."

"Thank you, Lieutenant. But you must hurry, young man. They are calling your carriage and Alice does not yet have her cloak. More haste, please."

"Mama, I will see you tomorrow. Shall I come to the palace?"

"No, I will come to your hotel at eleven o'clock. Goodnight."

"Baroness, we too should say goodnight," said Anne. "But before we leave I wish to introduce Sir Robert Whitfield, who is briefly in Vienna on business but who I am delighted to say was able to accept an invitation to join us this evening. Sir Robert, I have the pleasure to introduce Baroness Bartlett, a close companion of Crown Princess Victoria."

Whitfield froze. The grey-haired, fine-faced woman looked at him intently. Unable to speak, he took her hand in his and gestured to kiss it. She looked down at the signet ring on his litte finger. It bore the emblem of a falcon with outstretched wings above the letter *W*. She instantly recognised the unusual design. It was similar to the ring on the hand that had once held her close many years ago. She quickly withdrew her hand, looking again at Whitfield's face. Though older and puffy, the features were now unmistakable. This was the man who had betrayed her and taken away her child. His mumbled, half-swallowed words were too indistinct for her to hear.

"Sir Robert Whitfield?" an usher called out.

"Here," indicated Frederick Paul.

"Sir Robert, a police officer has asked to see you. He has certain information. He is waiting downstairs just beyond the main door."

"Are you sure it is me he wishes to see?"

"Most certainly," the usher replied. "Please come with me and I will direct you to him."

"Please excuse me," said Whitfield, deeply flushed, as he turned away from the Baroness and the von Deppes.

"What on earth is that about?"

"Perhaps I should go with him," offered Frederick Paul.

"Better not," advised the Baroness. "He is a man well able to take care of himself, by all accounts."

"How do you know that?" asked Anne.

"I believe he is known to the Prince of Wales and I understand the Crown Princess has encountered him more than once at court."

Downstairs, Chief Inspector Horváth was waiting. He led Whitfield across the courtyard.

"We have reason to believe you know a Herr Joiner. He says he works for you. Is that the case?"

"Yes, I know him," replied Whitfield hesitatingly, trying his hardest to speak with care. "I asked him to accompany me from London since he is more familiar with Vienna than I am. He was pleased to do so as he had business of his own to attend to. What has happened?"

"Herr Joiner has been involved in a fight. A man, an Englishman who was with him, is dead. The other person, not English and who appears to have been under some duress, is unscathed. Both are in our custody at present."

"What is all this to do with me?" asked Whitfield nervously.

"The Englishman is seeking your help."

"What assistance is he seeking?"

"Sir Robert, this man – Joiner by name – will most likely appear in court tomorrow charged with murder. Are you prepared to pay for him to be defended and indeed to testify in court regarding your connection to him?"

Whitfield swallowed. What should he say?

"What is the position of the other man?" he asked.

"He does not wish to press charges against Mr Joiner. Indeed he seems anxious to leave Vienna for Germany. We have no intention of stopping him. As you see, it all depends on you, Sir Robert."

"How can that be?"

"Some murky business was planned at a house in the vicinity of Ballgasse. I think you, Sir Robert, may know more than you care to admit. Indeed, you passed close by there yesterday in a cab, if my information is correct. The cab stopped for a few seconds. I wonder why. But let me come to the point, Sir Robert. As a man of the world and of significant wealth and influence, you will appreciate that we have many crimes to solve in this city – crimes of passion, common theft, you name it. At present we are spending considerable time seeking out revolutionaries anxious to foment trouble because they want to upset the present political order. My superiors wish to ensure that they do not succeed, that public security is maintained. In contrast, what happened at Ballgasse is less important. The solution is simple, Sir Robert. If you would care to cover the necessary expenses of our investigation into this matter, you can take Mr Joiner back to London, Herr Kiefer – the other detainee – will be helped on his way with some loose change, and we will dispose of the body. How does that appeal to you?"

Horváth raised his lantern to look directly into the eyes of his quarry. Whitfield knew he was trapped.

"I will help as you suggest."

"Good. Please come to this address tomorrow with this sum of money." He passed Whitfield a folded piece of paper. Whitfield opened it. On it was written in heavy ink a substantial amount of money and the name of a bank.

"I cannot raise this amount so quickly."

"If you go to this bank," Horváth said, pointing at the piece of paper, "and ask for Herr Kaczor, he will make the necessary arrangements for you to provide him with a guaranteed undertaking of payment from your bank, in return for which he will give you the corresponding sum of gulden to give to us. It appears you are a very wealthy man, Sir Robert, so we have no fear of your failure to pay." Gesturing towards the Hofburg, he added, "Besides, we know you would not wish to lose your reputation should this affair not be resolved in the way I have proposed. Once our business is completed tomorrow, all will be forgotten. There will be no paper record and you can escort Mr Joiner back to London without harm. One of my officers will accompany you as far as the border to ensure that is the case."

"So be it," replied Whitfield.

"I see your friends are waiting for you."

"Sir Robert, what is the matter? Is everything well with you? Can we help?" asked Frederick Paul.

"An acquaintance of mine who arrived in Vienna at the same time as me has got into a little trouble. The Chief Inspector asked if I could assist. I said I would. I will go to the police station tomorrow to secure his release. It seems he drank too much and fatally hit a man. I will go back to my hotel and rest."

With that he climbed into his carriage to return to his hotel. His life was now at a perilous point.

* * * * *

Early the next morning he was awoken by a message that a woman wished to see him. She had declined to give her name but insisted that he should join her as quickly as possible. On the card pressed into his hand were written the letters *RB*.

Rebecca Bartlett sat veiled in a private room she had requested. Whitfield sat opposite her. She raised her veil. Her face was drawn, her eyes full of bile.

"I wished to see in the cold light of morning the man who broke my heart. The man who cruelly took my daughter from me. The man who never had the courage to reveal his true identity. The man who promised marriage when he was already married. The man who promised to support his daughter in her childhood but who left her destitute. I see you for what you are – rich in money, worthless in scruples, wicked in deception. I smell the rotten sweetness of true corruption."

Whitfield looked at the face carved in granite.

"What can I do to make amends?"

"Nothing. There is absolutely nothing you could ever do to remedy what you did. I do not wish to have a penny of your tainted money. If I were the Lord, I would condemn you to eternal damnation. But I am not Him. All I can do is to wish it, to pray for it. And I will."

Whitfield made no response. There was clearly nothing he could say. She spoke again.

"There is one request it pains me grievously to ask and to which you must agree."

"What is that?" His words were scarcely audible.

"You must pay Herr Kiefer the sum of £3,000 in final settlement. If you do not I fear he will expose you as my daughter's father. This will become known in the London newspapers and to Her Majesty the Queen. While I have no care for your life, mine will be irreparably damaged by your scandal and my daughter's happiness in the von Deppe family ruined."

She thrust a sheet of paper into his hand.

"Please sign this promissory note to your bank. I will see that he gets it before his release from custody today."

"How do I know he will not ask for more?"

"He will not because I know, as you do, that he has killed three men in cold blood. If he asks for more the confession he signed, now in the possession of the police, will become public and he will be arrested for murder. But this is not an outcome you should wish for – it too could lead to your exposure, as in court your name will surely emerge."

"How do you know these facts to which you allude?"

"We live in a world of secrets in which there are sometimes strange fellowships that deliver justice."

Whitfield signed the promissory note. He handed it to her. She took it and, lowering her veil, left the room.

Later that day Whitfield went to the bank and police station to settle the matter as had been agreed the night before. He returned to his hotel room to pack for the journey back to London, leaving unanswered a message from Frederick Paul enquiring after his well-being.

A police officer accompanied Ernst Kiefer to his hotel to collect his belongings. Before departing he was shown into a room where he had been told a visitor wished to see him.

At one side of a table sat the same veiled woman. She motioned him to sit opposite her. For a moment neither spoke, neither moved. All that could be heard was the sound of the clock, accounting each second. Her voice broke the silence.

"Herr Kiefer, yesterday I met a villainous scoundrel. Today I come face to face with a liar. The experience in each case has been painful and distasteful."

"Who is the villainous scoundrel and who is the liar?" he asked.

Lifting her veil, Rebecca looked directly into his eyes.

"Sir Robert Whitfield is the former. You are the latter."

"How can that be?"

"You promised me you would not pursue the matter of my daughter's birth. Yet you did, breaking your word and deceiving me. You did so in order to feed your insatiable curiosity, and to gain money through blackmail. I find your behaviour abhorrent."

"I did it for you – to assuage your pain, so evident to me when we first met."

"Do not dissemble, Herr Kiefer. Instead acknowledge your shame, that you did it for your own selfish ends. That would be a nobler thing to do."

Her words cut him.

"Your grandfather, Anton Kiefer, was an honourable man who served the Countess Arabella well. You have behaved dishonourably and thus disgraced his memory."

Again there was silence. She was right. He was guilty of the sins she had laid at his feet. His pride had misled him. He had lied. He had killed a man in Berlin for money, he had killed another in London and now a third in Vienna. He felt a rope around his neck.

"What can I do?"

"You should return to Spain where you belong, to seek redemption, to make amends, to restore honour to the name of Kiefer. I may never be able to forgive you but I hope that others might."

"And if I choose not to return to a country I left long ago?"

"There is little doubt that in Germany you will be arrested for the murder of Herr Toller."

"I know nothing of Herr Toller."

"Herr Kiefer, speak the truth as you did to that man Joiner. If you do not speak the truth – on any matter – you will never find peace and satisfaction in your life. Unlike Robert Whitfield, you still have time to refresh your life, refresh your morals. At this fork in the road, you have one chance to decide in which direction to go."

He looked down.

She spoke again.

"Here is a letter from Robert Whitfield, undertaking to pay an amount of money to you on your return to Madrid – your thirty pieces of silver shall we call it. Take it and leave."

She pushed the letter across the table, lowered her veil and rose.

"I am no Judas. I did what I thought was best for you and your daughter."

"Herr Kiefer, there are the nameless who want to deal in secret things and there are those who wish to walk alone. Those who want to deal in secret things often seek to manipulate others and in so doing become corrupted by what they do, corrupted by their power over others. These nameless ones are all around us, unseen in their machinations. My daughter and I have chosen to walk alone, in the openness of sunlight, not with others in the dank, dark, suffocating air of corruption, feeding with accomplices on the weakness, frailty and insecurity of others. We all have choices to make. Now I urge you to make yours before it is too late. Goodbye, Herr Kiefer."

She left the room. He sat there for several minutes, listening to the sound of the clock. He recalled the lies he had told, his hubris, his deception, and the face of the man who had desperately clutched at him as he pushed him into the river in Berlin. He picked up the letter and tore it into pieces.

"Kiefer, it is time to go," said the police officer, placing his hand on the shoulder of the weeping man. "The train for Berlin will leave soon. You must hurry."

"You are mistaken, officer. My destination is Spain."

"I will tell my superior. I am sure you can be of assistance to us there."

"We will see," murmured Kiefer.

Later that morning Rebecca and her daughter sipped coffee at the Frauenhuber coffee house, where it was said Mozart and Beethoven had once played.

That evening three trains edged into the autumn night, one conveying the damned, a second the shamed, and a third a woman savouring the sweet taste of cold revenge, but now carrying a heavy secret – her daughter had brought tainted Whitfield blood into the von Deppe family, which still, she knew from conversations she had overheard at Herzberg, bore the legacy of the Countess Arabella's bitterness towards her father. She prayed that Robert Whitfield would soon be dead, taking his secret to the grave, and that Ernst Kiefer would remain silent. That left only her. Beside her in the royal train was Alice, asleep. In the book clutched in her hand was the letter she had received from Lieutenant von Dassanowsky.

As the trains rattled towards their destinations, the *Preußische Geheimpolizei* – the political police force in Berlin – received a report from Chief Inspector Horváth of the Austrian secret police on the Ballgasse affair. Though both departments concentrated on the suppression of political dissent, the alacrity with which the document was read reflected the appetite in Berlin and Vienna for the more salacious side of life, which sometimes offered enticing opportunities for blackmail. Sir Robert Whitfield's involvement in what had happened at Ballgasse and his acceptance of a suggestion that he pay a large bribe to a police officer in the course of an investigation afforded the possibility of securing information from him about British policies and intentions towards Germany and the Austro-Hungarian Empire – information he assuredly gained, according to Mr Joiner, from his apparent regular contact with high levels of the Foreign Office.

The report was promptly passed up the chain of command in Berlin. The next day Chief Inspector Horváth received a reply.

Most Secret

The Generalpolizeidirektor *has been asked to thank you for the discreet and sensitive way in which you have handled this matter, so ensuring no harm to the unimpeachable reputation of the Crown Prince and Crown Princess and the von Deppe family. This being the case, it would be inappropriate for Lieutenant von Dassanowsky to repeat his letter to the Countess Alice von Deppe. Her background, along with that of her mother, is not a matter for investigation under any circumstances.*

However, the information concerning Sir Robert Whitfield and his associate, Mr Joiner, is a valuable addition to our files and may be used in the future.

We have noted in our records that Herr Kiefer is en route to Madrid, where he intends to reside. On account of his mental state, we consider he has become unreliable and is therefore no longer a focus of our attention – at least for the present.
Heinrich Müller
Preußische Geheimpolizei
Berlin
Friday the 31st of October, 1873

Robert Whitfield returned to London, though Joiner was not with him. He was last seen in a waterfront bar in Calais. Soon a sharp November chill descended, extinguishing the remaining embers of summer past.

PART THREE: ADAGIO MOLTO
LOST IN AUTUMN 1880–1888

CHAPTER 9

The Diminishing of Trust

Robert Whitfield never recovered from the Vienna affair. It dealt a blow to his self-importance, deepened his guilt about the unworthy means by which he advanced his ambitions and wealth, and reignited his unshakeable prejudice – not only against the von Deppe family, who still plagued his life as they had done his grandfather's, but also against Germany. The unsavoury circumstances of the Vienna incident, the questions that still remained unanswered about Fletcher's death – into which some police enquiries had fortunately not been pursued – and Joiner's disappearance meant that for a while at least he appeared less in public and when he did so he was less ebullient. Moreover, the death of his wife, Emily, added to his introspection and weariness. What pained him more, however, though he tried hard not to acknowledge it, was that in Vienna he had seen Alice – even more striking a young woman than when he had first encountered her at Buckingham Palace – perform as an accomplished pianist in front of an aristocratic audience in the Hofburg, the seat of Habsburg power. Yet he was unable to avow her as his daughter. That fact, and the yet sharper pain of coming face to face with her mother, to whom he had behaved so abominably, often caused him great distress late at night or in the early morning hours – the price, he concluded, of his handshake with the Devil, the deed he could never undo. The only comfort was that Alice's mother would never disclose her daughter's paternity, nor could he think of anyone else who would, since Fletcher and Joiner were gone and Kiefer was unlikely to spill the secret for fear of his own neck. In the autumn of a man's years there is an inclination in quieter moments to reflect on life past. He avoided such moments; if he did not, he would be able to reflect only on the terrible misjudgements he had made.

The obscurity Whitfield sought did not, however, cause him to cease his periodic visits to the Foreign Office to see the Permanent Under Secretary Lord Tenterden and, occasionally, Lord Granville, the Foreign Secretary – not so much to provide information from his diminishing knowledge of events in Germany but to surmise, from their response to his seemingly innocuous questions or the warmth of the greeting he received, whether they had acquired intelligence from the imperial authorities about the affair in Vienna. But nothing appeared untoward, despite the fact that, unknown to him, the British ambassador, Sir Andrew Buchanan, had passed to his superiors a rumour that the Austrian secret police had approached Sir Robert during his short and unexpected visit to Vienna. The ambassador had added to his brief, unsubstantiated report the comment that it was likely any conversation, had it happened, would have been reported to the Berlin authorities because of the close contact between the two police services. His diplomatic colleague in Berlin said he had heard nothing from his sources. The ambassador's report was therefore filed away, following the decision that such a rumour should not be pursued in case it carried the risk of impugning Whitfield's integrity. That would be unwise, not least on account of Whitfield's financial links with the Prince of Wales and indeed the marital link between the von Deppe family and the distinguished British lawyer Sir Charles Hardinge, QC.

Nonetheless, a discreet decision was made within the Foreign Office that no matter of any political sensitivity should be discussed with Whitfield in future, just in case he inadvertently disclosed the information he acquired, however harmless it might be, in the wrong quarter. After all, the Foreign Office had good grounds to believe that there were German spies in London. They should not be encouraged in their trade. Since there was no knowledge in Berlin or Vienna of this Foreign Office instruction, their respective secret police authorities concluded that their decision to keep the Ballgasse affair secret had been right, that the other side had something delicate to hide. It was therefore appropriate to remain ready to exploit future opportunities for the possible blackmail of Sir Robert if he came their way again.

Due to his declining health, Whitfield sought to give more responsibility for the family's affairs to his two sons. Charles and his wife, Sarah, continued to enjoy the benefits of the Meltwater estate and Whitfield often joined them for long weekends. Whitfield's younger son, Arthur, continued, albeit reluctantly, to help his father with his extensive London property portfolio, of which the houses in Westminster and Mayfair were the most profitable. However, the largest source of income came from the substantial interest on various bank accounts and other investments that remained secret, locked away in large black ledgers, the dates on their spines going back more than a hundred years. Though Arthur was diligent in assisting his father it was not his sole preoccupation. His secret passion was painting and, little known to his father, he had rented a small studio in Islington. Here he led a separate and secluded existence. His life-model portraits of women, the occasional private sale of these pictures for high prices to lascivious Victorians to hang in sequestered rooms, and his bohemian lifestyle with its lack of sexual inhibitions soon attracted, like moths around a light, a small circle of exotic friends with similar tastes. One particular painting, which Whitfield had secretly asked a dealer to acquire on his behalf upon hearing of his son's activity, impressed him because of the delicate and sensitive way in which Arthur had depicted the frontal pose of a svelte young woman who wore only a mask. Though he could never admit to his possession of such an erotic painting, equally he could not bring himself to burn it, because the picture revealed a free spirit he had never enjoyed. He put the picture in a wooden box and hid it in the attic of his Westminster house. Arthur's secret weekend life, his evident sexual freedom and the cosmopolitan company he kept added to Whitfield's anxiety about the preservation of the family legacy, an anxiety increased by his lack of trust in his replacements for Fletcher and Joiner. He had become a lonely man, his mind increasingly troubled.

If there was anxiety in the Whitfield family, there was also evidence of growing concern at Herzberg, as the von Deppes became more exposed to the stresses and strains that the new imperial Germany was beginning to impose on the fabric of its society. In Russia the Tsarist ideology had long been orthodoxy, autocracy and nationality. Though a similar cry was not uttered in Germany, the Imperial Chancellor was nonetheless advocating and pursuing a policy of a stronger centralised government presiding over a state with territorial ambitions, and friendship with Russia rather than amity with England. This was at odds with the traditional approach of the elite – aristocrats like the von Deppes, diplomats and artists – who had a continuing strong attachment to charming, quaint England going back to Frederick the Great. This latter affinity was shared by Crown Prince Frederick Wilhelm who, strongly supported by Crown Princess Victoria, continued to advocate a less bombastic, more open-minded and laissez-faire approach to Germany's future, an attitude vehemently rejected by their son Wilhelm.

This dichotomy gradually became more noticeable at Herzberg, particularly when Joseph, his brother, Fredrick, and their two families gathered for weekends, often with close friends. To everyone's surprise, Joseph began to advocate the Imperial Chancellor's policy, which he believed was in Germany's best interests. If the German state was to flourish, then it had to compete with England. The softly spoken but strong-minded Beatrice condemned her husband's opinion as tasteless and disagreeable.

On one occasion, shortly after Christmas in 1881, this verbal skirmishing led to a sharper exchange of words over dinner at Herzberg. Victoria, on one of her frequent visits from London, had severely criticised Chancellor Bismarck for seeking to take Germany in a direction that its past monarchs had eschewed. In her view, such a path would surely lead to war and destruction.

"I admire you and your contribution to Herzberg's continuing musical heritage greatly," said Joseph, pompously, "but I deeply resent your unending advocacy of the virtues of English-style laissez-faire government. Your opinions demonstrate a certain arrogance on your part which I find out of keeping. Not living in Germany diminishes your understanding of what has to be done and the way it should be done. I urge you to restrain your uninformed judgements and in particular to desist from persuading Alice of your point of view. She may have been born in England but she has been brought up to be German, she is married to a German citizen and is part of a respected German family. She must therefore live as a German must do. So please, Victoria, no more of your views."

"Joseph," interrupted Beatrice, "how could you be so objectionable? None of us, regardless of our sex and regardless of whether we live in this country or not, is obliged to follow your misguided opinion, which incidentally others in this family do not share. In recent years you have changed, become more uncompromising. It is unbefitting. I do not know what has happened to you in that parliament building. I urge you to apologise."

Joseph hesitated, struck by his wife's harsh words, and then grudgingly apologised.

Beatrice hoped her husband's apology would be an end to the matter. But it was not.

"The worst thing that can befall us all," said Victoria, "is not to listen to or indeed respect the opinions of others. Perhaps as old age encroaches we are all inclined to become intolerant and narrow-minded. I must be careful to avoid such an affliction. I would add this. Though I may live in London and the music I perform is international, my blood is still German, just like yours, and the Kaiser is my king. Yet what I admire most of all about Britain is its freedom of expression. It will be a bad day if such a freedom is extinguished from Germany in the pursuit of an illusion to be greater than England. We should of course have strong policies but blended with the cultural openness for which we at Herzberg have long been standard-bearers. I will advocate this to my last breath."

There was a long silence after this clash of verbal arms across the table, eventually broken by Alice and Nicolas recounting their plans for a fresh landscaping of the garden in preparation for an outdoor performance of Mozart's *Requiem*.

"Let us hope there will never be a requiem for Herzberg," muttered Frederick Paul, who had said little during dinner.

"Amen to that," said everyone.

Still bruised by the earlier exchange, the family adjourned to the *Spiegelsaal* to hear Victoria play the piano. For Beatrice, Frederick Paul and Anne what had been said marked the worrying sign of a weakening of the generosity of spirit that had been such a hallmark of the von Deppe family over the years; it seemed a disturbing harbinger of a new and hard-nosed bluster with accompanying colonial pretensions and notions of a huge naval fleet.

As her cousin played the *Minuet* from Handel's opera *Berenice*, Alice was rereading in her mind the letter she had received the day before from Colonel Albrecht von Dassanowsky telling her of his appointment to the Austrian legation in Berlin.

> *My dearest Countess,*
>
> *It is with the gladdest of hearts that I tell you I have been appointed to my government's legation in Berlin.*
>
> *You are the most beautiful and entrancing woman I have ever encountered. Your visits to Vienna have been too rare over these past years. When you have come here to play, I have deeply valued sitting close to you, holding your hand when you let me and stealing a kiss when you are least expecting it. I long so much to hold you close. Together in Berlin within three months I hope we will be able to find more secret moments together.*
>
> *A bientôt,*
> *Your devoted admirer,*
> *Colonel Albrecht von D*
> *Vienna*
> *Tuesday the 11th of January, 1881*

Receipt of the letter caused Alice a tremor of intense concern. She recalled the beginning, seven years before, of what she had considered to be an innocent but amusing correspondence, starting with the letter he had delivered at the end of her first visit to the imperial city.

> *Dear Countess Alice,*
>
> *It was a great honour, privilege and above all pleasure to act as your escort to the Hofburg. What an evening it was – to hear you play Mozart with such confidence and lightness, to*

*dance with a beautiful woman so fleet of foot, and to enjoy your
amusing conversation. I wished the call for carriages had never
come.*

*I hope that you will return to Vienna before long, so that
we can renew our acquaintance.*
Your devoted servant,
Albrecht von Dassanowsky
Vienna

She recalled her carefully written reply:

Dear Lieutenant von Dassanowsky,

*Thank you for your kind letter. Your flattery on paper is
as skilful as your dexterity on the dance floor. I expected no less
of an officer of the cavalry.*

*You have left me with many happy memories, which I have
shared with my husband.*
Yours sincerely,
Alice von Deppe
Herzberg

He promptly replied:

Dear Countess Alice,

*Thank you for your kind letter in reply to mine. There is
nothing more to be said. I wait with great anticipation your
return to Vienna, which I hope will be soon.*
Your devoted servant,
Albrecht von Dassanowsky
Vienna

This exchange began an infrequent and discreet correspondence
– teasing but innocent in Alice's eyes, though not so for von
Dassanowsky. Here was a woman he longed to bed and in pillow
talk to find out more about her intriguing past, about her mother
with her royal connection and about her mysterious father. Might
he be Sir Robert Whitfield, as the interrogation at Ballgasse might
suggest? If his information was true and he succeeded in bedding
the Countess, this might offer opportunities for mischief-making.

The plain fact, however, was that he wished to see her undressed, in his arms, in his bed. The fact that she was married was inconsequential.

Though Alice did not disclose her correspondence – except on one occasion to Victoria, who urged caution – her excitement on the eve of her periodic visits to Vienna did not escape the notice of her husband or indeed her mother. Nicolas, who had an eye for women, much to his mother's disquiet, was amused and even impressed by his wife's many admirers; for Rebecca, pride at her daughter's musical achievements was tempered by anxiety over the risks she thought she was taking. Alice reassured her mother and husband that she was never alone on her journeys outside of Germany. Von Dassanowsky assured those who questioned him that his intent was harmless flirting, readily reciprocated by Alice. What might come of it could be of benefit to his superiors.

Closer to her than many others, Victoria considered Alice her musical protégée, a refreshing, confident spirit who might perhaps be the next guardian of Arabella's music book. Sometimes studying Alice while she played, Victoria observed a delicate femininity interweaved with traces of earthy sexuality, maybe reflecting her very first years in London's east end. She played her family role with grace and style, her freshness and laughter putting even the stiffest at ease. Yet there was an innocence about her – whether deliberate or genuine was hard to say – and this, combined with frequent coquettishness, made her highly attractive to men, as was often manifested at social events by the presence of handsome men seeking to be as close to her as possible. There were even occasions when Victoria saw in Alice a passing likeness to the Arabella in the portrait with the Empress Catherine of Russia.

She tried hard to persuade Alice to come to England, not only to play in concerts and to see more of London but to become part of her German circle of friends in rural Leicestershire, which included Count Friedrich Hochberg and the Imperial Chancellor's son Herbert von Bismarck, all living with great pleasure an English way of life. This friendship and informality Victoria thought would be agreeable to Alice. Yet the young and strong-minded Countess resisted these invitations. She had come to love Germany; she had happy childhood memories of Wannsee, Berlin, Leipzig and Dresden, which she was ever keen to renew; she spoke fluent

German; enjoyed horse riding; and had fallen head over heels in love with music. And now she had a child, Eva Victoria. Most of all she loved performing music in Vienna, allegedly to see more of the Empress Sisi but truthfully to enjoy the flirtatious company of a handsome cavalry officer, whose reticence about his army activities only served to make Alice more inquisitive.

As the years passed Victoria noticed a further change in Alice. She had become more self-willed, which suited her increasing contribution to the Camerata; it helped Victoria to ensure that, while its classical and romantic repertoire continued to flourish and it competed as best it could with Vienna's unassailable musical position in Europe, it was open to new compositions from composers such as Richard Strauss. Yet, despite her musical preoccupations, this sensuous woman loved being with men even more than before, continuing to attract new ranks of male admirers and teasing them with what some considered the promise of intimacy. Her flirtations did not help to ease the occasional family tension and led to sharp reproofs from her mother and even occasionally from her husband who, though still flattered that his wife should be adored by so many men, was becoming jealous of the attention she constantly received, to the point that he began to flirt with women. When that became apparent, Alice knew it was time for Scheherazade to enchant her husband in bed. The arrival of the newly promoted Colonel would put her to even greater test.

Throughout these years Alice was pleased that a calmer sea prevailed for her mother. Though the Crown Princess and her husband found life at court difficult and their son Wilhelm increasingly tempestuous, they travelled as often as they could to escape the formality of Berlin court life, frequently visiting London to be with Queen Victoria. From time to time Rebecca travelled with the royal party, providing her with the chance to see London and revisit childhood places. Yet Rebecca's preference was to remain in Berlin in order to be close to her daughter, about whom she frequently worried, and her grandchild.

As Victoria finished playing, Alice pondered how she should respond to the latest letter from the newly promoted Colonel von Dassanowsky. Late at night she went to Victoria's bedroom and, sitting on the bed, showed her the letter.

"Your correspondence with this man should never have happened. Your replies to his messages have, I fear, merely encouraged him. In Vienna he pays attention to you for all to see and openly displays affection towards you, which is unbecoming. It has not gone unnoticed here and has become the subject of comment. You rightly have many admirers. We women love the adulation of handsome men, particularly those in uniform, and it is fun to flirt. But it is necessary to be aware of others' perceptions. You must now bring this matter to an end before he comes to Berlin."

"It is true that I enjoy the adulation of men and I confess I play with their emotions. But it has only been a game. Nicolas remains my prince, to whom I will always be faithful. He is the father of my daughter and I hope before long to give him a second child."

"Are you carrying another?"

"Yes, I think so, but please say nothing until I am sure."

"You have my word, but this is an even greater reason for ending your dalliance with von Dassanowsky. You do not want gossips to speculate that the child is his."

Alice froze.

"It is not. It is Nicolas's," she said in distress. "What am I to do, Cousin Victoria?"

"Let me think, Alice. We will speak tomorrow."

The following morning Victoria and Alice walked in the garden at Herzberg.

"I have written to Charles this morning, delaying further my return to London so that you and I can attend an important concert in Prague in which I have been asked to participate. I know the proprietor there and can arrange for you to perform with me. You must write immediately to Colonel von Dassanowsky. Do not acknowledge his letter but say simply you will soon be on your way to Prague. Without your acknowledgement of his latest letter he will think you have not received it and will surely follow you there to tell you of his new assignment. In Prague, away from prying eyes, you will tell him that he must refuse his appointment to Berlin as your correspondence with him has become known and that, if continued, its disclosure and his presence in Berlin will cause grave difficulties for him and for you. He may concur or he may not.

Whatever he may say, Alice, you must be firm. Your association with him must end and he must not come to Berlin."

"I will do as you advise," replied Alice, "but please help me to compose this letter."

Less than two weeks later Victoria and Alice set out from Berlin.

Putting von Dassanowsky from her mind Alice was thrilled to arrive in Prague, the city of the composer she loved best. Victoria told her it was where Mozart had composed *Don Giovanni* and *La Clemenza di Tito* and where his symphony known as the *Prague* had been first performed in 1787. The two women were greeted enthusiastically and room was made for them to perform on the fourth night in the Estates Theatre. In the concert's first half, in front of a full house, Victoria played Mozart's *Piano Concerto No. 20*, which was received with rapturous applause. In the second half the two elegantly dressed women played Ludwig Abeille's *Piano Concerto in D Major for Four Hands*, the second movement of which Arabella had briefly referred to in her music book as intimately romantic, since it could be performed with a keyboard companion of trust. In the audience was Colonel von Dassanowsky, still recovering from Alice's earlier termination of their correspondence and her insistence that he decline his appointment to Berlin. He gazed intently at the young Countess in her shimmering green taffeta gown as she played the slow movement. She had toyed with him over the past years. Often he had sat close to her, held her hand, drawn her ever closer to him as they danced and kissed her on the few occasions she had allowed him to do so. He had become besotted with her. He would not let her go. With her hair pinned up revealing her long slender neck he lusted for her. He would bed her before her departure from Prague whatever she might say, whatever the risk. She would come to realise that they loved one another and so would agree to a new, more intimate relationship in Berlin. As the two women finished their performance he joined in the enthusiastic applause.

Following a late supper with friends and admirers, Victoria and Alice returned to their hotel. After a few minutes together Alice left Victoria's bedroom for her own along the corridor. She began to undress, first removing her gown, then the shift beneath it and then her corset. Before slipping into her nightdress she admired her slim figure, soon to swell with another child. For a while her contours would not emulate the Empress Sisi's. As she sat at the dressing table there was a knock at the door.

"Who is there?"

"I have a message from the Countess Hardinge von Böhm."

Alice was puzzled. Why should Victoria send her a message so late at night?

"Please push it beneath the door."

"I am not permitted to do that. The Countess asked me to hand you the message personally and to wait for your reply. She said it is urgent."

Slipping her dressing gown over her shoulders Alice went to the door. She hesitated and then turned the key, starting to open the door. Von Dassanowsky pushed against it, forcing his way in.

"Colonel, please leave at once. I have nothing to add to what I said earlier. Our association has ended."

Von Dassanowsky turned the key behind him and moved closer to her.

"Countess, you answer my letters with endearing replies. You smile at me. We sit together. We dance together. We kiss. But we are never alone. Now we are."

"Colonel von Dassanowsky, you have mistaken my politeness. Please leave or I will summon the hotel staff."

She made to pull the bell rope by the bed but he seized her arm, dragging her onto the mattress. Sweeping aside her dressing gown he tore at her nightdress, revealing her breasts. She tried to call out but he put a hand over her mouth.

"Countess, please listen. I love you. I have loved you ever since we first met in Vienna. For the past years you have tormented me – so close, yet never the love I expected to follow. I have no wish to take you from your husband but for us to have a secret friendship in which we can enjoy one another. Let go, Countess. Unleash your true feelings towards me I beg you."

She tried to break free from his grip.

"You will not have me. I have never wanted you, only to be friends. You must leave immediately. I implore you to go."

Alice fought him, managing to free herself despite his strength. She ran to the door and twisted the key. As she struggled to open the door he lunged at her, tearing her nightdress from her body.

"You will never have me. Never. I would rather die than succumb to you," she shouted.

At that moment the door burst open.

"Get out, you bastard. Get out," cried Victoria.

Von Dassanowsky fled, his face bruised and contorted in rage.

For the rest of the night Victoria comforted Alice. As the young woman lay asleep in her arms, Victoria reflected on what had happened.

Von Dassanowsky had reciprocated Alice's flirtation with the intention of beginning an affair. That was what men often sought. Her first husband had proved that. Apart from the appeal of Alice's physical attraction, such closeness would enable him to learn more about a woman who had come to fascinate him. From their exchange of letters and gestures he had become mistakenly convinced that Alice too wished for an affair. His longing to have her in his bed had grown so intense that his desire had become uncontrollable. Alice, in her innocence, had not seen the increasing danger to which she had exposed herself. He had sought her surrender; she had played with his emotions, secure in her battlement. In the end, that which had been denied to him he had sought to secure through force. What had happened was a consequence of her innocence and profound misjudgement. Armed with the impregnability of her reputation, bearing the von Deppe name and failing to realise the potency of her femininity and allure, she had driven him beyond distraction into an insane action. The final act in the drama had demonstrated how easily trust could be misplaced, how fragile it could be. She, Victoria, should know from her own first marriage.

Alice awoke.

"Will it be all right? Am I safe?"

"Yes, all will be well. But heed this warning. We live in a time of mounting apprehension. While you must remain as you have always been – embracing of all, feminine and bewitching – be wiser and follow the advice of the Countess Arabella. She once wrote, 'I will do what people want but only as I want it to be.' Like her be vigilant, be sparing in your trust."

"I will. Hold me tighter."

"Alice, forgive me."

"What is there to forgive?"

"I brought you to Prague. I was the architect of a plan that put you in needless danger."

"It is over, Cousin Victoria. I am now safe and much wiser. Besides my husband, I regard you as my truest friend. You saved me from a terrible fate. Henceforth I will place my unwavering trust only in you and him."

"Good. Now sleep and try to forget what happened."

The next morning she received a letter of apology from von Dassanowsky, delivered to the hotel in the early hours. She handed it to Victoria.

"Please, Cousin Victoria, help me. Neither Nicolas nor my mother must ever hear of what happened last night. If they do I will never be forgiven, expelled from a family to whom I owe so much. I just wish the Colonel would go away."

"He will, Alice, he will."

They stayed a further night in Prague so Alice could compose herself before returning to Berlin. After having her bruising treated by a doctor, making a report to the police and much sleep, she awoke calm the next day. As they made their final preparations to leave for Berlin, Victoria received news that the local police had found the body of Colonel Albrecht von Dassanowsky in an alleyway the evening before. He had been strangled.

Long before Victoria and Alice arrived in Berlin, an urgent and secret message arrived at the headquarters of the secret police in Vienna.

Most Secret

The Generalpolizeidirektor *has been asked to inform you that the recent conduct in Prague of the late Colonel von Dassanowsky was unbecoming of an officer and unforgivable. Despite earlier requests that you should transfer him to other duties far removed from Vienna, your investigations failed to reveal his persistent attempts to seek a close and unacceptable relationship with the Countess Alice von Deppe, one that she did not desire. Your assurances that his intentions towards her were harmless proved untrustworthy. Furthermore, the decision to assign him to your mission in Berlin was against our express wishes. Necessary urgent remedial action was therefore required. We thank you for your cooperation in the subsequent steps. You will wish to know that we have taken measures to improve our surveillance procedures to ensure that none of the Countess's family is ever again exposed to the risks that occurred on this occasion.*

We consider the case to be now closed. Consequently, there should be no further reference to these recent events, on the express orders of our highest authority.
Heinrich Müller
Preußische Geheimpolizei
Berlin
Friday the 25th of February, 1881

The communication received a curt reply from Chief Inspector Horváth in Vienna, acknowledging receipt and confirming closure of the case. Before filing the incoming telegram, the Chief Inspector recorded on it in his neat, unmistakable handwriting that Colonel von Dassanowsky, one of his best officers despite his sexual interest in the Countess, had been murdered by a German agent on Austro-Hungarian soil. This unfriendly action had breached the trust between the two authorities.

Some weeks later, Alice suffered a miscarriage. While Victoria well understood Alice's distress, she was relieved that possible personal and political embarrassment had been avoided, even though she believed Alice that the child was her husband's not von Dassanowsky's. Nicolas was not aware of his wife's pregnancy or of the miscarriage.

* * * * *

The winter of 1881 was bitter. Now frail and aware he was a man of the past, almost out of time, Robert Whitfield decided in early February to visit Meltwater once more. Though he would not say so, it was to bid farewell to the estate his grandfather had nurtured and cherished and which he had subsequently extended and embellished. Once a small house it had become an imposing architectural and social landmark. The von Deppe family might have their grand palace at Herzberg but Meltwater, made of sturdy brick and flint, was his seat of power.

Through gently falling snow, he caught his first glimpse of the house against the horizon of approaching dusk.

"Nearly there, Sir Robert," cried the coachman. "Another fifteen minutes."

"Good," he replied.

He pulled the blanket closer to his aching body, his mind filled with thoughts of the past. From here, over a century ago, that cursed woman Arabella set out, in an impetuous act of defiance, on a long journey – via a London whorehouse, he remembered, relishing the detail – eventually to marry her ageing count. He admitted that, judging by the portrait he had seen in Berlin, she was captivating, but it was still his unshakeable opinion, which he aimed to take to his grave, that her capriciousness, her selfish wilfulness had nearly brought his family to its knees. He had tried to forgive, holding out his hand in reconciliation to that arrogant family, but his gesture of warmth was spurned. You are deceiving yourself, Whitfield, accused a voice in his head. Speak the truth. Reluctantly, he conceded that yes, it was he who had condemned his gesture before it began. It was his envy of what Arabella had achieved that made genuine reconciliation impossible. His jealousy was an uncontrollable tyrant, forever defeating his good intentions, causing him to indulge in outrageous acts, including being an accessory to murder. He would never be able to assuage his guilt.

"We have arrived, Sir Robert."

He stirred.

It was a happy respite at Meltwater, for a while everything forgotten as he enjoyed the company of his family, the bonhomie and respect of friends, and the comfort of a well-appointed country house. But his ease of mind did not last. Despite his son's urging that he should stay longer, he decided to return to London. Feeling increasingly exhausted, he knew that he could no longer put off tending to a few final financial matters. Before his departure, he removed from the locked box in the attic his aunt's music book and put it in his portmanteau. He had resolved to commit one final act of cruelty towards her memory – to burn it. He knew it would be sacrilege but his irresistible jealousy drove him to this act of shameful vandalism, the destruction of a book on the pages of which was indelibly printed her spirit, which he had come so much to loathe.

On his return to London he began to put his remaining affairs in careful order, including completion of a fresh will and final instructions to his bankers. Arthur helped him, diligently carrying out each precise order his father gave. Two days later all that was left were six black ledgers and the music book. Dismissing Arthur for the evening, Whitfield instructed the servants to prepare a hearty fire in the library so that he could sit alone and, page by page, destroy in the flames his financial secret – long the source of the family's wealth – and the music book. Once done, no one would ever know. Only ashes would be left.

After supper on a tray he sat by the blazing fire, ready to begin his task, when he heard a voice.

"It is time."

Startled, Whitfield peered into the dark recesses of the library not reached by the light of the flickering flames. He saw no one. It was a trick of the fire, he assured himself, the sound of the sap in the logs. He opened the first ledger. Again, he thought he heard a voice, this time more insistent.

"Come, do not delay. It is time."

He called out. "Arthur, it is not yet time. I told you to be absent this evening. Go and paint another of your dreadful pictures. Do you hear me, Arthur? Go away."

There was no answer. Whitfield suddenly sat back in his chair, the books on his lap spilling to the ground as his body began to shake violently.

"No," his voice mumbled, "not yet," putting up his hand in a weak gesture of defiance. From his throat came a long deep moan.

An hour later Arthur returned from an evening with his friends. Entering the library to say goodnight, he found his father slumped in his chair, his eyes still open, full of fear. He closed them. Sir Robert Whitfield was dead but his secret and the music book remained unburned. His trust in himself had failed him. Arthur opened the window to let in the cold night air.

*

Two weeks later, on Friday the 11th of March 1881, Whitfield's remains were buried in Meltwater's parish church alongside those of his father and mother. Many attended, squeezing into the small church to pay their last respects to a man who had not been warmly loved but whose ambitions and wealth had brought greater employment to the estate and the surrounding villages. In the front pew across the aisle from the new generation of Whitfields were the Countess Victoria and her husband, Sir Charles Hardinge, who had brought a letter of condolence from Joseph on behalf of all the von Deppe family. Looking down on the coffin above the crypt into which it would soon be consigned was the plaque on the wall:

In honour of
Arabella, Countess von Deppe, once of Meltwater and the Whitfield family
1743–1816
Proud of England, her country of birth
A patriot of Prussia

In death as in life, Arabella continued to haunt the Whitfield family.

Following a memorial service in London – where the prevailing view was that the deceased would be missed but not lamented – and the reading of the will, life for the Whitfield family began to return to normal. Charles Whitfield inherited his father's baronetcy and with it Meltwater, from which income Arthur would receive an annual allowance. Their father's London property portfolio was placed in the hands of agents for letting, sale or further acquisitions, with a proportion of the accruing profits being shared between the two brothers and the rest reinvested in accordance with their father's last will.

When he moved from Westminster to a smaller riverside house in Chelsea Arthur took with him the six black ledgers and the music book, which he had placed in his late father's portmanteau. That summer, while on holiday in Cornwall with his young muse, Juliet de Burgoyne, he began to examine the contents. The music book entranced him, shedding a pleasing light on a woman whose memory his father had confined to the attic. Her words, *I will do what people want but only as I want it be*, summed up neatly his and Juliet's free-spirit philosophy. He decided to place the book with its musical exercises and precious original compositions in the safe keeping of the British Museum's library, on condition that its ownership rested with the Whitfield family and that it would be accessible to them at any time. However the six ledgers were a different matter. As each day of his scrutiny passed a dark story began to emerge which Arthur decided should no longer be hidden.

Later that year an extraordinary letter appeared in the London *Times* which would cause consternation at Meltwater, divided opinions in London and renewed hostility and division at Herzberg.

CHAPTER 10

Revelation of a Wounding Past

Despite an urgent appeal from his elder brother, Charles, not to do so, Arthur chose to reveal the dark secret of his late father's wealth and to do so in a most public and contentious way.

> *To The Editor of* The Times
> *Sir,*
> *I have considered carefully whether I should write this letter. After weighing the possible consequences I have concluded there is no impediment and accordingly I have put pen to paper. If you decide to publish it I hope that its contents may encourage others in similar circumstances to do likewise, for the sake of common humanity.*
>
> *Earlier this year my father, Sir Robert Whitfield, of Meltwater Hall in Norfolk, died at the age of eighty-three. At his funeral there was much praise for his wise judgement, unstinting kindness, fine works and generous giving. I wish to inform you that this appraisal requires a fresh assessment if it is to reflect a true reckoning of his life.*
>
> *Irrefutable evidence has come to me that my father, like his paternal antecedents, received income from the ownership of sugar estates in Berbice and Demerara in the West Indies. Examination of most private accounts reveals not only the*

sizeable monies gained from these estates but also the extent of the unremitting hard labour of the slaves obliged to deliver their produce. This income was spent on Meltwater Hall and the purchase of properties in London. No portion was spent on relieving the miserable conditions of those who worked on the estates. While the undisclosed association of the Whitfield name with the West Indies thankfully ended with the most welcome abolition of slavery in 1833, my father received substantial compensation from the government of the day for the loss of these estates. A proportion of this sum was invested in fresh undisclosed businesses in this country and for the purchase of yet more prestigious properties in London, thus further increasing the flow of income. Other money was spent on another extension of his home in Norfolk. There was still no gesture on his part to assist the descendants of those who had toiled against their will on his behalf. I consider this most recent lack of compassion to be lamentable and reprehensible. Accordingly, as one who was due to inherit from Sir Robert, I urge the executors of his will to take all necessary steps to ensure the stain on the Whitfield name from the long ownership of these estates is somewhat mitigated by generous donations to those who are seeking to improve the conditions in our colonies of those who were once slaves. I have decided to renounce my share of my father's estate, so that it can be used as I have recommended.

In conclusion, I hope this letter may lead to a more balanced judgement of Sir Robert Whitfield and a better-informed knowledge of the extent to which some have gained financially, at the expense of the Exchequer — which is to say, the public purse — from the toil of oppressed people. I consider it is better to be hated for what you are than to be loved for something you are not.

I remain, sir, faithfully yours,
Arthur Whitfield
Chelsea, London
Thursday the 17th of November, 1881

Arthur's letter conveyed his abhorrence of the disturbing and shameful contents of the ledgers. They revealed that his father had inherited from his father two sugar plantations in the West Indies, one with 195 slaves in Demerara and another with 200 slaves on a similar estate in Berbice, from which had come a handsome annual income. Each of the ledgers contained in neat handwriting reports of the size of the twice-yearly sugar harvests and the considerable income earned; a record of the number of slaves; and, from time to time, details of unpleasant measures taken to enforce discipline in order to increase harvest volume – this despite occasional references in the ledgers to an apparent decline in the consumption of sugar from the West Indies. One ledger listed in gruesome detail the harsh disciplinary action, including three hangings on the Demerara estate, taken to restore order following the slave uprising of 1823.

The last ledger ended with the claim for compensation his father had lodged with the Exchequer following the passage of the Slavery Abolition Act. In response he had received from the National Debt Office, on Monday the 14th of December 1835, the sum of £20,000, which according to the ledger was approximately half of the market value of the two estates. This substantial payment, added to the income from the Meltwater estate and the family properties in London, revealed that Robert Whitfield had been a rich man. To his shame, the ledgers showed that neither in earlier years nor in 1835 had any portion of the income from the West Indies or the Exchequer been spent on desirable public causes. What money had been paid in local poor relief in the Meltwater parish appeared to have come from the estate's own harvest income.

Some of the ledgers contained references to so-called London "ephemeral costs", almost entirely without explanation or detail. Arthur speculated as to what the purpose of these might be, but there was no clue. If they had been payments to good causes in the capital, they would surely not have been recorded in secret ledgers. Yet there was one entry that was more specific – a payment of £20 on the 25th of July 1850 to Mr and Mrs Fitch of Whitechapel for the adoption of a two-month-old child. Arthur re-examined the ledgers yet again to see if he could find more detail or, more specifically, a clue to the identification of the mother. His search was in vain. Since his father was unlikely to have made such a payment out of public goodwill, and the transaction was in a private ledger, he drew the conclusion that the child was perhaps his father's, a fact he had wished to hide from his family. Arthur frequently wondered what had happened to the mother.

* * * * *

During a weekend at Meltwater in late October, Arthur had told his brother of his intention to write to *The Times*, patiently explaining his reasons for doing so and showing him as evidence for his charge one of the ledgers. Pushing the ledger aside, Charles pleaded with him not to take such precipitate action.

"Arthur, what good do you expect to come from writing? I agree that slavery was abominable and for the Whitfields to take income from such a tainted source should have ended long ago. But what you propose will do the family name no good, harm our standing in the county, and more particularly cause unnecessary distress at Meltwater and embarrassment to me in my legal practice. You and your circle in London may live a carefree life but I have obligations to fulfil. A letter to *The Times* will make that more difficult. It is better to let these ledgers remain undisclosed and for you and I to agree on specific instructions to the executors of Papa's will to make donations to those charities you have in mind. I ask you – I beg you – please do not write the letter you have in mind. Besides, even if you do write your letter, no one will care."

Arthur paused. Should he say more?

"Charles, your view arises from expediency. Mine arises from principle. Papa should be unmasked for what he became – a grasping landowner with no scruples, determined forever to increase his wealth at the expense of others. He owned estates in the West Indies where there was great cruelty. In 1823 three men were hanged on the Demerara estate for rising up against slavery – hanged in the name of our family. We should expose this and show our readiness to make amends for the wrongs of the past."

"Arthur, listen to me. Why should readers of *The Times* – in this country and abroad – read of our deeds of the past? What possible good will come from it? While nothing may be said publicly, it will cause some to gloat in private and others to forget what Papa tried to achieve, albeit with a poor result – reconciliation with the von Deppe family. I promise you that we will work together quickly to set some good works in progress."

"You are a hypocrite," replied Arthur. "In the margin of the more recent ledgers Papa wrote reminders to himself that he should let you know the progress of his claim for compensation. That suggests you knew about the estates, despite your protestations to the contrary, and yet you took no action to prevail upon him to remedy what had happened for so long in our family's name."

Silence fell in the library. Charles looked down with some shame.

"It is true that he told me of his claim for compensation, but he gave few details. I chose not to press him. I should have done."

"That makes you guilty of being an accessory to his misdeeds," retorted Arthur. "All the more reason to expose this family's involvement with an intolerable trade – the purchase and misuse of slaves for the benefit of the Whitfields' comfort and financial well-being."

"Arthur, don't be so pompous, so self-righteous. Do not seek to elevate yourself to prosecuting counsel, jury and judge. It does not become you. I may have made a misjudgement but I am not an accessory to the charge you have laid at Papa's door. Let the past alone. Long ago this family suffered grievously from the decision of our great-aunt to run away from Meltwater. The Whitfields have been afflicted by its consequences ever since. Do not let you and I squabble in this way and perpetuate bad blood, or cause another breach."

Arthur paused and then choosing his words with deliberate care spoke again.

"You and I have opposing principles. Yours are to bury the past and so avoid the public discomfort of letting people know why we intend to make amends. You just wish to begin to support good causes without explanation. My principles are to confess our misdeeds. Our friends, acquaintances, the villagers of Meltwater may say nothing in public but in private they will be shocked by my disclosure. They will surely respect us more for being truthful – for revealing what happened. I believe that is the right thing to do. Any discomfort will be short-lived and while it lasts it will be tolerable because we will know we have followed the right course of action."

"I can see you are determined to write. Your mind must be befuddled by the laudanum I hear you take. So let me speak clearly.

165

What you intend to do is wrong, disloyal and damaging to what Meltwater stands for. You do not have my support and I will oppose you. I will seek possession of the ledgers before you do further damage. I have nothing more to say. You should leave."

"I will leave, saddened that we have not agreed. But I adhere to my opinion and intended action – which, I should add, is not the effect of the laudanum you have accused me of taking. Please know that I will continue to regard you as my brother and friend and I hope you will do the same, even though I know I have tested our bond to its limit on this matter. As for the ledgers, keep the one I brought with me. Let it be a reminder of a shameful past. As for the remainder, there is no need to seek their legal possession since I know you would not wish others to be aware of their contents. Instead I will see to their early destruction, as I have no wish to retain them under my roof nor do I wish my friends and acquaintances to read them. My letter to *The Times* will be enough."

At that Arthur left Meltwater without a further word being spoken or any gesture of fraternity or friendship. Like Arabella over a hundred years before, he dared not look back in case sight of the Hall would weaken his resolve. The publication of his letter on Wednesday the 23rd of November led to a lasting breach of trust between the two.

* * * * *

As Charles had predicted, the letter's publication prompted no public response, perhaps because readers were so taken aback by its contents but more likely because slavery was not a cause célèbre. Besides, who would wish to cast a stone of criticism when family disputes over wills were so commonplace. After two weeks there were only half a dozen replies to the editor – two scolding Arthur for his unseemly violation of his late father's privacy and the remainder supporting his call for the donation of some of the family wealth to relieve the suffering of the victims of slavery. None was published; they were simply passed to Arthur. There was silence amongst those who had been friends of Robert Whitfield. In their smoke-filled London clubs there was some muttering over port about disloyalty and speaking ill of the dead. Their social encounters with Arthur, already limited, became even more infrequent and when they did occur lacked noticeable warmth – just a doffing of the hat in the street. In the wider circle of Whitfield acquaintances the opinion was widespread that Arthur, in writing about his late father's financial affairs, had broken a code of behaviour, while others simply shrugged, adding that it was only to be expected of a painter of risqué paintings surrounded by a coterie of equally risqué friends. Yet for others it caused a private and adverse reconsideration of a man who had not been the most warmly regarded in their circle.

In the Foreign Office equally little was said, although there was regret that the letter had possibly drawn fresh attention to the earlier government decision to provide, at huge expense, compensation to slave owners and to the scheme of indentured labour from the Indian sub-continent, which had taken its place in the colonies. There were also expressions of relief that Whitfield had never been considered for a diplomatic appointment. A whiff of connection with slavery would not have been suitable amongst Her Majesty's overseas representatives. The imposition of competitive entry to the Foreign Office had been a welcome saviour in this case. But there was also quiet respect for a young man who had bravely, in public, opposed the iniquities of slaveholding. One or two officials suggested that he would be a good addition as a clerk to the Office's anti-slavery department.

In Norfolk the publication of Arthur's letter was unprecedented, stimulating much gossip and some lampooning in the *Freshchester Gazette*. In another local newspaper there was a cartoon of Robert Whitfield spinning in his grave in a blizzard of imperial Bank of England five-pound notes coming from the coffin, with black sugar workers, freed from their chains, trying to catch them. Amongst the close friends of Charles and his wife, Sarah, there was a mélange of sympathy, embarrassment and some *Schadenfreude*. Little was said at dinner parties and soirées, though the Whitfields did not require a vivid imagination to conceive what was probably being said about the family in private. Within Meltwater Hall opinions were equally divided, though never surfaced above stairs. Some of the older staff expressed the opinion that the Whitfields deserved this public reprobation on account of the legendary wrong Charles Whitfield's great-grandfather, Robert, had done to his daughter, Arabella. Above stairs all was placid; the staff who served at dinner remained tight-lipped, perhaps even being more obsequious than usual. As for Charles's legal practice in Norwich, there was little noticeable change and no apparent loss of clients. As elsewhere nothing was said.

Within two months of the letter's publication and in the absence of any legal approach from his brother, Arthur began to burn the ledgers. Two weeks later all was gone, except the page recording the payment of £20 to Mr and Mrs Fitch. If one day he could find the child for whom the payment was made he would seek to make amends for his father's consignment of such a young being to the hardship of Whitechapel.

* * * * *

There was, however, one reader who was intrigued by the letter: Charles Hardinge. He drew it to his wife's attention on the day of publication.

"Victoria, read this."

She read it carefully.

"How extraordinary," she replied. "I always found Whitfield odd. While he portrayed himself as a man of wise judgement, liberal opinion and an ardent pursuer of reconciliation with Joseph, it is revealed he was a covert receiver of income from the toil of slaves. I have said it before – you English are so good at hypocrisy."

Hardinge chuckled. "You have a good subject to discuss with the Schröders and the Deichmanns when they are next in Leicestershire."

"I suppose I should write to Joseph."

"If you do, won't it stoke his unfavourable prejudice towards this country? He never liked Whitfield. The plain fact is the two of them never got on – Joseph was always stiff towards him. Now, there's a Prussian trait for you. It goes well with British hypocrisy."

"I think I will write to Beatrice."

"As you wish, my dear," replied Hardinge. "And I will write to Arthur Whitfield."

"Why on earth would you wish to do that? We only know him as a passing acquaintance."

"My dearest Victoria, this young man, who I hear paints erotic portraits of women, has written a letter of the sort no gentleman would ever write. To reveal income is simply unbecoming. In a letter to a newspaper it is for many unforgivable. In the old days he would risk being challenged."

"Challenged to what?" asked Victoria.

"To a duel, except in this case the libelled is dead."

"But does he not have a brother, a lawyer?"

"Well remembered, Victoria, he does indeed. He has chambers in Norwich, where I began. All the more reason I should write – just in case we have a case of Cain and Abel."

"Surely not?" said Victoria.

"I cannot speak for your family but certainly in England even the most harmonious families begin bitter disputes over inheritance. Human nature will never change in that regard, particularly if family secrets are revealed, as appears to have been the case with Robert Whitfield. Lord knows what else may lie in those ledgers."

The next day Hardinge wrote to Arthur Whitfield.

> *Personal*
> *Dear Mr Whitfield,*
>
> *You and I are not well acquainted even though your family and that of my wife, the Countess Victoria, are linked as a consequence of a marriage long ago.*
>
> *The source and scale of a gentleman's income and how he chooses to spend that income are regarded by many in England as the most personal of matters. Your letter to* The Times *was, if you would permit my private opinion, a brave act of an upright young man, though some might describe your action as bordering on the indelicate, if not foolhardy.*
>
> *I wish you to know that if you encounter any legal hostility or adverse action arising from your letter I will be readily available for you to call upon for advice or assistance, in the strictest confidence, if you consider you have need for it.*
> *Yours most sincerely,*
> *Charles Hardinge, QC*
> *Gray's Inn*
> *Monday the 28th of November, 1881*

Hardinge received by return of post a polite acknowledgement expressing the hope that such a need would not arise. If, however, it were to do so, Arthur would avail himself of a most kind and generous offer.

* * * * *

As her husband knew she would, Victoria wrote to Beatrice, not only to tell her of the Whitfield letter but to relay the latest London society gossip – in which she gladly indulged. Her account included salacious stories about the Prince of Wales's latest rumoured mistresses, Agnes Keyser and the actress Sarah Bernhardt, and the spicy repetition of yet more stories about royal visits to Le Chabanais, the Paris brothel where it was reported HRH and his liaison had bathed in the most expensive of champagne.

Beatrice read Victoria's letter with amusement. Life in Berlin seemed so dull by comparison – a stuffy court, the tiresome manoeuvrings of the Imperial Chancellor and the political activities of socialists in the East. If only some of those she encountered in her social round at Wannsee, in Berlin and Herzberg had some sexual peccadilloes. Everyone was so boring. She recounted *The Times* letter to her husband and Frederick Paul. Neither made any comment, except Joseph's muttered, "Good riddance. I never liked the man. While posturing about reconciliation between our family and his, and proclaiming liberal principles, he was earning a fortune from slaves."

"Aren't we culpable of double standards too – proclaiming peace and goodwill while eyeing potential victims for territorial emasculation?"

"We are merely standing up for our rights, long denied to us."

"Joseph, what has happened to you? You have become such a curmudgeon. Where is that Herzberg élan? Your father would be appalled."

"Whatever you may say, Beatrice, I will have nothing more to do with that family. Any further attempt at renewed friendship I will reject out of hand, as did Arabella all those years ago."

A frequent reader of *The Times*, the Crown Princess had her eye caught by the Whitfield letter. She had met the deceased several times and not liked him. Though from an old landed family, he seemed to her a parvenu but she had said nothing, aware of the occasional private financial support he gave her brother to settle debts. She passed the discarded newspaper to her companion.

"Miss Becky, do read an extraordinary letter on page five. It's about that man Whitfield, who I believe you met in Vienna. His son has spilled some pecuniary beans."

Rebecca read the letter in astonishment but also with anxiety. Her visceral loathing of the man was all the sweeter now he had been subjected to public ridicule, pilloried by his own son. Yet Whitfield's public exposure for hypocrisy and greed only served to increase her fear about his being revealed as the father of her daughter. The disgrace that would fall on her and Alice would be unimaginable.

* * * * *

One afternoon early the next year, as the last rays of the winter sun rippled across Wannsee lake and briefly reflected on the ochre-coloured walls of the villa, a tall, greying, well-dressed man returned to his office after a brief conversation with his superior on the floor above. Heinrich Müller of the *Preußische Geheimpolizei* carefully placed the file on his desk. Flicking through its slim contents, his eye stopped briefly at the earlier report from Vienna on the Ballgasse affair. Taking scissors from the drawer, he slowly cut the Whitfield letter from his copy of *The Times*. After dating it, he placed the cutting in the file beneath a sheet of paper on which he wrote in neat black-ink handwriting:

> *Nichts weiter zu veranlassen. Akte geschlossen.*
> *HM*
> *Freitag, den 20. Januar 1882*
>
> *No further action. File closed.*
> *HM*
> *Friday the 20th of January, 1882*

He placed the file in a shallow box in his safe next to another, deeper box bearing the words *die Familie von Deppe*. He sat down at his desk once more and gazing out of the window recalled the words of Johann Wolfgang von Goethe:

Nothing is worth more than this day.
You cannot relive yesterday.
Tomorrow is still beyond our reach.

Müller took another sheet of paper on which he wrote a name in preparation for the next day. He locked the sheet in his desk and left for the evening.

* * * * *

In February 1882 Victoria announced that her last public performance as a pianist would be on Saturday the 10th of June at the Royal Albert Hall during the visit to London of the Camerata Herzberger. Aged sixty-two, she was beginning to feel stiffness in her fingers. She insisted that Alice and Paul Wilhelm should join her so that the audience could feast on a banquet of German music played by German soloists. As the plans advanced, Victoria was thrilled to learn that the Crown Prince and Crown Princess would be in London and intended to be present. The event was widely advertised. By the end of May all tickets had been sold, many to Victoria's German friends, including the Imperial Chancellor's son who once again was in London.

The concert – a glittering occasion – began with Haydn's *Symphony No. 44 in E Minor (Trauer – Mourning)*. Next Alice, in an elegant off-the-shoulder slim-fitting powder-blue décolleté gown, with her hair pinned up, performed flawlessly Johann Christian Bach's *Piano Concerto in E Flat Major*, earning ecstatic applause. After the interval Paul Wilhelm played with consummate skill Mendelssohn's *Violin Concerto in E Minor*. Following the second interval Victoria, in a flowing high-neck deep-red gown tight-fitted around the waist, took to the platform to wild applause to play with great majesty Beethoven's *Piano Concerto No. 5 in E Flat Major*. The audience was rapt as she played the second movement with great delicacy and poignancy. At the end she received a long standing ovation, led by her husband, for once almost overwhelmed with emotion. The conductor then announced a surprise addition to the programme. To Victoria's astonishment her daughter, Aurelia, stepped onto the platform to play the *Harp Concerto in A Major* by Karl Ditters von Dittersdorf. The audience listened in amazement to her first-ever public performance – in honour of her mother. The concert ended with a performance of Mozart's *Ave Verum Corpus*, sung by the Camerata's choir. As the audience left the Royal Albert Hall there was unstinting praise. The Crown Princess turned to her husband.

"Is there nothing those von Deppe women cannot do?"

He smiled back.

"It would seem not, my dear."

The post-concert soirée was a sumptuous affair. Praise for the Camerata, its choir and the soloists rang to the rafters. It was very late when carriages were called for the departure of the royal couple and their retinue. As Rebecca, equally emotional to see her daughter perform before such an illustrious audience, turned to follow the Crown Princess, Charles Hardinge whispered to her.

"May I have the pleasure of calling on you before your departure from London?"

"Of course, Sir Charles, I would be delighted to see you. But surely it is I who should call on you?"

"Not at all, madame, I will come to you. To where should I come and at what time?"

"Kensington Palace, if you please. It is where I have rooms. Shall we say ten o'clock? What is the matter you wish to discuss?"

"It is only a small matter, madame. Please do not worry."

"That is reassuring, Sir Charles. The sight of a lawyer – and such a senior one as you – can be disconcerting for any woman."

"Not you, Baroness, not you," he replied encouragingly.

* * * * *

The next morning Charles Hardinge and Rebecca Bartlett sat facing one another in the morning room of her apartment. From a leather folder he took a folded sheet of crumpled paper on which were written faded words and figures.

"I think you should have this – to keep or to destroy." He handed it to her. "Please look at the words I have underlined in blue pencil."

Rebecca unfolded it slowly and stared at the writing. Then, letting the sheet slip from her lap, she buried her face in her hands and gently sobbed.

"Baroness, allow me." Hardinge passed her a white handkerchief.

She looked up at him, her eyes brimming with tears, her face etched with deep fatigue.

"How could he have done such a wicked thing after he had promised me she would have a loving home?"

"He was a monstrous man without scruples," replied Hardinge.

"I have tried for so long to hide the identity of Alice's father. Now it is no longer a secret. How many more will know? How long before this becomes public knowledge? It will break Alice's heart."

"Baroness, it will remain a secret. Only you and I know. Arthur Whitfield, who found this page going through his father's secret ledgers, gave it to me because he thought I might be able to help find the child so he could make amends. I assured him I was best able to do what he asked. He knows the name of neither the child nor the mother and he will never do so because I will never tell him. If he were to ask, I will say I believe the child is no longer with us."

"That is most kind of you. Is this the first you knew about Whitfield's involvement?" she asked.

"No. It is not. I knew once we had found Alice," he replied. "The Fitches – the couple who adopted her – described in good detail to my investigator, Herbert Pettigrew, an unpleasant-looking man who accompanied to their tenement in Whitechapel a woman carrying your child in a basket. I soon realised that the man they had described was Joiner, employed by Whitfield along with another called Fletcher. During my acquaintance with Whitfield both men appeared to be servants but it was my suspicion they were more than that, carrying out various private tasks and acting as go-betweens. Only a man like Whitfield would go to so much trouble to hide his identity and culpability in this sad affair. If it had been Joiner's child, he would have found other, quicker means to dispose of it."

Rebecca visibly shuddered.

"I have never disclosed my knowledge of this matter to anyone, not even my wife, and Pettigrew died some years ago, poor man. Our conversation – the one we are having, I as your lawyer and you as my client – is in legal confidence. It can never be revealed without your consent because your right to confidentiality remains a fundamental principle of English common law. So, Baroness, it is entirely in your hands whether to reveal to Alice or indeed to anyone else the name of her true father."

"Thank you, Sir Charles. I cannot find the words to express my gratitude for your great kindness and diligence. And I greatly value your assurance of confidentiality."

"There is one other matter I should draw to your attention."

She looked at him, fear returning to her face.

"Do not be alarmed, madame." He pulled another document from his leather folder. "As the registration of births, deaths and marriages in England was not compulsory at the time, Alice's birth on Friday the 24th of May 1850 – the date the Fitches recall they were told by Joiner – was never recorded. To overcome this unfortunate fact, I invite you to sign this written statement in which you assert – quite correctly – that against your will your daughter was maliciously and cruelly removed to an unknown place by her natural father, his true name unknown and, on account of the passage of time, now believed to be deceased. You were therefore unable as her mother to take the necessary action to register your daughter's birth as you had wished."

Rebecca signed and dated the statement he placed before her. Hardinge then signed and dated his counterpart document, attesting to the statement she had just signed. He handed both documents into her safe keeping.

"Madame, to compensate for the anticipated lack of a birth certificate, I took the liberty at the time of Alice's discharge from the care of the Fitches, and in your absence abroad, to arrange her baptism. Here for your retention is the certificate of baptism, on which is stated her date of birth. The certificate does not divulge the name of Alice's father but it bears yours. I believe that completes our business. I repeat that what has transpired between us remains confidential. No one else will ever know unless you change your mind and make a disclosure."

"Sir Charles, once again I cannot find the words to thank you for what you have done. You are such a kind man. I will be forever indebted to you." She paused. "You may not agree but, other than to confirm her age if she were to ask again, I intend to say nothing to Alice."

"I agree that would be wise, Baroness. Let sleeping dogs lie. Besides, Alice is happily married, a pianist of distinction, and much loved, admired and embraced tightly by the von Deppe family and most of all by you, her mother, which is as it should be."

He looked at his pocket watch.

"My goodness, I have tarried too long. I am sure the Crown Princess has need of your attention."

He stood and took his leave. As he turned towards the door, she clasped both his hands and kissed his cheek.

"Thank you so much, Sir Charles."

Hardinge walked briskly across the park, his mind already turning to other matters, not least the problems beginning to preoccupy his wife's mind – the impending marriage of their daughter; whether on her death she should be buried in England or at Herzberg; and to whom she should give eventual guardianship of Arabella's music book, which he had never seen. And there was yet another matter on her mind: unravelling the still unresolved mystery of the letters *FB* in the miniature of Lady Thérèse.

CHAPTER 11

The Shadows of Uncertainty

With the steady passage of autumn, sunlight grows weaker, shadows of diminishing daylight grow longer and nights become darker. An inevitable consequence of this particular movement in the annual rotation of the seasons is the rapid fading from memory of the confidence and joy of the summer past, replaced by growing apprehension at what the encroaching proximity of chilling winter will bring. Thoughts of this nature passed through Victoria's mind as, in the approaching dusk, she and her husband, the last of the end-of-summer visitors to leave, walked arm in arm in the garden at Herzberg one evening in the third week of September 1882.

As she and Charles talked about minor matters, in her inner thoughts she recalled the year past. Little had appeared to change, apart from Joseph becoming gloomier about events in Europe and Germany's eastern provinces, and Beatrice regularly chastising him for the absence of his former joie de vivre and for becoming increasingly reclusive at Wannsee. Their grown-up children led lives of their own. Daniel Frederick, happily married to Birgitta von Trost, had become a senior official in the War Ministry; his brother, Nicolas Carl, still deeply in love with Alice, flourished as a lawyer; Catherine Elise was equally in love with her husband, Otto Wilhelm Thurnhoffer, a conservative-minded landowner and army officer but the bearer of a broad smile; while Elisabeth Beatrice had been married for seven years to Frederick Wolff, a theatrical proprietor in Berlin. Periodically they would all come together for weekends of family laughter, musical entertainment and riding, together with Frederick Paul, his wife, Anne, and their similarly grown-up children. The vivacious Jeanne Françoise had married Heinrich Stefan von Stolpe, a senior officer in the hussars, stiff in his uniform but highly amusing when not. Jacqueline Anne, much to her mother's delight, had married a French aristocrat, Raymond de Saint-Mar, a senior officer in the French army, so keeping the tricolour flying at Herzberg, as she loved to say in her usual provocative way. To Anne's regret they only came to Prussia once a year. And then of course there was Paul Wilhelm, the gifted violinist, performing regularly in Vienna. He and his devoted Wilhelmina, now a respected cellist, had bought a large house on the outskirts of Vienna, where they spent many months of each year during the concert season. And sometimes Anne-Sophie, Frederick's and Joseph's sister, and her husband, Heinrich Stefan von Rostow, would swell the number. In the closing weeks of the summer of 1882 all seemed unchanged, timeless. Each year at Herzberg metamorphosed seamlessly into yet another.

Later in the evening, while her husband and Nicolas talked about law in the library and Alice practised in the *Spiegelsaal*, Victoria went to the grand bedroom. Unlocking the secret hiding place, she removed Arabella's music book, its contents as rich as ever but mustier and more faded with the passage of time. Sitting at a small secretaire she leafed through the pages, rereading the letters, humming a few bars of some of the musical compositions, and glancing at the sketches and random diary entries on loose sheets of paper. What a remarkable life this woman had led, her legacy still not spent. Victoria looked once again at the miniature of Arabella's mother, the strikingly attractive Lady Thérèse Whitfield, née de Miron. Looking up at a painting of Arabella she had moved to the bedroom from the gallery below, Victoria could see that the likeness of mother to daughter was obvious, though it had to be said that the daughter was even more beautiful than the mother. She read again the words on the reverse of the miniature:

Dans ta face vivent sagesse, la beauté et l'esprit rare qui ni l'age ni froid doivent se désintégrer!

Du fond du coeur que vous avez rechauffé.

In thy face live wisdom, beauty and rare spirit, which neither
age nor cold shall decay!
From the depth of the heart that you have warmed.

With the portrait in her hand, Victoria sat beside the fire to recall her earlier conversation in London with Sir Frederick William Burton, Director of the National Gallery and a close family friend. On a previous visit to Herzberg she had decided to take the miniature to London for closer scrutiny, despite her promise to her late mother never to do so. She had decided that Sir Frederick, who was frequently praised for creating the foundation of the gallery's collection of eighteenth-century art and who had made several shrewd purchases from English private collections, would be a good man from whom to seek a fresh opinion to that expressed by the Director of the Royal Prussian Academy of Art to her grandmother, the Countess Elise Catherine. Over dinner at Carlton House Terrace one night in January she had asked Sir Frederick if he would kindly oblige with an investigation, no matter how long it might take. He had readily agreed and the next day took delivery of the miniature. It was in early July, shortly before her and Charles's departure for Herzberg, that Sir Frederick asked to call on her as he had some news from his investigation. Following pleasantries over afternoon tea, Victoria, barely able to contain her excitement, invited him to tell her what he had found out.

"It is often the case that works of art contain baffling uncertainties," he began. "Some artists lay out their wares for all to see. Others are more reluctant, either because they wish to tease us or to withhold secrets of their trade or their identity. The miniature you asked me to examine is in the first instance an exquisite and finely done piece of work. After careful study and seeking the view of another, I would endorse the conclusion of the Director of the Prussian Academy that the initials *RC* in the bottom right-hand corner are most likely those of Rosalba Carriera, famed for the quality of her miniatures."

"I wish to thank you, Sir Frederick, for that confirmation. Is that everything?"

"No, it is not," he replied.

"Please, Sir Frederick, don't play with me. Tell me all!"

"As you asked me to do, I have looked carefully at the letters *FB* in the narrow fine-lace border along the top of the sitter's bodice. They are obviously unrelated to the painter of the miniature since we can be reasonably sure that it was Rosalba Carriera. Looking at other circumstantial evidence with which I will not trouble you now, it is my supposition that they may refer to François Boucher. If the portrait was painted around 1742, as suggested by the personal historical facts you previously shared with me, then Boucher at that time was professor at the Académie de Peinture et de Sculpture in Paris. He already had a sizeable reputation as a portrait painter and later, in 1765, became *Premier Peintre du Roi*. He painted pastoral and family scenes, often using his wife and children as models. But he also completed more risqué work, you might say, though at the time that was not necessarily a widespread opinion. His later so-called *odalisque* paintings got him into some trouble as being unduly licentious."

"Where might Boucher fit with Lady Thérèse?" Victoria asked expectantly.

"I was recently in Paris and while there I went to the Louvre to look at a Boucher painting I had seen some years before. The painting, completed in 1742, is entitled *Diane sortant du bain* or *Diana leaving her bath*. In the picture there is an unclothed young woman alongside the naked goddess. Her hair is tied up and secured by a blue ribbon, similar to the style and colour in the miniature. Moreover, though the young woman's face is looking down, I believe it bears some passing resemblance to that of the sitter in the miniature. If that is the case, then it is therefore my tentative opinion – and I can go no further – that this young woman portrayed with the goddess Diana is likely to be Thérèse de Miron or, since she was married, Lady Thérèse Whitfield." He handed Victoria a photographic plate of the picture he had visited in Paris. "The figure in Boucher's picture is more voluptuous than the woman in the miniature but, allowing for the artist's preference for the voluptuous, you may still see some similarity in facial features and the style of her hair and the way the ribbon is tied."

For a moment or two Victoria could not speak, so taken aback was she by Sir Frederick's hypothesis.

"Do you think it conceivable, Sir Frederick, that she and

Boucher might have been lovers, that she expressed her love for him in the lace border?"

Sir Frederick replied with great care.

"It is indeed conceivable that Lady Thérèse and Boucher were lovers. If they were not, and of course still assuming that the sitter in the miniature is the same person as the woman beside Diana, then Lady Thérèse was certainly amiable enough to pose for Boucher without her clothes. Even allowing for the degree of sexual freedom at that time, this would have been a gesture of particular physical familiarity. However, we may be following a wrong path."

"Why do you say that, Sir Frederick?"

"At this time there was considerable jockeying amongst beautiful young women for the attention of the French king, Louis XV. Though he was married to Queen Marie Leszczyńska, it was well known that from an early stage in his marriage he had mistresses. For example there was much feuding around this time – 1742 – between the five well-known de Nesle sisters for the important role of *maîtresse en titre*. Other attractive women were of course presented at court to catch the royal eye. I recall reading some while ago an alleged list of such women and, though my memory may be playing tricks, it is possible that I saw the name de Miron upon it. If so, it could only have been around the time 1742, since you have told me that was when Lady Thérèse was in Paris for some length of time while her husband – Sir Robert Whitfield – was travelling. I asked at the Louvre whether such a list might still be found but they could not help me, bearing in mind much was destroyed during the Revolution. To find such a detail would be nigh impossible. Besides, I could not remain in Paris any longer. But let me say this. As the King was of the Bourbon dynasty – and I appreciate that what I am going to suggest may seem far-fetched – it is possible that the *B* in the initials *FB* may refer to that royal house. What the letter *F* may represent in those circumstances I find it hard to say. Perhaps it may have been the first letter of a nickname, which intimate lovers tend to give to one another. My restrained inclination, however, is to say that, while nothing can be ruled out, this fascinating task has led me to conclude that *FB* might after all refer to François Boucher. Finally, I have looked at the delightful portrait of the Countess Arabella von Deppe in this house and compared it with an almost full-face portrait of Boucher by Gustaf Lundberg, presented to Boucher's Academy in 1741. It is hard to see any facial likeness of particular significance between the Countess Arabella and Boucher, except perhaps the incidental similarity of his slight smile with hers. But who is to say whether I am right or wrong? You gave me a mystery. I may have solved it but I leave you with another."

Silence fell on the room as Victoria absorbed all that he had said.

"Thank you, Sir Frederick, for your kindness and your patient exploration of the miniature. Despite your careful choice of words, I believe you have confirmed its artist but, as you say, you have replaced one question with another. For me the new question is who was the father of the Countess Arabella? Was it Sir Robert Whitfield, or was it the *FB* commemorated in the miniature, possibly François Boucher or perhaps even the King of France? Unless more substantial evidence were to come to light, it would appear unanswerable. My opinion – speaking of course as a woman uninformed in the field of pictorial art and therefore making in its place a more emotional and perhaps irrational judgement – would be that Sir Robert was not her father. As the Countess Arabella herself once observed, it was unlikely that a gruff, humourless and opinionated Englishman with no love for the French or evident linguistic ability would rise to the use of such poetry as is inscribed on the reverse of the miniature – unless he copied it, which I would dismiss as a possibility. That would surely suggest the verse was written by an educated Frenchman."

"Or perhaps by an educated Englishman?" interjected Sir Frederick. "After all, Countess, it was not long ago that French was the language of the aristocracy, even in England."

Victoria, dismissing his suggestion with a gentle gesture, continued.

"Whether in those circumstances it was Monsieur Boucher or King Louis we shall probably never know."

Sir Frederick, observing the Countess would not be deflected from the opinion now forming in her mind, elegantly ceased his effort to sow further countervailing doubt. His English pragmatism was on this occasion no match for her German persistence. And persistence manifested by a woman of such intellectual strength of mind was even more potent. So he surrendered.

"I would share your intuition, Countess, on both points. But that is all it is – intuition. I trust we agree on that."

"We do," Victoria replied with a broad grin.

He smiled in return. Perhaps there had been mutual pragmatism after all.

"How can I thank you, Sir Frederick, for your effort and erudition? I am ready to pay any costs you and your staff have incurred."

"Countess, that is not necessary. You and Sir Charles have been the most generous of hosts to me over several years. Perhaps instead you would play to me some day."

"Let me begin your reward at once!"

While he sipped a cup of refreshing tea, she played Schubert's *Impromptu in G Flat Major*. As she did so, she pondered the question: should she share what she had been told with the family or say nothing?

The maid entered the bedroom to place fresh coal on the fire, disturbing Victoria's remembrance of her conversation with the Director. Before changing for supper *à quatre*, she placed the miniature back in the secret cupboard together with the music book. She had still not shared Sir Frederick's opinions with anyone, not even with Charles, nor had she reached a decision on who should be the music book's guardian upon her death. Should it go to London, eventually to be in the care of Aurelia, now twenty-five and married to William Folliot, an official in the Western Department at the Foreign Office, or remain at Herzberg, as she had promised her mother? She would have to decide before long. To those he thought sometimes procrastinated her husband often quoted Shakespeare's words: "Time is the old justice that examines all such offenders". She had no wish to delay her decision, or indeed excuses for doing so. Although it had been another blissful family summer at Herzberg, an island of seemingly perpetual tranquillity, she felt uneasy.

Behind the façade of bonhomie she sensed that, though like her they were unwilling to talk about it, others in the family were equally troubled by the growing social and political tension within Germany arising from widening class division, the signs of more concerted agitation against the Jewish community and the continuing differences within the imperial family. Similar circumstances were not far beneath the surface in the Hapsburg Empire, which no Strauss waltz could hide from the perceptive. Arabella had noted in occasional poignant jottings in her music book her worry about the slide towards war in Europe as Napoleon grasped power. She had frequently recorded her determination to safeguard the integrity and reputation of the family and its estate. Though the cost to the fabric of both during a decade of war had been devastating, through her willpower Herzberg and its dynasty had survived and flourished once again. Who, thought Victoria, would step forward to do the same if war ever came to Germany again? The family was ageing; the younger generation had different opinions and other interests. Her own loyalties were divided. Should she die in England or spend her last days in Germany, a country she had to admit she no longer regarded as her home? She had become assimilated into the English way of life and Aurelia would come to regard herself as British just as Alice, by contrast, now considered herself to be German by assimilation. In each case, where would their loyalties lie in the event of war between Britain and Germany? Pondering who should have the guardianship of a dilapidated music book was in many ways a silly preoccupation. Yet for Victoria, as it had done to her mother, it represented the thread that held the family and its musical heritage together. The fate of the book was emblematic of the fate of the von Deppes.

The Hardinges spent another week together at Herzberg. The week after, Charles returned alone to London. Victoria stayed a while longer in order to accompany Alice to Vienna, her first visit since the von Dassanowsky affair, where she was to perform. It was good to arrive back in the imperial city on Wednesday the 11th of October and the two women were fêted. They inevitably danced to Johann Strauss's music into the early hours with a succession of dance partners. But after more than ten days they returned to Berlin – via Salzburg, so both of them could pay homage to Mozart's city, and Munich. Back at Herzberg – after a brief encounter in Berlin with an emotional Strauss, about to leave for Pest, pained by his wife's desertion of him for another – Victoria finally made up her mind. Though aware of a deep pain of disloyalty to her daughter and equally aware of the risk of similar accusations from other members of the family, she had resolved that it would be Alice who would inherit responsibility for the music book's safe keeping. When Victoria showed her the book and disclosed her intention Alice cried, momentarily overwhelmed by the trust Victoria had decided to place in her. Through her tears she asserted that the von Deppe family had given her love, support and a purpose in life, driven by music. She pledged to her greatest friend and confidante that when the time came she would protect and defend the book to the last fibre of her being. That was the only way she knew to repay the debt she owed the von Deppes. The two women embraced and Alice was sworn to secrecy. The future for both of them was uncertain in a changing Germany but one thing was sure. The music book would in due course pass into the hands of a new and different generation.

The next day, Thursday the 26th of October 1882, Victoria boarded the train in Berlin to return to London. Whatever might now unfold in the remaining years of her life, she was confident she had made the right decision about the book.

After Victoria had gone, Alice, Nicolas and their child were alone at Herzberg. On the second evening following her departure, husband and wife sat reading by the fire in the grand bedroom, which Victoria had insisted they should henceforth use. It was illuminated only by the flickering flames and a single candle on the small piano. It was the first time in many weeks they had been alone. The only sound came from the crackling of the burning wood. Nicolas put down his book.

"Alice, do you love me?" He paused. "Do you truly love me?"

She looked up at his face half revealed in the firelight.

"Yes. I truly love you. Every time we are alone I remember the frisson I felt when your hand brushed mine at the opera – and the touching words you whispered:

> *If among these shadows you spy*
> *A wandering shade in search of rest,*
> *'Tis that of your faithful husband,*
> *Come to beg you for mercy.*

Sweet will my final breath be
If, after my death, you live on for me

As you see I have never forgotten them. The music and those words awoke in me an unexpected urge for you to make love to me. I had no experience of what it would be like but as the music continued I tried to imagine. And the more I imagined it the more I wanted you to kiss me, to take me. The remembrance of that moment means as much to me now as it did then."

He reached for her hand but did not speak.

"Why do you ask if I love you? Surely you know I do?"

"I am not always sure of that," he replied. "You are like a beautiful, perfect butterfly – admired, adored, loved but never within reach."

"My sweetest Nicolas, I am who I am, a contradiction of imperfection, anxiety, hope and the pursuit of perfection. But I am also someone still not used to happiness – even now I am sometimes afraid."

"Afraid of what?" he asked.

"That I will suddenly awake and find all of this – you, the house, our daughter, music – has been a dream. That I am like the little match girl, striking matches to keep warm and then I see the vision of Herzberg – this warm, comforting and embracing house. I strike match after match to keep it alive and then I have none left. You know the end of the story. I have no need to tell you more."

"Alice, it is not a dream."

"But when the day ends and I approach the stillness of the night that is when I am most afraid I will wake and find Herzberg a mirage, a figment of my imagination."

"Alice, if you are afraid, tell no one but me. Do you promise? So many people have faith in you, rely on you, need you to be strong. Do not disillusion them."

She looked at him.

"Nicolas, life is not a part in a play. I am who I am. Please accept that."

"I do, as others do. Alice, be as you always are – bold, spontaneous and embracing." He squeezed her hand. "I too sometimes have fears."

"And what can they possibly be?"

"That one day when I reach for you, you will not be there because someone has fallen in love with you and spirited you away."

"I am always within your reach. You reached for my hand at the opera. It was there. You reached for my hand a moment ago. It was there. I now offer you the other. For my part I reach out to you in bed, seeking for you to make me truly, deeply, part of you. It is you who is sometimes unreachable. That is why I sometimes flirt with other men – to make you jealous. There, I have said it."

"There is no need to do that," he replied. "I love you, Alice – that is the plain fact. I do and always will."

"But show it to me. I need constant reassurance because I was not loved until I came to Herzberg. Despite years of comfort, affection, being part of this remarkable family and having your child, I still wish, because of the fear I have described, to be told – every day – that I am loved. You may think it a silly thing to say. But it is a relic of my childhood, not knowing who my father was. Surely you understand?"

He nodded and kissed her hand.

"Enough of words and such gestures. Nicolas, profess your love for me as I do my love for you but profess it by deed. Show me your true love."

"Alice, I will."

"I do not want a promise of 'I will' as in a marriage vow. Prove it to me now. Strip me, possess me, play my body with passion as fingers do a keyboard or a bow the strings of a violin. If you do, my body will sing, sing in such a way as you have not heard before." She stood and began to undress. "Nicolas, come," she said, pulling him towards her.

She stood unclothed. With her back to the fire, he could only see the outline of her face, hidden in the shadow. As he reached for her, she unpinned her hair, flicking its long dark tumbling coils so they fell casually about her breasts. She undressed him and in the warmth of the fire threw away all previous restraint. He drank deeply from her full glass. They lay afterwards in the great bed, each embracing the other, his face buried in her hair. Clasped in his arms beneath a crimson quilt, Alice looked into the flames. Scheherazade had cast her ultimate spell over the king. He would never cast her out, not now. She was safe at last.

After a while, Alice slipped from his grasp, put on her silk gown, tied it loosely about her waist and sat at the keyboard, softly playing Monteverdi's *Pur ti miro – I gaze at you* – the piece that Victoria had shown her when they sat together to look at the music book. Nicolas woke and came to sit beside her, his fingers tracing the contours of her fingers, her hand, her cheek, her neck, her breast. She turned to him.

"My dearest Nicolas, I promise I will never leave. Never leave you, never leave Herzberg."

"And I will never let you go," he whispered.

They kissed.

Later as she lay awake, the carved Herzberg crest above her and Nicolas asleep beside her, the fire still cast comforting shadows. She turned towards Arabella's portrait above the mantelpiece. Her words to her husband had echoed her solemn promise to Victoria to stay at Herzberg to protect the music book and to keep alive the memory of Arabella. Later yet, still awake, she thought she heard a distant keyboard playing Bach's *Prelude and Fugue No. 1*. She went to the window but saw nothing; the *Spiegelsaal* was in darkness. Perhaps, she thought, the music was a trick of the wind or perhaps it was only in her mind. She sat down at the piano and softly repeated the refrain. The nearly spent candle beside her momentarily flickered and then burned brighter. Alice's destiny was sealed and another child conceived.

CHAPTER 12

The Price of Rivalry

The years that followed reflected the deepening of the autumn season. Life at Herzberg remained regular, sometimes dull and occasionally squally. While the spring and summer of each year still saw family gatherings on the estate with the same veneer of levity as before, it was becoming apparent that age and worry about Germany's future were beginning to take their toll.

Victoria travelled less often from England, though when she did come to stay it was for longer periods than before. When it was time to return to London she confessed she found parting from the estate ever harder. It was also more evident that Joseph was not well, appearing thinner and more stooped by the year. He joked it was his first encounter with old age. Though it was not in his opinion a time for cowards, he sought to be more relaxed and less disagreeable than in the past. Beatrice urged him to work less but her pleas fell on deaf ears. Frederick Paul seemed increasingly preoccupied at court, where he was not immune from the ever more vehement disputes between the Crown Prince and his son Wilhelm, whose views on Germany – how it should be governed and its territorial ambitions – were often diametrically opposed to those of his father and perhaps even more so to those of his mother, Vicky. Rebecca, still a discreet and trusted companion to the Crown Princess, was not immune from the manifestations of royal disagreement behind closed doors either. Though she found Wilhelm's tantrums distasteful and wounding – not to her but to the Princess – and occasionally considered leaving royal service, she remained at her post out of loyalty. Besides, she was aware that, as she had lived outside England for many years, to return to London now would be most difficult. Moreover, she had no wish to be separated from her daughter, her sole close companion, a fact she would never disclose to Alice.

Amidst the gloom of an ageing family and the increasing differences of opinion within it about the course of Germany's expansionist ambitions and the growing sharpness in relations with England, aggravated by British conflict with the Dutch settlers in South Africa, Alice gave birth in 1883 to a boy who, after some considerable debate, they called Carl Johann Richard – the second name at Alice's insistence in honour of the younger Strauss and the third added at Victoria's suggestion to mark the death of Wagner in February of that year.

A high point in the autumn of 1884 was the visit of Wilhelm, the Crown Prince's eldest son, to Herzberg. Trim, active and amusing, he proved an engaging weekend guest. His musical taste was lighter and more superficial than his hosts had imagined, much to the disappointment of the Camerata's string quintet. Though the dinner-table conversation saw much repartee on matters of the day, there were no mishaps of etiquette due to Frederick Paul's fine planning and his insistence on the need for tact, not least on the part of the increasingly outspoken Victoria. He implored Charles Hardinge, accompanying his wife on this occasion, to do his best to rein in her opinions and certainly to prevent her suggesting a ride around the estate as Wilhelm, because of his withered left arm, did not feel comfortable on horseback. Charles more than once placed a restraining hand on Victoria's wrist but his own observations of Wilhelm disturbed him. There was no evidence of tact when the future Kaiser had left. Once again the dinner table witnessed sharp exchanges. Victoria could no longer contain herself.

"Herzberg has been renowned as a place of music and reason. Why are we obliged to compromise its reputation in order to pander to a man whose views seem to lack judgement and taste? Heaven protect us when he eventually ascends the throne."

"Victoria," interrupted Hardinge, "you spend most of each year in England. Those with whom you socialise, your German country set, do likewise. There have been good social reforms in Prussia, which it is important to praise. So, please be fair in your appraisal."

"I am fair, Charles. But judging by his views this past weekend there is no sign of any understanding of the values espoused by his parents. His father supports the proposition, as I believe does his mother, that the state should not act against the popular opinion of its people. And to cap it all, he sat at this very table advocating the importance of German colonies."

"Victoria," interjected Joseph, "there you go again. You fatigue us all. Your view is as shrill as ever. Everything in London is good, everything in Berlin is bad. In that belief you are wrong. The fine principles of eighteenth-century enlightenment are in the past. We are now in an age of empire and if Germany is to take its place as an equal guarantor of peace in Europe it needs land. If others, like Britain and France, have overseas territories, why should not Germany also? *Der Alte Fritz* was no angel. He was constantly acquiring land to feed his own ambitions and by so doing laid the basis for a unified Germany. Yet no one, other than the Russians and Austrians, criticised him. You liberals must stop complaining."

"Joseph, enough!" protested Beatrice.

"Why should I desist?"

"Because, Joseph, you are one extreme and Victoria the other and never the two will meet."

The debate intensified around the table, with opinion more in favour of a new course for Germany as their royal guest had proposed.

"What do you think, Sir Charles?" asked Frederick Paul, who to this point had remained silent.

"It would be presumptuous of me to offer an opinion," he replied.

"I urge you to do so," insisted Joseph.

Charles Hardinge paused. Throughout his long association with the von Deppe family he had always kept his opinions to himself. Though he had been to Herzberg and Vienna many times, had travelled widely through Prussia with his wife and met the Crown Prince and Princess, he still believed he did not fully understand Germany. Now he was being pressed for his view following a weekend with the future Kaiser. As this might be his last journey to

Herzberg, since, unknown to Victoria, his doctors in London had diagnosed a weak heart, Hardinge decided to lower his guard.

"I apportion no blame in this debate – it would be impolite for me to do so – but since you press me it would be dishonest to deny I fear for the future. I say this for three reasons. First, my country and yours are intimately linked by royal blood. History is littered with examples of royal disputes, jealousies and rivalries. Such potential for aggravation applies as much to your royal family as it does to mine. Nor indeed must we forget the Romanov family link, adding its own lethal potency. Royal human nature is no different from ours in its wild unpredictability. I earnestly hope that my Empress, your Emperor and the Czar, all of the same blood, will play their part in ensuring that no catastrophic mistakes are made, that we adapt to circumstances in the interests of peace. Rivalry leads to the wrong decisions for the wrong motives. Too often I have seen in the English High Court examples of the bitterness such disputes can cause.

"My second reason is that while empire, which often motivates the irrational desire to acquire ever more territory, may bring the tangible benefits of income and colour on a map, in the longer run such benefits tend to bring nothing but trouble, and empires do not last for ever. One only has to look at the Austro-Hungarian Empire with its evident internal decay. The British Empire is beset by its own problems, not least with the Boers and with Ireland too. Moreover, the problems in one empire provide opportunities for exploitation by others. In Germany there appears to be sympathy for the Boers. There may be some justification for such a position and my government may assist that argument by not playing its hand well. In a rivalry, it is an opportunity for *Schadenfreude*."

He paused, puffing on his cigar.

"And your last reason, Sir Charles?" asked Frederick Paul.

Hardinge again puffed on his cigar as he decided what words he should utter.

"I am no military man. Raymond, Daniel Frederick and Heinrich Stefan have greater knowledge and expertise to contradict my opinion. But, since you continue to press me, in my humble view it would seem, on hearsay and upon the slender evidence I have seen, that we are now embarked on a course of creating new means to wage war – bigger warships, more lethal guns on the battlefield and the planning of more damaging tactics to achieve maximum casualties. It is a bleak future, in which misjudgement arising from rivalry between monarchs, the pursuit of land to outbid another and the cold-blooded planning of death are each akin to a man walking amongst barrels of gunpowder with a naked flame."

He drew again on his cigar, looking around the table to see the impact of his words just as he would survey a jury before concluding his argument.

"For me, an aged lawyer past his prime and a mere observer of this country, which has shown me great hospitality, patience and indulgence over the years and most of all given me the woman I love so much, these are my thoughts. I have nothing more to say."

There was silence around the table. Alice broke it.

"I speak as a mother. I wish my son and my daughter to grow up in peace in a world of beauty and equality. I love this house, aware of its proud history and unblemished reputation, of the good and bad times it has seen. But by all accounts good has prevailed and I wish that to remain the case. So I ask all of you who may have a hand in the affairs of Germany to make sure that we do not go to war because if Sir Charles is right, we, the innocent, may lose everything."

"Well spoken, Alice," said Frederick Paul. "We may not yet live in perilous times but we live at a time of apprehension. Sir Charles, I thank you for your wise observations. We respect them all the more because your infrequent opinions are so thoughtful. Before we rise let me say this. Germany – and Prussia in particular – is in social and political turmoil and matters are not easy at court. It is desirable that all of us speak with caution, keeping frank opinions to ourselves, as there are many who would be inclined to use such opinions to their own advantage."

"Are you telling us that we are becoming a state where free speech is not allowed?"

"Victoria, I am not saying any such thing. Alice put it well. Herzberg has an unblemished reputation. You yourself said it is known as a place of reason and music. Let that not be tarnished by sharing our opinions with a wider world where there are those who would make mischief, even perhaps against us. I urge discretion, that is all. Now let us adjourn. Alice, perhaps you would play for us."

The debate of that evening was replicated almost every year, some years more heated than others. The only conclusion on each occasion was that the horizon was becoming bleaker.

* * * * *

In the spring of 1885, shortly before retiring from his chambers at his doctor's insistence, Charles Hardinge received a letter from Sir Richard Hartley, whom he barely knew, stating that he had some personal information to disclose. Hardinge replied that he was no longer accepting briefs but Hartley insisted this was not his intention. He wished only to place in Sir Charles's hands some delicate correspondence rather than retain it in the Hartley archive.

The two met at Hardinge's club on the evening of Thursday the 23rd of April. Hartley was a tall, refined man with an estate in Suffolk and business interests in London. Hardinge had provided him with some legal advice some years ago but since then their paths had rarely crossed. After exchanging pleasantries in the library, Hartley explained why he had asked for the meeting.

"It appears from her correspondence that my great-grandmother, Lady Pamela Hartley, was for a long time a close acquaintance of Lady Thérèse Whitfield, whose daughter, Arabella, became – as you well know – the Countess von Deppe. Lady Pamela and Lady Whitfield were companions in Paris in 1766 when Lady Whitfield was seeking news of her daughter's whereabouts. They were still together in the city when news was received that Arabella had reached Potsdam and had become engaged to the Count von Deppe. It seems from her diaries that over the remaining years of her life my great-grandmother and Lady Thérèse kept in close touch and met often, until her death. Going recently through a folder of old family correspondence I discovered a letter from Lady Whitfield addressed to her daughter. Perhaps Lady Pamela had intended to pass it to the Countess Arabella but for some unknown reason did not. I thought you should have it without further delay, together with my sincere apologies for Lady Pamela's failure to forward it at the time. I have not opened it and therefore have no idea of its contents. I stand ready to answer later any questions you may have." He handed to Hardinge a slim, battered leather folder. With that Hartley took his leave.

Hardinge sat back and after a sip of his port and a puff on his cigar took the letter from the folder. He broke the seal and began to read. The letter was written in French, the handwriting was unsteady and the ink had faded in places, making some of the words hard to decipher.

Arabella, ma fille très chère,

I do not know if you will ever receive this letter. My death is close and it is difficult for me to write. I am persevering, with Lady Pamela at my bedside.

I taught you long ago the strict necessity in life of virtue and honesty. I confess to you that I have been unvirtuous and dishonest. It shames me to do so.

I married Sir Robert Whitfield because his youth and allure, his title and his ambition turned my head. He flattered me and my father, too, for my dowry. I gave him a son as he earnestly desired. Thereafter, he was no longer constant. I found out that he had dalliances in London. His desertion of our bed caused me much unhappiness and vexation. Why should a man have such freedom but not a woman?

I was struck by a sonnet written by John Donne about a woman's constancy. I cannot remember all of what he wrote but it began with these words:

> Now thou hast loved me one whole day,
> Tomorrow when thou leavest, what wilt thou say?
> Wilt thou then antedate some new-made vow?
> Or say that now
> We are not just those persons which we were?

I decided after a while that if my husband should mistreat me in this way then I had licence to do likewise in revenge. It all began on a visit to London where I met a Frenchman, Auguste Gaillard. He was handsome and amusing and I came to enjoy his company. In 1742 I accompanied Sir Robert to Paris. He did not like the city and said he had to travel south on business. I doubted his words. Perhaps he wished to join one of his ladies. But I did not care if that were his intention. I was pleased to see him go, to be free of his encumbrance for some weeks. I went to my parents' estate. But soon I tired of being there and returned to Paris in the company of my father, who said he had matters to pursue at court.

What a time that was! I was free, able to meet whoever I chose. As women do, I enjoyed the flattery of many handsome men, and also the close company of the artist François Boucher, who, in the absence of one of his models, enticed me, saying I was one of the most beautiful women he had encountered. I succumbed to his wiles. Later I even agreed to pose as the companion to the goddess Diana, for a painting of her leaving her bath. Both the goddess and I were unclothed. Though somewhat chilled in his draughty studio, with what abandon were we so! Unexpectedly, but not unwelcomely, I also encountered Monsieur Gaillard, who chanced to be in Paris at the time, and enjoyed his intimate attentions one afternoon. If that was not enough, my father informed me that he had arranged for me to be presented at court with other young ladies, amongst whom, I learned, were some seeking the King's personal favour. He said my presence would help his cause. My presentation at court was such an affair – full of laughter and joie de vivre. Think of it: me – a young married woman – curtseying with my bust all but exposed to His Majesty King Louis of France.

To my surprise, I later received an invitation to join other ladies at the Parc-aux-Cerfs. I chose to decline but the gentleman of the bedchamber said that to do so would offend His Majesty, as did my father, still seeking royal signature for the grant of land to add to his estate. So it was that two days after my arrival at the lodge I was royally bedded, and again the next day and indeed the day after that. There were yet more amorous embraces – for me amongst others – but some two or three weeks later I received word from my father that Sir Robert would soon be back in Paris. I insisted to all that I could not remain at Parc-aux-Cerfs, pleading a diplomatic incident if that were to happen. So I was released from my obligation, which was not painful as it was becoming clear that the King's gaze was already set upon Marie Anne de Mailly, already, rumour had it, in the ascendancy for the title of maîtresse en titre.

My parting royal gift was a miniature of myself, with an inscription on the reverse, that the King had apparently commissioned for his collection of so-called royal beauties and which he had now discarded. The gentleman of the bedchamber drew my attention to the motif in the décolletage. "C'est François Boucher," I replied. "Mais non, madame, c'est la famille Bourbon," he countered. We both laughed. My father patted my bottom as we left the lodge. He said I had secured for him the much sought-after royal signature.

After a short stay in Paris, Sir Robert, still reeking of the pungent perfume that announced his rentrée to the city, and I returned to Meltwater, where he bedded me roughly à l'Anglais, the brute. Immediately thereafter I declared I was with child, though in truth for some weeks already my usual blood had not come.

Considering you without question to be his, my husband showed little interest in your presence at Meltwater – another troublesome woman, he often remarked. While I confess François B and I took to the bed in his studio, I cannot say with any certainty he was your father. My intuition has always told me he was not. For most of my life that same intuition – reinforced, perhaps, by a mother's apprehension (more powerful than a young wife's vanity) at the implications of the alternatives – convinced me it was Auguste Gaillard; he was, if such could be said of any of the three, the safest. But I have always known, with no room for doubt in mind or body, that it was not Sir Robert who impregnated me in Paris. And now, with God's judgement imminent, I must confront my own judgement, honestly and without fear or bias: I am sure, as only a dying woman can be, that the King of France was your father. It is not only my vanity, to which I now freely admit, that leads me to conclude so. But who can prove it? In London and in Paris I was an unfaithful wife. I was so because I wished to be someone's mistress to spite my husband and to revenge his cruelty. Upon reflection, what an absurdity that was. All my strong principles discarded for the sake of cold revenge. Yet from that reckless decision I gained my precious daughter. My dearest one, you are worth a thousand principles.

As death stares me in the face and I grasp my crucifix ever tighter, I am full of remorse that I did not reveal the truth to you – I was unfaithful to my husband and I denied you both the knowledge of who your real father was and the life you should have had as his daughter. I have decided, almost at the last strike of midnight, to reveal my shame as I cannot take this heavy secret to my grave. Please, ma chère fille, forgive your mother, as my anguish is great. The only comfort I can offer you as you read of your mother's great sin is that Sir Robert, that ogre, is not your father.

I am entrusting this letter to Lady Pamela with the instruction that you should have it with my earlier letter saying farewell. Now I must cease writing as I am beginning to cough blood. I think my end is near. Adieu.

Votre maman,

Thérèse

Meltwater, Saturday the 13th of March, 1773

Near the bottom of the letter were one or two brown spots, possibly blood.

Hardinge lowered his hands to his lap, exhaling slowly. Was this letter, written by a woman close to death, an accurate recollection of past events? Was it one last act of spite by a cuckolded wife towards her husband, denying him as her famous daughter's father? Or were its contents, its sentiments, merely an expression of delirium? Or could it even be a letter written by someone – Lady Pamela Hartley – interpreting, truly or falsely, the words of another? In a court of law, the letter's veracity might well buckle under the weight of robust and skilful cross-examination. And in such proceedings, to reach a conclusion one way or another, it would be necessary to compare the handwriting with a letter written by the late Lady Thérèse of which the authorship was beyond doubt. That would be hard to do as the only source would be the Whitfield family, still riven by internal quarrels – unless there was such a document in the Countess Arabella's music book, of which he had heard much but seen nothing.

Yet the more he studied the letter the more conviction it seemed to convey – a letter from a devoted mother and Catholic, racked by guilt concerning her past indulgence in carnal pleasures, seeking her daughter's forgiveness and summoning the courage to reveal that her cherished one was illegitimate by an uncertain father, either the King of France or an accomplished and praised artist. The pain of such an admission must have been agonising. The final wound was that the letter had never been delivered. Consequently, Arabella had gone to her grave still believing that Robert Whitfield, whom she despised, was her father when according to the letter in his lap he was not. That mislaid undelivered truth, if truth it were, had poisoned the decades that followed, as he had observed at Herzberg and at Meltwater. If he were to reveal the letter to Victoria, it would surely inflame and perpetuate the ill feeling between a proud and distinguished family in Germany and a privileged family in England. Moreover, the troubled relationship between the two seemed to mirror uncannily the difficult and increasingly agitated relationship between the two countries. Was it not better for him to throw the letter onto the fire in front of which he sat, so that the truth would become ash? Yet who was he, a respected QC, to do such a thing? He could of course withhold the letter from his wife, but that would be equally unforgivable. Victoria might find it after his death and would think ill of him.

He knew instinctively that, if he gave her the letter, Victoria would draw only one conclusion: the famed Countess was of French royal lineage; there was no Whitfield blood in von Deppe veins. Even if that were true, what good could come from her revealing the letter? In Germany it might lead to ridicule, the blemishing of a finely established reputation. Given the present circumspection of Germany's relations with France that might be unwelcome. The English were pragmatic. By that measure he would seek to persuade her that it would be best quietly to reseal the letter and place it in the music book, leaving another generation to reopen it and to judge whether the time was more propitious to declare its contents. Finishing his port and calling for his coat he decided he had no choice. He would divulge the letter to her and manage the consequences as best he could.

Later that evening Hardinge was struck by Victoria's lack of surprise.

"I knew there was yet more to discover. I have been vindicated. Arabella was a most singular woman, as her music book, portraits and fame reveal. That could only have come from royal blood. You may seek to deride my opinion but it is a woman's intuition."

"I would not dare argue there is no such thing as a woman's intuition but I doubt it would survive scrutiny in a court of law," he replied, smiling.

"You lawyers are as dry as the dust on an unopened pile of legal briefs. You have no sense of the romantic. To think I might be descended from King Louis of France! Is that not the most fantastical of thoughts?"

Hardinge laughed.

"And do you intend to share this connection to the French throne with Joseph and Frederick Paul and their children, with Anne-Sophie, and indeed with Alice? How do you think they might react to such news? And what would Raymond de Saint-Mar say? Would they all leap into the air with joy? Raymond might, but I doubt there would be whoops of joy at Herzberg and Wannsee. Think carefully, Victoria."

She did not reply. Instead she looked again at the letter in her hands. She wished so much to write immediately to Beatrice. She tried to visualise her reaction and that of the others. Would it be welcome? Was there a risk it would be dismissed as irrelevant? And in the current fractious atmosphere in Berlin and Prussia might it be portrayed by others – their critics, rivals and the gossips – as a family overreaching itself? Her husband was right. Enjoy the letter and its revelation but conceal its existence from others, at least for the present.

"I will reseal the letter and place it in the music book for the next generation to decide."

"And who have you decided should be the next guardian of this sacred book I have never seen?"

"Charles, don't mock me. You will never see its contents. It contains too many of one woman's secrets and should be protected. And you as a lawyer should know the importance of confidentiality. I am sure you withhold many secrets from your chambers, and indeed from me. I do not seek to pry into what they might be."

"I do not mock you. I'm teasing you. Yes, confidentiality is important. But you have not answered my question. Again I ask, whom have you chosen to be the book's keeper when you no longer can be? I should be told if I am to ensure your wishes are upheld."

"It is Alice."

"Why Alice and not our daughter?" he asked.

"Aurelia is married to William and therefore her future lies in England. The book must remain at Herzberg. I considered others in the family but none seemed suitable for the responsibility and it has to be a woman as it has been so far – Arabella's daughter, Elise, and then her daughter, Elisabeth Mariette –"

"And so," he interrupted, "in accordance with the line of succession it should be Aurelia."

"Charles, I have explained already the book must remain in Herzberg. You may think it silly superstition but that is what I have decided, in fulfilment of Mama's wishes."

"Is that because you think the walls of Herzberg might fall if it came to London?" he said, laughing loudly.

"Charles, stop it. You English say the ravens protect the famous Tower of London and that if they are lost or fly away, the Tower will fall and the realm with it. If that tale is good enough for England, then keeping Arabella's music book safely at Herzberg is sufficient for me. I would have liked Aurelia to be the future guardian of Arabella's legacy but it cannot be. So it will be Alice. I have shown her the book. She was deeply touched that I had decided she should become its keeper upon my death. She is committed to Herzberg and to Germany. In that regard you could say she is following in Arabella's footsteps. It is my decision, Charles, and neither you nor anyone else will dissuade me."

Hardinge embraced his wife.

"My dearest Victoria, if I outlive you I will see to it that your wishes are respected. And Alice is an excellent choice."

"Why should you not outlive me, Charles? Is there something you should tell me?"

"There is nothing. Only that I look forward to a long and blissful retirement."

She looked at him quizzically but with a sweep of his arm he guided her upstairs.

* * * * *

201

The von Deppe family gathered once more at Herzberg to celebrate Christmas 1887. Events followed a familiar pattern – good food, much laughter and an abundance of music. Unlike previous years, however, it was decided to welcome the New Year on the estate and to do so by giving a concert at which the holders of grants of Herzberg lands, awarded to their ancestors by the family in 1810, would be the guests of honour. Such an event had not been held before and it was well received, renewing the bonds of trust and friendship between the von Deppes and those upon whom they still, to some extent, depended for income and produce. The concert was an opportunity to play solid German music, to dance, to sing lustily and to drink well, not least at the stroke of midnight to toast the health of the ageing Kaiser.

Before the family dispersed the next day it was agreed to break another tradition by accepting the invitation of Raymond and Jacqueline de Saint-Mar to celebrate Easter 1888 in Paris. While there had been less enthusiasm from Joseph and Frederick Paul, the weight of opinion amongst the younger members of the family was in favour of accepting. Besides, 1888 was a leap year and deserved to be marked in an unusual way. Alice was thrilled at the prospect of Paris, as was Jeanne Françoise, who insisted that she would drag her husband to the city of her mother's childhood. Victoria too welcomed the prospect of several weeks in France. She had heard much about the painter Claude Monet and the garden he was creating at Giverny. She would contact Monet's dealer, Paul Durand-Ruel, to see whether he had any pictures she could view and possibly buy. Moreover, it would be a splendid chance for her and Alice to meet the young and scandalous French composer, Claude Debussy. She had heard a performance of his *Suite for Orchestra*, composed in 1885, and now there was rumour of fresh compositions for the piano – so-called arabesques. Alice said excitedly she had read that all Paris was in love with Monsieur Debussy. She suggested it was again time to shake up the Camerata's repertoire – to inject some Gallic notes. Victoria agreed, though her mind was on the possibility of finding out more about the Parc-aux-Cerfs.

The prospect of spring in Paris was overshadowed by the death in February of Wilhelm Louis, son of Alexandra Véronique and her husband, Ernst Walter Henning. His death cut another link with

Herzberg's past, since Alexandra's grandmother had been the Countess Arabella. Victoria had enjoyed Wilhelm Louis's quiet humour whenever they had met at Herzberg. His wife, Julia, had died several years before, an event from which he had never truly recovered. She would retain warm memories of them both. Then on the 9th of March the Kaiser died after a short illness, at the age of ninety-one. A courteous but old-fashioned man he had been much revered, though criticised by some for not doing more to restrain the policies of the Imperial Chancellor. His son, Frederick, succeeded him. The Crown Princess was, according to Rebecca, overjoyed that her husband was at last Emperor and King of Prussia. There were reports, however, that the new monarch was already seriously ill. His son Wilhelm, the new Crown Prince, stood waiting to succeed him.

The Kaiser's death obliged Frederick Paul to withdraw from the trip to Paris but he urged everyone else to go. The visit was greatly enjoyed from the moment the von Deppes arrived in the celebrated capital on Tuesday the 27th of March. After the observance of Easter the following weekend, the Saint-Mars ensured that the following two weeks were filled with music, dancing and good food. Victoria met Monet and, courtesy of his dealer, bought two paintings for London and presented another to Alice and Nicolas. She and Alice even managed to hear a recital by Debussy and to talk to him afterwards. Everyone, even Joseph, was sorry to leave Paris. It was such a lively city, full of joie de vivre, invention and the unusual, unlike staid Berlin and imperial London. For Victoria the nearest equivalent was Vienna. As for Charles, he was feeling increasingly weary but even he had his spirits uplifted. Yet he detected a sense of fin de siècle, as he had done in Vienna the previous year. In Berlin Bismarck had persevered with his policies, which were aimed at greater power for Germany and were proving increasingly divisive; in Vienna the Viennese just danced, while the French seemed almost oblivious to the growing might of their neighbour. He was pleased to return to Carlton House Terrace. But within the month, on Sunday the 13th of May, he died in his sleep. Victoria was heartbroken. Not even her daughter was able to console her. The news of his death filled Herzberg with sadness, too. Charles Hardinge had brought English distinction to the family with his quiet manners and fine legal judgement. He had represented what was good about England. His funeral in London was widely attended. Amongst the mourners were Joseph and Beatrice, Alice and Nicolas, and the Baroness Rebecca. Now only she knew the secret of Alice's birth.

A month later, following the return of the von Deppes to Berlin, it was announced that the new Kaiser had died, to be succeeded by his son, now Kaiser Wilhelm the Second. The news shocked the nation and Herzberg, too. Frederick Paul, drawn and fatigued, accompanied by Anne, retreated to the estate to get some peace. Over supper on Saturday the 30th of June he warned the family that a new and perhaps darker era had dawned. Vigilance and discretion were essential, not least at Herzberg. Victoria, who had also come to stay for a while, in order to decide her future – whether to remain in London or to return to Germany – thought his words chilling. The family adjourned to the *Spiegelsaal*. There Victoria played Beethoven's *Sonata No. 14* – the *Moonlight*. It conveyed the mood of the evening.

In the royal palace *die Engländerin*, as she was popularly known despite being almost entirely German, was distraught. After years of waiting to become Empress she had had her beloved husband snatched from her. She was alone, left to defend herself against her tempestuous son, now the new Kaiser. Rebecca joined others in trying to comfort her, even though she herself was weary and lonely. Would she now be dismissed, she wondered, or asked to stay? If the former, where would she go? If the latter, there would be no prospect of escape from what would be a gilded prison. It seemed autumn had turned into winter.

PART FOUR: LARGO
THE BITTER WIND 1907–1918

CHAPTER 13

Rupture

The library windows were ajar onto the garden. A gentle breeze, unseasonably warm for late autumn, tugged limply at the silk curtains. A shaft of soft afternoon sunshine penetrated the room, highlighting two shelves of leather-bound volumes of eighteenth-century French philosophers, to which Raymond de Saint-Mar had recently added copies of Diderot and Rousseau. The mellifluous voices of easy female conversation drifted out onto the patio. It was late 1907, Monday the 28th of October to be precise. A bank of grey cloud massed steadily in the distance, with an occasional rumble of faraway thunder.

Three women sat talking: one grey-haired, stooped, with a sad reflective face beneath a blue broad-brimmed hat and wearing a long grey dress, listening to the conversation more than engaging in it; another, younger woman – perhaps twenty years younger, though nearing the end of her sixth decade for all that – of understated elegance with a lively and attractive countenance and beautiful hands, dressed in a slim-cut long-sleeved cream dress with a high enough hem to reveal slender calves and delicate ankles; and a third, a few years younger yet, with a still youthfully pretty oval-shaped face and dressed in an equally close-fitting soft-blue velvet dress with three-quarter-length sleeves, its length and cut in accordance with the latest London fashion. The light, sometimes frivolous conversation, weaving nonchalantly between English and German, was punctuated occasionally by shrieks of laughter. The three women, each displayed in their distinctive personal style, were the Baroness Becky, as she was fondly known by all; sitting beside her, her daughter, Alice von Deppe; and facing them, Aurelia, wife of William Folliot of the Foreign Office in London and daughter of the late Charles and Victoria Hardinge. They were gathered for afternoon tea, a long tradition at Herzberg.

"Have you enjoyed your stay in Berlin?" asked the Baroness, taking her first sip of Assam tea.

"Very much so," replied Aurelia. "William and I came expecting to stay only a few days. I wanted to see Alice, and William had to call on our ambassador. But Sir Frank prevailed upon him to stay a little longer, in case there was a chance for him to meet the Kaiser. That seemed unlikely until the encounter with the Emperor at the opening of the Hotel Adlon last Wednesday. William left for London two days ago but was happy for me to stay a few days longer at Herzberg. Alice and Nicolas have been such generous hosts, as they always are. She has given me some piano lessons to improve my style. Mama would be shocked that I had become so lazy, the more so since I long ago gave up playing the harp, and so have only one instrument to practise, but it is difficult to find time in busy London. I have listened to Alice and promised her I will do better."

"I am sure you do yourself an injustice," replied Baroness Becky.

"Yes, she does, Mama," said Alice. "Aurelia has inherited her mother's fluid style. Just regular practice for an hour or so each day will keep the cobwebs away. And Aurelia has taught me something new."

"And what is that, my dear? Is it a new method on the keyboard?"

"No, Mama, it is not to wear a corset." Alice burst out laughing. "I am free of restraint, just like Aurelia. You should try it, Mama!"

The Baroness frowned. "Alice, shush, the staff might hear you."

"Mama, don't be so prudish. Every woman will banish the corset soon."

Aurelia steered the conversation in a new direction.

"Baroness, if it is not too painful for you or inquisitive of me, I should like to hear about the late Dowager Empress. What was she really like?"

"There is little I can add to what is already known. She loved her husband devotedly and was greatly protective of him. They waited all those years, then he was cruelly taken from her within three months of ascending the throne. His death broke her heart. She missed him greatly during her last years at Friedrichshof."

"Were you with her when she died?" asked Aurelia softly.

"Her closest friends were. I joined them for her final hour."

"Was she ever reconciled with her son the Emperor?"

Becky paused. "No, I don't think they ever were." She paused again. "Almost a year after his father's death, the Kaiser was heard to say that an English doctor had killed his father and an English doctor had crippled his arm – all the fault of his mother, who allowed no German physician to attend her or her immediate family. What he said hurt her greatly."

The room fell silent. Only the ticking clock and the rustle of the curtains in the breeze could be heard, while outside the rumble of thunder grew louder.

"Aurelia," said Alice, "have you any news of the Whitfield family? I read some time ago that Arthur has become quite a celebrated artist."

"Indeed, he is much sought-after. His paintings and drawings command a good price. He eventually married his muse, Juliet de Burgoyne, and they had a son, Florian. The child spends most of his school holidays at Meltwater with his uncle and aunt. I think he will be going up to Oxford before too long. William thinks he would be good at the Foreign Office – a free thinker and all that – if, of course, he were to pass the entrance exam."

"Why does Florian go so often to Meltwater?" asked Becky.

"Arthur and Juliet's marriage is quite unconventional – she is mistress to a writer and Arthur has his own close friends in the world of art and literature. At least he and his brother, Charles, are finally reconciled after that wretched business of the letter to *The Times*. We did not see them at Charles and Sarah's dinner party two months ago, but we did encounter all three of them at Meltwater in June. Arthur did some excellent sketches of the house and he even drew me one afternoon on the beach. He said I was beguilingly attractive and asked quite out of the blue if he could make love to me. Despite his handsome looks and attraction I of course said no. So he said that, if he could not make love to me, he would draw me – the exotic woman who had rejected his advances. He drew me there and then and gave the sketch to me with a delicious kiss."

"How wicked and utterly romantic," Alice exclaimed. "Did you keep the drawing?"

"Oh, of course I did. It's finely drawn, flattering and indeed rather suggestive. I had it framed and keep it on my dressing table. William thinks it's erotic because my bust and legs are too exposed. I've told him it's my dressing room, not his, and I reminded him of his copy of Bertel Thorvaldsen's three naked beauties in his bathroom. If my drawing borders on the erotic, his statue certainly does – three curvaceous bottoms and six breasts. Touché, he said."

The three women laughed.

The thunder drew nearer and rain could be heard on the patio. The breeze had quickened and it had suddenly become chilly. Alice closed the windows.

"I hope that's not the end of a fine autumn," she said.

"Tell us of London," urged Becky.

"London bustles," replied Aurelia. "The King continues to enliven the social scene. My mother would have loved London now – the fashions, the new musical compositions – and I am sure she would have joined Mrs Pankhurst's Women's Social and Political Union. For her, to be a suffragette would have been a badge of honour. I have been tempted by them, too, but William has told me that, on account of his job, under no circumstances should I express any sign of support – though unknown to him," she whispered, "I give occasional donations to the cause. It is so sad Mama did not live longer. She had such a love of life. When she became gravely ill she could not decide whether to be buried alongside Papa in London or here at Herzberg, close to her mother. In the end she decided to be cremated and have her ashes scattered – some beside Papa's grave and the remainder at Herzberg."

"Typical Cousin Victoria, a foot in both camps," quipped Alice.

"Show more respect, Alice," interjected Becky with a friendly frown.

"Mama, I adored her," said Alice. "She taught me so much. She liked to tease and so do I."

"And Beatrice taught you much, too," Becky interrupted again.

"Yes, Mama, Aunt Beatrice, too," Alice sighed.

"I am sure your mother is fondly remembered in London, particularly for her music, as she still is here."

"Yes, Baroness, everyone remembers her. Her concerts were always full and a place at her supper table in Carlton House Terrace was always much sought-after. But the bad blood between the King and the Emperor is beginning to cast a greater blight on the relationship between Berlin and London. The Kaiser is always being rather offensive."

"And what of your son?" asked Becky, wishing to divert the conversation into yet another direction.

"Oh! Rufus is now eleven. He's growing up so fast," replied Aurelia. "I had wanted another child but, despite the best doctors in London, I was unlucky."

And so the conversation continued in ways that only women's conversations can. After perusing *à trois* the latest Fortnum and Mason fashion catalogue, the Baroness took her leave, despite her daughter's efforts to persuade her to stay for supper. They would be joined by Alice's son, Carl Johann, and her daughter, Eva Victoria, with her husband, Ferdinand Anton, on leave from his regiment of hussars. It would be an evening of military talk, but Alice would hear of her young granddaughter's musical education.

* * * * *

A month later Charles and Sarah Whitfield spent several days at 35 Chesterfield Street in Mayfair, a large property inherited from Charles's father. Charles discussed financial matters, including the charitable foundation he had recently established – much to his brother's approval – to support the continuing national anti-slavery campaign, and spent some time at his club, while Sarah shopped and saw her friends. Their stay was a chance to give a large dinner party. The Whitfield family were well represented: in attendance were their elder son, Sebastian, a banker, and his wife, Cecilia; their daughter, Priscilla Emily, and her husband, Henry, an official in the War Office; and their younger son, Horatio, a Coldstream Guards officer, and his fiancée, Harriet Knowles. Amongst the handful of other guests was Eyre Crowe, a senior clerk in the Western

Department of the Foreign Office and a friend and colleague of William Folliot, also present with his wife, Aurelia. Charles's brother, Arthur, had declined the invitation, pleading a prior engagement but commenting to a friend that had he gone he would have either choked on an excess of prejudice or suffered acute hunger from the inadequacy of free thinking. The conversation over dinner was light, amusing and uncontroversial. Over port it inevitably turned towards peace in Europe.

"Mr Crowe," asked Charles Whitfield, "would you value Germany as an ally in the preservation of peace?"

Crowe, born in Germany of a German mother and English father and speaking with the slight trace of a German accent, replied crisply, "With a combination of cautious optimism and troubling doubt."

"And what is the extent of your doubt, Mr Crowe?" persisted Charles.

"Let me explain," he replied. "England does not wish to oppose Germany. We continue to do our best to convince the Kaiser and his government that we remain faithful to the preservation of the balance of power in Europe, and in that regard do not consider our interests would be served by Germany being reduced to the rank of a weak power, as some – not least the Berlin press bureau – allege we do. Indeed, if we were to seek such weakness it would only risk a Franco-Russian predominance, which would certainly not be in England's interests. Furthermore, it would be neither just nor politic to ignore the claims to healthy expansion of a vigorous and growing country like Germany, which owes its enlargement so far to our cooperation, mutual accommodation and royal ties. Nor should we oppose the building of a fleet large enough to meet Germany's national defence needs. In short, there is no discrimination on our part. However, I have to say that this benevolent attitude would give way to determined opposition at the first sign of British or allied interests being adversely affected."

"Well put, sir," said Sebastian Whitfield, echoed by his younger brother, Horatio.

"So thought the Foreign Secretary," replied Crowe. "He considered the expression of my views on this matter earlier in the year most valuable. My memorandum was also sent to the Prime Minister."

"Did he express an opinion?" asked Sebastian.

"No, not to my knowledge," Crowe replied.

"And what, Mr Crowe, would be our response if the Kaiser endorsed actions and a military build-up out of keeping with the balance of power of which you speak?"

"There would be a limit to demands we found acceptable."

"Can you be more precise?" pressed Sebastian.

"Let me put it this way, Mr Whitfield, and I speak amongst friends. To give way to the blackmailer's menaces enriches him, but it has long been proved by uniform experience that, although this may secure for the victim temporary peace, it is certain to lead to renewed molestation and higher demands after ever-shortening periods of amicable forbearance."

"Does that point to the prospect of war?" asked Charles Whitfield, thinking of his financial investments.

"The blackmailer's trade is generally ruined by the first resolute stand made against his exactions and the determination rather to face all risks of a possibly disagreeable situation than to continue in the path of endless concessions."

The room fell silent.

"A sobering thought," said Charles Whitfield. "Let us hope that common sense prevails and that our King exercises his persuasive powers as the Kaiser's uncle. War would be a calamity for all."

"I agree," said Crowe, "yet the risk cannot be excluded."

"William, what news do you have of the von Deppes? You were in Berlin recently, I believe."

"Yes, Sir Charles, I was indeed in Berlin, and stayed longer than I had intended. But the ambassador, Sir Frank Lascelles, insisted I should do so in order to try to meet the Kaiser, which I did at the opening of the Adlon. We had a fleeting conversation – nothing of note, just pleasantries."

"And the von Deppes?" Charles pressed.

"The Countess Beatrice still grieves for her late husband but she is greatly comforted by her four children. Aurelia and I called on her at her Wannsee villa, a charming house with a lawn down to the lakeside. Her son Daniel, and his wife, Birgitta, and their son, Wilhelm, live nearby. Nicolas, still practising law, and Alice remain at Herzberg with their children, Eva Victoria, who is married, and Carl Johann, who is not. Oh, what an impressive place Herzberg is!

Eva has a beautiful little daughter whom they have called Arabella, in memory of the famous Countess. I had a long talk with Joseph's brother, Count Frederick – a rather secretive fellow, perhaps, as you might expect from a career at court. His wife, Anne, was a pleasure to talk to, as were some of the so-called Secessionist artists she, Alice, Aurelia and I met – artists who are reacting against the traditional framework. I especially enjoyed the conversation of one called Hagemeister. Aurelia was struck by his strong dark eyes, powerfully captured in one of his self-portraits. As for Berlin, there is a growing industrial proletariat, as some in the city call it. The working and living conditions are dismal in some areas of the city, with much poverty and desperation. Some of the hardship and misery of everyday life, and a sense of the resulting volatile atmosphere, featured in a number of the paintings Aurelia and I saw in an art gallery. As for Alice, she remains as energetic as ever and is working closely with the Camerata to maintain its reputation, despite stiff competition from the Berlin Philharmonic Orchestra. It is at her – and Paul Wilhelm's – insistence that the Camerata now regularly plays the music of Wagner."

"What is the family's opinion of the Kaiser?" asked Eyre Crowe.

"Count Frederick would not be drawn, though I detected some inner apprehension. Beatrice and Anne were more forthcoming – they considered him a dangerous buffoon. Their preoccupation is to maintain the family's musical and cultural reputation at all costs and to continue to protect the interests of the landholders around Herzberg, families granted land title by the Countess Arabella almost a hundred years ago. I would think the von Deppe family are as worried about the future as we all seem to be."

"Thank you, William," said Charles Whitfield. "It's good to see you and Aurelia back in London. Now, let's join the ladies."

The rest of the evening was light-hearted and Aurelia performed at the piano, her lightness of touch on the keyboard already revealing the result of Alice's advice to practise regularly. As the guests prepared to leave, Aurelia asked Sarah Whitfield the question she had wished to ask all evening.

"I see that Arthur has another exhibition planned for London in January. Are you and Sir Charles intending to go?"

"I don't think so," replied Lady Whitfield. "Charles and I

respect what he does but those with whom he mixes are not to our taste. That reply may appear snobbish but you will know what I mean. However, Arthur, Juliet and Florian are coming to Meltwater for Christmas – we've managed to winkle them out of Chelsea. It will be good to see Juliet again – terribly intellectual and a passionate advocate of the rights of women. She terrifies my Norfolk circle."

As William and Aurelia returned home, Crowe's somewhat chilling words stuck in William's mind, as it did in the minds of the others who had heard them. Of course, war would not come; it would be in no one's interests. Or would it? Such were the shifting sands of dynastic alliances and the unsteady temperament and exaggerated self-confidence of the Kaiser. William decided, in response to his wife's question as to what had been discussed over port, that he would not disclose Crowe's opinion for fear it would worry her and that she would divulge it in her next letter to Alice.

Christmas at Meltwater was a heady mix of the steady and the unpredictable. For once the long-lost sparkle of Christmas past was rekindled with boisterous laughter, games, music and the idiosyncrasies of the landed laced with the unorthodoxies of Chelsea Arts Club. The celebration of the New Year was equally enjoyable, with a party for many guests in the Long Gallery. Charles Whitfield, observing the festivities alone for a minute or two, felt there was a touch of the end of an era about it all. He sensed that the world his father, his grandfather and great-grandfather had created was at risk of slipping away as the dark clouds of a more menacing dominion gathered.

At Herzberg the family came together once again, but it was a much quieter affair than usual, with more restrained music, as everyone still missed Joseph, who had died a slow and painful death earlier in the year. Frederick Paul, now aged eighty-three but still spry, had become the sole remaining male survivor of the earlier generation of the wider family. The next generation – Joseph's and Frederick Paul's children – were rapidly ageing and would in turn soon be gone. Even Alice, keeper of the music book, would soon have to decide to whom she should bequeath it. She confided first to Frederick Paul and then to her mother that she would find this difficult. He had replied that she should take great care with her decision because upon his death the family would become exposed. She pressed him to explain his remark but he demurred. Following a New Year's Day concert at Herzberg for the estate staff and landholders and their families, Alice and Nicolas and their children went to Wannsee to call on Beatrice.

The next evening, on her return to Herzberg, Alice sat alone in the *Spiegelsaal* and played Beethoven's *Piano Sonata No. 14*, the *Moonlight*. Outside the wind blew and the snow fell heavily. She felt uneasy.

* * * * *

To the casual observer, one year – its rhythms and routines – can often seem much like another: a seamless transition of seasons and lives against an unchanging backdrop of the familiar landmarks of daily life. By the middle of 1908 little seemed to have changed at Herzberg or at the von Deppe villa at Wannsee or indeed at faraway Meltwater. Yet beyond these limited comforting horizons, the ground in Germany was shifting – imperceptibly to some, but not to others more intimately involved.

Dislike of Jews was becoming widespread and social division more noticeable, aggravated by urban poverty. While the Kaiser encouraged public education and welfare and promoted medicine in public health, to those around him or close to those who were he remained obsessed with his perception that Germany was isolated, potentially encircled. Determined to resist such a fate and that Britain, France and Russia in particular should treat Germany with respect, the Krupp Company, which produced steel and armaments, had become the world's largest, employing many thousands; and shipyards in Danzig, Hamburg, Kiel and Wilhelmshaven were still building dozens of battleships to match the number of British warships. This was an expensive commitment, of which Daniel Frederick was well aware from his senior post at the War Ministry. However, it was one the Kaiser was determined to fulfil and he insisted on a restructuring of the Navy High Command to ensure he got his way.

Yet, despite his best efforts and frequently contrasting himself – a thriving younger man – with the older, corpulent English King, the Kaiser was still mocked, even behind closed doors at Herzberg and Wannsee, for his lack of culture; for his musical preference for Verdi and Gounod rather than Wagner; and for his faith in official art to inspire the people of Germany, in contrast to the Berlin Secessionist art movement.

Already in the 1890s art had become the object of vigorous debate in the capital and in 1898 conflict finally broke out between the conservative academies and Secessionist artists, led by Walter Leistikow, who organised their own membership association and exhibitions – much to the excitement of the von Deppes. The talented painter Max Liebermann, son of a Jewish textile manufacturer turned banker, became the Secession's president. This artistic hubbub and self-confidence challenged old attitudes and, through the efforts of art-gallery owners such as Paul Cassirer, brought international art to the city and with it a wave of demand for the new-style, less adorned portraits. Nicolas commissioned such a portrait of Alice, showing her in a plainer à la mode style never seen at Herzberg before. The recent artistic patronage and the rapid expansion of Berlin, with its broad tree-lined avenues, pleasing department stores, new theatres and hotels – the Adlon Hotel by the Brandenburg Gate, opened in October 1907, was intended to match the Ritz Hotels in Paris and London – were changing the city beyond recognition. In the view of many, it was putting Berlin on a par with the finest capitals in Europe.

Though Herzberg remained a much used grand country house, and Wannsee was still a charming villa by the lake shore with the pleasures of sailing and swimming, and nearby Potsdam was a stylish place to frequent, it was Berlin that was becoming the greatest magnet for the von Deppes, older as well as younger generations. Alice, Beatrice and Anne became devotees of afternoon tea in the ladies' lounge at the Adlon, often joined by nieces, cousins and grandchildren. This enjoyment of an English-style life, despite the Kaiser's disdain for Britain and what he perceived to be its antiquated ways, was also reflected in the frequency with which the von Deppes' friends and acquaintances and indeed the social elite in general travelled to and fro between the two countries, so they could continue to embrace quaint English customs, buy fashionably stylish clothing in London and relish Britain's idiosyncratic rural comforts. For those who enjoyed such a life and its equivalent in Germany – whether at Herzberg or at well-known Nassenheide in Pomerania, the home of Count Henning von Arnim – it was unadulterated indulgence in nostalgia. This social interchange, the diversion of clotted cream, jam and scones and their ilk, masked for many the fact that the two countries were unknowingly already embarked on a path that would lead inevitably to war.

At Meltwater much the same rhythm applied – spring sowing, autumn harvest, shooting and dinner parties – while in London the pursuit of banking, property interests and soirées was the primary interest. The relationship between Charles Whitfield and his brother remained equable but still somewhat stiff. Arthur's son, Florian, was accepted at Oxford for the following year, while Arthur himself remained a lionised painter. In early 1908 he and Juliet travelled to Paris, where they met Raymond de Saint-Mar and his wife; Jacqueline introduced Juliet to the novelist Anatole France, with whom she immediately had a short affair.

While in Paris Arthur met Alice, who by happenstance was visiting with the Camerata, accompanied by her daughter, Eva Victoria. They thought him handsome and amusing. In the belle époque city with its many diversions and temptations they had tea à trois and a few days later he lured both to a performance at the Folies Bergère, with its depictions of demi-mondaines. They found the performance extraordinary, fascinating and hugely enjoyable. Arthur relished having two attractive women on his arm. In their brief encounters he found Alice's earthiness and attraction still irresistible but the young and charming Eva even more beguiling. He wrote a note inviting her to visit the Louvre with him one afternoon, hoping it might present an opportunity for him to seduce her later. He received a polite though somewhat coquettish refusal. On their last evening together, at the Grand Véfour restaurant near the Palais-Royal, as they laughed and flirted with him he drew a pen-and-ink portrait he entitled *Two Heads of Beautiful Women*, which he presented to them – to celebrate, he said, their allure and femininity. They parted into the night with promises to meet again and an invitation to Florian to spend several months at Herzberg before Oxford. Following a final goodbye, mother and daughter each received in turn the tightest of embraces capped with a passionate stolen kiss.

The next day, before her departure, Alice asked of Raymond de Saint-Mar a most personal request – to see if he could possibly find out the names of aristocratic women who once upon a time had shared Louis XV's bed at the royal hunting lodge at Parc-aux-Cerfs. She told him she sought this information in connection with some historical music research. Though surprised by her unusual request, he promised he would try, but warned her, as Sir Frederick Burton had done, that much of the monarchy's archive had been destroyed in the fires of the Revolution.

Such was the backdrop to the spring and summer of 1908. Two cruel blows soon fell.

While Alice was in Paris, her mother, Countess Becky, fell ill. Frail and living alone, by choice, in a small apartment in Berlin, she had been out walking with companions in the Tiergarten. Caught in a heavy rain shower, instead of going home immediately to change, she went to a shop on the Unter den Linden and thus in her wet clothes caught a severe chill. By the time Alice returned to Berlin her mother had been diagnosed with pneumonia. Despite Alice's care and the attention of the best doctors, Becky died a week later. Though she had led a fulfilling life as a loving mother and a companion for many years to the Crown Princess, later Dowager Empress, she had been denied the happiness of marriage. Moreover, she had lived with the ache of Robert Whitfield's cruelty towards her and the burden of the secret that he had been Alice's father. That undisclosed knowledge went with her to the grave. Her daughter would never know the truth. At Alice's request, the von Deppe family agreed that she could be buried at Herzberg. Margarethe, the late Dowager Empress's youngest daughter, who had inherited her mother's house at Friedrichshof, attended the funeral out of respect for Becky's service and companionship to her mother.

Later that year the elderly Countess Beatrice died of old age. Alice, still mourning the loss of her own mother and more than ever aware that with no English family of her own she was completely alone in the country of her adoption, grieved for the woman who had played such an important part in inspiring the search for her as a lost child in London, bringing her to Germany and accepting her as her own daughter. At Wannsee she had been given a privileged education and, under the wing of the late Victoria, had become an accomplished pianist. And it was at Wannsee that she had fallen in love. In the months that followed, Alice, sometimes accompanied by her daughter, would frequently visit the graves of Beatrice and her mother. On the latter's grave she would often lay flowers, to which was occasionally pinned a card bearing the words: *From your devoted daughter.*

* * * * *

Much of the following year, 1909, passed at Herzberg and Meltwater without undue incident, though the rivalry between Germany and England continued, marked by occasional flashes of public bad temper that revealed the Kaiser's disdain for his uncle, King Edward VII. The promised visit of Florian was repeatedly postponed. Towards the end of the year Frederick Paul's wife, Anne, died. French by birth she had always been lively and teasing. Raymond de Saint-Mar once described her as the best unpaid French ambassador in Germany. Whereas her husband was quietly spoken and discreet, his words always measured and precise, Anne would be deliberately mischievous and indiscreet, reminding German guests at her dinner table of the great contribution that France had made to European culture and politics – even the great Napoleon had played his part in challenging and overthrowing not just an ancien régime but antiquated ways of thinking, to be replaced by the advance of the rights of man. This assertion inevitably led to strong counter-assertions but with Anne's dexterous skill such verbal skirmishes always ended in laughter.

That Christmas, as usual, the younger generation of the von Deppe family gathered at Herzberg. It was as pleasing as ever, with music from the Camerata and much laughter. One evening Raymond de Saint-Mar confided to Alice that his search for the ladies of the Parc-aux-Cerfs had so far yielded little, but he would continue with it, despite his other preoccupations. Fearing from Raymond's tone, his assurances notwithstanding, that this avenue of enquiry was in danger of coming to a premature end, Alice decided to say more about the reason for her request, explaining that it was to do not with music research, as she had first claimed, but with the mother of a distant relative. She asked his forgivness for misleading him, and hoped that he'd consider the delicacy of the matter to be sufficient justification both for her deception and for her keen sense of his investigation's importance. As a mark of her trust she gave him Thérèse de Miron's name. He assured her of his forgiveness, understanding and discretion, and when he repeated his assertion that he would continue the search, she now felt confident he would.

There was similar pleasing festive activity at Meltwater, but past traditions on both estates were beginning to fade. The shadow of inevitable war was never far away.

* * * * *

In May of the following year, 1910, King Edward VII died at the age of sixty-eight. The Kaiser attended his funeral in London. Though solemn in public, in private he made it clear to those around him that he was pleased he would no longer have to defer to his late uncle. The relationship between him and George V would be one of equals. Frederick Paul made no comment. Meanwhile the frantic building of naval vessels in Germany continued unabated.

Later in September that year another mortal blow befell the von Deppe family – the death of Frederick Paul at the age of eighty-six. The funeral, at St Hedwig's Cathedral in Berlin, was impressive, with the mourners, including the entire von Deppe family, led by the Kaiser himself. The aged and much revered courtier was buried alongside his brother, Joseph, at Herzberg. Only his sister, Anne-Sophie, three years younger, remained, a widow following the death of her husband eighteen years before in a riding accident.

Shortly after Frederick Paul's death, and with the encouragement of the Army General Staff under the command of General Helmuth von Moltke, a number of officials met at the headquarters of the *Preußische Geheimpolizei* to consider not only possible candidates to fill the now vacant post of director in place of the courteous and diligent late Count von Deppe but also which of the candidates they should recommend to the Kaiser. It was necessary to choose someone who would be assiduous in ensuring that in the likely forthcoming war in Europe there would be no dissent, only full support for the fatherland's war aims, including no dissent from those who continued to enjoy the friendship of English families and life in English country houses. Following the Kaiser's approval of the appointment – only a formality since the choice was the officials', not his – and the sealing of the late director's personal files, the new director quickly drew up a list of those who would merit surveillance upon the outbreak of war if England became an adversary, which rumours of a mutual safety agreement between Paris and London suggested might happen.

Because of its historical links with the Whitfields and its musical bonds with London the von Deppe name was added to the list. With the final flourish of the new director's pen, the family had now become exposed to the risk of hostile surveillance, as Frederick Paul had warned Alice they might. In the appended file, Alice's name was high on the list of von Deppe family members. Born in England, she was perceived as a potential internal risk to Germany because of possible divided loyalties. Below her name appeared that of her daughter, Eva Victoria, because of her frequent travels to England and France, and that of Arabella, her granddaughter. Beside the latter name was written: *in England erzogen; möglich subversive – educated in England; possible subversive.*

The family's listing did not go unnoticed. A well-informed person in the *Preußische Geheimpolizei* heard what had been done and resolved to take action to protect the family if that were ever necessary.

* * * * *

Apart from the death of Anne-Sophie within a year of that of her brother, the years 1911 to 1913 passed by with little further interruption to family life at Herzberg and Wannsee. Alice remained greatly engaged with the Camerata's repertoire, while Nicolas continued his law practice in Berlin. Carl Johann, much to the misgivings of his father and mother, joined the army and was soon promoted to the rank of junior aide de camp to General von Moltke. He had not yet married, though he had already broken the hearts of several young women whose heads had been turned by the handsome officer. Eva Victoria, now aged thirty-one and whose husband had gained further promotion in the hussars, had become a pianist of some note and worked with her mother to maintain the Camerata's reputation as a chamber orchestra of quality in Potsdam. It was not easy to do so because of changing musical tastes and the advance of the grander orchestras such as the Berlin Philharmonic. Florian went up to Oxford, never, in the end, spending a few months at Herzberg. His letter of apology to Alice, in which he conveyed deep regret at not coming to learn at first hand about a country often vilified in the British newspapers, carried the implication that Charles Whitfield had counselled against it, his decision no doubt reflecting the darkening hostility towards Germany in England. In September, 1912, at her mother's insistence, the young Arabella, now aged twelve, went to boarding school in England near Bexhill-on-Sea, to become thoroughly schooled in the "English way". After spending an enjoyable month with Alice at Herzberg, Aurelia Folliot accompanied the child to her new school, though with reservations about how the other boarders would treat a child with a German surname. The following year, 1913, passed by with equal domestic passivity.

* * * * *

In June 1914 the German newspapers reported the scheduled courtesy visit of three light British cruisers and four dreadnoughts to Kiel, where they were greeted by the Emperor aboard his yacht *Meteor*. The tone was friendly, although, according to Daniel Frederick in a subsequent account to his family, behind the scenes mutual suspicion heavily outweighed the apparent cordiality. Moreover, he added, while the Emperor had, to his credit, accepted with grace the defeat of his yacht in a race with a British craft, privately it had irked him. William and Aurelia Folliot were present for the events at the Kiel regatta – garden parties and general festivities – joined by Eva Victoria. To the untrained observer the two nations were on good if still competitive terms.

On Monday the 29th of June Alice and Nicolas, at Herzberg, opened the newspapers to read of the assassination of the Archduke Ferdinand and his wife in Sarajevo. In the days that followed, Daniel Frederick was constantly at the War Ministry and Carl Johann similarly busy at the Army High Command, while Ferdinand Anton and his brother officers in the hussars gathered with their men in barracks to await further instructions. In London, comparable preparations were quietly taking place. William Folliot, just back from Kiel, read the latest reports from Sir Edward Goschen, the ambassador in Berlin, and those from Sir Maurice de Bunsen, the ambassador in Vienna. While the prospect of war between England and Germany remained uncertain, he told Aurelia to make immediate arrangements to remove the young Arabella from her school and prepare for her urgent return to Herzberg. In his opinion, if there were to be war, it was paramount that the child should be in safety at Herzberg, not separated from her parents in an enemy country. Aurelia did as William asked. The thirteen-year-old Arabella arrived at Carlton House Terrace on Saturday the 11th of July. The following Tuesday, the 14th of July, she left with Aurelia for Paris, where they would stay with Raymond and Jacqueline de Saint-Mar until the arrival of Alice and Eva Victoria on Saturday the 18th. Receiving a message from her husband that she should stay no longer in Paris, Aurelia returned to London on Tuesday the 21st. Alice, Eva Victoria and Arabella left for Berlin on Friday the 24th of July. On their way, they heard news that Austria had delivered an ultimatum to Serbia.

* * * * *

The following week, on Tuesday the 28th of July, Daniel Frederick summoned the entire family to Wannsee; only Carl Johann and Ferdinand Anton were absent, due to pressing military business. Over a simple supper he explained with great care, and in confidence, the situation that now confronted them.

"It is unlikely that the Serbians will accept the Austrian ultimatum. If that proves to be the case, Austria will in all probability attack Serbia. We have reason to believe that if Austria does so, the Czar will authorise Russia to come to Serbia's defence. If that happens, the Kaiser will judge that he has the necessary grounds to go to war against Russia and its ally, France. Such a step would be in keeping with the Kaiser's long-held view that our country must not be encircled by our enemies – Russia and France. The army is already implementing its mobilisation plan. These are difficult times. We must await the course of events. As for this family, we should say or do nothing to bring into doubt our loyalty to the Kaiser and the fatherland. There will be many ready to point the finger of disloyalty at anyone who speaks out."

A hush fell on the dining room.

"And what will the British do?" asked Eva Victoria.

"We do not know for sure. There have been recent messages from our ambassador in London and indeed reports of conversations between the Kaiser and King George that allege England will remain neutral. I am not certain that will be the case. If the British do not stay neutral, we may soon be at war with them. You do not need me to tell you what devastation this will cause to those like us who have had a warm and enduring friendship with the country we have long admired despite its idiosyncrasies. If there is war between us and England it is likely to be bitter and lasting."

After supper the family went into the long garden with its strong scent of roses. Alice walked to the water's edge arm in arm with Eva and Arabella. They spoke little, preferring to listen to the lapping water. Daniel Frederick and Nicolas walked several paces behind them.

"Nicolas," said Daniel Frederick, his voice low, "please take great care of Alice, and of Eva and her daughter too in Ferdinand's absence. But it is Alice I worry about most. She has devoted her life to Herzberg and Germany but she has never hidden her humble origins or her pride for England, her country of birth. Now at this difficult time she must be cautious and suppress all such utterances. She will have to talk openly of her love for Germany and of her loyalty to the Kaiser. And she will have to speak in German at all times, as indeed must Eva and Arabella – in public and at home, though not in the bedroom when staff are not present. We must do all that we can to support those we love. It will not be easy for them but they will manage with our help, I am sure. Will you do this for me and for the sake of the family?"

"Of course I will, Daniel. I will not allow this damnable business to break our family."

"Thank you," he replied.

They stood by the water's edge in the warm evening air. The boatman approached, keeping silent until Daniel Frederick registered his presence.

"The boat is ready, Count, if you still wish to go out on the lake."

"Thank you, Franz, I think we will."

The lake had long been a source of great family pleasure, whether they were afloat on its waters or gazing from the villa windows through the trees at its beauty. Its tranquillity and gentleness, even in the depth of winter, and the sight of its yachts scudding along in the wind had always brought great joy, inspiration and ease of mind, captured in a sunlit painting that hung above the fireplace in the library. On that July evening, at the water's edge, everyone sensed the ebbing of an epoch, like the ticking of a clock with its hands edging inevitably ever closer towards the witching hour.

The elderly elegant sailing boat slipped silently from the jetty and slid into the twilight, past the indistinct shapes of moored yachts, empty on the black rippling surface. Across the lake on the other shore there were few lights to mar the beauty of the night sky, laced with many stars and decked by a rising moon. No one spoke, each preoccupied with personal thoughts of times past, each apprehensive about what the future might hold. All that could be heard in the absence of voices was the sound of water lapping softly against the hull and the occasional puff of breeze in the linen sails. Alice, her shawl drawn tightly around her, looked back towards the villa from whence they had come. It had now vanished into the inky darkness. She imagined for a moment Franz the boatman, with his gnarled hands and weather-beaten face, as the mythical ferryman conveying their souls across the River Styx, that mythological boundary between Earth and the Underworld. The thought chilled her.

Arabella broke the silence.

"Uncle Frederick, do you know the story of Rusalka?"

"Tell it to me," he replied softly.

"She was a water nymph who wanted to be human since she had fallen in love with a handsome prince who frequented the lake. She sang a song asking the moon to reveal her love for him."

"And what did she sing to plead her case?"

Arabella sang softly.

Moon in the dark heavens,
Your light shines far,
You roam over the whole world
Gazing into human dwellings.

Moon, linger for a moment,
Tell me where my beloved is.
Tell him, silver moon,
That my arms reach out to him,
Hoping that for a brief moment
He will dream of me.
Shine on him, wherever he is,
And tell him of the one who awaits him.
If a human should dream of me,
May he remember me on awaking.
Moon, do not fade away.

"And was her wish granted?"

"A wicked witch told her that, if she became human, she would lose the power of speech and, moreover, that if she was betrayed by the prince both of them would be eternally damned. But the water nymph was undeterred. The prince found her, embraced her and led her from the lake. But soon he rejected the mute Rusalka, lavishing his attention instead on a foreign princess. Rusalka returned to the lake to ask the witch for the answer to her woes. The witch told her that she could only save herself if she killed the prince but Rusalka, still in love with him, refused, casting the witch's dagger into the water. And so Rusalka became a spirit of death, living for ever in the depths of the lake. Who knows, perhaps she lives in the depths of this lake?"

"That is indeed a sad story," remarked Frederick Daniel mournfully.

"Yes," Arabella replied. "It is very sad. I cried when I first heard how it ends. Whatever may befall me, if I ever meet a handsome prince, I will never relinquish my voice."

"I agree, my child," he replied. "Have no truck with witches or evil ones. You have a beautiful voice. Guard it, nurture it and, whatever tomorrow may bring, use it to assuage sadness and to lift the human spirit. Only the heavens know what we may face."

No one else spoke. The moon and the stars suddenly vanished; the breeze quickened. The darkness around them was complete, save only for the dim light of the solitary lantern behind the boatman, guiding the boat on into the night, his silhouette barely visible in the yellow rocking glow.

* * * * *

On the evening of Tuesday the 4th of August Daniel Frederick sent a message to Herzberg and Wannsee that Russian troops were massing in the east; that German forces had already occupied Luxembourg; and that, as a result of England's declaration of war on Germany, the General Staff had authorised the rapid invasion of Belgium and France. He added that the British ambassador and his staff were quickly leaving Berlin. On Thursday the 13th he sent a further message to say that England was now the enemy of Austria. Daniel Frederick remained at his desk in Berlin. His wife, Birgitta, joined his sister, Catherine Elise, and her husband, Otto, at Wannsee, together with his widowed sister, Elisabeth Beatrice, and his cousins Hildegard Eva, Wilhelm Frederick and Johann Wolfgang – his aunt Anne-Sophie's children – and their families. They strived to come to terms with the catastrophe. Moreover, urgent rearrangements were required to release male staff at the villa to respond to the military call-up.

At Herzberg, on Saturday the 15th of August, Nicolas similarly summoned the landholders and the estate and household staff to inform them that those men young enough to fight for the fatherland's defence were discharged of their obligations and could therefore join the army if the High Command so required. Alice insisted that Eva Victoria and Arabella come immediately to stay at Herzberg for safety and companionship. They arrived early the following week. In view of the anti-British sentiment in Berlin, as manifested against the departing British ambassador, and Daniel's recent warning of eavesdropping mischief-makers, Alice, Nicolas, Eva Victoria and Arabella agreed that henceforth English would not be spoken at Herzberg in front of the remaining domestic staff, with the same rule applying to conversations with their friends and any visitors. They would speak English only late at night, in the privacy of their bedrooms. Alice and Eva also agreed on plans to put the house and estate on a so-called "war economy" footing and to prepare for the safe storage of pictures if there were a prospect of a Russian invasion. Last, Alice and Eva burned several letters they had received in earlier days from Aurelia Folliot and Arthur Whitfield. This means of communication with English friends was now closed.

*

Late one evening Alice and Nicolas sat by the fire in the library. She took his hand in hers.

"Nicolas, I am frightened. I'm frightened of being alone, of bearing all this responsibility, and frightened that we may lose our son in battle. Nicolas, please don't leave me. The world I have been used to has been turned upside down."

"As long as I live I promise I will never leave you. Together we will get through this but it will not be easy. We will face grim times. And we must pray hard for the safe return of Ferdinand Anton." He put his arm around his wife. "Play something."

She paused to enjoy the reassurance of his hold, then moved to the piano. She played Chopin's *Nocturne in B Flat Minor*.

The following morning the telegram boy delivered a message from Raymond de Saint-Mar.

> *Leaving Paris; hope we will meet again sometime; T de M was indeed an honoured guest at Parc-aux-Cerfs. Raymond.*

"There will be no more of these enemy telegrams," the boy muttered menacingly.

That afternoon, while Nicolas was in Potsdam, Alice removed Arabella's music book from its secret place. She reopened the ancient letter that Victoria had asked her to place in the treasured book shortly before her death, and read it again. Though Raymond's message was still not conclusive proof, it appeared to confirm Thérèse de Miron's assertion that she had been bedded by the King of France at his royal "stable", with the conceivable consequence that perhaps Arabella was, after all, King Louis's illegitimate daughter. She put Raymond's telegram in the book and locked it away in its hidden niche behind the wall panel in her and Nicolas's bedroom. It was paramount that in the dangerous times ahead, with France a sworn enemy, there should be no knowledge, no suspicion, no basis for gossip, that von Deppe blood might be mingled with French royal blood. She realised that it would soon be necessary to decide what should happen to the book and its secrets were she no longer able to protect them.

*

At the beginning of September Alice sought in private the advice of Frederick Daniel and Nicolas.

"I believe we should disband the Camerata until the time is right for us to play again. I have discussed this with Eva and she agrees. If more men are required at the front, our musicians can volunteer for the call-up or, if they wish, they can join other orchestras and play Prussian martial music."

Nicolas opposed her decision.

"Alice, how can you of all people suggest such a thing? The Camerata has been in existence since its first public performance nearly one hundred and fifty years ago. It would be tragic to break that tradition. I am no musician but I would be greatly saddened to see Herzberg's link with music end in this way."

"In many ways, Nicolas, I agree with you," said Frederick Daniel. "Yet I understand what lies behind Alice's conclusion. She – and Eva – cannot bear the thought of the Camerata supporting an aggressive war effort they find hard to comprehend and accept, and the bloodshed it will cause. For the Camerata to continue – to be asked to play Prussian marches to inspire the fatherland – would in their opinion sully Herzberg's reputation. If I have surmised her feelings correctly, I would strongly agree. Have I explained your view correctly, Alice?"

"Yes," she replied softly.

"Then the question arises," he continued, "how to explain – to justify – such a decision. What would you propose to say, Alice?"

"I would say that in order to make our contribution to the war the Camerata will, for the present, cease to play, so that its musicians are free to support the national effort and Herzberg can use the money it will save to assist the treatment of wounded soldiers in the best way possible."

"That is an admirable explanation – tactful and hard for anyone to dispute."

"How do you intend to proceed?" asked Nicolas.

"Eva and I will arrange a farewell concert in mid-October at the St Nicholas Church in Potsdam – that's where the Camerata's first concert took place, on the 18th of January 1767. It will be open to the public."

"So be it, Alice. I will inform the Ministry of your intention so there is no misunderstanding."

On Saturday the 17th of October the Camerata gathered for the last time. For the orchestra and those intimately involved with it it was an emotional evening. By each music stand a lit candle had been placed. The church was filled to capacity, with all seats full and many people standing. The von Deppe family sat in the front seats of the nave.

The performance began with Johann Christian Bach's *Sinfonia Concertante in C Major*. Alice then played his *Keyboard Sonata No. 2 in D Major*, as had been performed at the very first concert. Paul Wilhelm, who had been in retirement for several years, then performed Mendelssohn's *Violin Concerto in E Minor*. His phrasing, his cadenzas and the serene melody in the second movement, reminiscent of Bach, showed no sign of his ageing fingers. After the interval, to the audience's astonishment, Arabella von Eisenwald, Eva's thirteen-year-old daughter, stepped forward to sing Vivaldi's *Nisi Dominus* after two weeks of intensive practice, displaying as she did so the delicate feminine mannerisms of an emerging self-assured and beautiful young woman. She completed the arias with surprising dexterity and confidence, even though her voice was still young and despite her inexperience and the challenging nature of the piece.

Arabella received rapturous applause. Thereafter followed the chorus *Die Himmel erzählen die Ehre Gottes* from Haydn's *Creation*, sung by the Camerata's principal singers and choir. Daniel Frederick smiled inwardly at Alice's and Eva's skilful choice of words about the triumph of light over dark:

> *The heavens are telling the glory of God,*
> *The wonder of His work displays the firmament.*
>
> *Today that is coming speaks it the day,*
> *The night that is gone to following night.*
>
> *The heavens are telling the glory of God,*
> *The wonder of His work displays the firmament.*

In all the lands resounds the word,
Never unperceived, ever understood.

The heavens are telling the glory of God,
The wonder of His work displays the firmament.

For some, these stirring words could be construed to refer to the forthcoming anticipated victory of Germany over its enemies, but to others, Daniel Frederick amongst their number, they would be a disguised message of the eventual triumph of reason over the present foolishness.

Following ringing applause, Alice rose to speak.

"Ladies and gentlemen, I will not speak for long.

"One hundred and forty-seven years ago, on Sunday the 18th of January 1767, the Schloss Herzberger Camerata, formed by the Countess Arabella von Deppe at the express command of His Majesty King Frederick II, performed for the first time in public in this church. Over the ensuing years the Camerata has played an ever-widening repertoire of music from across Europe, but notably from Germany and Austria. The orchestra has done much to bring the pleasure of music to many and to help keep alive the flame of the human spirit.

"At this difficult time in the fortunes of the fatherland, the Camerata believes it is right to put aside its instruments so that its musicians can, in different and appropriate practical ways, help to meet the great challenges that lie ahead. All of us hope that soon, when the present danger is over, it will be possible for us to meet again in this church and so resume the Camerata's contribution to the musical heritage of this land."

Her voice momentarily cracked. She paused, struggling to hold back her tears.

"So, ladies and gentlemen, from us – the Schloss Herzberger Camerata and the Camerata singers and choir – a heartfelt farewell. Long live the fatherland."

Sustained applause thundered through the audience. There followed the final item on the programme: a poignant performance of Haydn's *Farewell Symphony* (*Abschieds-Symphonie*). In the last, adagio movement the musicians one by one ceased playing, snuffed out the candle by each music stand and left the high altar until, at the end, there were just two muted violins left. There was no applause. The audience quietly left the church.

Late that night, after Nicolas had fallen asleep, Alice lit the bedside candle and slipped from the bed. Sitting by the almost extinguished fire she opened the note Daniel Frederick had thrust into her hand as they had said goodbye.

> *Dearest Alice,*
>   *Tonight you displayed the greatest courage and bravery. All of us are deeply proud of what you did, none more so than me. You follow in the footsteps of the great Countess.*
> *Daniel Frederick*
> *Saturday the 17th of October, 1914*

She took the music book from its place behind the panel and placed his note and the concert programme inside. Holding it tightly and with tear-filled eyes she looked at the portrait of the Countess Arabella over the fireplace.

"Forgive me, Countess," she whispered, "for ending what you began. I did so because I believe it was the right thing to do. How could I let war, begun by Germany, trample on your legacy? I will continue, so long as I live, to do all that I can to keep alive your honoured memory, drawing strength from the example you set in your own life."

She placed the book back in its hiding place. In bed she cried silently, full of sadness at what she had done and fearful of what lay ahead.

* * * * *

A few weeks earlier, on the afternoon of Saturday the 19th of September, at Meltwater, Sir Charles Whitfield had received a deputation from the village.

"How can I help you?" he asked.

"On behalf of the village," said the deputation leader, Mr Monks, "we request that you agree without delay to the removal of the plaque in the church, put up over fifty years ago by your father to commemorate the Countess Arabella. As we are now at war with the Hun it seems inappropriate that her German name should appear on the church wall. She chose to go and live in Germany and will be remembered there. On account of her long association with what is now our enemy, her name should be removed forthwith from public view. This may be painful for you. But that is our firm opinion and we would be obliged if you would consider our request. After all, Sir Charles, you have a son and a grandson at the front, and your brother, Arthur, a son likewise."

There was silence apart from the sound of the clock. Charles's inclination was to reject their proposition out of hand. Arabella had been a Whitfield; she had never betrayed or dishonoured her country of birth. Though some in his family had resented her and her achievements in Prussia, she deserved to be remembered alongside other Whitfields. He looked down at the headlines of the opened *Times* newspaper on his desk, giving the latest news from France and reports of anti-German demonstrations in London. To one side was the *Daily Express* of the 5th of August, which he had retained for his scrapbook of newspaper cuttings. Across the top was a bold banner:

England Expects That Every Man Will Do His Duty

and at the head of the second column the chilling headline:

War Declared on Germany

In response he had already instructed that all men on the estate and in the house be released to join the army. Whitfield turned to the assembled delegation. He knew he had no choice.

"I agree, Mr Monks," he replied icily. "I will send my man in the morning to remove it."

"There is no need for that, Sir Charles," Monks replied. "We assumed you would agree. We have therefore already removed it. It is in the hallway, sir, wrapped in cloth."

"Thank you," he snapped. "It is best that you now leave."

After they had gone, he removed the cloth from the stone. It was broken in half and chipped.

"You bastards," he whispered to himself. "Why could you not wait? This accursed war will drive us all into the abyss."

Rewrapping the stone he took it to his study and put it in a cupboard beneath the bookshelves. He sat down at his desk, put his hands to his face. Arabella Whitfield still haunted his family.

* * * * *

One evening in London, William Folliot and Aurelia sat reading after supper. She looked up.

"Have you had a hard day?" she asked.

"Yes," he replied.

"Is there any news to raise our spirits?"

"No, I'm afraid not. The situation appears bleak. No one knows how long this damnable war will last. In the streets there's optimism that it will all be over by Christmas. But I doubt it. The Germans have deployed a large well-trained army and are making rapid progress. Our soldiers are going to find it hard going and the French are taking casualties. The public mood here against Germany is hardening, as you can read in the newspapers. They are banging the war drum – 'Let's beat the Hun' and all that wretched jingoistic rhetoric. I know this war will be particularly hard for you, as your mother was German, just as it will be for Alice on the other side. I want you to know that I understand how you must feel, reading the newspapers and the hurtful comments about Germany."

"Thank you, William. It is painful but I will bear it. I have put away the photos of my mother and today I took down her portrait in the dining room. I have also asked for a fresh passport, so that 'von Böhm' is removed. Henceforth, I will just be Aurelia Folliot, née Hardinge."

"You are very brave, my dearest."

He put his arm around her.

"It is all so sad, so very sad. Why did it have to come to this? I can't even write to Alice. If I were to go the post office to send her a message, I would stand accused of consorting with the enemy. Damn the Kaiser and his generals." She buried her tearful face in his shoulder.

"Amen to that," he replied.

* * * * *

With the war only weeks old, the relationship between two families had already been irreparably ruptured. All contact had been severed. Now hatred took its place.

CHAPTER 14

On the Front

Now is the winter of our discontent
Made glistening scarlet by this loss of blood;
And all the clouds that lour upon this land
Remain aloft, unlike our youth unfutured.

Recoining the opening words of Shakespeare's *Richard III*, a play he had seen recently in London, Charles Whitfield, sitting alone in the library, wrote these lines in his private journal late on the evening of Saturday the 2nd of September 1916 as he recorded the death of yet another brave young soldier from Meltwater on the Western Front. Eleven men from the estate and village killed in just two years. One by one, loss by loss, Meltwater was slowly being drained of its lifeblood. Soon only the elderly would be left to tell tales of times past, and once they were dead there would be no one to carry forward their legacy. With this rate of attrition, the Hall would soon become a mausoleum. For over a year Whitfield had kept in his diary a running total of reported casualties, even though he knew that the newspaper accounts were not always reliable. He recalled what Aeschylus had once written: *In war, truth is the first casualty.*

It was now evident to all throughout the land that this year was proving even worse than the previous one. In February, the

Germans had attacked French fortified positions at Verdun. William Folliot at the Foreign Office, whose own son, Rufus, was at General Haig's headquarters, had informed him over a sombre lunch at their club that a massive enemy bombardment and determined attack had led to France suffering mounting casualties already totalling thousands of men.

Before retiring to bed, Whitfield looked at the family photographs on the piano, now never played. His first grandson, Charles, had been killed by a German sniper late the previous year. His second grandson, Frederick, who had visited Meltwater on leave in the spring, greatly aged and no longer the sparkling boy he had taught to shoot on the estate, had written home on the 2nd of July, the day after a determined Allied effort to break through German lines on the Somme, that he still lived. But, Whitfield wondered, for how much longer? According to William, contrary to the General's plan almost 20,000 British soldiers had perished on the first day. Yet still the battle continued. To add to the Whitfield grief, Henry, husband to Charles's daughter, Priscilla, wrote to inform him that their son, Aubrey, had fallen on the 1st of July in the attack of the 8th Battalion of the Norfolk Regiment on the 109th Reserve Regiment, part of the German 28th Reserve Division. His body had not been recovered. He had gone to the front not as an officer but enlisted in the ranks, out of solidarity with those who had worked for his family. Priscilla was inconsolable.

Apart from Frederick, Charles's granddaughter's husband, Franklin Grayson, still lived, and his brother's son, Florian. He looked at a photograph of the handsome young man who had left his studies at Oxford to join the Royal Flying Corps and was now a trained pilot with the rank of lieutenant. Three young men committed, as their friends had been, to the effort to defeat the Kaiser and his army. Would they return alive? Would peace ever come? Would the bloody, frozen stalemate stretching the long 475-mile line from Switzerland to the North Sea, which Frederick had sketched on paper for him and which he had kept folded in his pocket ever since 1915, break in favour of Allied victory? And if it did, what would be the cost?

Against this backdrop of loss, despair and bombastic newspaper headlines such as *Huns on the Run*, work on the Meltwater estate continued, but its pulse was increasingly hesitant. Whitfield and his wife, Sarah, who assisted at a nearby military hospital for the wounded, in buildings he had provided on the other side of the estate, attended the parish church regularly to pray that their family and the village be spared further loss of blood. Every time he looked up from his kneeler he saw the mark on the wall left by the removal of the plaque dedicated by his father to the memory of Arabella von Deppe, wrenched unceremoniously from the chancel wall two years before. Such an act of callous wantonness still pained him. In his private moments he sometimes wondered what the impact of the war, and the hatred it had engendered, had been on the von Deppe family. He knew from William Folliot that his wife, Aurelia, concerned daily about the safety of her son, was deeply distressed that all contact with Herzberg had been cut for over two years, thanks to the provisions of the draconian Trading with the Enemy Act. No one knew how the von Deppe family had fared.

* * * * *

At Herzberg the war had taken its dire toll. Death seemed to stalk the family. In October 1915, Nicolas Carl, Alice's beloved husband, died from typhus, which he had caught while visiting prisoner-of-war camps to check the authorities were correctly applying international law in their treatment of Allied prisoners. His death was a profound blow to Alice; she had lost the love of her life, her king. Though drawing comfort from her daughter and granddaughter, Scheherazade was alone. In the silent hours of the night she would peruse the ancient music book, seeking to find strength and consolation in the closing years of Arabella von Deppe, when she, too, had been alone, in the depth of the war against Napoleon. Alice began to consider to whom she should bequeath the treasury of memories from another age.

By the beginning of 1916, Daniel Frederick, now a widower, was frail, constantly fretting about his only son, Wilhelm Philip, fighting on the Eastern Front. In May he received the news that Wilhelm had died of wounds sustained during a Russian counter-attack. Heartbroken, Daniel's will to live was shattered and a month later he drowned in the lake at Herzberg, as his distant ancestor had done, though his death was announced as being the result of pneumonia. He was buried at Herzberg in a simple ceremony. In July Carl Johann requested an active command and shortly afterwards was posted to the Somme battle line. Ferdinand Anton, now a senior officer, was also given a command close to the same line.

Since the end of 1914, when it became clear the war would not be over quickly, daily life at Herzberg had grown bleak. There was much back-breaking toil for all as the number of household staff dwindled. The estate's previous tranquillity disappeared. In 1915, owing to the shortage of male workers, the Army High Command had established a prisoner-of-war camp not far from Herzberg. Carl Johann, then at General von Moltke's headquarters, told his father that he had read reports of Germany now holding over a million and a half prisoners of war, a number the army had never expected to detain for such a period of time. He admitted that, together with food shortages and the lack of labour on the land, these prisoners were an additional heavy burden and had often been put to work in poor conditions or sent to the Eastern Front, not least in reprisal for the French sending German prisoners to North Africa and the British using them as workers in France. Those in the nearby camp – a mixture of non-commissioned ranks of nationalities including Belgians, French, Italians and Romanians – were either kept inside to do tasks or sent to work on the land all day, only returning to the camp shortly before nightfall. Occasionally, Eva Victoria and Alice would walk close to the camp or would see men in the fields. The conditions they glimpsed seemed appalling, wretched huts, barbed wire and guards. Increasingly, small groups of malnourished prisoners would come even to the land owned by the grant-holders, many of whom had been called up, to work in all weathers under conditions of harsh control. Eva and Alice were repeatedly warned to have no contact.

Within the house all valuable items had been removed. Some of the less historic had been sold to contribute to the cost of the national war effort. The remainder, including all the portraits from the gallery and other principal rooms, had been placed in a secret store on the estate, just as the Countess Arabella had ordered during Napoleon's occupation of Prussia. All English, French and Russian books had been removed from the library and put into crates for similar storage out of sight. In every downstairs room except the library and the breakfast room, furniture was covered with sheets and the shutters closed. The only rooms largely left untouched were the *Spiegelsaal*, where Alice and Eva continued to practise – but only the music of German and Austrian composers – and the main bedrooms. The daily meals were basic, with Eva Victoria and Alice insisting that they, Arabella and the few remaining staff, mainly women, should follow the same basic diet as the general population. Any spare food was regularly collected by an army vehicle for distribution to nearby garrisons. The ladies put away their finer clothes, dressing in the same plain, unflattering, everyday garb. German was spoken at all times; nothing was ever written in English. Light in the evening was sparse, mainly from candles. But often, late at night, when everyone had gone to bed, Alice, Eva and Arabella would gather round the feeble fire in the grand bedroom, whispering in English poems by Wordsworth, Keats and Shelley, or reading excerpts from Shakespeare's plays. Had they been reported it was conceivable they would have been charged with treasonable behaviour and possibly imprisoned or perhaps shot. Sometimes, if it was too cold to sit by the fire, or if they heard footsteps, the three would slip into the four-poster and sit huddled under the bedclothes, talking in hushed tones. At the beginning of 1916 one of the Berlin newspapers had proclaimed the von Deppes a fine example of patriotic commitment. They subsequently received a letter of royal commendation.

Each day followed the same monotonous pattern, a combination of toil, meagre meals, lack of trust in those around them, who might be informers, fear of the future and, above all, an unquenchable hatred for the Kaiser for bringing such a calamity onto the heads of the German people, who after two years of war had already suffered profoundly. Yet despite their daily travails and the need for perpetual vigilance, Alice, Eva Victoria and her daughter remained outwardly in good spirits, often buoyed by music and the remarkable progress of the young Arabella in her singing and piano skills. Much Mozart was sung and an equal measure of Beethoven was played. Occasionally, when they thought it timely, or whenever visiting army officers from the War Ministry called, there would be an afternoon of singing Prussian military songs.

*

At the beginning of September, Ferdinand Anton and Carl Johann returned to Herzberg for several days' leave. They described the bloodshed on the Somme, though less graphically than was really the case. They both looked careworn and, late at night around the fire, expressed their sorrow not just for German army losses but also for the English casualties suffered as they sought to penetrate the German lines.

"Will it end soon?" asked Alice.

"Our generals claim it will," said Ferdinand, "that the English and French will collapse or run out of men. But I know from my brief visits to England before the war, from reading reports of prisoner interrogations and from their evolving tactics that will never happen. The English are stubborn, even more than us. They never give up. If anyone capitulates, it will be us."

"But Ferdinand," replied Eva, "that will surely not be the case. The Kaiser is confident, von Moltke equally so."

"Eva, be realistic. The army may not surrender but the spirit of the German people would eventually crack and with it the public support on which the Kaiser and his generals depend. If that were to happen, this accursed war will thankfully end, though what will happen thereafter heaven only knows." Realising what he had just said, he put his finger to his lips. "Do not repeat my words. Whoever is heard uttering them could be arrested for spreading defeat or even treason against the Kaiser."

No one spoke further.

Three days later Carl Johann and Ferdinand Anton left Herzberg for the front. After they had gone, Alice, Eva and Arabella went to the *Spiegelsaal*. There Eva and Arabella sang softly the aria *Soave sia il vento* – May the wind be gentle – from Mozart's opera *Così fan tutte*.

> *May the wind be gentle,*
> *May the waves be calm,*
> *And every element*
> *Smile in favour*
> *On their wish.*

In the heart of each was the unspoken fear that, unlike in the opera, the two soldiers would not return.

* * * * *

Monday the 4th of September – another week began on the Somme front. Lieutenant Frederick Whitfield, of the 9th Battalion of the Norfolk Regiment, read various signals in his dugout following early-morning inspection of men and kit – over 60 lbs of it. Morale was not high. General Haig had already, it was rumoured, reprimanded two fellow generals for the slackness of their battalions. While awaiting further instructions there was little for Frederick to do that day but to keep his men safe, only returning fire if there were sign of a further German counter-attack. Amongst the mail brought up to the front was a letter from his cousin Florian. It was evident from the guarded contents that he and his fellow pilots in the Flying Corps were having a harder time in the face of an apparent increase in German air activity and better aircraft. He scribbled a reply on damp paper with his almost exhausted pencil, which he hoped would pass the censors.

> *Dear Florian,*
>
> *It was a surprise and a pleasure to receive your letter and to read you are still up there with the larks. I enjoyed your landscape description. I have none to share. Peering periodically above the top – at risk of having one's head blown off by a Hun sniper – there is little pleasing sign of autumn because there are few trees with golden leaves to reflect the turn of the season. Most have gone, smashed to bits by both sides. All that is left to measure autumn is the earlier setting sun, the damper evenings and the already cold nights. I thought waiting to take the perfect shot in a half-submerged hide in a freezing Norfolk dawn was challenge enough to the soul, but entombment in our trenches is a fate worse than Dante could ever imagine. Meanwhile, we await further instructions for another push.*
>
> *I will be home in October or November for a week. Hope you will be on leave at that time too. Let's get drunk at least once. But if I fall before then I will have no regrets. It is a great cause for which we fight and I do so willingly to serve my King and country.*

241

Yours ever,
Frederick
Monday the 4th of September, 1916

Within the hour the letter was on its way, together with one to his mother, Cecilia, and yet another to his girlfriend, Cassandra, who had given him such sexual pleasure on his last furlough. She had given him her picture, now propped up above his bed of boards. She was an attractive young woman, different from other girls he had met – a bit of a bluestocking. He had resolved that on his next pass home he would ask her to marry him.

In the late evening, with the sentries posted and the men asleep as best they could in their cramped conditions, he recalled in his battered notebook the start of earlier battles. How simple they had said it would be: bombard the well-dug-in German lines with heavy guns; detonate underground mines; take their trenches with infantry; and then press home the advantage. It all sounded so bloody easy, he scribbled. Yet, despite the months of preparation, the stockpiling of shells and the mining, plans often went wrong, as had happened on the 1st of July. According to rumours he had heard, the Germans had apparently read a good-luck message sent the night before and a mine detonation had blown ahead of schedule. By the time the first wave of new recruits walked towards the German lines, the enemy was waiting. The reports he had heard spoke of immense casualties. "It was pure bloody carnage," as one account had put it. Yet still the battle waged to and fro along the line of the Somme River – a battle of attrition. He had seen many young men die. He flicked back to a poem he had written earlier in the year. He was no poet but his verses conveyed the horror of what he had often witnessed.

The Corporal's Bloody Day

Inky black into battle grey,
Battle grey into bitter blue;
So becomes the hue
Of another bloody day.

Time to move each frozen limb,
Locked night-long in crusted mud;
The guns of the Hun begin to thud
Atop the trench's brim.

"Sir, men ready for inspection,"
Barks the sergeant,
Midst his men shuffling to attention.
Knee-deep in slime,
Affection I convey
To weary faces, lifeless eyes.

"Will we make it home to Blighty?"
Asks the corporal,
Seeking reassurance.
"Yes," I shout above the din.
"You'll make it, Stripey."

Inspection done, I move along
To the tune of loading rifles, whistled Tipperary song.
All standing ready for the sergeant's fateful order:
"Lads, forward to the German border."

Sudden comes the eerie whistle,
Then the deafening cascade,
And vivid pink, floating in the wind like down of thistle.
Alas! No Blighty for poor Stripey, despite the promise made.

And so the day goes on
As other days have gone,
On into another accursed night
Of vanquished hopes and unrelenting fright.

He closed the notebook. There was nothing more to say. He shook his palliasse to disturb the hidden lice, wrapped himself tightly in his damp-smelling blanket and snuffed out the candle.

Several evenings later, enveloped in his great coat, sipping hot tea, Frederick put his diary aside, thinking about the past day – its

routine barely different from the day before and the day before that
— and recalling lost, happier times at home, until he heard the
sergeant making his late-night check to ensure the sentries were
awake.

"All present and correct, sir," he reported. "The Huns are
silent."

"Listening for movement on our side, I imagine," Frederick
replied.

"Yes, sir. Any orders from HQ?" he asked.

"None yet, Sergeant, none yet, but I'm sure it won't be long
now."

"I hope you're right, sir. Everyone's on edge."

"Amen to that," he muttered. "Goodnight, Sergeant."

"Goodnight, sir."

"And Sergeant, the wind has changed. Has everyone their gas
mask at the ready?"

"They have, sir."

The candle flickered in the gathering breeze that blew through
the open door of his burrow, hewn from compacted mud. Unable
to sleep, he wrote another poem in the silence of the night.

The Wish

The wind has turned from west to east.
Ominously now it blows and chills,
Portent-full of what it might convey,
Including silent wafting mist
With no mercy for those enveloped in its deadly breath.

If only this fickle wind would spare a thought
To bear me up towards my distant girl,
So I might lie encompassed by her gentle arms
Amongst the late-summer flowers
Beneath a sun set in sky of azure blue.

But as I write of such a longing,
Day has given way to wretched night,
And with the dark will surely come the son of Jove
With fateful order to engage our foe.

In the fast-ebbing time till then
I can only dream of tender love unfulfilled,
Because the fickle wind chose not to spare a thought.

He closed his diary and extinguished the candle.

On Friday the 15th of September he fell in battle as the 9th Battalion of the Norfolk Regiment, part of the 6th Division, moved north-east from Guillemont, accompanied by tanks, in the direction of the Quadrilateral, held by the Fifth Bavarian Division. His body was retrieved and buried hastily nearby.

Late the following week Sebastian Whitfield asked to see his father in London. In the library of his father's club, Sebastian showed him a telegram.

Post Office Telegraphs

Ostend
War Office London

To the Hon Sebastian Whitfield and Mrs Whitfield

Deeply regret to inform you that your son, Lieutenant Frederick Stafford Whitfield, of the 9th Battalion of the Norfolk Regiment, was killed in action on Friday the 15th of September 1916. Lord Kitchener expresses his sympathy.

Secretary War Office

Sebastian and Cecilia had lost their remaining son. Cecilia was distraught almost out of her mind. Sebastian too found it hard to keep his composure. Charles Whitfield asked the steward for a private room and there alone for the next hour or so he sought to console his heartbroken son. The only scions left were his own younger son, Horatio, and Franklin, Sebastian's son-in-law, currently attached as liaison to the French army. Would the bell now toll for them? And there was Florian, too.

* * * * *

By mid-September the German lines on the Somme were coming under greater pressure from the prototype of a new British weapon – the tank, which could cross vast stretches of terrain at speed, bridge trenches and flatten barbed wire. As there was accumulating evidence, including the preparation of fresh enemy trenches, that their defences would soon face another offensive, the German High Command decided to send troop and artillery reinforcements forward, together with aircraft from Verdun. Ferdinand Anton, now an experienced officer, was rapidly posted to the Thiepval Ridge area to reinforce local command strength.

Conditions on the front were deteriorating rapidly, like the weather. Thiepval had been held by the Württemberg Infantry Regiment since 1914 and still contained many pre-war-trained soldiers. It was well dug in. Ferdinand Anton found that of little comfort in the face of reports of significant numbers on the opposing side. The anticipated enemy preliminary bombardment using field and heavy artillery began on Saturday the 23rd of September in poor weather. After an initial skirmish on the 24th, the expected attack began on the 26th. A fierce battle raged over the next three days. Despite reinforcements, the German defenders of the ridge struggled against the sheer preponderance of men and weaponry, including British tanks, and suffered substantial casualties. Ferdinand Anton wrote in his diary of the enemy breaches north-west of Courcelette and Thiepval, adding that lack of reserves had forced the 7th Division to retreat in the east, while the success of the British 11th Division had caused Thiepval to be outflanked from the right, with the loss of the village and most of the garrison. He recorded a day or so later that enemy activity had still not ceased. The British were pushing on towards the Stuff and Schwaben redoubts. Ferdinand Anton knew that losing possession of these heights would deprive the German army of important observation posts. As he feared, attacks on the redoubts began on Sunday the 1st of October. The first redoubt fell on the 9th and Schwaben on the 14th, so exposing German forces in the Ancre valley. Counter-attacks failed. Ferdinand Anton noted in his diary the lack of reinforcements and the acute shortage of ammunition. In the last struggle on the 10th and 11th of November, fighting valiantly alongside his men, Ferdinand, wounded, was captured. His war was over. Carl Johann notified his sister that her husband had been injured and was now believed to be an enemy prisoner.

* * * * *

On Tuesday the 14th of November Lieutenant Florian Whitfield took off from Mont-Saint-Éloi, a Royal Flying Corps aerodrome beneath the ruined twin towers of the abbey near Arras, in his two-seater Sopwith Camel aircraft with Second Lieutenant Richard Arbuthnot, observer in training. It was a reconnaissance flight over German lines on the Vimy Ridge, to observe their army dispositions as part of preparations for a rumoured Canadian spring offensive against divisions of the German 6th army – a diversionary attack at the time of the French Nivelle offensive. As they swung back low to get a closer view, the plane was hit by ground artillery fire. With smoke coming from his engine, Whitfield headed for level terrain well behind the German front line. Struggling with the controls he managed to bring the burning aircraft down, landing bumpily in a field some distance beyond the enemy. He pulled himself from the cockpit and then dragged Arbuthnot from his seat. Blood was flowing from an open wound in the young man's chest. As a German patrol approached to capture them and the plane burst into flames, he died in Whitfield's arms. On Friday the 17th of November Arthur Whitfield received a telegram informing him that his son, Florian, was missing in action. That same day a German army patrol placed a simple wooden cross over a hastily dug grave beside the burnt-out remains of the aircraft.

Here lies the late English Second Lieutenant Richard Arbuthnot of the Royal Flying Corps, killed in battle on the 14th of November 1916.

Florian Whitfield was interrogated for information. He refused to divulge what he knew and was badly beaten as a result. Realising he would not break his silence his captors placed him on a transport train with other prisoners to begin the journey east. It was a long and at times chaotic journey.

On Wednesday the 13th of December he arrived at Steinhaus labour camp, a large rambling collection of rough wooden huts, clustered around a stone-and-brick building which, by appearances, was over a hundred years old. The camp was filled to the brim with mixed nationalities. He knew from accounts he had read that as an officer he should have been deposited at a camp for similar ranks, but in the transport mêlée following his interrogation he had become separated. This did not disappoint him as he had already concluded that a labour camp might provide a better opportunity for escape. He knew he would have to try his luck soon because eventually discovery of his rank would lead to his transfer, and in officers' camp there was no work, only confinement.

Two days after his arrival he was put into a work gang and sent out under guard to work on surrounding farmland, clearing the debris of autumn and preparing for the sowing of next year's crops. As he toiled he recalled similar labour he had seen done at his uncle's Meltwater estate and how, as a boy on his school holiday, he had enjoyed being with the farm hands as they went about their tasks, even on raw winter mornings. On other occasions he had gone out with the gamekeeper to observe partridge and pheasant and to trap rats.

The following week at Steinhaus the guards made some efforts to decorate the main building for Christmas. Again Florian – his rank still unnoticed – volunteered for work outside, his torn flying jacket, which he had managed to retain, providing a degree of warmth from the bitter wind. On Tuesday the 19th he joined a gang of about twenty men who were taken in a dilapidated truck to an area some twenty kilometres away, where they were detailed to pick up wood debris, chop it into shorter lengths and then place it in bags for shipment; Florian assumed the bags were destined for the front. He got talking to an older guard and asked about the large imposing house in the distance.

"That's Schloss Herzberg," the guard replied.

"Who lives there?"

"The von Deppe family – well known by all accounts," the man snapped.

Recognising the name, Florian asked no more questions. He continued to work outside for the rest of the week, two days of which were amongst the trees close to Herzberg. This, he decided, would be his best opportunity to escape. Should he go to the house and seek help, or should he leave the house well alone? After all, nothing had been heard of the family since the start of the war. He had no idea whether they would be friend or foe.

"Herzberg is a big house," he said to the same guard later in the week.

"Yes, it is. I went there once to collect food for the front. The men are away, defending the fatherland. The womenfolk are at home, waiting like so many for their men to return."

Florian did not respond.

"Why are you so interested in that house?"

"It's like my uncle's house in England – big but empty. We are all suffering from this war."

"Yes, we are," grunted the guard. "Things will never be the same. Those in the big house over there will be swept away if the fatherland goes under. Now, get back to work."

Christmas was a meagre affair at Steinhaus. There was little to eat, just singing to pass the time. Florian sat, watched and planned. His escape was lent urgency by the news that, now his rank had been discovered, he would be leaving Steinhaus early the next month. In the last week of the old year he again volunteered for wood collection. It was even colder and without gloves the task much harder. He tore two strips from his thin blanket to bind around his hands. As they returned to the camp he looked at the sky. The gamekeeper at Meltwater had taught him the rudiments of reading the weather, a skill he had developed in the Flying Corps. He calculated that at some point in the next day or two there would be snow, in which case wood collection would cease. Besides, footprints in the snow would be a gift for his pursuers. The next day he again volunteered to go to the woods, despite the piercing cold. Fortuitously the gang was larger, so making it easier, he thought, to slip away when the moment was right.

After they had paused for a crust of bread at midday the first flakes of snow drifted down. The guards urged the men in their charge to work harder. An hour or so later the snow began to fall heavily and the guards ordered the gang to reassemble for the return to Steinhaus. Florian made sure he was present for the roll-call on the edge of the forest and then, as the gang made its way back to the truck, he stopped to relieve himself before momentarily rejoining the line. One of the men fell and a guard struck him with his rifle butt, shouting at him to get up. The gang remonstrated. In the distraction, Florian seized his chance and slipped back into the forest. He crouched, listening, as the shouting continued. Then he heard a shot and the barking of orders. A few minutes later came the sound of the truck receding into the distance. He was now alone – an escaped prisoner. He waited. Once it was dark he walked along the edge of the forest in the direction of Herzberg, scuffing the ground with each step in an effort to disguise his footprints when they came to search for him in the morning.

The house was further away than he had thought. Avoiding small dwellings that he knew were occupied from each chimney's plume of smoke, he eventually saw the silhouette of Schloss Herzberg. It was larger than he had thought, too. He saw a dim light through a crack in a curtain. He had no idea of the time but thought it was now probably late evening. Shaking with cold he walked around the edge of the garden, sticking close to shrubs to minimise the trace of footsteps. He found an outhouse – probably abandoned stables – and went inside. He climbed into the loft where he found some hay. Burying himself in it he fell asleep from exhaustion.

The next morning he awoke to a young woman's voice reciting a poem in English. He stirred, sat up and looked at her, his hands above his head.

"Forgive my intrusion. I should not be here. I escaped from Steinhaus yesterday and rested here overnight. It was so cold."

She burst out laughing.

"You look so funny, like a scarecrow – hay in your hair, hay all over you," she said in perfect English. "You can put your hands down. I won't shoot you. I don't have a gun. What is your name?"

He paused. Should he reveal his true name or give another?

"My name is Florian. And what is yours?"

"My word, you are a bold young man. Arabella is my name."

Florian hesitated to respond.

She smiled.

"Lost for words, are you?" she said.

"No, not at all," he replied, "just surprised to see an angel in a hayloft."

"Angels know all about haylofts. That's where they found Jesus."

"I know," he replied.

She helped him to his feet.

She was tall, slim, with a fine-featured almond-shaped face framed with darkish ash-blond hair drawn back in a disordered pony tail. Her eyebrows were dark above large green eyes. Her neck was long, her hands delicate, her mannerisms exquisitely feminine. She wore a long black coat and around her neck was wrapped a thick knitted scarf. She was striking.

"I must leave," he said. "I do not want to put your family in any danger. Perhaps I could just have a drink of water."

"I think it is best that you stay here. It is still snowing and dogs are barking in the distance. They are no doubt looking for you. So you see, you have to stay because if you leave they will find you. Please don't go. I will return shortly with something to eat and drink. You may read my poetry book while you wait."

A little later she returned, accompanied by a much older woman – elegant in deportment but frail, with a deeply lined face. She walked with the support of a stick. Yet her voice was strong, as was her grip when she shook his hand.

"My mother is away in Berlin," said Arabella, "but this is the Countess Alice, my grandmother. Together we will help you."

They had brought with them some warm bread, a mug of hot ersatz coffee, a bowl and a jug of hot water. He washed his hands and face, drying them on the towel Alice gave him.

They sat and listened intently to his story. For over two years Alice had been denied contact with anyone from England. Now before her was an escaped prisoner – moreover, a member of the Whitfield family of whom her mother had spoken disparagingly. But that was the past. Here was a handsome young man, a pilot, from England and she was duty-bound to help him on his way. But time was not on her side. Eva would be back in a few days' time and the household staff would become puzzled by activity in the stables when all the horses had been commandeered for the front.

For the next three days Florian remained in the stables. Alice decided that she should keep to the house but let Arabella go there from time to time as the staff already knew it was her favourite place to read and practise singing. Indeed, there had been occasions when a handful of servants had stood in the doorway to hear her sing Mozart. During these three days Arabella spent an hour or so of each morning in the stables and again in the afternoon, sometimes singing or reading Goethe out loud. In quieter moments she and Florian would sit close to one another, leafing through the books she had smuggled out of the house. She listened to him read Wordsworth, Keats and Byron. As he did so, she sat looking at him intently, at his kind, handsome face etched with weariness. When she read to him, she would sometimes pause. Her eyes penetrated his with a warmth and stillness he had never seen in a woman before.

"How old are you?" he asked her.

"Sixteen," she replied. "And you?"

"Twenty-four," he said. "But I feel as though I have already lived for a hundred years."

"If that is so, you have discovered a magic potion to look so young."

They gazed at each other.

"You're a beautiful young woman, with a full life ahead of you when this damned war is over. Then you will be able to let more people hear your voice and you will marry a handsome young man."

"Are you a fortune-teller?" she asked with a smile.

"No, I am not – just a man who is lost."

"You're not lost. You may be far from England, a country where I once went to school, but you are here with us at Herzberg." She paused and put the tip of her fingers to his. "Most of all, you are with me."

He laid his hand on hers.

"Thank you," he said.

"Please kiss me."

He hesitated.

"I have asked you to kiss me," she said. "Why won't you?"

"It would be wrong for me to do so."

"Why? Are you afraid?"

"I'm afraid that if I kiss you I will want to kiss you again and again. So I had better not."

"Florian," she replied, using his name for the first time, "I want you to kiss me so I can kiss you. Then we will be on an equal footing."

He had never encountered such directness.

They kissed.

Later that afternoon Alice came to the stables. Arabella and Florian were reading poetry to each other.

"I have found someone to take you to the border with France. You will wear one of my son-in-law's military uniforms. He will have no need for it, as we believe he is a prisoner of the British. At a suitable spot on the Rhine your escort will guide you across the river to freedom. My daughter will be back from Berlin the day after tomorrow and my son could come before too long. He too is in the army. Early tomorrow morning you will leave us. Arabella will walk some distance ahead of you. Where she stops she will leave a small bag containing a book of German poetry. Wait there. A man will come and you will follow him. Trust us."

"I will," he replied.

Alice handed him a bundle.

"Here is the uniform of the rank of major my son-in-law once had. There is an overcoat and boots. Although your German is passable, you will say little to the man you will follow. Just obey his instructions – and those of others you will meet – and you should be safe. I ask you for the sake of Herzberg not to say where you have been for the past few days or who has helped you. God bless England."

She shook his hand and left.

"I will come later to say farewell," whispered Arabella.

Later that evening Florian could not sleep. He turned from side to side in the rough bed he had constructed in the hay. Suddenly, he heard a noise, then footsteps coming up the ladder.

"It's me, Arabella," she whispered.

"Arabella, what are you doing here?"

"I have come to be with you."

She lay alongside him.

"What is it like?"

"What is what like?" Florian replied.

"What is it like when a man makes love to a woman? I have read about it but never experienced it."

"It's the coming together of two people physically to express their love for one another."

"Florian, please, that is not what I asked. What is making love like? Do you know?"

"I know what it is like for a man and I imagine that a woman would feel the same."

"I wish you to make love to me so I can find out what it is like."

"Arabella, making love is not like a scientific experiment. People only make love together when they are in love. Besides, you are so young. It would be wrong – indeed irresponsible of me – to do such a thing."

"If I were a king's daughter I would be old enough to be married and possibly mother of my firstborn."

"But you are not a king's daughter and our countries are at war. How would that appear if people got to know?"

"Yes, it is wartime and who knows, I could be dead tomorrow. That is all the more reason why I should discover without further delay what it is like to make love."

"Why should it be me who does what you ask? Would you not wish to have the expression of physical love from the person you choose as your husband?"

She did not answer. Then she spoke again – yet another question.

"Have you ever made love to a woman?"

Florian hesitated.

"Yes. I have."

"How many times have you made love?"

"Once," he replied.

"Did you love the woman you made love to?"

"No," he said.

"If you did not love her but still made love to her, then you can make love to me without any obligation, can't you?"

This young woman had cornered him in argument.

"Arabella, you push me too hard."

Her reply came instantly.

"Florian, I wish you to remove my maidenhead. That is what it is called in Shakespeare, is it not? As your Herzberg host, I command it."

In the candlelight, her eyes shone, unblinking. He was taken aback by the sharpness of her mind, her precocious self-assurance and yet fleeting glimpses of childlike vulnerability.

He kissed her.

"If that is your wish, I will."

"At last," she murmured.

He helped loosen her clothes and led by her hands began gently to fondle her small firm breasts. She kissed him. Slipping beneath him with a provocative self-confidence she put her arms around his neck, instinctively pulling him closer down on her. He began to touch her sweet spot. She closed her eyes and began to move in rhythm with him. As their bodies quickened he gently penetrated her. She cried out in pain but urged him on. Suddenly her body stiffened as she reached her climax. He put his hand over her mouth to stifle her cry of pleasure. It was all over. They lay together, she tightly clasped in his arms. For a while they did not speak.

"Thank you, Florian. Now I know. You have freed me. I have become a true woman."

An hour or so later he woke as the first sign of light entered through a chink in the stable roof. Arabella was gone. Beside him were bread and lukewarm coffee, a razor, some soap and water, and a fragment of mirror. He shaved and dressed in the uniform, which roughly fitted him. Then he noticed a slip of paper.

> *To Florian,*
> *I love you, kindred spirit. But I already knew that before last night.*
> *Arabella*

He put the crumpled piece of paper in his pocket and went outside. After one last look at the stables, he began to walk. In the distance he saw her. After several minutes she bent down by a gatepost as though to do up her shoe, then she walked away in a different direction. In the further distance in another direction he observed a hunched figure shuffling along in the snow. Florian quickened his pace.

He followed the figure into the woods. Not far in, the man stopped. Though stooped and thin, he had steel-grey eyes that seemed to spark above his beard.

"Young man, you will do exactly what I ask. Whatever happens, do as I say."

"I will," Florian replied.

They walked through the wood side by side. In less than an hour they reached a road.

"Walk in front of me," the man said firmly, dropping back.

Florian did as he was told but was increasingly puzzled by his guide's apparent eccentricity. Before long a small military vehicle came towards them. Florian looked down to avoid drawing the driver's attention. The vehicle passed but in a minute or two he heard a car pull up behind them. Florian looked round. It seemed to be the same one that had just passed them in the other direction.

"What do you want?" barked a voice.

"In front of me is an escaped British prisoner from the Steinhaus camp. I saw him some way back. He asked for directions. It soon became clear to me that he is not a German officer. And he is not well. I suggest that you take us to the nearest police station without delay."

The young *Hauptmann* got out of the vehicle. He examined Florian's uniform and asked for his army identity card. As he did not have one he put his hands up.

"The old man is right. I am an escaped prisoner."

"I arrest you," said the *Hauptmann* in English. "Get in – both of you."

Florian obeyed, bewildered by what had happened. He turned to look at the old man beside him, who said nothing but gave him a reassuring pat on his arm.

On arrival at a rural police station, Florian was formally arrested. The insignia were removed from his jacket and he was pushed into a cell. He asked for a drink of water, receiving some beer in a stained metal cup in return.

The following morning he woke early. He was shivering with cold. His limbs ached from the wooden bench on which he had slept. He thought of Arabella. The cell door swung open. After a drink of cold and disgusting coffee, he was handcuffed and put in a larger vehicle in which he was driven, under escort, to what he believed was the town of Brandenburg. There was no sign of the bearded man. On arrival at what were evidently police headquarters he was immediately taken to a large room, bare apart from a table and two chairs. A large unpleasant-looking uniformed man faced him. Still handcuffed, he was interrogated about his movements since his escape. Over and over came the same questions and repeated blows. He simply answered with his name, rank and number. Despite being struck, he did not budge, only admitting that he had escaped, lived in the forest and stolen the uniform from a house. Yet another punch came. The pain was hard to bear. But he was determined not to crack. Others might betray him but he would not betray those at Herzberg.

After several hours of repeated questioning he was led to a cell. Shortly afterwards he received a bowl of soup, thin and almost cold. In the evening he was taken to an adjacent building with a rudimentary court room. Half an hour later he was asked to stand. Following a summary hearing, most of which he was able to understand, the sentence of the court was passed. He was to be shot the next day for masquerading as a German officer; for seeking to make unlawful and unauthorised contact with the German people; and for withholding important information about those who had committed a treasonable offence by protecting him. He was asked if he had any statement to make. In reply Florian repeated his name, rank and number and said that under the Hague Conventions he deserved the protection of the German state, an obligation that Britain fulfilled in respect of all German prisoners in its care. His statement was dismissed and he was returned to his cell to await his punishment the next morning.

Later in the evening the cell door opened. A different police officer entered. He spoke good English.

"Your sentence of death has been temporarily deferred. The secret police wish to interrogate you. Come, they are waiting to take you to their headquarters nearby."

Florian put his borrowed overcoat round his shoulders and once again, still handcuffed, was pushed into an unmarked vehicle and driven into the night. The journey lasted many hours. He shook with cold. The guard beside him gave him a blanket. At about three o'clock in the morning, if the clock in the building entrance was correct, he was placed in another cell. He was left alone for several hours. In daylight an elderly, clean-shaven, sallow-faced man with thick grey hair entered the cell. He sat beside

Florian on the stone bench. As the man spoke, Florian recognised the same gleaming eyes he had seen before in the forest near Herzberg.

"Listen carefully. In an hour you will be taken from this cell to a courtyard just behind this wall." He touched the stone behind him. "Here you will face a firing squad of two men. Unbeknown to them their guns will fire blanks. You will slump forward, shouting an obscenity, something like, 'You bastards can't even shoot straight. No wonder you're losing the war.' I will then step forward and shoot you with my pistol. It too will have a blank – only one. When the shot is fired, clutch your hands hard against your chest. This fragile phial of blood I give you now will disintegrate and stain your chest. I will kick you and pronounce you dead. Your body will then be placed in a sack and removed for burial. A short distance from here I will release you and then you will begin your journey to freedom in Spain."

"Why should you wish to go to this elaborate charade?"

"Young man, I have long wished to expiate my guilt for a terrible sin I committed a long time ago. I have not long to live on this earth. Now at last I have the chance to do so."

"Is it anything to do with Herzberg?" asked Florian.

"Yes," he replied. "Now, officer, some more play-acting. I am going to yell at you and draw blood. What is about to happen to you must look convincing."

The man with the frost-fierce eyes began to shout at him for withholding information and disrespecting the German state. He struck Florian several times, bruising and bloodying his face.

Several hours later, once across the German lines and into France, Florian was released from his bloodstained sack.

* * * * *

On Friday the 19th of January 1917, a week after Florian had left Herzberg, Alice received a message that he had been arrested and would now face trial. The sentence was likely to be death by firing squad. Arabella was distraught at this news.

"How could you be so callous as to place Florian's life in the hands of a man who would immediately betray him? What poor judgement you showed. If he dies, I will wish to die too."

Alice sought to comfort Arabella but she was beyond consolation. She began to fear for her granddaughter's state of mind. Eva Victoria, now back from Berlin and relieved to have received official notification that Ferdinand Anton was a prisoner in British hands, was equally unable to console her daughter, who had not eaten for days. The following week, on Saturday the 27th of January, Alice received a personal message from a senior level in the *Preußische Geheimpolizei* that a certain person had now crossed the Spanish border and, on the Kaiser's personal instruction, they had closed the file on Florian Whitfield.

Alice and Eva Victoria summoned Arabella from her room.

"We have received news that Florian is alive and now safe in Spain, beyond the reach of his enemies."

Arabella was overwhelmed, her eyes full of tears.

"I wish to see him."

"Why do you wish to see him?" asked Alice.

"It is because I love him."

"But you are too young to know of love, my child," her mother insisted. "He is safe. Let him be in peace."

"I cannot and will not," replied Arabella with a sharpness her mother had rarely witnessed. "I want to be with him. If you will not help me, I will run away and find him on my own."

Eva Victoria continued her efforts to dissuade Arabella. Alice intervened.

"Eva, once upon a time there was another determined young woman in love with a man who had gone from her. She would not be deterred. And she triumphed."

"And who was that?" asked Eva.

"It was Arabella's namesake, the Countess Arabella von Deppe." Alice recounted what Arabella Whitfield had written in her music book before she left home: *I will do what people want but only as I want it to be.*

"Those were brave words. Some thought them arrogant. But they were her watchwords throughout life and they served her well. Let Arabella go to Florian. Ferdinand Anton is not here to give his own advice but I am sure he would agree. There is too little happiness in this wretched world. Let Arabella find it while she can."

*

A week later, on Friday the 2nd of February, Arabella left Herzberg in the care of the aged Ernst Kiefer, who had arrived the day before, now discharged from his long service to the secret police on grounds of exemplary service in Prussia, Austria and Spain. After crossing the German lines by clandestine means just as Florian had done, Arabella and Kiefer made their way towards Spain.

Before Arabella's departure, Alice had revealed to her the precious music book and its hiding place.

"If you return to Herzberg, as I hope you will, I wish you to become the guardian of this book and its many secrets and memories. It is the heart of Schloss Herzberg. The Countess was a beautiful, caring, courageous and single-minded woman, who treasured friendship, loyalty and music just as I believe you do. She was loved by many. She fought for what she believed was right. Above all, she strived throughout her life for the integrity and respect of this house and the von Deppe family. These are dark times but as the bearer of her name perhaps one day you will also be the new standard-bearer for this estate and what it has stood for over so many years. There are many pictures of the Countess, all safely stored undergound, but here to take with you is a miniature of her painted by one of the many artists who sought her patronage. The Countess Beatrice gave it to me as a keepsake. I now give it to you to have with you at all times."

Together they leafed through the treasured book, with its musical compositions, diary entries, note, anecdotes, letters and writings and occasional drawings and sketches.

"Guard it well, Arabella, guard it well," said Alice as she returned the book to its hiding place.

"I will, Grandmama. I promise you I will."

The next day Alice said farewell to her only grandchild and a tearful Eva Victoria, worn down by her mother's insistence that she could not hold Arabella back any longer, bid au revoir to her only child.

Shortly afterwards, the ground floor of Herzberg became a military hospital. One of the admissions in early May of 1917 was Eva Victoria's brother, Carl Johann, wounded in the French Nivelle offensive.

CHAPTER 15

From Evening into Night

Florian's journey from sentence of death before a firing squad to promised freedom was long and arduous, all the more so because of weakened health and malnourishment. His condition was equally evident to his escort, a refined and distinguished Spanish woman – straight-backed, with dark-grey hair and severe in look except when she smiled – who, after crossing the line of war, had been instructed to take him speedily through France to Hendaye in the far south-west and then across the Spanish border to Irún for onward travel by train to Madrid. She had pressed Ernst Kiefer at the beginning of the journey as to why the young aviator had not been allowed to rest on French soil a safe distance south of the front line; indeed, why he had not been conveyed to the International Committee of the Red Cross for repatriation to England. The elderly Kiefer was adamant that, unless the young man was dying, he should make haste to Spain where he could enjoy true respite and peace as Kiefer's own grandfather had done with the famous woman who had been his companion. Besides, Spain was neutral, offering welcome security. The Red Cross were already aware, he said, that Whitfield had not been executed and was on his way to a place of safety where he could recover his strength and, once the war was over, decide his future. Kiefer did not disclose to Florian's escort his true motive: he was driven by his belief that he could assuage his past guilt only by providing safe haven in Spain, his homeland, for the descendant of the woman he had once betrayed.

By the time they reached Irún Florian's condition had deteriorated, becoming feverish. Admitted to hospital, he stayed for several days. Once his temperature had improved and his determination to continue their journey had been restored, he and his companion, whom he had now identified as Doña Elena Carmen García Kiefer, took the train to Madrid. Here they would pause before going further south. Florian's spirits rose markedly when, after their arrival in the city, Doña Elena revealed she had received a telegram that a young woman, Arabella von Eisenwald, was following him to Spain. Having spent three days in Madrid, Doña Elena and Florian resumed their journey south by car in bitterly cold weather. With another sudden deterioration in her charge's condition, Doña Elena changed direction and headed north-west for the ancient walled town of Ávila, where she knew of a good and trusted doctor. Given the diagnosis of severe malnutrition and its contribution to likely pneumonia, she decided that, for the present, they would go no further, a decision she quickly telegraphed to Kiefer.

* * * * *

Receipt of the War Office telegram reporting that Florian was missing in action added further to the grief already afflicting the Whitfields. The dark-red stain of loss seemed to be spreading across the family like spilt ink through blotting paper. The despair lifted somewhat when the German authorities, in response to International Committee of the Red Cross enquiries, stated that the young officer had escaped from their protection. This was followed some two weeks later by another report that he had been recaptured and would be tried for the commission of certain offences against the German people. William Folliot was unable to offer any additional information to the Whitfields, now plunged once again in deep distress. Yet Arthur and Juliet Whitfield remained calm and stoic, an unusual response but one that perhaps reflected their compliant approach to life and fate. The anguish at Meltwater deepened when a further message was received that the officer had been tried and sentenced to death for serious offences, including espionage, unbecoming a prisoner of war, in turn followed by another terse report, through separate official channels, that the sentence had been commuted. A week later, Folliot examined another, highly unusual, cryptic message, which Arthur Whitfield had received from an anonymous sender.

> *So went Christian's fair son*
> *From fields of grass to house of thrall.*
> *On he journeyed to the mountain hall,*
> *Bewitching there the fairest daughter*
> *Before evading stain of slaughter*
> *For the warmth of Rodrigo's sun.*

In Folliot's opinion, though he could not rule out a cruel hoax, it seemed, despite its oddity, to bear a hallmark of authenticity. He showed it to Aurelia.

She studied it carefully and looked at one or two music books.

"It's a puzzle, which I think I have solved!" she suddenly exclaimed.

"Tell me, Aurelia. What is it?"

"The words are surely a play on the lyrics to Grieg's *In the Hall of the Mountain King*. It was an orchestral piece he composed for Ibsen's *Peer Gynt* in 1876. Surely 'fields of grass' means airfields where planes take off and land. 'House of thrall' could be the prison camp where Florian was taken after capture. 'Mountain hall' in German can be translated as *Schlossberg*, perhaps a subtle reference to Herzberg. The reference to 'Bewitching there the fairest daughter' is harder, but if I am right and *Schlossberg* is indeed Herzberg, it could be a reference to Arabella, Alice's granddaughter. She would be about sixteen now. If my supposition is correct, that would be yet further proof he was at Herzberg after his escape. As for 'evading stain of slaughter', it is possibly an allusion to not being executed. As for 'the warmth of Rodrigo's sun', that I deduce is a reference to Spain, since Rodrigo was another name for El Cid, the great Spanish soldier who defeated the Moors. And the fact that you think the message was sent from Hendaye, on the French-Spanish border, is a further indication that Florian is now in Spain. Last but not least, the sender is someone with musical knowledge and an unusual sense of humour."

She sat back with evident satisfaction, as she sometimes did after solving a crossword puzzle.

"Aurelia, you are brilliant."

"I hope, if we are indeed correct about Florian being at Herzberg, that Alice and her family did not suffer any retribution if, upon his capture, the authorities found out where he had been hiding."

"I hope so, too," replied William.

This latest message, and Aurelia's "decryption", provided a measure of comfort to the Whitfield family in the weeks that followed.

* * * * *

Arabella's journey took her in a different direction. In the almost silent company of Ernst Kiefer she travelled south from Berlin to Halle, where they were joined by a middle-aged woman called Hanna Kovács, then to Würzburg and Karlsruhe and, following some delay at the border, on into Switzerland and Geneva, from where they crossed into France. Day after day they travelled, by car or by train, making slow but relentless progress. Though an inexperienced traveller, Arabella had learnt from her journeys to school in England before the war to be observant. She was struck by the ease and comfort of their passage. The people at their overnight accommodation or who helped them on their way seemed always to expect them and to have everything ready. Moreover, there never seemed any shortage of money. She noticed too that when they stopped en route, they often saw people queuing, their faces war-weary, their clothes dishevelled. On a few occasions in Germany she overhead mutterings of malice towards the Kaiser and the generals for bringing hardship to the local population and its way of life. Once they were in France she noted that her two companions became more relaxed and talkative as they travelled towards Hendaye, though between themselves rather than with her.

Hanna Kovács was tall and physically striking, her face open and self-assured, with large brown eyes and thin lips that conveyed perhaps either the suffering of previous pain or the potential for cruelty. Her face was framed with thick black hair pulled tightly back in a chignon. She reminded Arabella of her boarding-school house mistress. Expensively dressed, she sometimes fussed over Arabella's limited travelling wardrobe, which comprised her long black coat, worn with the familiar grey knitted scarf and a black broad-brimmed hat, beneath which she wore a green ankle-length dress or a similar one in red.

They waited two days at Hendaye in a small nondescript hotel. Arabella was confined to her room, reading her well-thumbed books of English poetry, Shakespeare and a short history of early English music with some examples of pieces by John Dowland. The volume on music, which she had inherited from her distant relative Victoria, had become one of her most cherished personal possessions, not least because it had been annotated in places in Victoria's distinctive handwriting. Moreover, when she pressed its pages to her nose, she could almost smell that redoubtable person.

On the third day, Kiefer took his leave.

"Miss Arabella, I must travel ahead to Madrid to attend to pressing business. Early tomorrow morning, you will follow by train with Madame Kovács."

"When might I expect to see Florian again?" Arabella asked.

"That is hard to say," Kiefer replied. "If the fates are in our favour, it will be soon."

Later that day Arabella crossed the border with Madame Kovács and after lodging overnight in Irún they left early the next morning for Madrid. Though the sky was clear and the sun shone, it was bitterly cold. Arabella's coat provided reasonable warmth; the scarf she wrapped tightly round her neck.

The train journey was slow. Madame Kovács proved in its early part a woman of few words. With her face behind a veil, she read a thick book but would occasionally look up into the distance as though searching for someone or something on the horizon. As the train made its slow progression towards Madrid, however, her manner eased, responding to Arabella's gentle but persistent questioning about her life.

Her father, Alexander, who had made a fortune in textiles, and her mother, Adele, both Jewish, had come to live in Vienna when younger like so many other Jewish families following the 1867 *Ausgleich*, which had granted equal rights to all citizens of the

Austro-Hungarian Empire. Life had been good to the Apstein family – music, dancing, the theatre and travel. Their large Viennese apartment with its luxurious interior reflected her father's success but also the family's cultural difference from those around them. Hanna recounted how her mother had been one of a select few to be painted by Gustav Klimt, a much sought-after Viennese society artist. She showed Arabella a small photograph of the painting. The dark-haired woman, wearing a white dress with a delicate but noticeable pattern and edged in fur, was indeed striking. There was an aura about her. Hanna said her parents were proud of the picture and of another by Klimt of her father because they demonstrated the high social position that the Apstein family had achieved as part of Vienna's western European culture, but not as gentiles. She then showed Arabella another picture of a spacious and well-appointed drawing room in which her mother's portrait hung above the fireplace. A beam of sunlight shone across the room from an open window. Hanna paused to dab her eye. Continuing, she said that the family became uneasy as the years passed and prejudice towards the Jews in Vienna grew on account of their wealth and promoted difference. The increasing frequency of anti-Jewish cartoons in the newspapers and journals did not help. While some Jewish families had dismissed these hostile opinions, hers had not.

The conversation stopped as the train pulled into a station. Once it resumed its bumpy journey Arabella asked Hanna to tell her more of her story.

"I met a handsome young man in 1905 and at once fell in love with him. As he was not Jewish my parents urged me not to marry him, despite his position at the imperial court. His parents were also unhappy at the prospect. But after a while we convinced both our families that we would not be separated and therefore it would be better for them to give their approval than see us elope. In the spring of 1907 we married in the synagogue and afterwards we were blessed in the Catholic cathedral. We were so happy, so much in love. We moved to Budapest, where Franz was given a more important imperial position. During this time my father died. His death affected my mother greatly. Eventually, in 1914, on the outbreak of war, we returned to Vienna as Franz had been offered a commission in the army. At first he was in army headquarters, but soon after he sought a field command. He was killed in battle in 1915, not long after the death of my mother. She died of a broken heart, unable to bear the loss of my father."

Hanna stopped once more to dab her eyes with a small lace handkerchief.

"I lived alone in my parents' apartment for a while. But I soon decided to sell it and move to a smaller one. Last year I met Herr Kiefer. He encouraged me to travel to Spain, his country of birth, to begin a new life and perhaps to find new companionship. I could not make up my mind. Then he asked me to accompany you to Spain. I decided without further ado to let my apartment and here I am – a widow with a sad story, a companion to a young woman at the start of her life."

"We are like ships in a convoy, Madame Kovács. I do not know how much Herr Kiefer has told you but I am travelling south to be reunited with a man with whom I have fallen in love."

"How old are you?"

"I will soon be eighteen. My mother says I am too young to fall in love but I dispute that. Besides, Juliet fell in love when she was very young and no one ever criticised her for that. In this world of dreadful war I consider it is important to find love for as long as possible – you and me, Madame Kovács, must we not?"

"Arabella, I agree. Perhaps you would like to tell me more of your story, about your home, your family and the young man with whom you have fallen in love. And, please, call me Hanna."

So for the next hour Arabella told her about Florian and Herzberg. By the morning of the following day, when the train pulled into Madrid, both had become the firmest of friends. Ernst Kiefer was waiting at the station to greet them.

"Tomorrow, Miss Arabella, you and I will leave for Ávila by road. The journey will take several hours but if we begin early we should reach our destination by nightfall. And before you ask, yes, Mr Whitfield will be there. He eagerly awaits your arrival. I am sure Madame Kovács will help you buy some fresh clothes for the journey." He gave Hanna some money.

The next morning, on Tuesday the 13th of March, Arabella and Hanna Kovács said goodbye, pledging to meet again and wishing each other happiness. Then Arabella got into a large black chauffeur-driven car. Kiefer sat beside her.

"Miss Arabella, it had been my intention that you and Mr Whitfield should meet at my family's farm in Andalusia, but so far that has not been possible because he has been unwell – his time in the prison camp and his travails thereafter greatly weakened him. My niece, Doña Elena Carmen García Kiefer, who was accompanying Mr Whitfield south, decided to halt at Ávila so he could receive medical attention, which he has done. I understand from my niece's latest message that he is improved and the prognosis good. I will not stay in Ávila but Doña Elena will be with you while I travel to Andalusia. She will do whatever is needed to care for you both."

"Thank you," replied Arabella, full of suppressed excitement at the prospect of seeing Florian but troubled by Kiefer's report of his health.

By late afternoon, after a long journey through countryside that seemed to Arabella to be a living antiquity, they entered the ancient walled city of Ávila, set in an undulating landscape. Within a short while they had stopped outside a *pensión*.

"Wait here, please," said Kiefer.

Some minutes passed before he returned.

"Please, Miss Arabella, please come. This *pensión* is at your and Mr Whitfield's disposal for as long as necessary."

They climbed a steep wooden staircase and turning left entered a spacious, low-ceilinged, wood-panelled room. On one side was a large four-poster bed with heavy red curtains. On the other were a table and four chairs. Ahead was a blazing fire beside which sat Florian, reading. His thin pale face lit up on seeing Arabella. He stood slowly to greet her, opening his arms to receive her as she rushed towards him.

"My darling Florian, at last," she said as she held him tightly. "At long last, we are together. I am so happy."

"Yes, dearest Arabella, at long last we are together."

They kissed.

"Arabella, I wish to introduce you to Doña Elena, who has looked after me so patiently. Doña Elena, I introduce to you the Countess Arabella von Eisenwald, the young woman I love so much."

Arabella curtsied to Doña Elena.

"I thank you and Herr Kiefer for all that you have done to make this moment possible," she said, almost overcome by her excitement.

"Doña Elena and I will now leave you in privacy," said Kiefer. "Shall we have supper at eight o'clock?"

Florian and Arabella nodded.

For many days thereafter the two talked, read together and sometimes, hand in hand, despite Florian's fluctuating health, walked short distances along the town's cobbled streets and even occasionally to the exterior of the city walls. At night they sat beside the fire, where Arabella would play the guitar she had found and quickly mastered, and sing songs from her Dowland book. Later she would lie in a cot bed alongside the four-poster, holding Florian's hand as he tossed and turned during frequent feverish nights. Often she would cool his forehead with a damp cloth. Sometimes in his sleep he would call her name as he emerged from yet another nightmare. A doctor came regularly to see him, reassuring both that recovery would come. By late March, as the sun rose higher in the sky, his condition, like the weather, began to improve once again and with it his spirits. He began to eat more and the doctor came less often. Doña Elena made arrangements for them to move from the *pensión* to a small house in a street close to the cathedral where they could be alone. It had a small courtyard, in the middle of which was a fountain.

One afternoon in late April, after Easter, Arabella returned to the courtyard from visiting Doña Elena and attending Mass in the Cathedral of the Holy Saviour. Caught in a shaft of sunshine she stood for a moment to smell the scent of the early spring flowers in pots around the walls, unaware Florian was gazing at her from the darkened doorway. She was dressed in a loose floral dress tied about the waist; one sleeve had slipped from her shoulder and the low-cut bodice revealed the upper part of her breasts. Her hair, now even longer, fell in soft tumbling waves about her shoulders. Her shawl slid from her arms to her feet as she bent to pick some petals from the stones. He watched her closely. She was truly beautiful, a Renaissance image. She suddenly became aware of his presence. Her hands placed to his cheeks she kissed him gently. He put his arms around her waist and pulled her towards him.

"I have long waited for this moment," he said.

"So have I," she replied.

"Come." He took her hand and they went upstairs. She closed the door behind her, turning the key in the lock.

"So we are not disturbed," she said.

He smiled. They spoke no words as they lay together. He slipped easily into her.

"Now there is no distance between us," she whispered.

They made love, not febrile, lustful love as young lovers sometimes do, but as in the pleasing notes of the softest adagio, the gentlest andante. In their tender passion they floated upwards effortlessly, like ethereal spirits, into a timeless realm of sublime pleasure far above the hour of the day. Afterwards, in the wake of sweet and exhausted abandonment, as they slowly drifted into the dreamscape of sleep entwined in each other's arms, they swore the deepest love to one another. In the later hours of the night Florian awoke, the pain in his chest dull but unrelenting. He sipped some water. In the candlelight he looked at the half-uncovered young lover beside him, soft and still. His eyes followed the contours of her body, the exquisite shape of her breast, the gentle curve of her back, her sculptured thigh. He pulled the coverlet over her, silently kissing her mane of hair. She was like the flame of the candle still burning beside him – yellow and clear, light blue on the inside and an aura of intense dark blue on the outside. He lay back and recalled the song she had sung him that morning as she plucked the chords on the guitar. The beauty of her lilting voice and the tender notes her slender fingers drew from the strings almost pained him with their sublime perfection; perhaps they were the sound of heaven itself. He loved her so much, had done so ever since they sat side by side reading poems to one another in the stables at Herzberg. This precious gift would not be his for much longer; the doctor had warned that his illness had caused profound and lasting damage. His life would last at the most a few months, a secret he would not yet divulge though he suspected Doña Elena already knew. As he turned to extinguish the candle, Arabella reached for his hand and clasped it tightly to her chest.

The next day Arabella wrote to her mother.

Dearest Mama,

I hope you will receive this letter safely. Herr Kiefer has promised me that you will do so, however long its passage to you takes.

You will already know from the message he kindly sent you earlier that I arrived in Spain without harm or incident over a month ago. Herr K and Madame Kovács from Vienna were good companions and cared for me on the long journey. From Madrid Herr Kiefer and I drove to Ávila, a beautiful and ancient walled city. Here I was reunited with my Florian. He has been grievously ill and remains sick but a local doctor and Herr K's niece, Doña Elena, the kindest of ladies, have nursed him. I am now helping them to get him better. He was so pleased to see me. Perhaps my presence will indeed help him to regain his strength more quickly. I go regularly to the cathedral to pray for him.

I do not know the future; none of us does, so long as this hateful war continues. I will stay by Florian's side until he is better and able to decide what he should do – whether to remain in Spain until the war ends or to try to return to England. I love him more than ever and intend to be his constant companion in whichever direction he travels. I will not forget you and Papa or Uncle Carl, and certainly not my dearest grandmother, Alice. Though I greatly miss you all and Herzberg too, I am so happy to be with my Florian.

I will write again soon.
From your loving daughter,
Arabella
Ávila
Friday the 27th of April, 1917

The weeks that followed and the warm sun rising ever higher in the sky seemed to herald an improvement in Florian's health. He and Arabella walked more often beyond the city walls; he helped with some of the daily domestic tasks. He began to learn to play the guitar and even to sing some simple Spanish ballads, serenading her on her birthday. At night they lay together, two lovers oblivious to the world beyond the counterpane and the sound of the cicadas. This idyll of blissful love did not last.

In the middle of June Florian developed a fever. He had gone down with fevers in the past but this one was longer and more intense than any he had suffered before. His condition steadily worsened, aggravated by the heat of the day lingering long into the evening. The doctor came regularly and prescribed medicine, but it made little difference. Florian's cough, always present, became more destructive. By day and by night Arabella tended her patient, rarely allowing Doña Elena to take her place at his bedside. Late on the afternoon of Monday the 25th of June the doctor came once again. After examining Florian, he broke the news to Arabella and Doña Elena that, unless there were a miracle, he was unlikely to last beyond the next day. For the next few hours Arabella sat beside him, putting damp cloths to his brow, moistening his lips in between his racking coughs and holding his hand tightly. By the early hours he was finding it increasingly difficult to breathe, his voice almost inaudible. He looked at the care-paled face and tear-reddened eyes of the beautiful young woman he loved with his entire soul.

"I love you," he whispered. "Forgive me for inflicting this misery on you. In our short time together we have loved so much. That will last me until such time as you join me wherever it is I go. I will wait all eternity for you."

"Florian, please don't leave. Please stay with me. Please, please I beg of you, stay. You are my sun by day and my silver moon by night. You are my very being."

He took her hand.

"Arabella, I cannot stay. I have to confront what awaits me."

"Florian, you must stay. You are the father of the child I am bearing."

He turned and smiled weakly, lifting her hand which he put to his lips to kiss. His eyes filled with tears.

"My angel Arabella," he rasped. "If it be your wish, when the war is ended, let our child help you seek reconciliation between our two families. Remove if you can the barriers of past misunderstanding and hatred. It is a single chance to mend what is broken. All will be in your hands. Play your music, sing your songs. You read to me at Herzberg that music can be the sound of God absolving the world of its guilt. Play to our families, play to people everywhere the sound of God."

"I will, Florian, I will."

An hour later Father Felipe came to marry them and to administer the last rites. Just after dawn on the morning of Tuesday the 26th of June Florian Whitfield died in Arabella's arms. She cradled his emaciated body just as Mary cradled the dead Christ in Michelangelo's *Pietà*. Doña Elena came to sit beside her.

"Let him go, my child. Let him go on his way."

Arabella wept inconsolably, repeating over and over again, "Why should this be?"

Summoning help, Doña Elena loosened Arabella's grip and slowly Florian was removed from her arms. She was overwhelmed with grief. The hastily summoned doctor gave her a sleeping draught.

Late the next day a small cortège made its way to the great Gothic cathedral, entering through the Gateway of the Apostles; in the Saint Secundus chapel Father Felipe said Mass for Florian Whitfield. Before his body was taken from the cathedral, Arabella stood before the coffin and played John Dowland's *Tarleton's Resurrection*. Afterwards his body was laid to rest in an open field just beyond the city wall. A week later she wrote to her mother.

> *Dearest Mama,*
>
> *It is in great sorrow and despair that I write this letter.*
>
> *My darling, sweetest Florian died on the 26th of June, of pneumonia. I am broken-hearted – that he is gone and that he will not see his child, the child I am carrying.*
>
> *Shortly before Florian died, Father Felipe received him into the Catholic faith and married us at his bedside. The next day Doña Elena and Herr Kiefer arranged for a funeral Mass in the cathedral. Afterwards we laid my husband to rest in a field just outside the city wall. I sat by his graveside until dusk, as I could not bear to leave him alone.*
>
> *Life is so cruel.*
>
> *Shakespeare wrote in one of his sonnets:*

> For never-resting time leads summer on
> To hideous winter and confounds him there;
> Sap check'd with frost and lusty leaves quite gone,
> Beauty o'ersnow'd and bareness every where:

But not even Shakespeare's fine words can convey the cruellest and bleakest winter in which I am now enveloped. Yet the one gleam of light in this landscape of darkness is that I carry his child with love and pride. Our son or daughter will be a living reminder of the man I loved, taken from me after such a short time.

I am resolved to remain in Ávila as I am not strong enough to travel in my present condition. Doña Elena and the nuns of the Convento de San José will care for me at the birth of my child. Do not try to find me. I wish to be alone in my grief. Once my baby is born and I am well enough to travel I will strive to go to Paris, however difficult that may be, until this accursed war is over. Once it is I hope we can be reunited at Herzberg.

I send my deepest love to Papa in England, to Carl Johann and to Grandmother Alice. I think of you all often.
Arabella
Ávila
Tuesday the 3rd of July, 1917

Over the following months correspondence between Spain and Herzberg was intermittent and full of risk. Moreover, Herr Kiefer, now in rapidly declining health due to his advanced age, was reluctant to trade on the residual goodwill of his previous employers as conditions worsened in Germany or to expose the von Deppe family to greater risk. In distant Germany Alice assisted him by restraining Eva Victoria, understandably distraught at what had happened to her daughter, from such foolish actions as travelling to Spain through enemy lines or writing indiscreet letters. She insisted that Arabella was in safer hands in neutral Spain than in Germany, where the position was growing increasingly desperate as the enemy blockade tightened its grip. Nevertheless, Alice incurred the frequent and bitter admonition from her daughter that she, Alice, had encouraged Arabella to leave Herzberg against Eva Victoria's wishes and, as a consequence, Arabella had been led astray, marrying an enemy and bearing his child. Alice rebutted each accusation firmly and sought to comfort Eva Victoria.

In early January 1918 came a brief message from Doña Elena that Herr Kiefer had died in November but that the Countess

Arabella had given birth to a boy. There followed shortly a letter from Arabella.

> *Dearest Mama,*
>
> *As I hope you will already know from Doña Elena I gave birth to a son on Friday the 14th of December at the Convent of St Joseph. He was delivered safely. He now proudly bears the name Stefan Florian Whitfield von Eisenwald.*
>
> *Madame Kovács is coming soon to Ávila and together we will leave for Paris once the weather improves. I will try to pass a message to you once I am there.*
>
> *Your loving daughter,*
> *Arabella*
> *Ávila*
> *Friday the 11th of January, 1918*

The letter did not reach Herzberg until March, coinciding with the news that Carl Johann had returned to the front line as the hardship in Germany deepened. This intelligence brought great sorrow to Alice. Now ill, she yet clung tenaciously to life, hoping to meet her great-grandson, Stefan, to embrace Arabella once again and to bequeath to her the music book.

As for Arthur and Juliet Whitfield, they received official notification through the International Committee of the Red Cross that, despite efforts to treat him, their son had died of pneumonia in Spain from the harsh conditions he had endured in German captivity. He had been buried at Ávila. It was followed in early 1918 by a separate message, from Doña Elena, conveyed via the British embassies in Madrid and Paris and the Foreign Office, informing them that shortly before his death Florian had married Arabella von Eisenwald and that she had since given birth to their child, a boy. Before long she intended to travel to Paris, where she would wait until the war ended so she could return to Germany. Charles Whitfield received this news with astonishment and personal relief. Fate had intervened in a remarkable way and perhaps, he thought, it might in due course open the way to a possible lasting reconciliation between the two families and thus finally heal the rift that had split them since 1766.

EPILOGUE

"Will the Sun forget to streak ... ?"

War-weary and barely recovered from the wounds he had sustained during the Nivelle strategy, Carl Johann returned to the front for the German army's spring offensive of March 1918. Its initial success moved the front line to within seventy-five miles of Paris. But the High Command's jubilation was short-lived. The offensive was halted, victim of overextended supply lines. Further attacks were mounted towards the Channel ports and in July Carl Johann was involved in a bold attempt to encircle the French city of Reims. Yet again the attempt failed to press home early advantage as the enemy re-engaged in strength. During March and April the army's casualties had risen ever higher – reaching, it was reported, more than a quarter of a million. Carl Johann knew from his last visit to High Command headquarters of the devastating reports of a disintegrating Germany. Anti-war marches were becoming frequent and he was acutely aware of falling army morale. Despite another major push in early August, the army lines fell back in the face of enemy attacks elsewhere along the front. Carl Johann sent a message to his superiors that his severely depleted and exhausted force could not sustain their position much longer. Within weeks it would collapse. His message followed many others in a similar vein, collectively conveying the unavoidable conclusion – impending defeat.

By early November, following the installation of a new government in Berlin, a German republic was declared, a month after the dissolution of the Austro-Hungarian Empire. News quickly reached Carl Johann and his soldiers that the Kaiser had been removed and had fled the country, soon followed by the announcement of the cessation of hostilities, to begin on Monday the 11th of November. The war was over; defeat for Germany was underlined by American, British, Belgian and French troops entering the Rhineland. Sick, fatigued and full of malice towards those whom he believed had betrayed his men, Carl Johann began his slow journey back to Berlin.

From Herzberg, Eva Victoria and Alice surveyed Germany's devastation. Since the start of the war civilian deaths had steadily multiplied, due in large part to food shortage and malnutrition. Herzberg mirrored the impact. The surrounding farmland, once the pride of the grant-holders, was in poor condition in the absence – through call-up and civilian mortality – of labour to sow and reap; the house had been used as a military hospital and in its much-needed service as such its previous historic lustre as a place of music and culture had largely been hidden behind a veneer of blood and the echoing nightmares of wounded soldiers. Many of the von Deppe family had died. Most heart-breaking of all was the loss of contact with Arabella. There had been no recent news of her whereabouts. In her grief – a lost daughter, a bitter brother and a husband a prisoner of war in England – Eva Victoria had aged. Only Alice remained defiant, a stout defender of the Herzberg spirit. Eva, steeped in resentment at what had befallen her family, never ceased berating her mother for persuading her to let Arabella go. Alice continued to give no quarter.

"We agreed that she should go, rather than lead a miserable, unhappy existence at home. She safely reached her destination. She fell in love with a handsome young English pilot, just as you did with a handsome young soldier. They married, as you did. He died but she carried his child. She did what she wanted to do. We chose – you and I – not to stand in her way but to liberate her spirit. She seized the opportunity and secured a year of happiness. That is more than can be said for the intolerable suffering of the German people, all for the sake of overweening imperial ambition."

Eva tried to challenge her last assertion. But Alice would have none of it.

"Nothing can ever assuage the guilt of the Kaiser and his generals for what they have done. They have weakened us so much that now ordinary people are dying from this new and dreadful epidemic of flu."

Eva fell silent.

"Let us try to use what strength we have to bring some order back to Herzberg. We may have little money left but let us use it to provide work to those who need it most and, with their help, to restore this estate as a symbol of integrity."

* * * * *

At Meltwater there was profound relief that the war was over but sadness at the terrible cost in bloodshed throughout the land. Charles Whitfield knew it would take time to restore the Hall and the estate to something of its former glory. He was determined, in his few remaining years, to set about the task. Yet in his heart he knew that Meltwater would never be the same. In January 1919 a memorial service was held in the village church to mourn and remember the war dead. A large plaque was ceremoniously placed over the faded outline of the previous memorial to Arabella von Deppe. Florian's name was listed amongst those it recorded but little was said about him at the gathering at the Hall afterwards. Hatred of Germany was too visceral. Charles knew that it would be too insensitive to talk of Florian's young wife, his great ancestor's namesake, and the birth of a new Anglo-German generation. The prospect of reconciliation between the two families, for which he privately yearned, was not even a distant possibility. It had been extinguished. The broken plaque was removed to the attic. The music book Florian's father had conveyed to the British Museum remained forgotten in its bowels.

* * * * *

Hanna Kovács arrived in Ávila, unlucky in love and unable to return to Vienna in the face of reports she had heard of increasing anti-Jewish sentiment. She and Arabella had become refugees, unable to return to their respective homelands – either because their way was blocked by war or because they were no longer welcome. With Doña Elena they travelled to Madrid in order to secure travel documents. The German ambassador warned them that until the war was over they would not be able to enter France as both would be regarded as enemy aliens and illegal entry would mean risking arrest. It would be best for them to remain in Spain, in the safety of its neutrality. Heeding the ambassador's advice, they found basic accommodation in Madrid. After seeing them settled in their temporary sanctuary, Doña Elena returned south to Andalusia. Arabella earned a little money from music tuition and from singing and piano playing in one or two restaurants and cafés. Hanna stayed home and cared for Stefan.

One evening Arabella fell into conversation with an attaché at the British embassy, Benedict Gibbon.

"Why are you living in Madrid? I am sure there are many in London who would like to hear you play and sing."

"Mr Gibbon, I cannot play in England because I am German. And, in case it crosses your mind, I am not some sultry spy."

"But you speak such excellent English, with no trace of an accent."

"That is because I learnt English at boarding school in England. Our language mistress taught us well."

"Who looked after you at holiday time?"

"Either I would return to Germany or my parents would come to England to see their friends, and sometimes I would stay with my distant cousin, Aurelia Folliot. Her husband was an official at the Foreign Office."

"You are related to Mr Folliot at the Foreign Office, Mr William Folliot?"

"Yes," replied Arabella in a matter-of-fact manner.

Gibbon spent the rest of the evening hearing Arabella's story.

"I do hope we can meet again soon," he said.

"Perhaps," replied Arabella drily.

The next morning Gibbon sent a telegram to the Foreign Office for Mr Folliot's attention, reporting his conversation with Arabella and asking for instructions. She would make a good spy, he suggested.

William Folliot discussed the communication with his wife,

Aurelia.

"William, do whatever is necessary to secure a laissez-passer for her, her child and Madame Kovács to travel to France immediately."

"That won't be easy."

"Stop finding obstacles, William. She is part of my family, for heaven's sake. She is only eighteen years old and she is the widow of an English pilot who was given refuge at Herzberg and with whom she fell in love. She is a young mother, surviving on a pittance, singing and playing in bars. She should be on prestigious music platforms not languishing in Madrid, perceived by Mr Gibbon as a potential spy for England."

"And if I am able to do what you ask, what do we tell the Whitfields?"

"Nothing, you tell them nothing. Sebastian is rabidly anti-German, his father is weak, and Arthur, Juliet and Horatio are indifferent. It is better that Arabella and her child do not come to England and become a target of hatred on account of their nationality. I will visit her when she reaches Paris."

Under two weeks later the British embassy in Madrid received instructions to issue a laissez-passer to Arabella, Stefan and Madame Kovács. Within a month, on Tuesday the 9th of July, the three crossed into France at Hendaye and slowly made their way to Paris, where four days afterwards there was a tearful reunion behind closed doors in an apartment rented by Aurelia. She was struck by Arabella's composure and serenity after all that she had endured.

Over the coming months the four lived discreetly out of sight as hatred of Germany reached new heights. Following the signature of the armistice at Compiègne and a tearful goodbye to Hanna Kovács, Arabella and Stefan left Paris with Aurelia for Germany. They were horrified by the destruction, degradation and human misery they witnessed as they journeyed slowly towards Berlin. The closer they got to their destination the greater the chaos. Without warning anyone, Arabella arrived at Herzberg on Wednesday the 11th of December. Aurelia decided that she would delay her own arrival there until the next day, so she would not distract from what would be an emotional reunion.

Arabella walked down the long, unkempt driveway, Stefan in a rickety pram. At last, between the few remaining trees, she saw the house she had left almost two years before. Its fabric showed palpable neglect and the surrounding garden appeared overgrown and unloved. She climbed the steps to the portico. After pausing to look back down the driveway, she turned the handle of the large double door. It opened. Holding Stefan in her arms she entered. The hall was dark; her footsteps echoed on the bare floor.

"Who is there?" a woman's voice called out.

"It is me, Arabella. I have come home," she replied.

A white-haired elderly woman, stooped but proud-looking, walked slowly towards her from the gloom, supported by a walking stick in her left hand; the recent hardship had aged her beyond her years. She stopped as though suddenly turned to stone.

"Grandmother, it is me, Arabella. It is truly me. And this is Stefan, my son."

Tears flowing down their cheeks, they embraced, kissed one another and then embraced again.

"My darling Arabella, I thank God you have returned. My prayers have finally been answered. You are so grown-up, so mature and more beautiful than ever."

They embraced again, neither speaking. Then they walked through the musty shuttered house to a small room at the back, once used as a night watchman's parlour but now a modest living room. Here Arabella was united with her mother, the joy of their reunion washing away past recrimination and despair.

Later, as her mother sat with Stefan on her lap, Arabella visited every corner of the house with Alice, opening some of the shutters in the empty rooms from which hospital beds had only recently been removed, discussing which might be restored to life and how. The only room unchanged was the *Spiegelsaal*, still with its piano, still in tune. The next evening, while Alice and Eva told Aurelia of all that had happened at Herzberg in the intervening years, Arabella returned to the music room she had loved as a child, with its painted frescos. She lit the candles on the grand piano where her mother said she had often sought solace after Arabella had left. Against the wall was a bookcase on which had been placed music scores. She pulled out a yellowed one. It was the score of Bach's

Prelude and Fugue No. 1 for the piano. She sat down and began to play.

Later that night Arabella went with Alice to the grand bedroom.

"We kept this room for ourselves," Alice told her. "Selfish you might say, but other than the *Spiegelsaal* this was our private kingdom, the beating heart of a wounded family. This room is where it all began in 1766, when your famous namesake became the Countess Arabella von Deppe and opened a new and illustrious chapter in the story of an old and forlorn family."

The young Arabella looked at the portrait of the beautiful countess above the fireplace.

"From henceforth," continued Alice, "this is your room, not mine. This is where you and your son will sleep. I insist. It is sad that Florian is not here to share it. Neither you nor I – indeed, none of us – knows what the future holds in the midst of the debris of this war. But this house and its fate lie in your hands. My time is almost over. It is for you, not me, not your mother, not your father on his return, and not Carl Johann, to decide whether Herzberg will be your home or whether you wish to leave for a future somewhere else. Last, dearest Arabella, I give you this precious key to the music book. Despite all that has happened in the past it is still here."

They sat together on the great bed, leafing through the book on Alice's lap. Arabella again looked up at the portrait of her namesake. As she did so, Alice observed her granddaughter's apparent veneer of outer coldness, a protective shield of numbness hiding the pain of the tragedy she had experienced in Spain. But behind it she glimpsed her inner peace, that serene calm that follows a raging storm. She observed too her compassionate glance and the trace of sadness of human loss etched in her young face, in her dark-green expressive eyes.

"The Countess was remarkable. I wish I had met her," said Alice. "She was strong, clever, capricious, wilful, heroic and sensual – a most extraordinary woman who brought great respect and fame to Herzberg."

"If she was as you describe, then she was similar to Cleopatra," observed Arabella. "At least, that is how I consider Shakespeare portrays the Queen of Egypt. Hers was a tragic story set against a backdrop of war, just like mine, but with the difference that my

Florian was not weak like Antony. Florian died a hero."

"He did indeed," replied Alice, taken aback. "You have every right to be proud of your husband and of your son," she added, anxious to reassure the self-possessed young woman still looking at the portrait.

"I am proud of them both, certainly, but the burden of my alleged treachery for deserting Germany to marry the enemy and my responsibility for such a young, defenceless child – all weigh heavily on me. How can I bear that weight and still carry the expectations you and others have of me to safeguard Herzberg's future? I am frightened I may fail and that if I do, people will think even more badly of me because I did not have the strength and determination she had." Arabella, tearful, turned towards Alice. "What has become of us? Life is full of pain, suffering, hate and cruelty. I have seen it, experienced it. The certainties of her age, the certainties you were taught and I was taught, they have all gone, crushed. We live in disorder, not order. The world around us is harsh, unforgiving and bleak. And my faith is crumbling."

Alice took Arabella's hand, shaken by her anguish. What could she possibly say to answer her?

"Life asks so much of us. At times what it demands can seem overpowering, suffocating and destructive. And, yes, life can be cruel. I came to Herzberg as a child to be united with my unmarried mother, who had been forced to give me away at birth, without ever knowing – to this day – the identity of my father. In my early years I found the legend of this house and the von Deppe family intimidating. But over the years everyone embraced me and from the moment of my marriage to a man I adored and cherished, Herzberg became a warm and pleasing refuge in which I always felt secure, even during years of war and hardship. Whether you will follow in my footsteps here only you can decide. I – indeed everyone – will respect your decision. After all, it is your life that matters, not the stones of this ancient house of faded glory. As for your faith, that is a personal journey on which you are embarked. You alone will know where and when it might end. I can offer no advice except to say that in whatever you do in life be guided by your conscience, not the voices of others."

They sat side by side on the bed, holding hands in silence. There was nothing more to be said.

*

Two weeks later, after Christmas had slipped quietly past, the exception to its muted pianissimo being Ferdinand Anton's unexpected, emotion-filled return, Alice died in her sleep at Herzberg, eased of her burden as keeper of the music book and exhausted by life, yet, on the eve of her death, feeling she had been delivered from lifelong exile to an uncompromised childlike self, joyful and loved.

One evening not long after Alice's funeral, Arabella sat in bed, propped by embroidered eighteenth-century pillows retrieved from the underground store rooms. Stefan lay asleep in his grandfather's army cot. A fire crackled beneath the Countess's portrait. Arabella opened the music book. From it slipped an envelope bearing words written shakily by her husband shortly before his death.

> To my bella doña, Arabella, here is the only gift I possess. I give it to you as a measure of the depth of my love.

She pressed the envelope, which contained a lock of his hair, against her lips. Before closing the book she began to leaf once more through some of the yellowed sheets of paper, a tumble of secrets, memories and musical transcriptions from a time long past. One short, faded transcription in a woman's hand caught her eye; it was a sarabande – a slow court dance – composed, it seemed, many years ago in France. She hummed the melody and began to imagine a scene – perhaps at Versailles – with elegant, beautiful women in revealing low-cut gowns, their pearl-dusted breasts bathed in candlelight, dancing opposite handsome, finely dressed courtiers. Their bodies moving gracefully to the persistent lento beat of the music but never touching, the performers of the ritual stately steps were yet intimately drawn together, charged and held by pulsing magnetism, their eyes afire with physical passion and their silent lips withholding unspoken lustful profanities. The music ended. Before replacing the book, of which she was now the custodian, she withdrew Florian's envelope, deciding to keep it with her, not locked away in a secret place.

*

Three months later, as a chill early-April wind blew outside, a small group of elderly musicians gathered one afternoon in St Nicholas's Church in Potsdam. Despite the rapidly worsening lawlessness, the social and political rancour, and the activities of the *Freikorps*, which Carl Johann in his bitterness had now joined, hundreds came on foot, on bicycles and in dilapidated cars to witness the re-formation of the Herzberg Camerata and to hear music of a quality and richness they had been denied for so long, its place taken by martial and bombastic tunes designed to raise the national mood and support for the army.

The orchestra opened with a rousing performance of Beethoven's *Seventh Symphony in A Major*, with its stirring fourth movement lifting spirits in the face of catastrophic defeat. As the thunderous applause and cheering ebbed, Arabella stepped forward to sing *Fra quest'ombre* from Hasse's opera *Solimano*, explaining that the aria had a special significance for her family a generation ago and she wished therefore to dedicate it to all those who had perished on the battlefront.

> *If among these shadows you spy*
> *A wandering shade in search of rest,*
> *'Tis that of your faithful husband,*
> *Come to beg you for mercy.*
> *Sweet will my final breath be*
> *If, after my death, you live on for me.*

She followed with Daphne's aria *Felicissima quest'alma* from Handel's cantata *Apollo and Daphne*, accompanying herself on guitar, playing together with the Camerata's flautist and strings.

> *How happy is this soul*
> *Which loves naught but freedom.*
> *There is no peace, no calm,*
> *For one whose heart is fettered.*

The audience sat enraptured by such a tender voice, whose notes seemed to hang in the air like ethereal particles floating in a shaft of sunlight. When she finished, a dazed ripple of applause became a roar of approval.

After the main performance of Beethoven's *Pastoral Symphony*, a great cheer arose as Arabella stood to sing the Queen of Sheba's aria from the last act of Handel's oratorio *Solomon*, alongside a young tenor from the Camerata choir.

The Queen of Sheba

Will the Sun forget to streak
Eastern skies with amber ray,
When the dusky shades to break
He unbars the gates of day?
Then demand if Sheba's queen
E'er can banish from her thought
All the splendour she has seen,
All the knowledge thou hast taught.

Solomon

Adieu, fair queen, and in thy breast
May peace and virtue ever rest.

The Queen of Sheba

Ev'ry joy that wisdom knows
May'st thou, pious monarch, share!

Solomon

Ev'ry blessing Heav'n bestows
Be thy portion, virtuous fair!

The Queen of Sheba

Gently flow thy rolling days.

Solomon

Sorrow be a stranger here.

The Queen of Sheba and Solomon

May thy people sound thy praise,
Praise unbought by price of fear.

The audience would not let Arabella go. To its profound delight she and the handsome tenor sang Adam and Eve's duet *By thee with bliss* from Haydn's *Creation*. After so many years of hardship, death and cruelty, many of the audience were moved to tears by their affecting rendition.

Exuberant applause still ringing in her ears, Arabella and Stefan returned to Herzberg that evening in the company of her mother and father, who were speechless with pride at their daughter's accomplishment. Before going to bed she went to the *Spiegelsaal*. Sitting at the candlelit piano, she gently touched the keys and began to play Bach's *Prelude and Fugue No. 1*. As she did so she saw an encroaching speck of light. The room became warmer; its earlier chill had gone. As she continued to play the speck grew larger and then fragmented into a swirling white dust of minute points of light that slowly gathered into a pivot of radiance, gradually forming into the figure of a woman in a long flowing white-and-cream dress, its muslin blown by breaths of air that Arabella could feel on her flushed cheeks. Though still indistinct, the figure fleetingly appeared to have the translucent image of the Countess in the picture above the fireplace in the grand bedroom. As Arabella continued to play, the woman seemed to lock her hands together in a moment of rapture. Then she slowly receded back into a single speck of light, only to burst once again into myriad motes of brightness that swarmed into a ball of radiance before finally exploding in a cascade of intense light that seemed to envelop Arabella. The candle flames on the piano flickered. Arabella ceased playing, transfixed by what she had seen.

Suddenly the door opened. Arabella turned to look. It was her mother, carrying Stefan. Eva having left them alone, Arabella placed her son on her lap and began to play Beethoven's *Moonlight Sonata*. He watched her fingers, entranced. Slowly he fell asleep. If only Florian could be here, she thought, her eyes moistened by tears.

That night, with Stefan beside her, she once again leafed through the music book. A faded piece of paper fell from the sheaf of pages. She read the words:

I will do what people want but only as I want it to be.
Arabella

Meltwater
1764

She put it back, but before tying together the ancient covers of the music book with the frayed gold silk ribbon, she inserted a small sheet in her own handwriting.

Goodnight, sweet Florian.
Never forgotten, always in my mind – in the morning, in the afternoon and in the evening – I with you and you with me. But you are always closest in the silence of the night, that most secret, most intimate and most lonely of times. I reach for you in the emptiness of my bed but you are not there to take my hand. You are gone. All I have are memories.
Wherever you may fly amongst the stars of eternity, I wish you safe passage.
Soave sia il vento.
Goodnight, sweet Florian.

She put the book down, beside an unread one, a 1906 edition of Friedrich Nietzsche's *Der Wille zur Macht* – *The Will to Power* – which had arrived mysteriously several days before, addressed to her. She extinguished the candle and lay back on the pillows looking at the flames of the fire reflected on the wall, just as her namesake had done on her wedding night over a century and a half before. Tomorrow she would finally decide whether to remain at Herzberg and seek to follow in the illustrious footsteps of the famed Countess, but in her own way, against the backdrop of a defeated, shattered and embittered Germany; or, regardless of the calumny of betrayal she would surely incur, to refuse to bear the heavy legacy of upholding the history of this Valhalla of the gods and its musical tradition and begin a new life far away. Whatever her decision it must be for her son as well as for her. Perhaps tomorrow her luminous visitor would help to choose the path she should take.

She fell asleep, exhausted as much from the expectation of the new day as from what had happened in the day that had passed.

* * * * *

AFTERWORD

Two items had been consigned for sale at a leading international auction house in London on Tuesday the 23rd of October 2012. One was a British passport issued at the Foreign Office in London on the 3rd of October 1853 to Mr Robert Whitfield, his wife and son for the purpose of travel on the continent. On its own it carried no particular significance. Rather, its value lay in its connection to the other, more substantial item for sale, which had already aroused much interest amongst prospective bidders. It was an eighteenth-century music book, bearing on its front cover the crest of Frederick the Great of Prussia. Presented to a young English woman, Arabella Whitfield, on her marriage on the 18th of March 1766 to Count Carl Manfred von Deppe, the inside bore the following inscription in the King's distinctive handwriting:

> *To the Countess von Deppe, in admiration and deep appreciation for cheering an old man's heart at the end of a long winter.*
> *Frederick*
> *King of Prussia*

The book had only recently come to light when brought to London for sale. Eighteenth-century music books – or commonplace books, as they were sometimes known – are not infrequent in auctions of rare manuscripts and books. Though the crest on the cover and the inscription inside were unusual, the financial value lay in the book's contents, which included a surprising array of letters – many of a most personal nature – and a selection of musical transcriptions, amongst them a handful of original compositions, including Mozart's *Nine Variations in D on a Minuet by Jean-Pierre Duport* (K. 573), signed and dated by the composer in the spring of 1789. To connoisseurs of music and historical documents the book and its unique contents were a rich treasury of memorabilia, far surpassing an earlier music book – still in the possession of the British Museum – which the young Arabella Whitfield had received on her seventeenth birthday from her French-born mother, Lady Thérèse Whitfield. The book's possession by the descendants of the Countess was accountable up to the Second World War, when in the chaos of the latter years of the conflict it disappeared from its secret resting place at Herzberg.

The sale, which had been eagerly awaited by several highly interested unnamed buyers, had already been deferred for several months to allow experts appointed by the auction house to examine, authenticate and document in detail the book, its history and its precious contents and to check certain other matters. This thorough work was essential in order to ensure that the auction catalogue contained a comprehensive description of the book and what was inside it and that there would be no challenge to the vendor's right to sell. Moreover, it was necessary to establish an accurate indication of the price it was likely to fetch in bidding. The last of the enquiries was resolved in late July 2012, when the auction house received a letter from a leading expert in DNA analysis.

To the Chief Executive Officer,

My colleagues and I write to you in connection with the intended auction of the music book that once belonged to the Countess Arabella Mariette von Deppe, who died on her estate of Herzberg, near Berlin, on the 25th of April 1816. You asked for our assistance in connection with certain matters concerning the book's contents, notably, a letter written by Lady Thérèse Whitfield dated the 13th of March 1773. In the letter she asserts that, during a prolonged stay in Paris after her marriage to Sir Robert Whitfield, she had enjoyed a brief liaison with King Louis XV of France and that Arabella may therefore be the daughter of the King rather than of her husband. You were of the opinion that if the assertion could be proved to be correct it might have some bearing on the value of the music book at auction. We undertook to conduct our enquiries as quickly as possible. Our study is now complete.

In order to reach a definitive view on whether Lady Whitfield's statement was correct or merely imaginary, we sought to carry out certain scientific tests to compare the DNA of the Countess with that from samples that might help confirm her parentage. With the kind assistance of your office we were able to secure several samples with good provenance, which enabled us to carry out the study. These consisted of hair from Louis XV, and a molar tooth from Sir Robert Whitfield. We compared these samples with a lock of the Countess's hair — which her daughter, Elise, had placed in the music book upon her mother's death, in her lasting memory — in order to see if there was a DNA match with either of the samples from Louis XV or Whitfield. We were able to extract adequate DNA from all the samples and to carry out DNA profiling by amplifying a number of short tandem repeats (STRs). As the DNA in such samples is degraded, we were not able to obtain a full profile for each individual but we were able to type a sufficient number of markers from which to draw a conclusion. The profiles indicate that Sir Robert Whitfield could not be the father of Arabella. However, the profile obtained from the hair of Louis XV was consistent with him being her father. I attach a dossier containing our detailed findings.

From our detailed analysis the match probability is sufficient to suggest that the Countess von Deppe was the daughter of King Louis XV of France. Our conclusion would therefore appear to bear out Lady Whitfield's assertion in 1773 that her husband was not her daughter's father and that it could have been the French king.

We therefore conclude it would be safe for the sale catalogue to speculate with considerable confidence that the Countess Arabella was an illegitimate child of French royal blood.
Head of the Department of Genetics
University of Leicester
Thursday the 26th of July, 2012

Upon receipt of this letter, and after careful scrutiny of the accompanying dossier, the auction house decided that there was no need to seek a second opinion. Instead it proceeded to publish details of the contents of the music book in the catalogue and to set the date for the auction. By the day of the sale the auctioneers had received numerous and significant intentions to bid. Bidding opened at under £1 million, but within a matter of minutes the level had risen sharply, becoming a contest on the telephone between four anonymous bidders, one of whom was thought to be German. Shortly thereafter, only two bidders remained. After further bidding, the music book was sold for a record price.

The sale of the music book received immediate post-auction publicity on account of the unusually high price but speculation about the buyer was soon overshadowed by the record price fetched by a van Gogh painting.

For the next three years nothing further was heard of the music book. Then out of the blue there appeared a short news story that the book had been bought by a Russian buyer and was now in a private collection in St Petersburg. Within a month or so there followed a further report, from an anonymous source – datelined New York – that the book was in the possession of a private foundation belonging to a rich descendant of the beautiful Countess Kseniya Sokolova, once the wife of Nikolay Sokolov, one of Catherine the Great's courtiers and lovers until his death in 1769. The story recounted that the Countess von Deppe and her husband had known the Sokolovs during their stay in St Petersburg in 1767–1768 and, according to Kseniya's diary, the Count von Deppe had frequently spent time in her company during the many hours his wife attended the Empress. The story speculated that the principal reason for the purchase of the book may not have been solely for investment purposes but because of a possible family link to the von Deppes. Nothing further was said in the media. Besides, what had been written was a mere footnote to the sale, for a record price, of a music book three years before.

Before its sale in London the vendor of the book had made personal copies of a selection of the letters it contained. In the light of the latest story she re-examined some of the correspondence and was struck by a reference in a letter dated the 14th of November 1790 from a dying Waldemar Drescher to the Countess:

... and soon became jealous whenever I saw him and you together, enjoying the fruits of a friendship and a love I could never have and which once I believe he may have betrayed by a certain use of words in a moment of weakness.

Moreover, there was the passage in a farewell the Countess wrote on the 20th of March 1816 shortly before her death:

My life has been blessed in so many ways, with a loving husband – even if he withheld from me the truth about what happened to my late brother in Paris and, according to Herr Drescher, may have betrayed me in another unknown way ...

Though it was only supposition in the absence of any proof, the vendor concluded that the references to an act of betrayal may have been an allusion to a brief affair between the Countess Kseniya and Count von Deppe while his wife spent private hours with the Czarina; and that, moreover, the liaison may have resulted in an illegitimate child who never met its natural father. The current descendant of that child – with much money to spend – may have wished to acquire the book and its contents in order to have a voyeur's insight into a family with which they were once distantly linked. The vendor recalled reading the words of the sixteenth-century German mathematician, astronomer and astrologer Johannes Kepler:

Truth is the daughter of time, and I feel no shame in being her midwife.

For a moment or two she considered the possibility of assisting in the birth of the final revelation in the story of Arabella von Deppe and her husband by offering an off-the-record interview to the newspaper that had carried the story. But upon further reflection she decided it was best to let sleeping dogs lie. After all, a disturbed dog might bite.

* * * * *

As for the decision Arabella made when she woke at Herzberg that morning in April 1919, and the events that ensued, that is a story for another day.

The End

ACKNOWLEDGEMENTS

To finish three books in three years was almost as great a challenge as my completion of the 2014 London Marathon. Though this third book took only seven months to write, my first and warmest thanks go to my wife, Audrey, for giving me this amount of time and space to complete the task I had set myself. I am deeply grateful to her for allowing me to escape so many family duties.

I have also received the support and advice of a small and invaluable team of people whose efforts deserve abundant recognition: Jenny Langford, a dear friend who once again helped greatly with research, checking and occasional suggestions; my daughter Caroline, for her impeccable knowledge of the attribution of paintings and the characteristics, idiosyncrasies and techniques of individual painters; Lady Fiona Fraser, for her advice on the writing of poetry, which I have attempted for the first time in this book; Madame Odile Castro, for her advice on French aspects of the story; and last but not least Bianca and Jürgen Freymuth-Brumby, our close and long-standing friends in Berlin, for their factual contribution. All have been my core team and without them I would not have crossed the finishing line.

Beyond this team, my warmest thanks go to Sue Tyley, my highly professional and knowledgeable copy editor, who, as with the two previous books, helped buff and polish the manuscript; to Niall Cook, who did the artwork and advised and assisted in countless other ways; and to Julia Bell, Senior Lecturer in Creative

297

Writing and Convenor of the MA in Creative Writing at Birkbeck, University of London, who, even though I was not one of her students, was always ready to find time to answer my questions. I add to this list Eleanor Christian, a lawyer and close family friend, who once again kindly advised on some legal aspects; and Tony Mulliken and Fiona Marsh and their team at Midas PR, for their commitment, advice and support.

I also convey my gratitude to the late Kate Crowe, formerly of the FCO Historians, who gave me excellent advice about what the Foreign Office was like in 1853, when the story begins, and who answered innumerable subsequent questions; to Professor Patrick Salmon, the FCO's Chief Historian, and to his excellent team for their valued assistance; and to Dr Nicholas Draper of the Centre for the Study of the Legacies of British Slave-ownership at University College, London. In his expert guidance on the abolition of slavery, Dr Draper advised me that the compensation of £20,000, the sum the Whitfield family received, would amount to £16 million in today's terms, using the average-wage method. My special thanks also go to Dr Turi King, Lecturer in Genetics and Archaeology at the University of Leicester. Leader of the international research team that provided the overwhelming evidence leading to the identification of the remains of Richard III in 2015, she gave me expert advice on the DNA references in the book. Without her contribution I would not have been able to solve a mystery of paternity. I also express my thanks to Clive Harris, the battlefield historian, who taught me much about the Battle of the Somme, stripping away the myth to reach the truth of what really happened. Finally I warmly thank Julia Rafferty, an accomplished freelance photographer, for her assistance; John Needham, another valued friend, for the loan of several helpful reference books; and the artist David Cooper, for his initial ideas on the design of the book's cover.

I read widely to understand the different geopolitical forces that flowed and ebbed during the period leading up to the start of the First World War, and to learn more about the dreadful First Battle of the Somme. Amongst the books I consulted I wish to acknowledge the following in particular: *The Nineteenth-Century Foreign Office: an administrative history* by Ray Jones; *The Foreign Office Mind: The Making of British Foreign Policy, 1865–1914* by T. G. Otte;

The Foreign Office: An Architectural History by Ian Toplis; *Noble Endeavours: The Life of Two Countries, England and Germany, in Many Stories* by Miranda Seymour, lent to me by Mrs Gabriele Fyjis-Walker from Germany, whose late husband, Richard, taught me the art of good Foreign Office drafting; John Suchet's *The Last Waltz: The Strauss Dynasty and Vienna*; Douglas Haig's *War Diaries and Letters 1914–1918*; Andrew Roberts' *Elegy*, about the first day of the Battle of the Somme; *The Somme Battlefield: A pocket guide to Places and People with Secret Maps* by Ruaraidh Adams-Cairns; and *The Rise and Fall of Prussia* by Sebastian Haffner.

My thanks go to Classic FM and BBC Radio 3 for providing me with a rich and pleasurable selection of eighteenth- and nineteenth-century music from which I was able to select pieces that might have been played by the Camerata Herzberg at the Schloss, in Berlin and in London and, moreover, played and sung by some of the characters in the book. A number of these pieces helped to inspire particular scenes in the novel; I have listed them in Appendix 3.

APPENDIX 1
The Whitfield Family Tree

The Whitfield Family

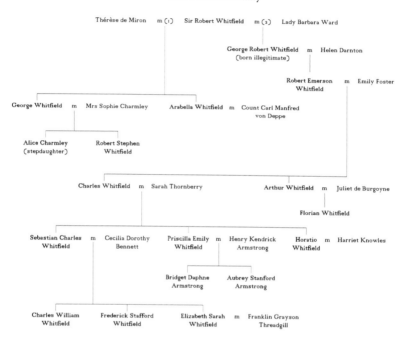

APPENDIX 2
The von Deppe Family Tree

The von Deppe Family

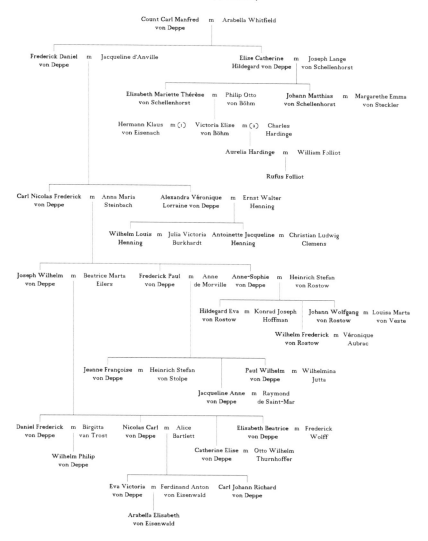

Count Carl Manfred von Deppe m Arabella Whitfield

Frederick Daniel von Deppe m Jacqueline d'Anville

Elise Catherine Hildegard von Deppe m Joseph Lange von Schellenhorst

Elisabeth Mariette Thérèse von Schellenhorst m Philip Otto von Böhm

Johann Matthias von Schellenhorst m Margarethe Emma von Steckler

Hermann Klaus von Eisenach m (1) Victoria Elise von Böhm m (2) Charles Hardinge

Aurelia Hardinge m William Folliot

Rufus Folliot

Carl Nicolas Frederick von Deppe m Anna Maria Steinbach

Alexandra Véronique Lorraine von Deppe m Ernst Walter Henning

Wilhelm Louis Henning m Julia Victoria Burkhardt

Antoinette Jacqueline Henning m Christian Ludwig Clemens

Joseph Wilhelm von Deppe m Beatrice Marta Eilers

Frederick Paul von Deppe m Anne de Morville

Anne-Sophie von Deppe m Heinrich Stefan von Rostow

Hildegard Eva von Rostow m Konrad Joseph Hoffman

Johann Wolfgang von Rostow m Louisa Marta von Veste

Wilhelm Frederick von Rostow m Véronique Aubrac

Jeanne Françoise von Deppe m Heinrich Stefan von Stolpe

Paul Wilhelm von Deppe m Wilhelmina Jutta

Jacqueline Anne von Deppe m Raymond de Saint-Mar

Daniel Frederick von Deppe m Birgitta van Trost

Nicolas Carl von Deppe m Alice Bartlett

Elisabeth Beatrice von Deppe m Frederick Wolff

Wilhelm Philip von Deppe

Catherine Elise von Deppe m Otto Wilhelm Thurnhoffer

Eva Victoria von Deppe m Ferdinand Anton von Eisenwald

Carl Johann Richard von Deppe

Arabella Elisabeth von Eisenwald

APPENDIX 3
List of Musical Pieces

A selection of the music that inspired the book:

Ludwig Abeille
Piano Concerto in D Major for Four Hands

Carl Philipp Emanuel Bach
Keyboard Concerto in D Minor

Johann Christian Bach
Keyboard Sonata No. 2 in D Major
Piano Concerto in E Flat Major
Sinfonia Concertante in C Major

Johann Sebastian Bach
Prelude and Fugue No. 1 in C Major

Ludwig van Beethoven
Bagatelle No. 25 – Für Elise
Fifth Symphony in C Minor
Piano Concerto No. 3 in C Minor
Piano Concerto No. 5 in E Flat Major
Piano Sonata No. 14 – the Moonlight
Piano Sonata No. 25 in G Major
Septet in E Flat Major
Seventh Symphony in A Major
Violin Sonata No. 5 in F Major

Johannes Brahms
Piano Sonata in F Minor
Violin Concerto in D Major

Frederic Chopin
Berceuse in D Flat Major
Nocturne in B Flat Minor
Waltz in E Flat

EDWARD GLOVER

Karl Ditters von Dittersdorf
Harp Concerto in A Major

John Dowland
Tarleton's Resurrection

Antonin Dvořák
The Song to the Moon (from the opera Rusalka)

John Field
Piano Concerto No. 5 in C Major

George Frederick Handel
Felicissima quest'alma (from the cantata Apollo and Daphne)
Minuet (from the opera Berenice)
Sarabande
Will the Sun forget to streak … ? (from the oratorio Solomon)

Johann Adolf Hasse
Fra quest'ombre (from the opera Solimano)

Joseph Haydn
By thee with bliss (from the oratorio The Creation)
Keyboard Concerto in D Major
Keyboard Concerto in F Major
Symphony No. 44 in E Minor – Trauer
Symphony No. 45 – the Farewell
Symphony No. 101 in D Major
The heavens are telling the glory of God (from the oratorio The Creation)
Trumpet Concerto in E Flat
Violin Concerto in G Major

Johann Nepomuk Hummel
Piano Sonata No. 2 in E Flat Major

Felix Mendelssohn
Symphony No. 2 in B Flat Major – the Lobesgang
Violin Concerto in E Minor

A MOTIF OF SEASONS

Claudio Monteverdi
Pur ti miro (from the opera L'incoronazione di Poppea)

Wolfgang Amadeus Mozart
Ave Verum Corpus
Clarinet Quintet in A Major
Piano Concerto No. 18 in B Flat Major
Piano Concerto No. 20 in D Minor
Piano Concerto No. 23 in A Major
Soave sia il vento (from the opera Così fan tutte)

Giacomo Puccini
Intermezzo (from the opera Suor Angelica)

Jean-Philippe Rameau
Les Sauvages (from the ballet Les Indes galantes)

Franz Schubert
Impromptu in G Flat Major

Robert Schumann
Kinderszenen

Michele Stratico
Violin Concerto in G Minor

Johann Strauss the Younger
Tales from the Vienna Woods

Antonio Vivaldi
Nisi Dominus
The Four Seasons

ABOUT THE AUTHOR

Edward Glover was born in London in 1943. After gaining a history degree followed by an MPhil at Birkbeck College, London University, he embarked on a career in the British diplomatic service, during which his overseas postings included Washington DC, Berlin, Brussels and the Caribbean. He subsequently advised on foreign ministry reform in post-invasion Iraq, Kosovo and Sierra Leone. For seven years he headed a one-million-acre rainforest-conservation project in South America, on behalf of the Commonwealth Secretariat and the Guyana Government.

With an interest in 16th- and 18th-century history, baroque music and 18th-century art, Edward was encouraged by the purchase of two paintings and a passport to try his hand at writing historical fiction.

Edward and his wife, former Foreign & Commonwealth Office lawyer and leading international human rights adviser Dame Audrey Glover, now live in Norfolk, a place that gives him further inspiration for his writing. Edward sits on the board of trustees of the Welsh environmental charity Size of Wales and is vice-chairman of the Foreign & Commonwealth Office Association, an associate fellow of the University of Warwick's Yesu Persaud Centre for Caribbean Studies and a board member of The King's Lynn Preservation Trust.

When he isn't writing, Edward is an avid tennis player and – at the age of 71 – completed the 2014 London Marathon, raising £7,000 for Ambitious about Autism.

Printed in Great Britain
by Amazon

70215842R00196